DEATH OF A

Born in 1974, Fiona Campbell studied Psychology and Zoology at Bristol University before doing a PhD on social learning in animals. After working for Unilever, including several months in Tokyo, she completed this novel for the Manchester Metropolitan Writing MA. She works as a policy director for environmental campaigning charity ENCAMS.

FIONA CAMPBELL

Death of a Salaryman

VINTAGE BOOKS

London

Published by Vintage 2008

1 3 5 7 9 10 8 6 4 2

Copyright © Fiona Campbell 2007

Fiona Campbell has asserted her right under the Copyright, Designs
and Patents Act 1988 to be identified as the author of this work

First published in Great Britain in 2007 by
Chatto & Windus
Random House, 20 Vauxhall Bridge Road,
London SW1V 2SA

www.vintage-books.co.uk

Addresses for companies within The Random House Group Limited
can be found at: www.randomhouse.co.uk/offices.htm

The Random House Group Limited Reg. No. 954009

A CIP catalogue record for this book
is available from the British Library

ISBN 9780099503699

The Random House Group Limited supports The Forest Stewardship
Council (FSC), the leading international forest certification
organisation. All our titles that are printed on Greenpeace approved
FSC certified paper carry the FSC logo. Our paper procurement
policy can be found at: www.rbooks.co.uk/environment

Printed in the UK by CPI Bookmarque, Croydon, CR0 4TD

MUM, WITH LOVE

Part One

ONE

Kenji Yamada stifled a yawn as the crowded train rattled into Tokyo station. Commuters gathered on the platform pushed forward expectantly. It was Monday, early morning rush hour on the Yamanote line. He had been unable to reach the doors of the last train, but now there was only one other person standing in front of him and he was determined not to let this one leave without him. By stepping on backwards, wriggling and squirming, he was able to force his way into the carriage where he watched – helplessly – as the doors snapped shut, trapping his box-like briefcase between their thick rubber lips. Even had he been able to move, tugging and pulling would have been pointless. The case would not budge. He simply had to wait until one of the three grey-suited platform attendants prised the lips apart and knocked it free, allowing the doors to close unimpeded.

A shout echoed along the length of the platform. An attendant waved a white baton in the air, high above his head. The train lurched off, moving uncertainly at first and then with increasing speed, bowling fiercely along the tracks. As the next station approached, the train slowed and juddered to a stop, losing Kenji his grip on the clammy chrome bar overhead. With nothing else for support, he was forced to lean heavily first to the right and then to the left before returning to a near upright position. On one side an elderly gentleman smelling of stale whisky and fresh tobacco smoke acted as a buffer; on the other a young woman wearing a perfume with an overwhelming odour of roses that did little to mask the smell of perspiring bodies and unwashed hair permeating the carriage. Kenji's nose twitched and he sneezed, managing to keep his lips firmly pressed together.

When the old man got off, Kenji was able to squeeze himself into the corner next to the door, where he extracted a copy of the *Mainichi News* from the pocket of his raincoat. Leiko Kobayashi's review of the best and worst television programmes from the preceding week was printed every Monday and he liked to be among the first in the office to read it. But today Kenji got no further than the front page. Nissan, he read with dismay, was shedding over a thousand workers from its manufacturing plant in Kanagawa. Or rather it had done so already. Several weeks ago, in fact, but it had managed to keep the news quiet until an employee – disgruntled by the provisions that had been made for him and his colleagues – went to the newspaper. There was a large black and white picture of the man standing outside the manufacturing plant: alone and waving his fist in the air.

Kenji emitted a low whistle. He had always regarded the motor industry as untouchable – the one thing that would stand firm when everything else was falling down around it. He was not alone in this. Everybody thought so. If it wasn't the case, what hope was there for the rest of them? Things, he realised with a shudder, were starting to look very bad.

'Shibuya, the next station is Shibuya,' an automated female voice trilled over the public address system.

He pocketed the newspaper and left the carriage, stumbling slightly but quickly regaining his balance as he joined the long line of people who shuffled slowly towards the exit. From here it was a short walk through lightly drizzling rain to the office block in which he worked. There were too many people around to put up an umbrella, so he let the rain fall on to his head, where it rolled off his well-oiled hair and splattered his glasses. The building in which he worked came into view through the blurred lenses. It was a modest eleven storeys: three of which were occupied by NBC and included the programme research unit of the light entertainment division where Kenji worked.

He took the lift to the seventh floor and walked out into a windowless passageway lit overhead by harsh fluorescent strip lights and covered underfoot by a coarse, rust-coloured carpet. Extensively labelled cardboard boxes awaiting collection by the mail room were stacked along the length of one wall, all the way to a double set of opaque glass doors. He keyed a four-digit security code into a pad on the door handle and there was a cheerful beep. The code was changed on the first Monday of every month. Today. And it had been clearly written on a small piece of paper sellotaped to the glass with a note that read, 'Don't tell anyone, but here's the new code.'

He pushed against the door, into the office.

It was open-plan and divided into two halves by a wide aisle. Within each half, rows of desks arranged face-to-face ran at right angles to the main walkway. Kenji's desk – like those of his colleagues – was equipped with a telephone and a personal computer. A two-drawer filing cabinet was slotted into the space beneath the desk leaving just enough room for his legs alongside. Having long ago exhausted the capacity of these drawers, he had taken to piling paper files on his desk and the floor, building a low wall on either side of his chair with boxes of videotapes on which were recorded pilot episodes and the entire series of shows. The desks were arranged in order of rank and only the head of programme research, Shin Ishida, who sat at the far end of the row directly beneath the window, enjoyed an uncluttered working environment. With his position came additional storage space in a vault in the basement. Not to mention other privileges such as subsidised membership at the Maruhan Golf Club just outside Tokyo and use of the corporation's condominium in Hawaii.

'Good morning,' Kenji greeted several of his colleagues who were sitting at their desks, already at work. They looked up, smiled, returned his greeting but nothing more. There was a time when one of them might have asked him about his weekend and he would have enquired after their son's baseball match or wife's birthday dinner. But there had been little of that lately. In fact, nobody said very much of anything to him anymore. Not even to remark upon the weather.

Having dropped his briefcase on his desk, Kenji hung up his coat and went to the nearest drinks dispenser. He selected a cup of strong black coffee sweetened with sugar that never managed to dissolve but always sat in a clump of translucent granules at the bottom of the cup. Back at his desk, he turned on his computer and checked his watch. It was 8 a.m. A full hour before the Monday morning team meeting. He got down to work.

High-pitched music began to wail from the extensive system of loudspeakers distributed throughout the office. Jumping up, Kenji joined the rest of his colleagues trooping towards meeting room one: a small, cramped, dusty space with no windows and an air-conditioning unit that either whistled when it worked, or groaned and shuddered when it didn't. The walls were painted a shade somewhere between yellow and brown, which used to cause him to joke with his colleagues that an entire family of smokers was locked in the room overnight after they had all gone home. 'Ah, the Watanabes must have been back again,' he would say at the start of a meeting. Or, 'The Watanabes must have been busy last night.'

Comments such as these had never failed to raise a laugh. Once. These days he just kept quiet. It seemed like the safest option. There was nothing definite that Kenji could put his finger on, but he felt certain that his colleagues' behaviour towards him had cooled considerably over the last few months. Certainly they were polite, but he was no longer invited out for drinks after work. Occasionally he caught a look in someone's eyes and it wasn't as friendly as it had once been. Several times colleagues had stopped talking if he suddenly happened upon them. There was only one possible explanation. They blamed him.

Taking a hard plastic seat in the corner of the meeting room away from the others, he pretended to read the contents of his notebook as he waited for Shin Ishida to arrive. Which he did, minutes later, pushing confidently into the room, his assistant, Akira Eto, scurrying in his wake.

'Good morning.' Ishida straightened his claret tie and smoothed down the front of his dark blue suit as he greeted the team. He had a small and unexpectedly stocky physique. Even Kenji's wife had commented when, last year, the team and their families had visited an *onsen*, and Ishida had stripped down to reveal large muscles in his calves and powerfully defined forearms. She had looked accusingly at her husband's puny body beside her, as if to say, 'Why can't you be more like that?' But it wasn't just Ishida's impeccable dress sense, strong physical appearance or position within the corporation that commanded the team's respect. It was the straight way he held his back, the grace of his movements and the calm, dignified manner in which he spoke to everyone, no matter what their rank or the situation. He was in his late fifties. His otherwise jet black hair was showing signs of grey around the temples, and he required an enormous pair of black-framed prescription glasses. When not talking, he would methodically clean the thick lenses with a white cloth covered with polka dots. Kenji wondered if he repeatedly laundered the same one or kept a large supply at home.

Ishida cleared his throat and began by making a number of announcements about work already in progress and on the horizon. 'I am particularly excited,' he said softly so that everybody leant forward in their seats, 'by a piece of work currently being undertaken by our Innovation Managers.'

Kenji turned to where a group of three men was sitting in the opposite corner of the room. None of them wore ties. All had their shirts open at the neck and tended to favour smart casual trousers rather than suits.

'This involves a group of extremely creative viewers who will be helping us to identify novel game show formats. We have recruited an author, a film maker, a graphic designer. And I am told that their ideas are different. Very, very different. But – ' He momentarily bowed his head. ' – these are still tough times and the only way in which the corporation will get through them is if we all pull together and persevere.'

Thinking about the Nissan factory in Kanagawa and that solitary, angry worker, Kenji nodded his head in agreement as a low murmur of consent passed around the room.

'We must work hard,' Ishida concluded. 'But we must also get a good night's sleep.'

When he sat down, it was amidst appreciative laughter and polite but nonetheless heartfelt clapping. He immediately began to clean his glasses as Eto came forward. A gaunt, bird-like man with a small, egg-shaped head and thin hair, Eto took loud, deep intakes of air whenever he spoke such that clients often feared he was about to suffocate. In his hand was a well-thumbed book: its spine bent and the pages that had fallen out secured back in place with strips of sellotape that bore prints of his long, thin fingers. He opened it, having already selected a proverb that Ishida deemed suitable for the current climate, and began to read. 'Today's proverb is – ' He inhaled deeply. ' – one kind word can warm three winters. So act considerately towards your colleagues and support them in their work.' The book snapped shut and he moved back as if surprised by the sound. This was usually the cue that signalled they should all stand and go back to their desks, but only after they had shouted, in unison, Nippon Broadcasting Corporation's motto – 'Working hard to fulfil our promise to every viewer everywhere.'

Before the occupants of the room could leave, Ishida was on his feet again, coughing politely. 'Excuse me, please. Before you go, I believe that we have a birthday to celebrate today. Something of a milestone if I understand correctly.'

Kenji hung his head.

'So if everybody could join me in wishing Yamada-san a very happy fortieth birthday.'

He blushed. A hot crimson glow spread across his face as colleagues turned to pat him on the shoulder or reached across chairs to offer him their good wishes. As this was taking place, the door to meeting room one opened and Ishida's secretary rolled in a trolley laden with fresh pots of coffee, pristine white cups and a large selection of cream cakes.

'Please help yourself.' Ishida waved an arm benevolently in the direction of the trolley and then left the room.

'Come, Yamada-san, you must go first.' One of Kenji's colleagues pushed him towards the trolley, past chairs and smiling faces. He felt warm, as though someone had just wrapped him in a soft blanket. 'Perhaps my suspicions were wrong,' he pondered. 'My colleagues bear me no grudge after all.' He began to feel enormously relieved and lighter than he had done in months as his hand hovered above the cream cakes.

'Take the largest one,' someone shouted.

'Hey not that one,' another voice joked as he appeared to pause. 'That one has my name on it.'

NBC was the only company that Kenji had ever known, the only job he had ever had. Six months ago he had celebrated twenty-two years of service with his colleagues over dinner and been shocked when he realised that this was longer than he had been married, longer even than he had known his own, late father. His mother, too, had passed away and while he had a wife and two children, and an incumbent mother-in-law, the company felt like family. Whenever a new show aired he felt sick with nerves. More so if it was one that he had been responsible for testing. If it did well, he allowed himself to think that he had played some small role in its success. If it did badly he was inconsolable for days. The only way to escape the black cloud hanging over him was to apply himself harder, to work even longer hours.

Throughout the Seventies and Eighties, NBC was the network that took the largest share of viewers, and was renowned for its news and documentary programmes. The last twenty years had seen a rise in the number and popularity of light entertainment features, especially game shows, and the network had lost its competitive edge. A light entertainment division was rapidly formed but had never been able to match the output of its major competitors. Increasingly NBC had turned to independent production companies that promised a change in their fortune but too often failed to deliver. Just recently a quiz show had been commissioned from the production company, Miru TV, in which mothers and their daughter-in-laws competed in pairs to win a luxury holiday. Kenji's focus groups had given the pilot episode a lukewarm reaction. They had wanted to know where the drama was. The action. The suffering. He had given what he regarded as one of his best presentations ever to the production team involved, ending with a great idea for re-working the show.

'Pit mother-in-law against daughter-in-law,' he implored the team passionately. 'The winner gets to take either the son or husband on holiday with her. Or, if you really want to shake things up, the wife doesn't have to take her husband. She can choose a friend instead, maybe even a lover.'

Even though Kenji was a research manager and his loyalty lay with the programme research division, it had always been his dream to work in production. He was bursting with ideas for new game show formats and spent hours devising them on the train to and from work. He had never been one for crosswords. Whenever he got the chance, he would share his ideas with colleagues although they were usually too busy to listen and he did not press them as that would have appeared overly forceful. This meeting was the best opportunity he had ever had to present one of his ideas and he could tell that the team was interested. A buzz of conversation started at one end of the table and soon everybody was talking at once.

'Excuse me, please,' a loud voice had spoken out. It belonged to the show's executive producer, a man called Abe E. Kitahara, who was both charming and persuasive. There was little Kenji could do but listen as Kitahara explained to the team that Kenji's focus groups had got it wrong and it was imperative they stick to the original format or they would lose this chance of success. Kenji had been dismissed from the meeting.

NBC had eventually pulled the show – viewing figures were disastrously low and every episode ran over budget. This was the first time the network had had to do something like this and it made people nervous. Their wretchedness was magnified by data that Kenji subsequently collected which suggested that the show had adversely affected NBC's brand image. There was no point in saying 'I told you so.' If anything, he blamed himself for not having spoken out, or been stronger, and felt that his colleagues did too. Especially those who were at the meeting and had witnessed the meek way in which he had backed down to Kitahara. But this impromptu birthday celebration indicated that maybe he was wrong. Or if he was right, then at least some bridges were now being mended.

He filled a cup with fresh coffee and chatted amiably before taking the largest cream cake – at everybody's insistence – back to his desk. The cake consisted of sheets of sweet, flaky pastry sandwiched together with a fat layer of cream and a generous spread of strawberry jam containing substantial lumps of real fruit. Just as he was walking out of the door, a voice called out after him, 'Hey, Yamada-san, perhaps we should leave a little something for the Watanabes. What do you think? They must get hungry in here at night.' Everybody laughed and when Kenji got back to his desk he took a large bite out of his cake. The cream squirted out of one side and landed on his freshly laundered shirt. He chuckled as he wiped it off with a handkerchief.

At midday the loudspeakers wailed again. He finished what he had been doing and broke for lunch.

Before the speakers were installed, it had been easy to forget about eating and work straight through lunch, snacking occasionally on the sweets and crackers that he kept stored in the top drawer of his desk. That was before a disgruntled American employee, seconded to the corporation, had complained that adequate provisions were not being made for the workforce and that people were not encouraged to take regular and well-deserved rest periods. Six months later, workmen appeared throughout the office, mounting the speakers that were, from that moment on, used to remind everybody when the official working day started and ended, when they could begin to claim overtime and when it was time to eat. Many employees ate at nearby restaurants or bought food from convenience stores. Other married male employees, like Kenji, had the lunch boxes that their wives prepared for them stored in the fridge at the back of the office and ate while sitting at their desks.

Once he had finished eating, Kenji caught the lift down to the ground floor and went for a short walk. He did this every day since reading in one of his wife's magazines that it aided digestion – he suffered from terrible stomach aches, especially after eating. He also took the opportunity to smoke several cigarettes in quick succession, cupping his hand around the glowing white stick to prevent it from getting wet in the rain. By the time he returned to his desk it was 12.40 p.m.

The rest of the day was spent organising a focus group to gauge reactions to the pilot episode of a new soap opera: sending out videotapes to the participants; booking a room in a downtown hotel; organising a facilitator and preparing a discussion guide. At 5 p.m. the part-time and temporary contract workers began to drift out of the office, signalling to him the start of overtime. Last month he had amassed forty-three hours, although only entitled to claim twenty.

The sound of polite coughing caused him to look up.

'Ah, Yamada-san. I am very sorry to interrupt your work, but need to speak with you. Can you please come to see me in meeting room one. I will be there in fifteen minutes.' Without waiting for an answer, he nodded and left.

Kenji could not imagine what Ishida wanted to speak with him about. It was quite unheard of that he should call one-to-one meetings as the team always met together. 'I wonder if he would like to wish me a happy birthday,' Kenji thought. Then, having convinced himself that this was indeed the case, did not give the matter another thought until, fifteen minutes later, he got up from his desk and went to meeting room one carrying his notebook and pen.

The first thing he noticed was that the layout of the room had changed. A small table sat at the front with two chairs, one of which was already occupied by Ishida, positioned beside it. The remaining chairs had been stacked, one on top of the other, and lined up against the back wall. The second thing he noticed was that on the table next to the vacant chair, was a glass tumbler filled with water and a box of tissues.

'Thank you for coming. Please sit down.'

Sitting down on the edge of the chair Kenji crossed his hands in his lap: first one way and then the other.

'It is not good news, I am afraid.'

Kenji frowned. He was suddenly reminded of an incident at school when he was eight years old. The school's secretary had interrupted the maths lesson to ask if Kenji Yamada would accompany her to the headmaster's study. He had trailed after her, down the long corridor, burning to ask why he was being summoned, but too frightened to utter a word. It turned out to be a case of mistaken identity. A window had been broken by a football and the boy seen running away from the scene was wearing a backpack of the same distinctive design and colour as Kenji's. 'No harm done,' the headmaster said jovially, drawing their meeting to an end. But Kenji had never been able to forget the fear that gripped him on that long walk to the study; the cold, clammy sweat that covered his body and the hammering of his heart.

Ishida's voice brought him back from his memories.

'As you are aware, the light entertainment division has been underperforming for many, many months. Some might even say years.'

When Kenji looked down he was surprised to see that his hands were shaking and, in an attempt to steady them, he opened his notebook and gripped the pen in a position ready to take notes. His mouth was parched and he wished desperately that he could take a sip of water, but feared he might spill the cold liquid down the front of his shirt that already bore evidence of a cream cake. He usually kept a spare shirt at work in case he needed to freshen up, but had forgotten to replace the last one he had used.

'The board of directors have met several times to decide how best to resolve this problem. This morning they came to a decision.' Picking up a piece of paper, Ishida began to read. 'Two things are obvious. First, in the current climate NBC is unable to compete against other networks providing light entertainment shows. Second, this particular marketplace is volatile and subject to extreme change. Therefore, it is with considerable regret that the board has decided the light entertainment division will cease to operate and NBC will return to its original specialisation – news and documentaries.'

Kenji was disappointed, although relieved. The team had been expecting this news for a long time – there had been rumours – and now it was here. Of course he was upset, but perhaps moving to another division would be exactly the boost he needed. And now he knew what Ishida wanted to talk to him about he could relax.

'The last eight years of my life have been spent working in this division. It has been a very happy time and I am saddened by the news. But my confidence in the board is strong and I look forward to the new challenges that lie ahead of me.'

Ishida cleared his throat. 'Obviously the programme research team will have to be disbanded. Wherever possible we have tried to find employees a place elsewhere. Unfortunately this has not always been possible. Not everyone has been accommodated.' He stared hard at Kenji. 'Budgets are tight. There have been many cutbacks over recent years in every unit, not just ours.'

Kenji's first thought was for his colleagues; those who had joined the corporation only last year during the annual intake of graduates. Could it be that Ishida was implying that these men and women would lose their jobs? When he joined the corporation twenty-two years ago it was with the understanding that it would be a job for life, but he appreciated that this was not the case for the next generation. 'My length of service,' he had thought on any number of occasions, 'provides me with immunity.'

'We have tried very hard,' Ishida continued, 'to match someone with your tremendous experience and many skills to another team. It is unfortunate, very, very unfortunate that we have been unable to find you a place.'

Kenji was confused. 'So I will be moved to another unit instead? Production perhaps?' he asked hopefully. Perhaps this was the chance he had been waiting for. Was it possible that word had got back to Ishida about his ideas for game show formats? Kenji would be happy wherever they put him but production would be a dream come true.

'That is not an option. Instead we must ask you to retire.'

'Retire.' Kenji repeated the word but it still made no sense to him.

'Yes, retire.'

'But,' he stuttered, struggling to get the words out, 'I am only forty years old.' Then he found himself giggling, the situation suddenly seemed ridiculous. 'Today is my fortieth birthday. I am too young to retire.'

'I am afraid that there is no other option.'

'No other option?' Then a thought suddenly occurred to him. 'Ah, I see. This is a joke. A joke because it is my birthday.'

'No, this is not a joke.'

One look at Ishida confirmed that it was not. Kenji's own face crumpled and he began to scratch his neck absentmindedly, creating long red weals with his fingernails. 'But I have worked here all my life. Twenty-two years. How can I be retired? I don't understand. I met my wife here. She was an office lady. You will remember her. Ami. We have two children.' Turning in the chair, Kenji looked at the door and thought about his colleagues sitting outside. 'They are . . . were my friends. I see them every day.'

'I really am very sorry, but it is out of my hands.'

'You can't do this to me.' Kenji was unable to keep the rising panic out of his voice. 'The network has always been good to me. It gave me the deposit for my family's home, my health insurance. What about our summer trip?' The network provided bi-annual trips for all employees and their families. Last summer there had been a trip to an *onsen*. Next month they were going to Tokyo Disneyland. 'What will I tell my wife? And my mother-in-law? She has just moved in with us. Her husband died. I am supposed to be providing for her.'

Ishida remained motionless for much of this speech but as Kenji's voice grew louder, he began to shift uncomfortably in his seat. He prepared to stand. 'Really there is no other way. Now, you must take some time to gather yourself together. Then please collect any belongings from your desk and leave the office. It is important that you disturb your colleagues as little as possible. We do not want them to be upset.' As he walked towards the door he took off his glasses and began to clean them with the white cloth covered with polka dots.

Kenji stood with him and followed him to the door, pleading, 'I will work harder. I will be more diligent. There will not be any more mistakes. Not like the last time. I knew I should have spoken up. Been more insistent. It won't happen again.'

Ishida didn't turn back. Alone in the meeting room, Kenji slid down the back of the door until he sat slumped on the floor. He had not meant to. His legs had simply buckled beneath him. A strangled sob escaped from his throat. How would he tell his family? He had let them down. And his colleagues? How could he face them, look them in the eye? He felt sick and dizzy. Slapping the floor with the palm of one hand, he muttered, 'Come on, pull yourself together.' Standing up, he took a few tentative steps. His legs felt extremely unsteady and, fearing that they might give way at any minute, he walked as quickly as possible out of the door and through the office.

Back at his desk he opened his briefcase and stood staring for several seconds at the brown lining before realising that he had nothing to put in it. There was no longer any need to take some paperwork home just in case he might get the chance to go over it on the train, and he had no personal belongings of any kind: no photographs of his wife and children, no paperweight or pens. Everything he used, from the calculator to the pencil sharpener, belonged to the network. Everything that is except for the golf ball ficus. Picking the plant up and snapping his empty briefcase shut, he scurried towards the door, trying to be as inconspicuous as possible.

The senior managers, seated at the far end of the row of tables, did an excellent job of pretending not to see him go and earnestly continued with their work. The junior employees were, however, less aware of the need to preserve Kenji's dignity and one called out as he passed.

'Yamada-san, where are you going so early and with that plant? You must have a secret lady friend that your wife doesn't know about.'

Kenji stuttered until finally managing to make a feeble excuse about a doctor's appointment.

Seeing the expression on his face, Kenji's colleague apologised for his outburst. 'Yamada-san, I am sorry. Good luck at the doctor's and, all being well, I will see you tomorrow.'

Outside the office block, Kenji put his briefcase down on the ground and buttoned up his coat. 'I am forty years of age,' he thought, 'and I no longer have a job.' What should he do now? He could not face telling anybody, let alone his wife. And if he went home now she would be suspicious. She would fret and fuss. 'Why are you home so early?' She was used to him getting home at nearly midnight every evening. 'Was there not enough work to keep you at the office? Did you not go out with your colleagues?' she would demand and the red flush she experienced when anxious would creep up from the base of her neck like prickly heat, colouring her entire face.

There was nothing else to do but go in search of a bar.

TWO

Kenji buried his face in the palm of his hands. He sat slumped across the bar, balanced precariously on the edge of a high stool with a chrome frame. The beige polyester suit he had collected from the dry-cleaners only yesterday was crumpled and stale. His off-white shirt was open at the neck and his burgundy tie stuffed deep into the pocket of the coat that was hanging from the back of his stool, its hem trailing in spilt beer. He had been drinking for just under two hours and, as the bar filled up around him, had attracted a number of curious stares. It was not just his dishevelled appearance that aroused attention, but that his right arm was hooked protectively around a potted house plant.

Removing one hand from his face, he groped at the counter in front of him for his glass. It contained a single mouthful of whisky that would swell to two, maybe even three, when the ice cubes melted: more than enough to see him through the next half-hour, when he would leave Gas Panic to catch the last train home to Utsunomiya. But his search proved fruitless as his hand closed repeatedly around thin air.

'It was here a minute ago,' he muttered.

Pounding music assaulted his ears and throbbed inside his spinning head, while the flashing strobe lights from the dance floor made his every movement appear to be in slow motion.

He looked at the bartender standing in front of him, wiping

18

down the sticky counter with a damp, dirty dishcloth.

'What can I get you?' she demanded, making the question sound more like a challenge.

Kenji waved both hands in front of his chest, the movement causing the stool on which he was sitting to rock. 'No, thank you.' He had had more than enough whisky already and was aware of it sitting heavily on his otherwise empty stomach.

The bartender pointed angrily at a poster pinned to the wall immediately behind her. Squinting, Kenji attempted to read the oversized script that was Gas Panic's drinks policy, printed not only in Japanese, but also in English and Spanish. If you weren't holding a drink at all times, the poster read, then you would be asked to leave.

'Whisky.'

She served the drink, slamming it down on the counter before moving on to her next customer. He reached out, picked up the glass and took a small sip that slipped down his throat like molten lava. His stomach reacted violently, sending a reflux of acid bile up into the back of his mouth. Swallowing it back down, he grimaced.

Just then somebody knocked into the back of his stool. Clutching the glass to his chest to avoid being coerced into buying another whisky that he did not want or need, he turned around. Behind him a fight had broken out between two American girls, both of whom, he saw, wore braces on their teeth. He watched in astonishment as they pulled each other's hair, slapped one another around the face and scratched at bare skin. A young Japanese man with a shaven head and tattoos down both arms, who appeared to be the cause of the altercation, looked on uninterestedly in a cloud of his own cigarette smoke.

The Gas Panic bar was located on the second floor of a three-storey building. A large, warehouse-style room, the concrete walls had been left exposed. Fat, black air-conditioning ducts snaked across the ceiling, raining down large drops of condensation on to the crowded dance floor where a 'no requests' neon sign pulsed on the front of the DJ's booth. A well-stocked bar ran along one length of the dance floor, red vinyl booths along the other with additional seating – narrow benches and tables bolted to the floor – at the back of the room.

Kenji had never been to Gas Panic before and did not intend to come again. But for tonight it served him well as there was little, if any, chance of bumping into his colleagues. Former colleagues, he reminded himself and, even though such thoughts were painful to him, could not help wondering what they were doing now. It was a Monday night so, he reasoned, they would have gone out after work for something to eat and drink. Had things worked out differently, he might have joined them and together they would have toasted his fortieth birthday. Perhaps they toasted him now? Or did they try and block him from their minds as they topped up each other's glasses? After all, the entire team was being disbanded and Kenji was not the only employee it would prove difficult to place elsewhere within the organisation. They would be concerned for their own positions, their mortgages, their wives and children. Kenji himself became more morose as his own thoughts turned, not for the first time that night, to the lifetime mortgage on the family apartment in which he lived with his wife, two young children and querulous mother-in-law.

Groaning loudly, he kneaded his temples with considerable force as though the pressure alone would banish such thoughts from his mind. He looked longingly at the floor and imagined what it would be like to curl up in a ball there; to stop eating and drinking; to fade away to nothing. Not only nothing, but something that had never existed in the first place. How could I have been so stupid, he asked himself over and over again, dwelling on every last detail, every clue that he had missed: the hushed conversations that stopped the moment that he appeared, the knowing looks. Someone could have taken him to one side and warned him what was coming. Then he might have been able to do something about it. Change Ishida's mind. Work harder. Be a better employee. And if that did not work, then at least he would have been able to slip away quietly, dignity partially intact, instead of scurrying out of the office, head bowed, carrying an empty briefcase and a plant; the taste of cream cake still in his mouth.

Staring mournfully at the floor he felt a hand pressing down on his shoulder but did not look up. He already knew that it was another of the girls who had been using him to hoist themselves up on to the bar where they would dance, watched by the men below, before tiring of the music or, in some cases, falling off. Out of the corner of one eye he watched as a pair of black stilettos teetered in his direction. He looked up; tried to warn the owner of the shoes that she might fall and injure both of them, but was too mortified to say anything. Above him stood two pale, bare legs, hardly covered by a short denim skirt that did little to hide the white lacy knickers beneath.

The girl, sensing her own unsteadiness, got down from the bar, leaning heavily on Kenji as she did so. Her backless, black-sequinned top gaping open at the front. Embarrassed, he looked away.

'Hey, you're real cute,' she slurred, tickling Kenji underneath the chin. 'Do you speak English?'

He tried to answer, but the words would not come out. Instead his mouth simply flapped open and closed. The girl did not seem to notice.

'Cute plant.' She picked it up. 'Where did you get it from?'

Kenji grabbed the plant back and clasped it to his chest, fondly stroking the leaves as he remembered better times and better places than this. At least thirty inches tall and potted in an octagonal ceramic bowl, the golf ball ficus was so called because the four braids of which the trunk was composed had been cultivated and sculptured to grow over a golf ball that now could not be removed except by cutting the branches. On top of the earth, stood a three-inch plastic man: golf club raised in the air behind his head, he was preparing to swing. The plant had been a present from his wife to mark his tenth year of service at NBC. It had also been a symbol of their shared hope that after a decade of loyal and faithful service, he would soon be considered for the type of promotion that meant taking up golf so that he might play with the other senior managers and section heads. But the last ten years of his career had been dogged by budget cutbacks and continual restructuring. So while the ficus was everything a good house plant should be – lush, green and healthy – sometimes he had not been able to look at it, it seemed to be mocking him. On several occasions he had tried to kill the thing off by starving it of food and water. But a thoughtful colleague never failed to step in if they thought that the ficus looked in need of care.

'My wife,' he whispered and belched loudly. Acidic bile flooded into his mouth. The music seemed to be getting louder and the floor had started to lurch beneath him, turning his stomach and causing his head to spin. 'An earthquake?' he said to the girl who looked back at him dumbly.

'You'll have to speak up I can't hear you.'

'Earthquake,' he repeated, this time grabbing the girl by her bare arms as the floor lurched again, more violently. Mistaking this for a fumbled pass, she began to giggle; a giggle that quickly turned into a scream and then a wail when he threw up all over her and the bar. People turned to stare as two bouncers appeared out of the shadows. Picking Kenji up under both arms they marched him out of the bar – his feet barely touched the ground – and pushed him down the flight of stairs that ran along the outside of the building. They threw his coat and briefcase down after him, but after a quick exchange of words, decided to keep the plant.

'Please,' he begged, climbing halfway up the stairs only to be blocked by one of the men. Realising that to protest was pointless, Kenji struggled into his coat, picked up his briefcase and began to stagger up the road in the direction of Roppongi station, pausing momentarily to retch, once again, in the gutter.

At Roppongi station he stood midway along the platform, swaying slightly, as he waited for an underground train. He had to be at Tokyo station for the last bullet train to Utsunomiya, a journey of 100km. It arrived a few minutes later and he staggered on, collapsing gratefully into an empty seat next to the door. He felt better for having thrown up, but a pounding headache and desperate thirst replaced the nausea. As he searched in his pockets for the painkillers that could be taken without water, he looked around the carriage. It was busy, although most people were standing or sitting in the front or the back of the carriage. The central section – where he had got on – was empty except for another man. A few seconds later he began to realise why.

The man smelt rancid: the combination of a dense, musky body odour and a strong chemical that put Kenji in mind of a futon on which he had slept while honeymooning at a guesthouse in Osaka. (When he had asked the owner what the smell was, he was told, curtly and quietly, that it was used to kill bugs.) The man's hair grew down past his shoulders; further possibly, had it not been tangled in thick clumps where particles of dust, dirt and skin had become trapped. A thick layer of grime covered his face, and sores had broken out in weeping clusters at both sides of his mouth. His fingernails were long and pointed, dirt wedged beneath their surface, and he wore muslin bags tied around his feet with the same twine that he used to keep his trousers in place. Muttering and repeatedly shaking his head, he waved one hand about in the air as if there were a fly bothering him. Then he leant forward, opened his mouth and allowed a long stream of dense, discoloured spittle to drip from his mouth to the floor of the carriage.

'What are you looking at?'

Kenji, who had not realised he was staring, turned away, but it was already too late.

'What are you looking at?' the man repeated, growing louder and attracting stares from the other passengers in the carriage. 'Haven't you ever seen a man down on his luck before? Come on, answer me.'

Apologising, Kenji got up from his seat. He had to get off at the next stop and willed the train to move faster. But the man had also stood up and was muttering loudly as he moved closer; bringing with him a smell so overpowering that Kenji felt his stomach preparing to heave again. After what seemed like an eternity, the blackness outside the carriage turned to light and Kenji jumped through the doors the moment they opened, praying silently that the man would not follow. Thankfully he merely leaned out of the carriage, shouting after him.

'I used to be like you too. I used to have a job, a family, a home.

23

But look at me now. They took it all away from me. Every last bit. And they can do it to you too. Be warned. They can do it to you too.'

Kenji's hands were still trembling when he boarded the bullet train to Utsunomiya. It crawled out of Tokyo station, moving slowly past the tall buildings that crowded the train track, their walls black with the dirt that they had absorbed over the years. Overhead a mass of confused electricity pylons and cables crossed one way and then the next. Suddenly sober, he stared out of the window into the black night sky punctuated not by stars, but neon lights that illuminated signs advertising beer, restaurants and bars. He closed his eyes and when he opened them, caught sight of a man's reflection staring back at him. At first he did not recognise him: the man in the window looked so tired, so old and haggard, whereas he had always thought of himself as being reasonably young. Forty, yes. But he certainly did not look his age and never had. At least not until today.

Ami, Kenji's wife, once confided in him that his youthful appearance singled him out over her other suitors. Although they had dated when Kenji first joined NBC, it had not lasted. Ami wanted a man with better prospects. A few years later, when they were both in their mid-twenties, Ami had still not managed to find a man to fit her high standards, and Kenji's prospects were looking up. After a long engagement, they were married and shortly after they had saved up enough money towards a deposit on a place of their own, the twins were born. On the day of their wedding, Ami had told him, 'I chose you because you are a decent man who wants to get ahead. And you have good skin. You will age well.' She did not want to imagine herself growing old with a wheezing, grey-haired man who could not climb flights of stairs without growing breathless.

Utsunomiya station was deserted except for the lone guard who was always there. Tonight this seemed ominous as Kenji walked through the ticket barriers and on past the darkened coffee shops and the department store with its shutters pulled down. Even the kids who hung out on the bridge connecting the station to the main road, listening to music on their ghetto box and practising break-dancing moves in cycle helmets and knee pads, had gone home.

It was a short walk home where everything was in darkness. Not bothering to turn on any lights, he went straight to the bedroom. Ami was sleeping soundly, happily unaware. He undressed and climbed into bed beside her. She stirred slightly, mumbled something, but did not wake. He wanted to touch her, to be held by her. But it was a long time since they had done anything like that. He contemplated waking her, telling her about his job, but imagining her reaction, sank down on to the futon where he lay on his back, staring at the ceiling, trying to ignore the hole that was opening up inside him. At 3 o'clock in the morning, lulled by the regular rhythm of his wife's breathing, he finally fell asleep.

THREE

'Wake up. I have been calling you for over an hour. Don't you realise you're going to be late for work?'

Slowly, because sudden movements were painful, Kenji opened first one eye and then the next, raising himself up on both elbows. His head was pounding, his tongue felt as if it was covered with a layer of finely ground glass, and Ami was staring at him from the bedroom door. He rolled over on to one side and checked the time on his digital alarm clock. He moaned and fell back down on the futon. It was 8.03 a.m.

He had been dreaming. Dreaming about the Queen of Hearts Banquet Hall in Tokyo Disneyland where he had found temporary employment as a waiter. When he reported for duty on his first day, he was handed a pile of clothes and instructed to change. Ten minutes later he arrived on the restaurant floor wearing an exaggeratedly tapered pair of white furry trousers, a bright yellow jacket over a bottle green waistcoat, a red cravat and a long pair of snow-white, downy ears.

Just thinking about the row of suits hanging in his wardrobe at home made him want to flee the restaurant. But before the opportunity arose, a young woman in a long blonde wig thrust a damp dishcloth into his hand and shepherded him in the direction of a recently vacated table. 'Clean this,' she told him, smoothing down the front of her blue dress, 'and then bring the next customers over.' She pointed in the direction of a party of four, waiting at the front of the banquet hall to be seated.

He did as instructed; cleaning one table after another until he was covered with sweat. All the other workers seemed to vanish mysteriously until he was the only one left, cooking, serving, taking orders and cleaning tables. He thought things could not get much worse, and then they did. Walking towards the front of the banquet hall, he stopped dead in his tracks, causing the long, white, downy ears on top of his head to quiver. The next group of people waiting for a table were his colleagues from NBC. They were followed by his wife, children and mother-in-law, whose heads were bowed in shame.

Waking up to the reality of his life was not much better than this awful dream.

'If you hurry I can drop you off at the station,' Ami called impatiently from outside the door.

He had no choice. He would have to tell her what had happened. Rolling out on to the floor, he stood up, pushed both feet into a pair of slippers and pulled on his dressing gown. As he shuffled down the corridor towards the kitchen, his entire family came into sight. The twins – now nine years old – were sitting at the table eating breakfast. Yumi's hair had been neatly plaited and secured with pink ribbons. He watched her legs, swinging underneath the table, kicking back and forth until she caught her brother on the shin.

'Ow,' he yowled. 'Mum, she kicked me.'

Although they were twins, Yoshi was considerably smaller than his sister and, Kenji had always thought, resembled him in temperament. Yumi on the other hand was more like her mother.

'What's going on now?' Ami continued washing dishes in the sink.

Kenji opened his mouth to speak but no words came out. Nobody had even noticed him standing there.

'She kicked me,' Yoshi whined.

'Apologise to your brother.'

'It was an accident.'

'I . . .' Kenji began, but was interrupted by his mother-in-law: a small, wizened old woman with soft wrinkled skin.

'Has anyone seen my magazines?' she demanded, retrieving a pair of glasses from the front pocket of the floral housecoat she wore every day over polyester trousers and a long-sleeved cotton blouse with ruffled cuffs. 'They were here last night.' She picked the children's lunch boxes up off the counter and looked in their school bags that were hanging off the back of their chairs.

The way his family spent their mornings was not usually something that Kenji witnessed and he was glad of it. But he knew what the old lady was looking for. Ami had told him after she had first moved in that her mother was adamant she would pay her way. With no money to speak of, the old woman entered competitions in every single magazine that she could lay her hands on and donated her winnings to the household. She had proved to be quite successful although the prizes tended to be of little use. Trays of dog food were stacked up, one on top of each other, in the hallway next to the front door; a pair of winter tyres for a Jeep were pushed beneath Yoshi's bed; and several large jars of pickled vegetables were piled next to the washing machine.

'I could keep this family afloat with the prizes I win,' Eriko muttered defiantly and pushed past Kenji, out of the kitchen. It was then that Ami noticed her husband.

'What are you doing standing there? You should be changed already. If you hurry I can drop you off at the station when I take the children to school.' As she spoke she rubbed at the kitchen counter with a damp cloth, the large curls on her head bouncing lightly.

'I have something to tell you.'

'What is it? Don't you feel well? Do you have to go to the doctor?'

'No, it's nothing like that.'

'Well it will have to wait then.' Throwing the cloth in the kitchen sink, Ami walked towards her husband, turned him round and urged him down the hallway to the bathroom.

'We need to talk,' Kenji protested weakly, allowing himself to be pushed into the bathroom as if he were one of the children.

'No time.'

The door closed and he collapsed on the toilet seat. What was the point? He had tried but she wouldn't listen. It was best just to go along with her for now. Maybe going to Tokyo today wasn't such a bad idea. He could go and see Ishida, beg for his job back. No, he was too proud for that. It would be better to find a new job. It wouldn't take long. He was a man with a great deal of experience and contacts. Then Ami would not have to know, at least until it was safe to tell her. It was decided. He would go to Tokyo and look for a new job. Feeling if not confident then at least hopeful, Kenji stood up, washed his face and brushed his teeth. After putting on a clean suit he returned to the kitchen where Ami handed him a lunch box that he put into his empty briefcase and followed everybody into the car, where he sat in silence in the front passenger seat until they reached the station.

'Have a nice day,' Ami called as he closed the door and she drove off.

FOUR

What else does a man need to find a job besides a mobile phone and a collection of business cards, Kenji thought as he left Tokyo station and walked into the first coffee shop he came across. One of his many contacts was sure to help.

'Large black coffee please.' He placed his order with the gangly young man behind the counter, pointing at a large, round, icing sugar-dusted pastry. 'And one of those.'

After paying, Kenji carried his order to the corner of the coffee shop where he sat down. On the table, he placed his mobile phone, a stack of business cards and a packet of Lucky Strikes. He lit a cigarette and started sorting through the cards, wondering who he should phone first. The answer was obvious. Masao Jo was a senior executive at a research agency based in Naka-Meguro, whose services Kenji had often employed when conducting large-scale studies NBC did not have the capacity to run alone. Confidently, he dialled the number.

'Ah, Yamada-san.' Jo sounded pleased to hear from Kenji. 'How are you?'

They exchanged pleasantries for a minute or two before running out of things to say.

Jo was the first to break the silence. 'What can I do for you, Yamada-san? Do you have a study with which you need our assistance?'

'It is a more delicate matter than that.' Kenji began to talk, at length, about the recession, the restructuring and budget cutbacks at NBC and their recent decision to move out of the light entertainment sector.

'That is very unfortunate,' Jo soothed. 'Also very strange. I had not heard any rumours and normally I am the first to know. My contacts are excellent.'

Kenji hesitated. Would he be able to say the words out loud? 'I have been obliged to retire due to the recent restructuring and find myself in need of alternative employment. I was hoping that you might be able to assist me. Perhaps your agency is in need of a senior research executive?'

Jo apologised, repeatedly. 'That is very sad news. For you and for your family. Unfortunately business is bad for everybody, my agency included. Please be assured that if I do hear of anything I will be in touch. Thank you very much for your call.' He hung up so quickly that Kenji did not have a chance to speak.

Sitting at a table directly across from Kenji was an old woman with leathery skin. She smiled at him. He looked away, ashamed, and only when she had left the coffee shop, did he make another call. This, and all the others that followed it, were worse than the first. As soon as he mentioned losing his job, the tone of the conversation changed. The person on the other end of the line became less affable, even suspicious. How had he lost his job? Why was he retired? It was very unfortunate but no, they did not know of any jobs.

His entire day was spent being rejected in this manner until at last it was late enough for him to go home without arousing Ami's suspicions.

The rest of the week passed in much the same way. Every morning he woke from a restless sleep filled with strange dreams in which he stacked shelves in supermarkets, served customers in 7/11 or directed traffic into an underground car park. Day after day he dragged himself out of bed and travelled to Tokyo, where he studied the job advertisements in newspapers, searched the websites of suitable companies and signed up with recruitment agencies.

'What did you study at university, Yamada-san?' a young lady at the Tokyo Recruitment Agency asked him, fingertips hovering over the surface of her keyboard. There was a framed photograph on the desk showing her in full graduation gown flanked by an elderly man and woman, and a certificate on the wall indicated she had recently graduated from Waseda University with a degree in human resources management.

'University,' Kenji spluttered. 'I didn't go to university.'

The girl's eyelids fluttered momentarily as she tapped at the keyboard. 'How many languages do you speak?'

'I speak only Japanese.' He was starting to panic. Why was she asking him all these questions? Surely what mattered was that he could work and that he wanted to work. 'I have twenty-two years' experience with a large corporation and an unblemished record. I joined NBC after leaving school and rose to the position of programme research manager by hard work and merit.'

The girl began twisting the thin silver band on the little finger of her right hand. 'Any professional development qualifications?'

'I was too busy working to take any courses,' he snapped. But he wasn't angry with her, he was angry with himself. Why hadn't he taken any courses? Were they even offered? So why hadn't he insisted? Probably because he had never insisted upon anything in his life. Would he even know how to?

The girl smiled. 'I'll submit this form and we'll see what matches our database finds for you. It will only take a few minutes.'

There were three. Each offering half the salary he had been paid by NBC. With a mortgage and a family to support he could not afford to take such a pay cut. His pride would not let him.

'These are all junior positions,' he exploded.

'Nowadays most companies require that their employees not only have a degree but at the very least can speak English. Unfortunately, you have neither of these qualifications.'

'I have twenty-two years' experience.'

'I am sorry, but these are the only matches our computer found for you. Would you like me to arrange an interview?'

'No, thank you.' He pushed back the chair and left the office.

On the street outside he paused to light a cigarette. At the end of the month, his wife would be expecting him to transfer his salary into their shared account, of which she would then give him a monthly allowance. Thankfully he had had the foresight to put aside some savings into a personal account. How long he could use this to stave her off he was not sure. Maybe a month or two at the most.

Three weeks passed without even the hope of an interview. He was commuting to Tokyo now with unwashed hair, several days of stubble on his chin and wearing a crumpled suit. After yet another morning of unsuccessful job hunting, Kenji stopped for lunch in a Shinjuku ramen bar. The place was empty except for an elderly man in a blue canvas cap and matching jacket who was sitting next to the door. He was hunched over a large steaming bowl of noodles, sucking them into his mouth, hot and straight out of the broth while drawing in a cooling intake of air at the same time. The result was a loud slurping noise. Once the noodles were finished, the old man picked up his bowl and drank the remaining soup with equal gusto. The chef looked on, wiping the palms of his hands up and down the front of his already stained apron.

The door flew open and somebody clattered through it. Everybody – the chef, his elderly customer and Kenji – turned around to see who could be making such a noise. It was a man, in his fifties probably, although his hair and clothes seemed to suggest somebody much younger.

'Not you again,' the chef roared. But there was something about his voice that told Kenji he was not entirely displeased to see this odd man who carried a battered, brown leather suitcase. 'What do you want this time?' the chef continued. 'Have you come to bother my customers?'

The man smoothed down the front of his suit. It was made from a shiny black material with a faint silver dart detail running all the way through it. 'Pah,' he said, gesticulating with his free hand. 'What customers? I don't see any customers.'

'They heard you were coming, that's why.'

The man laughed, good-naturedly, hauled the suitcase on to an empty stool and began to open it. The chef stopped him. 'I have had enough of buying from you. Nothing ever works properly, everything breaks. So sit down and eat, or you can leave.'

'Okay, okay.' The man removed a white handkerchief from his breast pocket and waved it about his head as he ordered. 'I'll have the same as him,' he said, nodding at Kenji who was eating a bowl of Chinese noodles in broth with sliced pork and a leek garnish. The chef busied himself preparing the food and the man sat down at the counter, a few feet from Kenji. In spite of himself, Kenji found that he was watching him out of the corner of one eye. He bounced, like a child, on the cushioned stool while playing with a pair of chopsticks: beating out a fast rhythm on anything that was close to hand. His feet were tapping too. They were encased in a pair of black leather boots: the toes of which tapered to a long point and – because they had become detached from the soles – were held in place by several layers of black duct tape.

'Come on. A man could die of hunger in this place,' the man shouted and then suddenly jumped up and moved to the empty stool beside Kenji. 'Have I got something for you, my friend.' He opened his suitcase and removed a pair of red chopsticks sealed in a plastic bag.

Now that he was up close, Kenji could see one of his eyes was dark brown, the other green. He couldn't help staring.

'Strawberry-flavoured chopsticks.' The man slid the plastic bag across the counter to Kenji. 'Dissolve in your mouth as you eat. Makes everybody's food taste good. Even mother-in-law's. Even his.' He nodded in the direction of the chef.

'I have all the chopsticks I need.' Kenji slid the plastic bag back across the counter.

Undeterred the man reached into his suitcase and brought out a pair of bright orange, plastic underpants. 'Inflatable underpants, for the gentleman that wants to avoid drowning while travelling on the subway should there happen to be a flood.' Again Kenji declined. 'You are a hard customer to please.' The man laughed and reached into his suitcase once more, bringing out a small fan. 'But I suspect I have just the thing for you. Cools noodles down in seconds.' The fan consisted of three white plastic blades that sat on top of a square battery pack with a bulldog clip attached to its base. Clipping the fan to Kenji's bowl, he switched it on and the blades began to rotate: at first slowly and then with increasing speed. At that moment, Kenji was lifting noodles to his mouth. They became trapped in the whirring blades which then whipped the chopsticks from his hands and blew hot broth all over his suit and newspaper.

'I am so sorry. So very sorry.' The man flew into action, turned off the fan and grabbed a handful of tissues with which to blot Kenji's suit.

'That's all right,' Kenji told him firmly, stood up and went to the other end of the counter. The man looked sheepishly at Kenji as he ate his own food which the chef had left in front of him. Then, a few minutes later, he joined Kenji at the end of the bar. They ate together in silence.

'Look,' the man said, breaking the silence. 'I'm sorry. I can get a bit over-zealous at times. A guy's got to make a living you know.'

'It shouldn't worry you.' Having noodles splattered all over him seemed to be exactly what Kenji deserved and he wasn't about to get upset about it.

'My name's Izo Izumi.' He offered Kenji his card. 'And you are?'

'Kenji Yamada.'

Indicating the sodden newspaper, Izo asked, 'You're looking for a job?'

Sitting a bit straighter on his stool, Kenji asked, 'Do you know where I might find one? A job in research perhaps. I worked for NBC for many years. I have lots of experience.'

'Me?' Izo shook his head. 'No. I'm too much of a free spirit to be tied down by an office, a boss. I did it for a while. I trained as a lawyer and worked for a firm here in Shinjuku.'

'A lawyer?'

'I don't really look the type, do I? But it was back when things were booming.'

It seemed like a long time ago now, but Kenji remembered it well. Limitless expense accounts. Eating out every night with clients in Tokyo's best restaurants. Extravagant outings for employees and their families.

'Most of our clients had more money than sense.' The salesman became sombre. 'Men who should have known better getting sued by young girls when they found themselves pregnant. Then their wives found out and wanted a divorce, not to mention custody of the children, home and any cars. I even dealt with a custody battle involving a dog once. A very handsome poodle, but a dog nonetheless. Then the cases dried up. Nobody had any money to take young girls out, let alone get divorced. We went under. I lost my job and couldn't find another one. You see, I was recently qualified and not very good either. I only got the job because my uncle twisted a few arms. I was a wreck. Wandering around Tokyo, not knowing what to do with myself. Then one day, I was sitting in a bar getting drunk when this guy came in.'

He turned and looked at the door through which he had burst a short while ago.

'He was carrying a brown leather suitcase much like this one here. I thought to myself, hey, that guy must be going on holiday. Then he opened the suitcase and all the regulars in the bar crowded around him. He had all kinds of stuff in there. Beer mats, drinks umbrellas, fancy soaps, instant noodles. Cheap too. They kept pressing money into his hands and soon the case was empty. I said to myself, Izo, you could make a living like that. So with the little money that I had left I got myself a suitcase, a few suppliers, and now I'm a travelling salesman. I can never stay in one place for too long or I get itchy feet. No wife, no kids. Nobody to think about but myself.'

'Doesn't it get lonely?'

'Lonely? Me? You must be kidding.' The wide grin plastered across Izo's face waned slightly. 'I've got a girl in every town. Best way to be. What about you? Are you married?'

Kenji told him about his family.

'Being out of work must be pretty tough for you. How did your family take it?'

'They don't know.' Normally a private man, Kenji was surprised by how easy it was to open up to this stranger. 'It was my hope that

36

I would be able to find another job before it was necessary to tell them. Now I am not sure. It has been three weeks already.'

Izo chewed on his bottom lip. 'Shall I tell you a secret?' he asked, leaning across the gap that separated them. 'Shall I tell you how to make money without having to do another day's office work in your entire life?'

Kenji tried to sound casual. 'Sure.'

'You ever play pachinko?'

'Pachinko?' he repeated, thinking about the parlours he had frequented in the days before his marriage; about the rows of upright pinball machines and the weary men who sat, mesmerised, in front of them. 'Years ago.'

'So you know the basic rules, right?'

He remembered the rules. First you buy a supply of small, shiny silver balls that you place in a tray at the bottom of the machine. Next you turn a dial handle: spinning it quickly if you want the balls to cascade rapidly down the face of the machine; slowly if you require a more sedate pace. Then it's just a case of sitting back and watching the balls as they bounce off a maze of pins and levers. If you are lucky they drop into an open slot and more balls fall out of the machine into the tray. At the end of the evening Kenji would exchange any leftover balls for cigarettes at a counter located at the front of the parlour. Other prizes were on offer and could be traded for cash at a nearby back-alley shop but all he had wanted was cigarettes and, anyway, most of the time he went home empty handed.

'You lose,' Kenji shrugged. 'But you don't play to win.' He was referring to the hypnotic effect that the bright lights and military-style marching music played in the parlours had had on him.

'Then you don't know the secret.' Izo seemed pleased with himself. 'It's all in the pegs,' he told Kenji. 'Every night, after the pachinko parlour closes, an employee opens each machine and adjusts the pegs with a small hammer. Most machines he sets so that the player will lose all his balls. But on a few – different ones each night – he spreads the pegs wide enough so that lots of balls will fall into the payoff slot. Whoever gets this machine the next day will be a lucky man and anybody watching him will be encouraged to hope that they too will win.'

'I've heard that before, but it's not actually true.'

Izo looked offended and Kenji tried to think of something he could say that might make amends.

'How would you know? Which ones had been fixed?'

'You arrive early. Before the parlour opens. Then when it does, run quickly up and down each aisle until you spot the one that has been set to pay out. In the beginning this will be difficult and you will need to carry a ruler to hold up against the glass face and measure the distance between the pegs. Be discreet or they'll throw you out. Then later, when you become a real pro, you will be able to tell just by looking.'

'How much can you win?'

'How much did you get paid by your company?'

Kenji hesitated but then told him, and when Izo explained that a pachinko machine could pay out even more than that, he was amazed. 'So why are you a travelling salesman? Why do you not play pachinko all the time?'

Izo put both hands over his ears and shook his head madly as if there was a wasp trapped between his ears. 'It was the noise that got to me. All those steel balls dropping down the front of the machine. It was like sitting in a tin shack during a hailstorm. I couldn't stand it. My head would be screaming at the end of each night. So I got out of it. I haven't played for years now. Anyway – ' He looked at his watch and jumped up suddenly. ' – I've got a train to catch.' He made to leave but before he went handed Kenji the pair of red chopsticks. 'On the house,' he grinned. 'Take care and be lucky.' Slapping him hard on the back, Izo exchanged a few friendly insults with the chef and left.

Kenji wanted to ask him to stay a little longer. Instead he jumped up and ran to the window of the ramen bar where he watched Izo disappear down the street. When he returned to his seat, the chef cleared away his bowl and smiled broadly at him. 'Crazy guy, that one.'

Kenji nodded. Sure Izo was crazy, but perhaps he was just the lucky break that he had been looking for.

FIVE

'Hey, what do you think you're doing?'

When Kenji was a child and his mother caught him committing some misdemeanour or other, she would pinch the top of his right arm between her fingers and demand to know what he thought he was doing. Kenji would yelp and protest, but it didn't take long before they were friends again. His mother was a mild-mannered woman who was slow to anger. If she did pinch him, it was because he deserved it and after he had been punished he would try desperately hard to make it up to her. There was nothing he liked more than the time they spent together, telling stories. As they walked through the neighbourhood, on their way to the shops or to Kenji's school, his mother would point at a stranger and whisper in his ear, 'Tell me about him? What is he doing here? Where is he going?' Kenji's responses were always elaborate. He was a pirate who had sailed the Caribbean Sea and had come to Japan to retire. He owned a three-legged cat and was on his way to the fishmonger's to buy their lunch. That evening he intended to play cards with his neighbours and win all their money. By contrast his mother's stories were simple but heroic. He was an ordinary office worker. Every day he wrote out long lists of numbers on pieces of paper and added them up. Once he'd finished, he filed the papers away in a large cabinet where they were never seen again. During the day he was a sad, lonely man, but at night he came alive when he painted the most beautiful pictures anyone had ever seen. Kenji's mother saw beauty in everything and everyone, even the most ordinary of people. She said that deep down everyone had a secret passion or desire, a hidden talent. For years he thought he might have harboured one. That's why he'd kept a notebook filled with ideas for TV programmes.

'What do you think you're doing?'

Although spoken some thirty years later, these words had the same effect upon him. He froze and the ruler he had been holding up against the face of the pachinko machine fell out of his hand and on to the floor. Slowly he inched round until he was facing the direction from which the voice had come.

The man standing behind Kenji was enormous: his girth completely spanned the width of the aisle running between the two rows of pachinko machines. It wasn't just his size that made him stand out among the other pachinko players and grabbed Kenji's attention. He wore a voluminous Hawaiian shirt that depicted an orange sun setting over a volcanic mountain. A reddish-blue sea lapped at the sandy base of the mountain where mango trees grew, casting long shadows over the ground. Kenji considered trying to run round past him, but it was impossible. The man's legs were planted firmly on the floor beneath the shirt: large and solid as any sumo wrestler's, and all but bursting the seams of the light-beige cargo pants in which they were encased. The man's feet were strapped into a pair of open-toed sandals, above which his ankles were just visible. Although he tried not to, Kenji could not help but notice that where the rolls of fat ended, where they could not spill any further down the man's legs, deep red fissures cut into his skin.

The man did not look like a security guard. But the Maruhan Tower did not look like any kind of pachinko parlour Kenji had ever visited before.

There were five floors: each one equipped with an extensive range of videogames, slot machines and pachinko. Music thumped from the speakers, occasionally penetrating the wall of sound created by thousands of metal balls cascading down the vertical faces of several hundred pachinko machines. The machines themselves were not the purely mechanical creatures Kenji remembered. Each was encased in brightly coloured plastic and equipped with a video screen where animated characters danced and cheered when a steel ball disappeared into holes in the face of the machine.

Once a ball disappeared, it activated three reels, causing them to spin. If the pictures on the reels matched when they stopped spinning, more balls fell out of the bottom of the machine and could be exchanged at a prize counter. And it wasn't just the cigarettes Kenji had played for. There were designer handbags and sunglasses on offer, and digital cameras. The parlour too was different from what he remembered. There were even plush velvet love seats for couples on dates, an extravagant water fountain and a no-smoking section. But what surprised him most were the posters in the foyer.

'Every Wednesday night is ladies' night,' he read out loud. 'And on these nights the Maruhan's honourable male customers are respectfully asked to remain at home.'

'Since when,' Kenji had said, turning to the well-groomed usher who had greeted him on the way in, 'did women play pachinko?'

The usher had smiled and repeated the message on the poster.

'What are you doing, salaryman?' the man in the Hawaiian shirt asked again, shifting his enormous weight from one foot to the other.

Kenji looked closely at the floor, which was decorated with cartoon characters, but could not see his ruler. Thankfully none of the other patrons were paying him any attention. They sat mesmerised in front of machines, sponge plugs stuffed deep into both ears and cigarettes hanging from their bottom lips. The pachinko pros among them were easily identifiable by the yellow plastic trays overflowing with steel balls stacked high at their feet.

'I don't mean to cause any trouble,' he muttered and bowed apologetically. 'I will go.'

Head down, he ran towards the escalator and rode it to the ground floor. Thinking that all must now be safe, he took a deep breath that caught in his throat the moment that a large hand landed on his back. He stared at the nails on the end of the fingers: they had been bitten down to the quick.

'What's your hurry?' the man in the Hawaiian shirt asked cheerfully. They were standing on the street outside the Maruhan Tower and despite the cold air, beads of sweat had broken out all over the fat man's forehead. He wiped them away with a handkerchief, his breathing deep and irregular.

'Are you a security guard?' Kenji asked and the man chuckled, his eyes closing and disappearing behind two enormous apple-shaped cheeks. It was a mirthful sound that rose from the very depths of his belly and caused his entire body to rock back and forth. Unable to help himself, Kenji giggled along and when asked, agreed to accompany the man for something to eat.

Several minutes later they were both sitting on hard plastic chairs in McDonald's: Kenji nibbling unenthusiastically on a hamburger while his companion, who had introduced himself only as Doppo, devoured a large burger, French fries, chocolate milkshake and apple pie.

'So what was with the ruler?' Doppo asked in between mouthfuls of food, and as Kenji explained, silent mirth rocked his body again and the yellow plastic seat creaked and groaned beneath his weight. 'It must be a long time since you last played pachinko,' he said and Kenji agreed that indeed it was. 'You don't really see machines like that anymore. The ones where they alter the pins every night. Some of the more rural areas or neighbourhood parlours have them. But these days,' he said, pausing to wipe his mouth with a napkin, 'most machines are controlled by computer circuits. Although that doesn't mean they can't be beaten. You've just got to know how.' Doppo placed the napkin on the table and looked searchingly at Kenji. 'I can show you if you like.'

'You would show me?'

'Sure. Why not?' The large man shrugged. 'I was following you back at the parlour for quite some time. You looked like you were up to something and I wanted to know what. When I saw you slip that ruler out of your coat sleeve I said to myself now there's a man that could use a break. I'm something of a player myself, you see. Ever since my wife died, really.'

The smile disappeared from his face. Kenji searched for

something comforting to say, but could think of nothing. Instead he offered him his uneaten fries. Doppo smiled sadly.

'No, thank you. I've eaten enough and I promised my daughter that I'd do something about this waistline.' He patted his stomach. 'She is never happier than when nagging me about something. She wants me to give up everything. Pachinko, smoking, eating junk food. And she is always pestering me to come and live with her and her family in Hawaii. Ever since my wife – her mother – died five years ago she has not stopped. Yesterday I finally decided to take her up on her offer. The climate will suit me, I get on well with her husband, and her two children are polite and well-behaved. Perhaps I can learn to play cards.'

He did not sound convinced.

'So you'll give up pachinko?' Kenji asked.

'It looks like I'll have to,' Doppo replied, removing an inhaler from the top pocket of his shirt and sucking deeply on it. 'But not – ' He put the inhaler back. ' – before I have taught you how to win.'

SIX

Kenji checked his watch. It was 8.45 a.m.: more than an hour to go before his meeting with Doppo. To pass the time he drank several cups of strong, sweet black coffee in the nearby Tokyu department store and when he returned to Shibuya station, brushing pastry crumbs from the breast of his suit jacket, found it quieter than when he first arrived.

Standing next to the long row of ticket machines just inside the station's west entrance, he watched as a middle-aged man carrying a raincoat and a briefcase not too dissimilar from his own, walked through a barrier and out of the station into the plaza. He thought about his mother and what she might have said to him had she been there. 'Where's he going in such a hurry?' she would have asked. The man was certainly hurrying. He also wasn't looking where he was going, because he bumped into a schoolgirl who was dawdling across the square, staring at a music video on the large screen that hung from the side of a tall building on the opposite side of the road. The impact caused her to stagger and then, under the weight of the large bag of books she wore thrown across one shoulder, fall to the ground with a loud smack revealing the white soles of her plimsolls. Apologising profusely, the man helped the young girl to her feet before hurrying on across the square.

Perhaps it was all the caffeine he had drunk but, as he waited for Doppo, Kenji became aware of a strange sensation rising up inside him. It was one that he struggled to name but had experienced before in a spacecraft simulator at an exhibition in Yokohama. It had been late in the day. The conference centre was virtually empty and he was the only person floating around inside that tube; rolling first one way and then the next; feeling free, rootless, and completely unencumbered. When the simulation ended and he dropped heavily to the floor, he begged for one more go only to be informed – politely but nonetheless firmly – that it would not be possible. Bereft, he had boarded a train at the station thinking that he would never recapture that feeling. And yet here it was again. He was floating.

'Morning, salaryman.'

'Doppo.' Kenji beamed, taking in Doppo's enormous frame and his colourful shirt. The top few buttons were open, revealing a gold medal on a chain that pinched the flesh of his thick neck.

Kenji strode towards Doppo. Inside the otherwise empty briefcase he was carrying was the bento box Ami had prepared for him and it rattled loudly as he walked.

'We need to get you some new clothes, salaryman.' Doppo laughed, but not unkindly. 'Those parlours can get pretty hot and stuffy when a man's been playing all day long.'

Nodding solemnly, Kenji loosened the knot in his tie. It was royal blue and embroidered in silk thread with small men playing golf. Another present from Ami. 'I thought about smuggling some clothes out of the house. But I don't want my wife to become suspicious.'

'Still haven't told her, huh?'

'The longer I leave it the more difficult it becomes. I keep thinking I'll get a job soon and then I'll tell her but it never happens.'

'Well, how about we get you a little number like what I've got on?' Doppo performed a small pirouette in front of Kenji. 'You can always leave it in one of the station lockers. But first things first. Let's go play pachinko.'

Kenji was so excited that he almost whooped with joy. He hurried after Doppo, out of the station and into the warm sunlight where the schoolgirl was still standing, staring up at the same video screen, shading her eyes with one hand.

A small, orderly queue was waiting patiently on the sidewalk outside the Maruhan Tower. Doppo greeted a number of people who were standing in line; they nodded politely in his direction but glared at Kenji. So intense were their stares that he was glad when, a few minutes later, the shutters rattled open and two young men in ushers' uniforms unlocked the doors. Immediately, Doppo moved back against the wall, bidding Kenji to do the same. The queue, which had continued to grow after they joined it, surged forward and in through the open doors.

'Let them go,' Doppo shrugged as people pushed past them. 'We're in no hurry. At least not today.'

Once the rush was over, they entered and took one of four parallel escalators travelling to and from the third floor. Ahead of them an elderly gentleman was running up the moving steps. This surprised Kenji as he did not look like a man who could, let alone should, be travelling at such speed. As the escalator continued its ascent the third floor came into view and they saw the old man, now carrying a yellow plastic tray full of silver balls, racing to a machine in the far right-hand corner. He was beaten to it by a middle-aged woman wearing a head scarf and large, round, black sunglasses. He threw the cloth cap he was wearing to the floor in frustration and retreated to a nearby machine, from where he glared at the woman in the head scarf, jumping up from his seat each time she made the slightest movement.

'Already we have our first lesson.' Doppo grinned at the confused expression on Kenji's face. 'Who do you think sets the machines' win ratios?'

Kenji shrugged. 'Government?'

'Right. But the parlours manipulate them. It's illegal, but overlooked by the officials. Jackpots are increased on busy days when they are more likely to be noticed. Customers think that it's a good parlour and so they come back. And no matter what kind of day it is, at least a few machines are always set to pay out big, for much the same reason.'

Music began pumping out of the speaker immediately above

46

Doppo's head. He raised his voice until it was just loud enough to be heard.

'The electronic circuits that control the win ratios are altered every three to four days. If you're a serious player then you will be in here just before closing time, checking out which machines are paying out big. These are the ones that you make a beeline for the next day.' Doppo nodded in the direction of the man in the cloth cap. 'Come on, I'll show you around.'

They began to stroll slowly along the nearest aisle. Kenji stopped expectantly a number of times thinking they might choose a machine to play, but Doppo kept on walking and talking.

'Hanemono are the easiest machines to play. They're the ones in which the pins are altered every night. The ones that your friend told you about. But they don't have any here and they're not worth bothering about anyway. They're less expensive and less risky to play, but the wins aren't so spectacular. What we want to focus on – ' Doppo finally paused next to a machine very much like the one in front of which he had challenged Kenji yesterday. ' – at least for now, is this kind of instrument here. These are called deji-pachi and you play them in the normal way using the dial to propel the balls up into and down the face of the machine.'

In a small notepad, the same one Kenji used to make notes of his ideas for TV shows, he recorded Doppo's every word. The speed at which the dial was turned controlled the speed at which the balls dropped down the face of the machine and bounced off the nails that created various valleys and dips. There were also a number of holes in the face. If a ball dropped in some of these holes you won; others you lost. It seemed simple enough and Kenji found that he was anxious to make a start. If this was it, the way that he could make a living, then why waste time? His savings were rapidly dwindling and Ami was starting to get suspicious, asking him questions about work whereas in the past she hardly asked him anything at all. Except perhaps what he wanted for lunch.

Failing to notice Kenji's mounting anxiety, Doppo continued talking. 'The winning and losing holes will change depending on what type of machine you play. So it's always best to check first.'

'Sure.'

'You will need to ask or have a look at what everybody else is doing. At least in the beginning. Now, if you get a ball into a winning hole you activate this slot machine here . . .' Doppo tapped the centre of the glass screen. '. . . and if it comes to rest on three matching symbols you win more balls.'

'I understand. Can we . . .'

'Wait. That's not everything.' Lowering the sound of his voice, Doppo leant forward conspiratorially. 'Some people believe that if they spin the dial in a certain way or lean against the machine slightly it gives them more control over the way in which the balls fall down the face. Others find that holding a magnet against one side helps. But before you start trying to outwit the machine you must learn how to play.'

Satisfied with his explanation, Doppo nodded and marched to the end of the row where he turned left and left again into the next aisle.

'Aren't we going to play?' Kenji trotted after him, failing to keep the note of frustration out of his voice. The pad and pencil were now forgotten and stuffed into the back pocket of his trousers.

'There's more to show you.' Doppo scratched his head and turned away from Kenji just as his face crumpled in disappointment. 'The machines in this row are called kenrimono and they're for serious gamblers. You don't want to start playing these until you're absolutely ready and you know what you're doing.'

'Why?'

'Because you could win or lose the equivalent of a day's salary in a matter of hours.'

So that's why they had waited. Now he understood the delay. These were the machines that he would learn to play. There was no point wasting his time on the others. No, these were where the real money could be had. Kenji rubbed his hands together in excitement as he thought about going home, for the first time in months, with a wallet full of money. Maybe – he thought about the gift counter they had passed on the way in – he might even go home with a few presents. He sat down on the stool in front of the machine and lit a cigarette.

'You'll show me how to play?'

'Not now, no. It's better that you perfect your technique first. On the easier machines.'

'But what harm will it do?' Kenji cajoled Doppo until finally he gave in.

'Now listen carefully, because this is complicated stuff.'

Doppo sat down next to Kenji who was expectantly spinning the plastic dial that launched the steel balls into the machine.

'When you play these machines you earn certain rights and to win you must have a detailed knowledge of these rights and how to use them to your advantage. Take this machine. If it's cold – that means if nobody has been playing it for at least thirty minutes – you have a 1 in 300 chance of winning. Unless you manage to get a ball into this hole here. If you do that then you can win between 300 and 6,500 balls depending on how many you have already lost. The more you lose, the more you stand to win. So it's good practice to lose for as long as you can afford to. Then, for the next thirty seconds of play, you will have a 1, in 30 chance of winning and can drop a ball in any hole except for this one here. If you drop it in this one your chances of winning go down to 1 in 3,000 for the next sixty seconds.'

'So I just sit back and do nothing, huh?' Kenji ground his cigarette out in the ashtray that protruded from the side of the machine.

'It doesn't work like that because if you lose less than 1,000 balls during this period, the clock will reset itself and the sixty seconds starts all over again.'

'Okay. It sounds easy.'

'Don't be too confident. It's much harder than it looks.' Doppo looked at his watch, frowning. 'I hate to leave you but I must run some errands. Will you excuse me for a short while?'

'No problem.' Kenji almost cheered. With Doppo gone he could be let loose on the machines.

'While I'm gone why not take a look around and watch a few people play? See if you can't pick up some tips. They're a friendly bunch once you get to know them. Just say that you're a friend of mine.'

49

After waiting for as long as he could bear, Kenji purchased 10,000 yen of steel balls and carried them to the kenrimono machine where Doppo had lectured him. He spun the dial and launched some silver balls up into and down the face of the machine. Missing the winning holes completely they disappeared at the bottom, so he tried again, and again and again. Within ten minutes every single ball had disappeared from the yellow plastic tray and he had won nothing.

'Damn thing must be broken.' He kicked the base of the machine, stubbing his toe painfully. Deciding to try his luck elsewhere, he purchased more silver balls and moved to another aisle. This time he spun the dial more quickly, propelling the balls with greater force and lost everything in five minutes. It was not until he was 30,000 yen down that he finally admitted defeat.

'What's wrong with me?' he muttered, looking around the parlour. Everybody else seemed to be winning, so why couldn't he? Had Doppo taught him the wrong rules? He didn't trust that guy. He hardly knew him. Maybe he wasn't as much of a pro as he had claimed to be. And where was he anyway? He had gone to run a few errands, but that was nearly an hour ago. What was the point? Picking up the now empty yellow plastic tray, he carried it to a nearby counter and threw it down angrily. Who did he think he was fooling? Kenji Yamada the pachinko pro? Kenji Yamada the loser more like.

He strode purposefully towards the exit, his cheeks flushed with anger.

'Kenji.' Doppo walked off the escalator. 'Where are you going in such a hurry? I thought that we could grab some lunch.'

'Food. Is that all you think about?' Kenji retorted, walking on to the moving steps, ignoring the wounded expression on Doppo's face.

'Wait for me.' Undeterred, Doppo hurried after him. 'I've arranged to meet some friends for lunch. They're pachinko pros just like me and I thought that it'd be good for you to speak with them.'

Kenji did not stop. He did not even look back. 'I have to get out of here,' he thought, shuddering, because he had got it wrong yet again. Why was he always so foolish, so gullible? Did he have to accept everything he was told?

'Please, don't give up just because you've lost some money. Everybody loses in the beginning. That's why I left you. I saw that you wanted to play and I knew that you had to get it out of your system. It's only once you lose and it really stings that you can learn to play.'

'You let me lose on purpose.' Full of anger, Kenji span around. 'That was the last of my savings. That was all the money I had in the world. What am I going to do now? What will I tell my wife?' It was several seconds before he realised that Doppo was bent over double and struggling to catch his breath. He ran back up the steps towards him. 'Are you okay? What's the matter? Is there something that I can get you?'

Doppo waved him away. 'I just need to catch my breath,' he panted.

'Come on. Let's go outside and get some air.' Grabbing one of Doppo's meaty arms, Kenji clung to him until they were outside.

Doppo leaned heavily against the side of the building.

'You mustn't try to run before you can walk. Or you'll be disappointed,' Doppo wheezed.

'Please don't talk,' Kenji implored as the big man sucked deeply on an asthma inhaler. 'You'll make yourself worse.' He felt terrible. Why had he run off like that, making Doppo come after him when he knew that he wasn't a fit man?

'Promise me that you won't give up?' Doppo asked after several minutes had passed, when his breathing had returned to normal.

'No,' Kenji shook his head. 'I won't give up. It's the very least I owe you to try again.'

'Good. And you will come to lunch with me?'

'I can't.' Kenji patted his empty pockets as his cheeks flushed with shame.

'I would be offended if you didn't let me pay. After all I was responsible for you losing your money.'

Although it embarrassed him greatly, Kenji agreed and the two men set off walking together in silence.

'Doppo, over here.'

The restaurant's interior was overrun with a reddish-brown bamboo wood. The floor, the walls, the ceiling, the tables and chairs, the blinds pulled down over the windows: everything, it seemed, was assembled from this one basic material. And with the only light provided by small bulbs, covered by glass pendants that hung from the end of long insulated cables to within one foot of the table tops, it took several seconds before Kenji's eyes had adjusted to the gloom and he was able to discern a large party sitting in the corner of the restaurant, waving in their direction. They were making their way to the table, past the open kitchen and office workers on their lunch breaks, when Kenji felt a sudden pang of anxiety. What if he was recognised? What if he bumped into a former colleague? He didn't recall anybody having mentioned this restaurant, but to be safe he kept his head bowed and walked in the shadows.

He counted at least a dozen people seated around the table. Each one greeted Doppo warmly, bombarding him with questions.

'How's your asthma?'

'Is your daughter still nagging you to go and live in Hawaii?'

'Imagine that. I wish my daughter would nag me to go to Hawaii.'

'I wish my daughter would go and live in Hawaii.'

Somebody laughed. Somebody else slapped him on the back.

Hanging back in the shadows, Kenji felt self-conscious and sorry for himself. This man had gone out of his way to help him and how had he repaid him? By acting like a petulant child, sulking when things had not gone his way. Okay, so maybe he had been too confident. Or maybe he just wasn't cut out to play pachinko. Either way, it wasn't Doppo's fault.

'Let me introduce you to my friend.' Doppo pulled Kenji forward. 'Salaryman, meet everybody, everybody, meet Salaryman.'

'Hello, Salaryman,' the entire table sang out. In spite of himself, Kenji smiled and was glad to sit down when room was made for him at one end of the table. Doppo sat at the other.

'Hello.' Kenji bowed to an elderly woman sitting at his right. She

52

was wearing a blue T-shirt with the words 'Las Vegas' across the front.

'Are you a player?' she croaked, lifting, slightly, the sun visor that sat on her head, casting a green glow over her face.

'No, but Doppo is trying to teach me.'

'Oh, he is, is he?' The old woman dragged on a cigarette, the filter of which was stained with red lipstick. 'He never shared any of his secrets with me. His oldest friend.'

'Must you moan so?'

Kenji noticed a wiry young man to his left.

'Don't get your knickers in a twist, Professor,' the old woman teased.

The young man grimaced at her and turned towards Kenji. 'Doppo's game is not as refined as it could be, but he is the best teacher anybody could hope for.'

'You are a professor?' Kenji asked.

The old lady cackled. 'In name only. He plays pachinko so that he doesn't have to teach. He works at the university but he hates teaching. He hates students.' She laughed again. 'Imagine that. A professor who doesn't like young people.'

The Professor grew serious. 'That's not true and you know it. I am engaged in an important research project that can take me away from my other activities.'

Kenji wanted to know more but a waiter arrived, laying bowls of deep fried vegetables, meat and fish on the table followed by a large bowl of steaming white rice. Kenji tucked in and was surprised by how hungry he felt. The food tasted good. Better than anything he had eaten in a long time. He found he was enjoying himself and talking animatedly to the two people sitting next to him.

'How do you know Doppo?' he asked the Professor, picking up rice with his chopsticks.

'I was an impoverished student desperate to make money. Doppo found me wandering around a pachinko parlour, hatching a plan. He taught me how to play and I've never looked back.'

Kenji realised he had misjudged Doppo.

'If you will excuse me . . .' The Professor stood up once they had finished eating and put some banknotes on the table. ' . . . I have a lecture to deliver this afternoon. It was a pleasure meeting you. Please take my business card.'

'I'm sorry, I don't have one.' Kenji blushed.

'Perhaps next time.'

'Can I get a lift with you?' the old woman croaked.

'As long as you don't smoke in my car.'

'He treats me like a mother,' she winked, and then they were gone.

Noticing the empty chair beside Kenji, Doppo came to join him. There was a food-stained napkin tucked into the neck of his shirt. 'Did you have fun?'

Kenji nodded and gestured at the remaining people seated around the table. 'They all play pachinko? No one works in an office?'

'Only the Professor. And some might disagree with that.'

'Imagine.' Rubbing his stomach, Kenji sat back in his chair.

'I have something for you.' Doppo handed Kenji a parcel wrapped in tissue paper. 'Just a small gift.'

Kenji tore the tissue paper open, revealing a brightly coloured Hawaiian shirt, and laughed loudly.

'Do you like it?' Doppo asked uncertainly.

Kenji unfolded the shirt and held it up against him. 'I love it.'

SEVEN

'Damn.'

The moment he heard the sound of the shutters rolling up, Kenji began jogging up the hill, but was too late. By the time he arrived, the doors to the Maruhan Tower had been unlocked and the people who had been waiting outside were already sitting at their preferred machines. If only he hadn't stopped for coffee, but Kenji had been playing pachinko for several weeks now and the more successful he was, the easier he tended to take things. Perhaps he was starting to become too laid back.

It was Monday morning – the start of another working week – and just like every other week, he had planned it out, intending to spend the day here at the Tower. Only now he had lost the chance of getting on to a good machine and going to another parlour would be pointless. The machines there would be occupied too. So he decided to while away a few hours playing for recreation rather than money, hoping that later in the day one of the better machines might become available.

As he walked slowly through the third floor of the parlour, taking more time than he usually did, a machine in the furthermost corner caught his eye. It had fewer flashing lights than the others, made less noise and was without an LED screen. Kenji could not recall having seen any of the regulars play it. He had never even noticed the machine himself before now. If he had then he would certainly have played it. From the moment he launched the first few balls down the face, it became apparent that the win ratios had – at some point – been set unaccountably high and, the machine forgotten, never returned to normal. No matter what he did, he could not help but win. He simply launched the balls up into and down the face of the machine, and sat back. Wherever they disappeared – into one of the holes on the face of the machine or the trough at the bottom – more fell out into his yellow plastic tray.

Two hours must have passed before he decided enough was enough. It took three trips to the prize counter before he had delivered each tray of balls; exchanging them for seven large plastic bars, each with a faux black pearl embedded in its centre.

Leaving the Tower he turned into an alleyway that ran along the back of the building. Treading over discarded rubbish, empty cardboard boxes and small mounds of vegetable peelings thrown out of the back of restaurants, he arrived at an unobtrusive door. It had no handle or lock and could only be opened from the inside. If he hadn't known it was there, he would almost certainly have never noticed it.

Tapping lightly on the cracked red paint, he waited until it opened and a nose appeared in the gap.

'Oda.' Kenji wanted to be as quick as possible. These back alley trips still made him nervous, even though he had been several times before.

'What do you want?' Oda snapped, opening the door wider but looking over his shoulder as he spoke at the television droning in the background.

According to the other pachinko pros, he spent hours watching American soap operas; talking back at the set, mimicking the tone and intonation of the actors. As a result he now spoke Japanese like a Texan and dressed like one too in worn blue Levi's, a checked shirt and a belt with a large, brass buckle.

Silently Kenji handed over the bars. Oda grunted and slammed the door shut. Standing in the alleyway surrounded by oily puddles and the smell of putrefaction, Kenji began to wonder if Oda had forgotten all about him. He was just about to knock again, when the door flew open and Oda stuck out his hand. Kenji took the thick brown envelope that was being thrust at him and Oda's hand immediately disappeared and the door was shut.

'Now go away and leave me alone,' a muffled voice shouted.

Kenji checked that no one else was standing in the alley before opening the envelope. Suddenly he felt breathless. It was stuffed full of notes. Possibly more notes than he had ever seen before in his life. The thrill of winning was something that he would never get used to. Nor would he ever forget the enormous relief that flooded through his body when, at the end of his first month's play, he was able to deposit money into the family's bank account. Things were going so well that he had been obliged to set up a separate bank account. This he called 'Yumi and Yoshi's university fund'.

He kissed the brown envelope and looked up at the sky. 'Thank you, Doppo. Thank you, my friend.'

It had been an easy win. Perhaps too easy which is why, the next day, Kenji decided to return to the Tower and the same machine. This time he earned ten plastic bars.

'Not you again,' Oda muttered when he opened the door.

On the third day, when Kenji won twelve bars, Oda did not say anything at all, just stared at him intently.

On the fourth day, when Kenji returned to the Tower, he realised that he was being followed from the moment that he went in through the entrance.

Pausing at a machine and pretending to study it, he was able to discern the reflection of the manager – an efficient, young university graduate – in the glass face. Moving off again, he stopped and started several times just to make sure. There was no doubt about it. She stopped walking when he did, and started when he did. She wants me to know that she's there, he realised. Up one aisle, down the next, the hunt continued.

He looked around the parlour. This had never happened before and he didn't know what to do. If only Doppo was here. How stupid it had been to come back on the fourth day. He had been lazy, complacent, foolish. No longer a complete novice, he knew the rules. The pachinko parlours had a relationship of sorts with the pros. They tolerated a small number of them but got very jumpy if the numbers became too high, or if they felt that anyone was pushing his or her luck. By coming back for another day Kenji had pushed his too far.

'You've broken the single most important rule.' He could all but hear the disappointment in Doppo's voice as he hurried towards the exit.

'I know, I know.' He shook his head. 'What do I do now?' he asked, imagining that his friend was there with him.

'Keep your cool,' Doppo counselled, 'and get out of here.'

Fighting the urge to run as the manager's heels clicked loudly in his ears, Kenji walked on to the escalator. The manager did not follow him. His hands were still shaking when he paused outside the Tower to light a cigarette before running off down the street and losing himself in the crowds. Then he began to laugh. At first quietly and then more manically. It was, he realised, the most excitement he had ever experienced in his whole life.

'Drink?' the Professor asked, standing up and forcing one hand into the front pocket of his black jeans.

'Large whisky, please. No ice,' Kenji replied, coming up behind the Professor and collapsing on to the wooden chair that had been reserved for him. Doppo looked at him quizzically but he pretended not to notice. Making a mistake was one thing, but admitting to it was something else entirely. Now that the excitement had faded, he was feeling anxious and his hands were shaking.

Several minutes passed in silence before the Professor returned from the bar. Kenji knocked back his whisky and then jumped up to buy a beer. This he drank more slowly and by the time the glass was drained, felt calmer and more relaxed. Looking around at his friends – Doppo, the Professor and the old lady, Michi – he allowed himself a smile. It was now – safe among friends – that he was able to realise, to admit even, just how close he had come to falling off the edge. Losing his job had shattered his self-confidence. He could not bear to remember how wretched he had been, traipsing around Tokyo, receiving knocks day after day. Now, though, everything was different. He was earning money – more money than he had ever earned – and he had friends. True friends. People who could be relied on. It felt good to belong, to be a part of something.

And – his smile grew wider – he was a natural when it came to pachinko. He had a talent for it. Or so everybody said, and who was he to argue? His method of play was perhaps heavy-handed, but he was especially good when it came to spotting machines that were hot. In this respect he was better even than Doppo and Michi.

'How do you do it?' they demanded, but he was at a loss to explain.

'I don't know. They just seem to give off an energy. It's like they throb, pulse, vibrate.'

Putting his now empty beer glass down on the table, Kenji concentrated on his friends. Michi was speaking.

'He called me a cheat.' Michi exhaled smoke through her nose so that it gathered under her sun visor until she waved it away.

'And were you?' the Professor asked.

'Of course I was. Those suckers deserved it.'

'What will your son say?' Kenji asked, opening a packet of Lucky Strikes and offering them around. Doppo hesitated before taking one. 'If he finds out?'

Michi snorted. 'He won't.'

Her son's intellect was not something the old woman had a tremendous amount of respect for. Nor for the daughter-in-law with whom she lived in an apartment block in Tokyo. They assumed that Michi spent her days engaged in pursuits befitting an elderly lady: reading, taking moderate exercise, silent contemplation. What they did not realise was that she was a regular at most of the downtown pachinko parlours and played weekly poker games with the other elderly tenants in the same apartment block, usually winning from them a large proportion of their meagre allowances.

'The old fool was sitting beneath a security mirror,' Michi persisted. 'I could see his hand.'

Leaning across the table to tap the ash off the end of his cigarette into the ashtray, Doppo turned to Kenji. 'How's your day been?'

It was apparent to Kenji that Doppo was trying very hard to make the question sound casual, but was unable to keep the note of worry out of his voice. Like all good teachers, he was concerned with Kenji's progress and while he now played alone, and successfully so, his former teacher still maintained a watchful eye.

'Good,' Kenji lied. He did not want to worry his friend who was already fretting about the imminent arrival of his daughter from Hawaii. She was, he had confided repeatedly, certain to be critical of everything and demand that he come and live with her immediately. While he was not against the idea, he did not feel ready to leave Tokyo. At least not yet.

Doppo did not say anything. He just stared at Kenji. Michi and the Professor sat silently, watching the two men. The bar was all but empty. The only sound was that of Doppo's breathing – heavy and laboured.

'Okay, so I lied,' Kenji admitted. He found deceiving Doppo – even if for his own good – completely impossible. 'I didn't let the trail go cold at the Maruhan. I won three days in a row.'

'How much?' Doppo asked, and when Kenji told him everyone cheered.

'More than I've ever won in any one week.'

'Any one month.'

'What happened?'

'I went back today and they followed me,' Kenji admitted.

'I knew it,' Doppo exclaimed, slapping his immense thigh with the palm of one hand. 'You're okay though? They didn't hurt you?'

Kenji shook his head. 'Aren't you cross with me?'

'You're cross with yourself.'

He nodded.

'And you're not going to make the same mistake again in a hurry.'

'No.' He shook his head emphatically as the Professor and Michi stared at him sympathetically.

'Well, then, I'm happy.'

Starting to feel like a young child being patronised by those older and wiser than him, Kenji was relieved when the barman turned on the television immediately above their heads and everybody looked up.

'At last, the much awaited arrival of the cherry blossoms in Tokyo,' the newscaster announced as she faded from view and a map of Japan appeared in her place. It showed where the blossoms had first appeared in the southern plains of Kyushu and were spreading, at a rate of thirty kilometres per day, north-east across Japan, heading for Hokkaido.

They left the bar shortly after the news piece ended, lingering on the sidewalk outside. There was a definite chill in the air. Kenji pulled his coat tightly around him and stamped his feet against the ground.

After saying goodbye, the Professor and Michi walked away, up the hill.

Kenji watched them go and then turned back to Doppo. 'When does your daughter arrive?'

'Tomorrow afternoon.'

'I guess I won't see you for a while then?'

'Not for a couple of weeks, no. I have to be on my best behaviour.'

'Well, have fun,' Kenji offered and then on impulse, leant forward and gave his large friend a hug.

EIGHT

'Wake up, Yoshi,' Kenji spoke softly, rocking his son gently back and forth.

Mumbling incoherently, Yoshi rolled over to face the wall and then very suddenly sat bolt upright in bed. He was wearing a pair of dark blue pyjamas covered with cartoon characters that Kenji did not recognise and his hair was flattened against one side of his head, standing up on the other.

'I should take a picture,' he thought, sadly. 'In case I ever forget this moment and how my son looks on waking.'

'What is it? Am I late? Where's Mum?'

Ruffling Yoshi's unruly hair, Kenji laughed. 'It's time to get up. We're going cherry blossom-viewing.'

'When?' Yoshi stared at his father disbelievingly.

'Now. Breakfast will be ready in five minutes. Your favourite. Rice omelettes.'

Yoshi grimaced. Even the words seemed to taste bad to him. 'I haven't eaten rice omelettes since I was four.'

Not to be put off, Kenji kept the note of disappointment out of his voice. 'I'm sure we can find you something else to eat. Up you get.' He whipped back the duvet cover allowing Yoshi to swing his short legs out on to the floor and into a pair of slippers. Yoshi looked at his clock.

'Dad,' he wailed, 'it's 6 a.m. Nobody gets up at 6 a.m. on a Saturday.'

'We have to leave early if we want to get a good spot.'

'Who am I going with?'

'Why all the questions?' Kenji snapped and immediately regretted it. Although hurt by his son's lack of enthusiasm, he could hardly blame him. This was possibly the first outing that they had taken as a family since the twins were born. When they were one week old, he and Ami had taken them out in their pram for a walk in the park. It was winter and cold but the couple were so excited they did not notice. A few weeks later, Kenji was promoted. It meant more money, but longer days and less time to spend with his family. Even at weekends he was often too tired to do anything other than lounge in front of the television, watching baseball and drinking beer. At least, he had consoled himself at the time, he was providing for his family and they were comfortable.

But that wasn't living. Things were different now. He had more energy. He felt like a new man. If he could just maintain his excitement today, the children were certain to be swept along.

'You're going with me, of course. So hurry up. You can help me make the picnic if you like.'

As he left the bedroom and started walking down the corridor, Kenji heard Yoshi sink back down in bed and sigh, 'Oh, boy.'

Ignoring this Kenji sang out, 'Everybody, time to get up.'

The first to emerge into the corridor was Eriko: her hair in rollers and covered with a net. 'Have you finally gone mad?' she demanded.

Kenji took a deep breath and turned to look at her. 'Okay, mother-in-law, if you insist. You can come too. Nobody gets out of cherry blossom-viewing today.' Grabbing her by both shoulders he planted a large kiss on her cheek.

'Get off me, you mad man,' she squealed, wriggling free. 'Get off me.'

It was 10 a.m. before the family arrived at Ueno station. It had taken much longer to mobilise everybody than Kenji had expected and, as a consequence, they had got here much later than he would have liked. The best spots were almost certain to have gone judging by

63

the number of people heading in the direction of Ueno Park's west gate, where they followed a broad tarmac path heading north.

'Did you know,' Kenji asked, taking Yoshi's hand in his right and Yumi's in his left, 'that this is Tokyo's largest open public space?'

The two children both looked up at their father, blinking because the sun was shining fiercely.

'I almost forgot.' Dropping the twins' hands, he rummaged in the front pocket of his rucksack until he found what he was looking for. Two pairs of children's sunglasses that he'd won at pachinko: one set of red frames, the other yellow. He handed them to the twins and smiled encouragingly as they put them on. 'Very handsome. Now show your mother and grandmother.'

Spinning around quickly, Yumi shouted eagerly, 'Look, Mum, look at what Dad got us.'

'Very pretty.' Ami forced a thin smile.

'Don't you look lovely,' Eriko agreed with more conviction.

Between them they were carrying a bright blue coolbox containing the picnic that Kenji had prepared for their cherry blossom-viewing party. Not accustomed to making picnics, he had bought most of it from the delicatessen hall in the Tokyu department store. Everybody had their own meal box containing deep fried fish cakes, braised eggplant, rice and a soba and vegetable salad. He had been careful to remove all of the wrapping from the food, put it in a plastic bag and throw the bag away in a bin outside the apartment. It seemed like a lot of trouble to go to, but he knew that if Ami found the evidence she was certain to complain about the expense.

The twins casually slipped their hands back into Kenji's. He was surprised that such a simple act would please him so much.

'What was I saying? Oh yes. This park is home to . . . Go on, have a guess. How many museums do you think?'

'Two,' Yumi shrugged.

'One hundred,' Yoshi squealed.

'Kenji, don't get them too over-excited,' Ami advised sternly.

Ignoring her, Kenji continued in his instruction. 'There are no less than five museums. There are also two temples, one shrine, a large pond, a zoo, and 1,200 ancient cherry trees. Imagine that.'

'Wow!' Yoshi exclaimed. Not because of what his father had said, but at the path stretching out in front of them. It was lined, on both sides, with the gnarled, towering trunks of cherry trees: their branches, pregnant with blossoms, stretched out overhead, forming a dense canopy. The sun was all but hidden but the light still shone blindingly through the abundance of pale pink blossoms.

'Look, look! Aren't those pretty?' Yumi pointed at a long line of red and white paper lanterns strung up between the trees and swaying back and forth in the same light breeze that lifted petals from the branches to dance on the air currents before releasing them to fall down on to the heads of Kenji and his family.

'It's snowing.' Yoshi danced back and forth on the balls of his feet, both arms outstretched and the palms of his hands held upwards. All around him other young children were similarly enchanted and their parents took photographs. Kenji removed the family's digital camera from the case hanging around his neck and did the same. He aimed the camera at Yoshi and studied the image. It occurred to him that his father had taken an almost identical photograph of him when he was Yoshi's age. The picture had sat in a frame next to the futon where his father slept until the day he died. This had always struck Kenji as odd. His father was an unresponsive, uncommunicative man who seemed to tolerate his son rather than feel any affection towards him. Why then did he want the picture beside his bed? So that Kenji's face, partially obscured by a flurry of blossoms, was the last thing he saw at night and the first thing to which he opened his eyes in the morning?

Now that he was older, Kenji understood something of the disappointment his father must have felt. He had been a postman all his life. For forty years he trudged up and down the same streets, delivering mail to the same doors, seeing the same faces. At weekends he disappeared for hours with his camera. When he came home, he locked himself in the bathroom that functioned as a makeshift darkroom, and afterwards there were dozens of photographs hanging out to dry on a line suspended above the bath tub. He specialised in portrait photography. Kenji often wondered if the reason his father showed him so little affection was because he saved it all up for his subjects. Perhaps he had even dreamed of becoming a famous photographer, but was forced to live a life of routine and drudgery by the mere existence of a wife and child.

The one thing Kenji feared most as a young man was that he would grow to be like his father – sullen and uncommunicative towards his family. He feared that he already had. The transition had been gradual, but he hoped it was not reversible. As a child, the only real time he ever spent with his father was when they went cherry blossom-viewing. They would trudge through the park in silence as his father took photographs. This was the first time Kenji had been cherry blossom-viewing with his family and he was determined it would be an event to remember. In his rucksack, he carried a number of surprises: board games, a karaoke machine and a bottle of the best sake that he could find in case the spring day turned cold. Perhaps he had been foolish to spend so much money, but why not? He could afford to treat his family and they deserved it.

'Do you know why this time of year is so special?' Kenji asked the twins.

They shook their head.

'When the cherry blossoms arrive it means that winter is over. That's why everybody has come here to celebrate today. It is a time of new beginnings. Children enter school, graduates start jobs and transferred employees take up new positions. But the blossoms don't last long. See the wind is already causing them to fall. In a week they will be gone completely. Do you understand?'

Yumi and Yoshi nodded sagely.

'It's a new beginning. Time to start again,' Kenji whispered. 'Everybody deserves to start again.'

Onwards, the Yamadas continued to march slowly through the park, beneath the blossoms, past many large parties of families, friends and office workers who had already laid out large blue plastic sheets beneath the trees and were enjoying their picnics. Kenji could not see where they might squeeze in but then spotted a small space between a party of red-faced salarymen and a large bin.

Ami wrinkled her nose.

'Come on,' he urged, removing a blue tarpaulin sheet from his rucksack and spreading it out across the ground.

'The germs.'

'It'll be fine. I promise you.'

Reluctantly she put the coolbox in the centre of the mat. After removing their shoes and placing them in a neat row on the ground, the family sat down and looked at each other, uncertain of what to say or do next. Unable to wait a second longer, Kenji pulled the karaoke machine from his bag.

'Where did that come from?' Ami spluttered.

'A present,' Kenji declared proudly, 'for my family.'

'A karaoke machine. There are many other things we need more,' she spat back, unable to keep the anger from her voice.

'Well, we can have them too.'

'Let's sing something, Dad,' the twins begged and so they did. Kenji went first. His favourite song by Elvis Presley, 'Love Me Tender'. He knew all the words although he wasn't, at all times, entirely sure of what he was singing. The twins went next. Yumi singing a pop song that she liked; Yoshi the theme to his favourite cartoon show. Both were terribly out of tune and could not keep in time with the music, but Kenji thought they were the best singers that he had ever heard and even whispered to Ami they might have a career in music.

'They should learn to play the piano,' he suggested.

'They already do.'

Once the children tired of singing the family ate lunch. Afterwards, they played some board games and cards; Yumi and Yoshi jumping on top of their father whenever he got anything wrong. Throughout this Kenji witnessed his wife's face getting more and more furious. She hardly spoke, not even to her mother, and ate very little. There was nothing he could say that would cheer her up and later that evening, when they finally got home and the children were in bed asleep, she turned on him.

'What is going on?'

He struggled to answer. 'What do you mean? Today? Cherry

blossom-viewing? I thought you would enjoy it. I thought that everybody would.'

Ami appeared to be thinking something over. 'Is something wrong at work?'

'Everything's fine at work,' he lied, feeling himself blush a hot, deep red.

'What about our trip to Tokyo Disneyland? Why was that cancelled?'

'Budget cutbacks,' he replied, pretending to be absorbed in the task of opening a can of beer.

'Why, then, do you seem to have so much money?'

'It was a bonus. Just a one-off to thank us for our hard work.'

Ami seemed to consider this for a number of seconds and then asked, the curls on her head shaking as she spoke, 'Are you having an affair?'

He laughed, stood up and took his wife's stiff body in an awkward embrace. 'Don't be ridiculous. Can't I just be happy to spend time with my beautiful wife and my children without there being something wrong?'

Over her shoulder he could see an unwashed cup sitting in the kitchen sink. As he stared at it, Kenji vowed to be more careful. That was two mistakes he'd made in the last week. He couldn't afford to make a third or the game would be up.

NINE

Kenji checked his wallet though he already knew what was in there. It was stuffed full of 10,000 yen notes: money left over from last week following his wins at the Maruhan Tower and that he had not, as yet, had the opportunity to bank. Studying the wallet he realised it was starting to look old. The stitching was frayed and the brown leather had become discoloured where it had come into contact with liquid. Lain on a wet bar, for example. 'Maybe I should get another one?' he smiled to himself. 'A bigger one.'

'Excuse me, please.'

A middle-aged man pushed past. As Kenji watched the back of his raincoat flapping in the wind, he realised that he had come to a standstill on the sidewalk across the road from the train station and was blocking people's way. He found himself doing that a lot lately. Just stopping to stare at something, not realising everyone else had somewhere to get to. 'I guess that I'm just not in a hurry anymore,' he thought, moving back and watching the man cross the bridge spanning the road and hurrying towards the station. It suddenly occurred to him how grateful he was not to be like that. Not always concerned with where he had to go and getting there as soon as possible. In fact, he realised, slipping his wallet into his back pocket, he didn't even have to go to Tokyo today if he didn't want to.

Doppo's daughter was staying with her father in Tokyo on a two-week vacation from Hawaii. The Professor had gone on what he called 'a study tour' of Osaka, and Michi was on her best behaviour after a fellow resident in the apartment block where she lived with her son and daughter-in-law had lodged a complaint with the concierge. Her card games, the old man claimed after losing three times in a row, were rigged. With everybody otherwise engaged there was no obvious reason for Kenji to make the tiresome journey to Tokyo, so he contemplated rewarding himself with a day off. 'I could stay in Utsunomiya,' he realised. 'Take things easy.' After all the tension and drama of the last few months, he felt that he had earned it.

'That's decided,' he said out loud and strolled across the bridge to the station where he kept his clothes – jeans and an assortment of garish Hawaiian shirts Doppo insisted upon giving him – in a locker. After changing in the men's toilets, Kenji left the station and chose a small coffee shop nearby. He sat down in a booth in the corner and ordered a cup of strong black coffee and two jam-filled doughnuts from a waitress who jumped when he spoke to her.

Kenji opened his newspaper and read it from cover to cover; even the advertisements for sayonara sales and piano lessons in the classifieds section. It wasn't until he heard a small cough that he became aware of the waitress, hovering next to the booth.

He looked up, smiling broadly. 'Nice day, isn't it?' The truth was that it was so dark and gloomy in the coffee shop – the blinds were rolled down and covered with many years of dust and grease – it was impossible to tell what kind of day it was outside. But Kenji was in a good mood – the best mood he had been in for a long time – and he wanted to share it. There was no doubt, this was fun; taking things easy and not rushing to get to the best machine before everybody else. Then once he'd won enough for the day, hunting out a machine to play for the next. In fact, things had been going so well for him that maybe he didn't need to work so hard from now on. A three-day week would quite easily see him earning just as much money as he had at NBC. He could take the other two days off. Start a course. Maybe even learn English.

'You must order something else or leave,' the waitress whispered with a slight movement of her head in the direction of the counter where the chef was staring at him. He wore a white muslin cap and was chewing on a matchstick. Each time his mouth opened, Kenji caught sight of his yellowed teeth.

'Another coffee, please.'

'It's not enough.'

'Doughnuts then.'

She scurried off.

An hour later, Kenji left the coffee shop and headed for Utsunomiya's only Internet café: a small, cramped room with no windows or air-conditioning in the basement of a building. It was empty when he arrived – all the kids were at school – and he was able to choose his own computer. He sat down at the machine and checked his email account for a message from Doppo. Finding none there, he spent some time browsing pachinko sites. It was through these sites that he had learned many of the techniques he used to his advantage, and about what the different parlours in Tokyo were up to. Other pros kept the sites up to date with all the latest information. Maybe a parlour had had a new game installed, or a new one had just opened so the machines were paying out big for a limited time. Others advertised electronic play gadgets to enhance your game. He tended not to bother with these as he found his game was just as good, if not better without them. He was a purist, so the Professor said.

At lunch time, he ate a simple meal of rice and omelette at the restaurant next door and then made his way to the library. It was several years since he had last visited, but it was exactly as he remembered it. The reading room was not so much a room as a windowless corner of the ground floor sectioned off by two rows of grey metal shelving units. A selection of out-of-date magazines and newspapers were on display, resting on shallow sloping racks that could be lifted up to reveal neat piles of past editions on a hidden ledge beneath. Low, deep, wide chairs were arranged in the shape of a horseshoe around the reading area. The varnish was peeling off their wooden frames, and the dark aquamarine fabric covering the lumpy foam cushions was stained. Overhead, harsh fluorescent lights illuminated the area; each covered with a rectangular plastic guard through which the bodies of long-since dead flies were visible.

In spite of the shabby surroundings he liked it here. The peace and quiet suited his contemplative mood. It occurred to him that the library might become a regular haunt if he decided to take things more slowly. It was exactly the kind of place that he needed. For most of the day it was deserted and he could sit in the corner of the reading room with a book. When Doppo had lent him a detective novel he tried to remember how long it was since he had last read a book, and was shocked to admit that it had been more than twenty years.

It was 6 p.m. by the time he left the library. Standing outside, he wondered what to do next. It was too early to go home so he decided to go to the nearest pachinko parlour. Not to win any money, he reasoned, just for a little game to while away the hours.

He walked in the direction of the train station, slowing when he saw the pachinko parlour in the distance. The front was covered with bright, flashing neon lights and whenever a customer walked through the automatic doors, the sound of metal balls falling and pounding music escaped. Just as he too was about to walk through the doors he felt the mobile phone in his pocket vibrate. On the display screen he saw that it was the Professor calling.

'Professor,' Kenji exploded happily, moving away from the parlour doors so that he could hear. 'How's things? Are you learning lots in Osaka?'

The Professor inhaled deeply. 'I have something to tell you. I don't quite know what I shall say.'

Kenji's entire body turned cold. It was as if someone had poured a bucket of ice cold water over the top of his head. His stomach twisted into knots. 'Tell me what? What is it?'

'It's Doppo.' The Professor's voice was barely audible. 'He's dead. He died of a heart attack this morning.'

The plastic casing that surrounded Kenji's mobile phone split cleanly in half when it hit the floor.

TEN

It was obvious she was Doppo's daughter. They shared the same round cheeks coloured with a touch of pink; small, bright, black eyes and black glossy hair. He had worn his hair short and spiked. Hers was long and smooth and, from a certain angle, when it caught the light, created the impression that there was a halo resting above the crown of her head.

When the priest kneeled down on a cushion in front of Doppo's coffin and began to sing scripture in a low, deep, reverberating voice, she started to whimper. Then, looking up at the poster-sized, colour photograph of Doppo on the wall above the coffin – a big smile on his face and wearing his signature Hawaiian shirt – her whimper became a sob and then a howl of anguish. A tall, thin man standing to her right, held her around the shoulders throughout the service as though she might fall to the ground at any minute, while a young child clutched her left hand, looking more terrified with each passing minute. She stood suspended between the two. As he watched them, Kenji clutched at the collar of his coat. It was not cold, but he too needed something to hold on to in case his legs gave way and he was becoming increasingly conscious of the looks that his Hawaiian shirt was attracting. He had worn it as a mark of respect. Now he worried that it looked disrespectful.

The last funeral Kenji had been to was for a colleague who had died of *karoshi*, or death from overwork. A heart attack bought on by stress. After the funeral he made a number of promises. He would give up smoking, drink less, and work fewer hours. He even started doing callanetics in the mornings and went for long walks at the weekends. None of his good intentions had lasted, and he thought of this now as he said goodbye to his friend.

After the priest had left the room, tables were laid out and covered with plates of food, soft drinks, whisky and beer. Kenji, the Professor and Michi took a little food, more from politeness than hunger, and hung back in the corner. They did not know anyone else there and none of them felt much like talking. Then Kenji saw Doppo's daughter walking towards them and panicked.

'What will we say?' Kenji looked from the Professor to Michi and then back at the Professor as he watched the woman who looked so much like their old friend approaching. Michi's eyes were puffy and she did not reply. She had said very little all day. In fact he had failed to recognise her when she first came to stand next to him. He had never seen her in anything other than jogging pants and T-shirts and today she was wearing a simple black dress.

'I don't know what to say to her.' The words caught in his throat.

Then she was standing in front of them, wearing a simple pitch-black kimono and carrying prayer beads in one hand. He put his glass of whisky down on a nearby table, changed his mind and picked it back up again.

'Thank you for coming. I am Umeko Suzuki. Doppo's . . .'

'I know who you are,' Kenji interrupted without meaning to do so. Although the room in the funeral parlour was filled with people, it suddenly seemed as though it were utterly silent and his was the only voice that could be heard. It sounded loud and unnaturally high. Pausing, he continued more softly, 'I would have recognised you anywhere, I mean. You look so much alike.'

She smiled sadly, though the comment seemed to please her.

'I thought that perhaps you knew my father well.' She indicated the shirt that Kenji was wearing.

'Yes, it was a gift.' Feeling awkward, he played with the lapels of his jacket, drawing them closer together.

'I must say – ' She looked about the room in which all the tables and chairs had been pushed back against the walls. ' – that I was surprised by the number of people who came today. I did not realise he had so many friends. Now perhaps I understand better why he would not come to Hawaii. He did not want to leave all of you behind.'

Some friends we were, Kenji chastised himself. Each and every one of them had known that Doppo's health was poor. That he should have lost weight, given up smoking, cut out the junk food and almost certainly have stopped playing pachinko. Yet not one of them had ever said anything to him about it. They should have encouraged him to go to Hawaii where he would have been better cared for.

'I let him down,' Kenji confessed loud enough for her to hear. 'He was my best friend. He saved me. But when he needed help I let him down. I should have convinced him to take things easier, to give up smoking, to cut down on the beer. But I never said anything. I was too selfish.'

Clasping Kenji's hand, Umeko laughed. 'Nobody could tell my father what to do. Not even my mother could tell him what to do and he worshipped her.' A sob escaped from her throat as she spoke and a single tear rolled down her cheek. Her husband was trying to get across the room to her side but people kept stopping him, to pass on their condolences.

'Tell me – ' She gripped Kenji's hand so tightly that the blood stopped flowing to his fingers. 'Do you have children?'

He nodded. 'Two.'

The Professor and Michi drifted away.

'Then you must promise me one thing.'

'Anything,' he replied. He would promise her the world to rid himself of the awful burden of guilt that he felt.

'That you will never play pachinko again. For the sake of your family. For the sake of your health. Look at what it did to my father. It robbed him of his life.'

What could he say? He couldn't tell her that such a promise was impossible. That what Doppo had rescued him from was far worse for his health than pachinko. So instead he promised her that he would never play again. Just at that moment, her husband reached the corner of the room where they were standing and their conversation ended.

Kenji moved away, but watched them for several minutes. Their foreheads were pressed lovingly together and their hands clasped. It was not long after that he left, without saying goodbye to his friends or Umeko. Tears rolling down his face, he stumbled up the hill towards the station, making the long journey home in a trancelike state. The entire way, all he could think about was the twins and how much he wanted to throw his arms around both of them at once and kiss their soft hair.

'Where have you been?' Ami demanded the moment her husband walked into the apartment, closing the door behind him. Spotting his puffy face she lost some of her force. 'Where have you been?' she repeated, a note of fear creeping into her voice.

'At work,' Kenji shrugged. He had spent an hour walking around the neighbourhood, trying to regain some composure before coming home, but could feel it slipping already. He wanted to tell Ami everything. To share a moment of tenderness with her like the one that he had witnessed between Umeko and her husband. Was that what it was like to be truly in love, he wondered? Had he and Ami ever been like that? Surely there must have been a time, once?

'Don't lie to me.'

'What do you mean?' Kenji walked past her and into the kitchen, where he collapsed on to a chair. 'What are you talking about?'

'I called you at work.'

It was like being kicked in the stomach. Not once in all their years of marriage had she ever called him at work. If she wanted to speak to him at all she rang his mobile phone and if she could not get through, left a voicemail.

'I spoke to Ishida. He said that you no longer worked there.'

'I have been moved to another department,' he protested weakly, knowing it was feeble to pretend. He started crying. Tears coursed down his face. He was crying not just for Doppo, but for the loss of his job and the hundred indignations he had suffered since.

'What's wrong with Dad?' a small voice asked and when Kenji

turned around he saw Yumi standing behind him in her pyjamas.

'Nothing, sweetheart.' There was fear in her eyes, like the young child at the funeral today, and he wanted to take it away. 'Your old Dad just had some bad news today that's all.'

'Go to bed, Yumi,' Ami ordered, and reluctantly the young girl did.

Certain that she had heard the bedroom door close, Ami sat down opposite Kenji. 'Ishida told me that you had lost your job.'

Kenji struggled to think of something to say to her. 'Yes, I did. Today. I lost my job today. That is why I am so upset. But don't worry I shall find another one. I already have some ideas.'

'Six months ago. He told me that you lost your job six months ago. Is it true?'

Several seconds passed in silence before he spoke. 'Yes.' He nodded and broke down into uncontrollable tears as Ami watched, a look of disgust on her face, as he confessed everything, every detail. How he had lost his job; the endless search for a new job; and the manner in which he had been supporting his family ever since. As he spoke he hoped to feel her arms circle his shoulders but they remained rigidly clamped to her side, her expression growing more stony with every word. When he finished he allowed his head to hang down limply, not daring to meet her eyes.

'You will never set foot in a pachinko parlour again,' she hissed through gritted teeth. 'Do you hear me? Never.'

It was the second promise he had to make that day.

Part Two

ELEVEN

For yet another night, Kenji had fallen asleep in the canary yellow, faux-suede armchair where he was now sitting. It was not until Ami threw open the last pair of curtains, that his eyelids flickered open and he found himself staring at the particles of dust dancing in the beams of early morning sunlight that flooded the sitting room. He had never much cared for the armchair and matching sofa. Not only was the colour offensive, but the armchair in which he had slept was narrow and shallow. Every muscle in his body now felt tense and stiff, but not even this would induce him to return to the bed he used to share with his wife and while she had certainly noticed his absence, she did not comment upon it. She did not comment on much lately. At least not to him.

He turned his head to the right, staring out of the crack in the sitting room door into the hallway where Yoshi and Yumi were standing, chattering quietly as they waited for their mother to take them to school. They had always been polite, well-behaved children, but now even more so; treating him like a housebound invalid who required peace in order to recuperate. From the kitchen he could hear the sound of Eriko, where she sat hunched over the table, scratching her name and address on to a large pile of competition prize entries that she had cut from magazines and newspapers. Some of them belonged to the household, others had been donated by friends and neighbours when they had finished reading them. An entire boxful stood by the apartment door and she was slowly working her way through it.

Kenji's mother-in-law had always been frugal. After he married Ami, she presented the couple with a large envelope filled with money-off coupons she had been saving since they announced their engagement. Ami had thrown the envelope straight in the bin, even though she told her mother the coupons had been extremely useful. This was a sign of encouragement to the old woman and every week thereafter, an envelope containing more coupons dropped through the letterbox with their post. Further back still, while the couple had been dating, Kenji was invited to dinner. The food always came from tins. Eriko believed fresh food was wasteful – it never lasted more than a few days whereas tinned food could be kept for months. As a young man eager to impress his girlfriend's parents, Kenji had claimed to find Eriko's behaviour endearing. But now that she was living with them, following the death of her husband, her behaviour had grown more bizarre and he couldn't be so kind. The woman was a menace.

It was exactly five weeks since Doppo's funeral and, faithful to his promise, Kenji had not played pachinko in all that time. Instead he had renewed his search for an 'honourable job', as Ami insisted upon calling it. This time at home and under her watchful eye. He had, as before, very little luck. Eriko, on the other hand, was prospering. Last week she had won an electric bike and sold it to a neighbour, using the money to buy a computer for the children. They had been delighted, but it spelt trouble for him. The more the old lady won, the more she seemed to despise her son-in-law. Whereas before they had simply ignored one another, now Kenji had to endure her insults all day long.

'I could support this family,' she never tired of telling him, 'with the prizes I win.'

'Really?' he had replied in mock admiration. 'And tell me, what exactly do you plan to do with all that dog food stacked in the hallway?'

Ami opened the last curtain and turned to face her husband. 'Once you have cleared away the breakfast dishes I would like you to wash some clothes.' Standing in front of him, she was holding both hands on what had once been an ample pair of hips. Now they were almost svelte and stretched across them was an aquamarine lycra catsuit she would never have considered wearing before. Kenji wasn't afraid to admit, it was a shock to see her dressed this way. Until now she had always favoured loose, shapeless clothes. This outfit was extremely tight. And she was also wearing her hair in a new style. As she spoke, Ami adjusted the white towelling sweatband around her forehead and patted her hair that, just permed, looked light and fluffy.

If he had been asked while he worked at NBC where the family's washing machine was kept, Kenji would not have been able to answer. Now he was intimately acquainted with the appliance and its strange nuances. The way the door had to be teased open and the noise the machine made once the spin cycle started because one of the feet had come off.

'Don't forget that Inagaki-san is expecting you at 11 a.m. sharp.'

Kenji wondered how he could possibly forget as Ami had gone to great lengths to remind him every day for the last week. As a personal favour to Kenji's mother-in-law, whom he described as 'an unwavering source of comfort and friendship to my mother', Inagaki had agreed to see Kenji and discuss whether there might be a position for him at Fuji Bank. Kenji was hopeful, his wife even more so.

'I have hung out your best suit for you.'

He nodded as Ami bent down to kiss him on the cheek. But she obviously changed her mind and just brushed back the hair from his face as he had seen her do to the children.

'Good luck,' she said, straightening up. 'And don't forget to go to the supermarket after you've been to the bank. The shopping list is on the fridge.'

The door slammed behind her and the house sat in silence except for the low hum of the refrigerator and the scratching of Eriko's fountain pen.

Kenji understood just how much of his family's future depended upon whether he was offered a job at Fuji Bank: the sensation was crushing. But not so humiliating as when Ami had cheerfully dusted off the sewing machine she used to make her clothes on before they were married, and started to take in excess work that the neighbourhood tailor could not cope with.

'You can't,' Kenji had protested, horrified. 'What if the neighbours were to find out? They will think that I cannot support my own family.'

Without a hint of malice, Ami had replied, 'You can't.'

It was not long before word of his wife's sewing skills spread and she began attracting customers of her own from all over Utsunomiya, even receiving commissions to make wedding dresses. The house always seemed to be buzzing now – with the sound of her sewing machine or the women who came to be fitted – while scraps of cloth and lengths of thread covered the floors. An affable woman when it suited, Ami soon became firm friends with many who employed her services. They often went out together on shopping trips where Ami bought nothing for herself but instead watched her friends spend their money. More recently she had started to attend aerobics classes with them and found that she enjoyed herself, and had a talent for some of the more choreographed lessons.

Surrounded by women and sewing all day, Kenji had begun to experience a new kind of madness. It was not enough that he had been stripped of his pride and sense of purpose, now he was forced to endure the same four walls all day, every day. He had always been an active man, but now the weight was starting to pile on – the band of his trousers cut into his waist – and he felt constantly lethargic. If he managed to sleep at night, then he struggled to wake up the next day. He was nothing but a walking apparition, a stranger in his own home. No matter where in the house he went or how obliging he tried to be, he always got in someone's way.

This time last week, as he sat on the low three-legged stool in the bathroom, bailing hot water out of the square deep tub and pouring it over his body, Ami had banged on the door.

'Yumi and Yoshi have to get ready to go to school,' she said. 'You must come out now and see to yourself later.'

He tried getting up earlier, he tried getting up later. There was always someone who deserved to be in the bathroom more than he and now it was several days since he last washed.

Recently, he had taken to visiting Doppo's headstone at the cemetery in Tokyo once a week. Sometimes he talked to his old friend, told him what he was up to. But most of the time he just sat still, getting colder and colder until it was time to go home. He missed Doppo desperately. He would even have enjoyed seeing the old crowd – the Professor and Michi. Of course it would have hurt, remembering what had been, but they could have spoken about Doppo: his kindness and big heart. It might have helped. But Ami forbade it. What he needed now was something to take his mind off missing his friend and feeling that he had failed his family, that now his wife was the head of the household.

'I need a job,' he thought, standing up and going into the kitchen where he began to wash up the breakfast dishes.

TWELVE

'Yamada-san. Please come in.' Inagaki ushered Kenji into his office, indicating that he should sit on the empty chair beside his desk. 'Would you like some coffee?' he asked graciously.

'No. Thank you.' Kenji sat down, surreptitiously looking around Inagaki's office. It was by no means the largest office he had seen – about eight feet by four – and it felt even smaller because of the desk and filing cabinets that were crammed into it. But that he had even been given a space of his own away from the other employees must signify that this was a man who could make decisions. Kenji felt hopeful.

As if sensing what Kenji was thinking, Inagaki explained. 'I see a great deal of clients each day. Many of them are very important and we discuss some personal issues.'

'I understand.' Kenji nodded, studying Inagaki's pinched face, his thin lips and cheekbones that swept up both sides of his face like large tick marks, his skin bore the scars of adolescent acne. There was something familiar about him. Perhaps they had met before, Kenji thought. Given that he too was a customer here, it was not unlikely that their paths had crossed.

'I understand something of your situation from my mother and may I say that I offer you my full and deepest sympathy.' Inagaki spoke assuredly. 'These are tough times indeed, for all of us.'

'It has been difficult.'

'My mother thought that I might have a job for you here at the bank. "Mother," I told her, "I cannot give just anybody a job. It would be seen as an abuse of my power and then the floodgates would open. Every relative, every friend and acquaintance would come knocking on my door whenever they found themselves out of work."'

Inagaki straightened the tie around his neck.

'I explained to my mother, "Yamada-san is a businessman. He will understand. If he wants to make a career for himself in banking then he will, like everybody else that comes to see me, have to start out at the bottom." You are a hard-working man, I know, and your mother-in-law has assured me that you will be glad of any opportunity. So now if you would like to accompany me.'

'Accompany you?'

'Yes. This way.'

Inagaki stood up and in doing so brushed against a picture frame on his desk. The frame fell backwards revealing a black and white photograph of a handsome woman with her hair swept up into a bun which sat on top of her head and large diamonds studs piercing her small ears. Elaborate handwriting was scrawled across the bottom of the print. She looked familiar.

'Is that . . .' Kenji asked.

'It is,' Inagaki replied curtly, picking up the frame and inspecting it for any damage. 'I am the president of her fan club.'

'. . . Hana Hoshino.' Thinking about it, Kenji recognised the face of the television presenter who had been popular in the 1980s. He wondered what had happened to her and was about to ask, but he saw that Inagaki was in no mood to talk.

He moved out from behind his desk. Kenji noticed for the first time that he walked with a stick, dragging his seemingly lifeless right leg along behind him. It did not stop the bank manager from moving quickly, however, and Kenji was forced to jog to keep up as they made their way to the lift. Once inside, Inagaki pressed the button marked basement.

'When you said,' Kenji spoke cautiously, afraid of offending his potential employer, 'start out at the bottom, what exactly did you mean?'

Inagaki appeared not to have heard. 'How are your children? Are they well? You must pass on my regards.'

It was oppressively hot in the basement. When the lift doors opened a warm, heavy air immediately filled the confined space. The walls were covered in an eggshell-blue paint that had long since started to crack and peel. Overhead all manner of pipes and ducts hung from the ceiling, grumbling and moaning as they transported gas, water and air to different parts of the building.

Immediately opposite the lift, two large swing doors led into a room lit with harsh fluorescent lights. Each of the four walls was lined with pigeonholes, the lowest of which started at waist height. In the centre of the room was a rectangular, battered table, around which a number of men stood sorting mail. Each was dressed in a blue shirt, blue trousers, and black shoes. Some were young, under twenty-five, Kenji guessed, but most were old enough to be grandfathers. When Inagaki entered the room, the doors swinging violently in his wake, each man uttered a polite greeting, although their hands did not stop moving and sorting mail, even for a second.

Feeling a slight pressure on his back, Kenji allowed himself to be guided to the end of the table where the oldest sorter stood. His back was hunched, the vertebrae having fused into this position, and his head bent over as if looking at something interesting on his chest. When his name was called, Soga looked up. It was the one part of his upper body that seemed to have any range of movement. His complexion was sallow, the skin on his face paper thin and wrinkled.

'Soga-san, this is Kenji Yamada. He will be joining us in the mail room from tomorrow.'

'The mail room,' Kenji repeated, incredulously.

'I'd like you to show him the ropes. Now, Yamada-san, if you'll excuse me I have a meeting to attend. I hope that you will be very happy with us here at Fuji Bank and I look forward to seeing you once you have started your duties.'

'But,' Kenji stuttered, following Inagaki out. 'I thought . . .'

Inagaki turned back to look at Kenji whose sentence trailed off into mid-air. 'What did you think?'

Kenji didn't reply. All sense of hope that he had felt on the way here today, had evaporated. He felt deflated. 'Nothing. Thank you, I am very grateful for your help.'

'Remember, bottom up,' Inagaki called cheerfully as the lift doors closed, leaving Kenji with no other option than to return to the mail room where Soga handed him a polythene bag containing a uniform and told him where and when to report for duty the next day.

Standing outside the bank, Kenji sucked deeply on a cigarette, feeling the smoke burning his lungs. After Doppo's death he had vowed to give up but was already back on twenty a day. With nothing else to do he would quite easily have smoked more but the meagre allowance Ami gave him did not permit such extravagances. He imagined his friend standing next to him now, a look of disappointment on his face.

'I know,' he shook his head, trying to get rid of the image. 'I can't do it,' he announced boldly to nobody in particular. 'It is beneath me. Ami will understand. I will make her see.'

Imagining that Doppo smiled and patted him encouragingly on the shoulder, he headed away from the bank, towards a nearby bin where he threw the uniform inside before catching a bus back to the apartment. Inside Ami was sitting at the kitchen table, her sewing machine in front of her and a long piece of ruby-red silk draped out across the surface, beneath a needle that didn't stop moving as she spoke. She looked up at her husband, over the top of the half-moon glasses she used for sewing.

'How did your interview go?'

Pouring himself a glass of water, Kenji took several gulps before sinking down opposite her. He began to explain. About his high hopes for the interview and that he would be offered a position befitting of his years of experience. How he knew how much his family depended upon him to get this job. How difficult he found it to see Ami reduced to making clothes when it should be he who provided for the family. It grieved him that she now earned more money than he did. He grew more and more ashamed every day.

Ami stared at her husband, the sewing machine now silent. 'Did he offer you a job?'

'Yes, but . . .'

'He offered you a job. That's good news.' She looked back down at the piece of silk on the table in front of her.

'But . . .' Kenji began to explain that the job was working in a mail room, and was not befitting of him at all. And he would be earning substantially less money than he had at NBC. He could not accept it.

'You will take the job,' she said, taking her time over each word, 'and that is all there is to it.'

'But . . .'

'If you want to continue looking for another job then so be it. But in the meantime you will not refuse Inagaki's kind offer.'

'You don't understand.'

'I refuse to say another word on the matter.'

'I am not a child. You cannot treat me like the twins.'

She did not look up. She would not be drawn on the subject.

He had to make her listen. He had to make her understand just how much this meant to him, how strongly he felt. There was only one thing for it. 'If that's what you think then I may as well give up all hope now,' he shouted angrily before storming out of the kitchen.

He opened the door to the cupboard in the hallway. Tucked away in the corner was a tartan bag containing three golf clubs that Ami had bought him a number of years previously. They had remained there ever since, unused, though he had always harboured the vague hope that he might have recourse to them if ever that promotion he hoped for came his way. It never did and now he would be working as a mail room attendant he'd certainly never need them. Making no attempt to be quiet, he dragged them out of the cupboard and to the front door. Ami knew how much they meant to him. If she saw him doing this then she was certain to realise how strongly he felt and stop him.

'Kenji,' she called from the kitchen just as he was opening the front door. He held his breath. She did understand after all. He had made her understand. 'Did you get the shopping?'

THIRTEEN

The automatic doors opened slowly, as if the mechanism controlling them had grown tired. Kenji stood on the mat outside the supermarket entrance, waiting patiently. When the doors were half open, they stopped. He looked around for someone who might explain what was happening. Finding no one, he decided to brave the doors, squeezing between the gap and into the shop.

It was like falling into another world – one full of blindingly bright light and loud, tinny music. Shelf after shelf of neatly stacked products, freezers and cabinets, stretched out in what seemed like endless, identical rows. Clutching the long list Ami had given him to his chest, he wondered how he would ever be able to find anything. It could take hours, he realised with trepidation, grabbing a nearby basket and edging further into the shop because he was blocking the path of other customers trying to enter through the malfunctioning doors. Silently he cursed his wife. It was obvious that she had done this to punish him and was probably sitting at home, this very minute, sniggering at the thought of him wandering helplessly through the supermarket, too proud to ask for assistance.

Of course she had tried to give the appearance of making things easy for him. The list he held in one hand had been written out in the same order that he would encounter each item as he passed through the shop. There was even a floor plan that plotted the best route to take through the aisles. But she must have known how bewildered he would feel in a place like this. In fact, he had even dared to suggest that for the length of time it had taken her to prepare these instructions, she would have been better off going shopping herself. Whereupon she had snapped at him. 'Next time it will not take me so long because you will know what you are doing.'

Looking at the long aisles – full of tins, bottles and plastic-packed goods, labels arranged facing outwards – he wondered if he would ever know what he was doing. The floor plan did not help matters. If anything, it bore such little resemblance to what was now confronting him that he wondered if he was in the wrong shop entirely. There was no point turning back now, though. He was here and if he took things slowly, one item at a time, he could get through this.

Taking the first item on the list – apples – he looked around him. Evidently he was standing in the grocery section. Boxes of fruit and vegetables were arranged on waist-high, shallow, sloping shelves lined with a sheet of plastic grass and lit overhead with mushroom shaped bulbs. He could see potatoes, tomatoes, beansprouts, oranges and watermelons. But none of these items were on his list and he couldn't find any apples. Wandering hopefully from shelf to shelf he eventually stumbled upon what he was looking for – large, perfectly round pink apples that were so impossible to find because each one had been wrapped in a white mesh polystyrene jacket. Picking up four, he dropped them into his basket where they landed with a loud thud. The noise caused a supermarket employee, standing nearby, to stop what she was doing and look up.

'If you drop them like that they'll bruise,' she smiled, handing him a brown paper bag. 'Why not give those to me and choose some more.' She bent over his basket and picked out the apples. The movement caused her beige- and orange-check dress to tighten around her waist.

Blushing furiously, Kenji looked away until she was standing up straight once more, clutching the apples to what he couldn't help but notice was a very generous bosom bulging beneath her uniform.

'Is this your first time?'

As she spoke he noticed that she had a small gap between her two front teeth.

'Yes,' he confessed. 'I don't know where to start.'

'Do you know something? I wish more people were as honest as you. It's very refreshing. We get a lot of men in here that are in the same position. But they won't admit that they don't know what they're doing until they've been in here for over an hour, wandering helplessly around. It's nothing to be ashamed of, I tell them.'

'The same position?' he repeated.

'Yes.' She sat a pair of spectacles that were hanging on a chain around her neck on the bridge of her nose and studied him. 'You are divorced, aren't you? Or maybe separated?' She bowed slightly. 'I'm sorry. I shouldn't have been so presumptuous. It was rude of me.'

She started to turn. He tried desperately to think of a way in which to stop her. There was something about her. The way she looked and the tone of her voice. Both were infinitely soothing and immensely reassuring. Just being in her presence made him feel that things were going to get better. But how? He knew before he had said it that he shouldn't, that it was dishonest. No matter though. It didn't stop the words from coming out.

'Yes, you're right,' he muttered quickly, as though saying it quickly might mitigate the lie. 'I am separated. Six months ago.' It was not completely untrue, he reasoned. It was, after all, six months ago that he had been forced to leave NBC which was a separation of sorts and the effect had been just as catastrophic for him.

'Perhaps I can help you then?' She held out her hand for the list.

'I would be very grateful.'

Breathing an enormous sigh of relief, he pushed the list at her. She smelt fresh, like cucumbers, and as she studied the piece of paper, he found himself staring intently at her. Hers was the kind of face that it was a pleasure to linger on: oval with a full forehead and a delicately rounded chin, she had a small, slightly up-turned nose; two large, high cheeks and full, almond-shaped lips to which a layer of damson lipstick had been carefully applied. Her black hair was secured in a tidy bun, and stray, loose curls hung around her face. He was shocked to find himself imagining what her skin felt like and thought about stroking her cheek. No doubt it would be soft. If pressed he would have described her build as plump, maybe even slightly overweight, but could not think of anybody that it suited more.

'Let's see. My, this is quite a list.' She giggled. 'You must have a big appetite.'

He thought fast. 'My sister and her two children are coming to stay.'

'That's nice. It'll be company for you. Let's take this one at a time.'

As she looked at him through her glasses, he found himself wishing that he had taken more care over his appearance. It felt like months since he had given even a minute's thought to how he looked. Even for the interview at Fuji Bank this afternoon – he shuddered to remember it – he had allowed Ami to dictate what he should wear, how he should comb his hair and shave.

'Obviously this is where you will find all the fruit and vegetables.' She indicated the surrounding cabinets while waving the tip of a biro over the list. 'The frozen food section is at the very end of this aisle with the fresh fish, meat, milk and yoghurts. Curries and noodles, they're on aisle two. Bottom left.'

Moving expertly through the list, she scribbled instructions on the piece of paper, occasionally looking up at him. No matter how hard he tried, he could not pay attention to what she was saying. Her mere presence – soft, warm and intoxicating – was a distraction to him. Finally she finished speaking.

'That should get you everything you need.'

Thanking her profusely and unable to think of anything else to say, he had no option other than to walk away. Turning back to capture one last look at her, he walked straight into a table. The display of watermelons came crashing to the floor where several split clean in half, splattering their pink, juicy flesh everywhere.

'Hey, watch out,' a voice shouted.

Aghast, he clapped one hand over his mouth and immediately dropped his basket, bending down to pick up any watermelons that could be rescued. It was then that he noticed something unusual about them. They were square.

'They are no ordinary watermelons,' the voice continued. 'They were grown in specially made plexiglass containers.'

'I am very sorry,' he spluttered. 'It was an accident.'

'Accidents don't come cheaply. Not in my store.'

As the young man spoke, spittle escaped from his mouth, landing on Kenji's right cheek. He wanted to wipe it away but did not want to draw the young man's attention to what he had just done.

'I will pay for the damage.' Kenji reached for his wallet.

'You've ruined three and they cost 10,000 yen. So that's 30,000 in total.'

'That's not possible.' It was more money than he had in his wallet and if he came home without the shopping Ami was almost certain to suspect him of having played pachinko. 'I can't . . .' Before he could think of an excuse, a voice interrupted.

'Rambashi-san, it was my fault.'

Spinning around he saw the woman who had helped him just moments before.

'I distracted our customer when I tried to tell him about our special offer on oranges. If I hadn't, then he would have seen the table and the watermelons would be intact.'

The look on Rambashi's small, square face said that he was not entirely convinced. But with little else to do, he marched off, swinging his long, wiry arms and called out over his shoulder, 'Clean it up. Now, before a customer slips on it.'

It was not until he had disappeared into the storeroom at the back of the supermarket, that Kenji finally spoke. 'I don't know what to say. Thank you. Again. Thank you.'

She put one finger to her lips. 'It's our secret. Now get on with your shopping or you'll get me into even more trouble.'

He watched her go, surprised to find he was smiling.

FOURTEEN

'I do not understand.' Soga scratched his balding head, the skin on which was shiny, as though it had just been polished with a cloth. 'Please explain to me one more time how you happened to lose your uniform.'

'It was not so much lost as stolen,' Kenji replied uneasily. He had felt hopeful on arriving at the bank this morning; buoyed up by his experience at the supermarket last night. Just thinking about the woman who had helped him made him feel good, but the more Soga said, the more of this sensation drained away from him. Soon he felt nothing at all but grim resignation.

'After I dropped my keys in the gutter, I put the parcel to one side as I looked for them. By the time I retrieved my keys the parcel had gone. I saw some kids running down the road, laughing, but they were too far for me to chase after them.'

'You are one man,' Soga persisted. 'How can I give one man two uniforms?'

Kenji thought about the child he had seen on the way to the bank this morning: prodding a dead sparrow with a long stick by the side of the road, repeatedly over and over again even though it was obvious the poor creature was dead.

'Perhaps you could take the money for the stolen uniform out of my salary?' he offered quietly.

Tutting loudly, Soga hobbled off in the direction of a large locker at the end of the mail room. 'Before commencing employment as a mail attendant a new recruit is given one uniform,' he called out. 'He should not receive another uniform until his first has worn out beyond reasonable repair. Yours, I think, has not.' Opening the locker with one of the many keys that hung off a large ring he kept in his pocket, Soga removed two cellophane bags and handed them to Kenji. 'It will not be so easy for me to give you any more uniforms, so please be careful not to lose this one.'

Bristling, Kenji took the uniform to the men's locker room where he changed into trousers that were several centimetres too short and a shirt so voluminous he felt like a young boy dressing up in his father's work clothes. Staring at his reflection in a full-length mirror, he frowned. He had to take this job. It had been hopeless to protest. Ami was immoveable and now refused to even speak about the subject with him. Dejected and frustrated, he reported back to the harshly lit mail room where, one by one, the other attendants slowly drifted in. When they were all present, Soga made a number of announcements before introducing Kenji to his colleagues. A few cast suspicious glances in his direction, the others were completely uninterested in his presence.

'Since it is your first day – ' Soga handed Kenji a white rectangular badge with 'trainee' written across it. ' – you will be accompanying Yamanote on his route today. He will show you what to do and then from tomorrow you'll be on your own.'

Turning to his right, Kenji smiled feebly at the man called Yamanote and found that he was already gone; pushing a two-layered white mesh trolley out of the swing doors and into the lift. Hurrying to catch up with him, Kenji bowed quickly and bid him a polite good morning. Yamanote simply grunted and then retreated back into the silent contemplation that occupied him for most of the day as they worked their way down from the top floor of the bank, stopping off at each of their designated collection points and filling the trolley with the envelopes that they picked up there.

Once they had finished their round, they took the trolley, which was now full, back to the basement, and spent the rest of the morning sorting through the mail. The first task was to divide the external from the internal mail. The internal envelopes were then posted into pigeonholes beneath which a label denoted their final destination, while the external envelopes were franked and packed into large sacks for the post van that arrived shortly before lunch.

After the van had been filled, all of the mail attendants clocked off. Most ate in the men's locker room, staring blankly into space. Kenji found the atmosphere so oppressive that he took his lunch box outside and sat on a bench at the side of the road to eat. It was loud and there were lots of people walking past, but he didn't care. The noise of traffic lumbering by was a distraction from the images of Yamanote's expressionless face as he pushed the trolley through the bank, and of Soga's crooked back. Not to mention his long, thin, crippled fingers ravaged by arthritis. Was this what he had to look forward to, he wondered?

'Why?' He could hear the disappointment in Doppo's voice as he imagined his friend sitting next to him on the bench. It was comforting, at those times when he was most down, to pretend that his friend was still alive and coaching him as he had always done. 'After everything I taught you, why would you want to work here?'

In his head, Kenji tried to explain. 'I made promises, to your daughter and my wife, I would not play again.' Finishing his lunch, he went back inside.

The next day, he was allocated his own route and was given a wire mesh trolley that he pushed back and forth through the building before returning to the mail room to sort the envelopes in silence. He was slower than the other attendants and often hadn't finished sorting by the time that the post van arrived. The driver would wait, smoking a cigarette, impatiently tapping his fingers on the bonnet, or lie across the front seat listening to music on an oversized pair of headphones.

It was not an overly strenuous job, but with each passing day, getting up in the morning was becoming more and more difficult when in fact it should have been easier. When he'd worked at NBC he had woken at 6 a.m. every morning and did not generally get to bed until after midnight. Now he was always in bed at 10 p.m. and didn't get up until 8.30 a.m. He spent so long in bed not because he felt especially tired, but because he could not bear to be awake and the longer that he could put off having to think about getting up and going to work the better.

Then, on the first day of his second week, something unexpected happened: Inagaki appeared, limping through the swing doors of the mail room. It was the first time that Kenji had seen him since being offered the job and was apprehensive about this moment. The bank manager was friendly and civil, which only succeeded in making the hairs on the back of Kenji's neck stand up on end. He didn't like him and he certainly didn't trust him. This man had humiliated him when he was at his lowest point. It made him angry just to be in the same room as him.

'Yamada-san, how are you settling in?' Inagaki assumed an expression of genuine interest.

'Good,' Kenji nodded, gritting his teeth. There was something so familiar about this man but try as he might, he could not put his finger on it.

'I'm glad to hear it. Now if you wouldn't mind coming with me, I have a very important job for you to do.'

The other men looked up from the mail that they were sorting and glared at Kenji. Intrigued and even slightly hopeful, he followed Inagaki out of the swing doors and up to the ground floor where they passed through a security door and into the main foyer. Kenji started to feel light-headed. Had he misjudged Inagaki? Was the job in the mail room simply a test? A way for him to prove his merit? And now this was it, the chance that he had been waiting for. Start from the bottom up, that's what Inagaki had said and he was most certainly ready. He wondered if he might get his own desk, a telephone and a computer. Even if he had to share, it wouldn't matter. Just so long as it got him away from the mail room and the other attendants. Perhaps he should mention that now to Inagaki and put his mind at ease. Except the bank manager was walking quickly ahead of him and Kenji was having difficulty keeping up.

The bank was busy and there were a number of floor attendants on duty, directing customers to the seated waiting area and then on to the service points as they became vacated. Inagaki continued past

99

the waiting area, to a small cupboard in the far left-hand corner which he unlocked with a long thin key. The door creaked open revealing an assortment of cleaning materials.

'There has been a small accident in the manager's bathroom on the fourth floor. One of the toilets has become blocked and flooded. Please remove the blockage and then clean up. You will find everything you need in here.'

'Excuse me?' Kenji was not quite sure if he had heard Inagaki correctly.

After repeating the story, Inagaki turned and walked away, leaving Kenji staring after him, his mouth hanging wide open, desperate to say something, but too shocked to speak. Indescribable anger boiled up inside him, but most of all he felt deeply embarrassed and ashamed. Who did that man think he was? He was not a cleaner. He was a respectable salaried man. Or at least he had been until now. Look at what he had been reduced to. If it wasn't for the fact that he had a family to support, he would storm upstairs right now and tell that weedy, limp-legged stick of a man exactly what he could do with his mop and bucket. But he did have a family to support and bills to pay. So instead he picked up the cleaning equipment and made his way to the fourth floor. Some time later he returned to the mail room, his uniform sodden. Soga refused to allow him another one to change into and so he passed the rest of the morning drying out, feeling more and more frustrated with each passing minute.

'The man is a tyrant,' he exploded over the dinner table that evening.

Eriko would not hear a word said against him. 'He has been very good to our family,' she said, her thin lips forming a line.

'He has a cruel streak.'

'He's had a hard life,' Ami interrupted and, knowing it was pointless to disagree, Kenji simply sat back and listened as the two women gossiped. As they spoke, it became apparent why Inagaki looked so familiar. They had been at school together, in the same class even. The young Inagaki was a shy child and teenager, with bottle-thick glasses and a pronounced limp who always hid in corners, and whose father had run away with another woman. Kenji knew that the young Inagaki had suffered at the hands of his former classmates but was certain that he had played no active role in the bullying. He hadn't tried to stop it, however, but why would he? It was not wise to draw attention to oneself, for you could never tell in which direction those bullies would focus their attention next.

This clearly wasn't how Inagaki saw things. Every day he called down to the basement with some job or other for Kenji to perform. Always appearing gracious and calling Kenji out of the room, away from the other men, before he told him that he wanted him to scrub the floor in the men's locker room, sweep the bank's frontage, polish the signs on the managers' doors. At least now Kenji understood why. He was having his revenge. It wasn't long before the other men in the mail room became jealous, thinking that he was being groomed for a better position. Now they did talk to each other, but only ever about him and behind his back. The atmosphere was unbearable, reaching its peak whenever Inagaki came limping through the doors.

'Yamada-san, your most urgent assistance is required,' he called out, and Kenji followed him, burning with fury. What else could he do? Inagaki was the boss and he couldn't afford to lose another job, no matter how much he hated it. If only he had someone he might talk to. Confiding in a dead friend had its advantages, but wasn't as good as the real thing. Meeting up with Michi and the Professor, however, wasn't an option. If Ami found out she would be furious. Looking at his watch as he trailed after Inagaki, Kenji wondered if he might make it to the supermarket and back in his lunch hour.

101

FIFTEEN

'I'm glad we bumped into each other again.' Kenji took a sip of coffee and was surprised to find that it had turned cold. It seemed like minutes since the cup had been refilled. Dai was such good company and easy to talk to. It made him happy just to hear her giggle. It seemed foolish now, how nervous he had felt about revisiting the supermarket and hoping to see her. Many times he had thought about turning back. He was glad now that he had not.

'Me too.'

Emboldened, he continued. 'I know it sounds silly. I hardly know you. But just talking to you about all these things – my job, Inagaki, Doppo – has made me feel so much better.'

'Perhaps that is exactly the reason why,' Dai commented, dabbing her lips with a paper napkin. She looked even more pretty today than he had remembered and was wearing a burnt orange lipstick that matched her eyeshadow. 'It is always much easier to talk about the things that hurt the most with someone who does not know you so well. And it has been a very difficult time for you. Losing your job, your wife, your best friend. All in the space of six months. It is important to get things off your chest or else – ' She looked around the restaurant in which they had chosen to eat lunch as if searching for the right words. ' – you'd go mad.'

Kenji nodded and looked away. Dai patted his hand. Her skin felt soft and smooth, but her kindness made him feel worse. It was a terrible thing to have lied to her. The first time it had happened, it had been a simple misunderstanding. The words had slipped out before he had the chance to stop them. This, on the other hand, was much more deliberate. He had even gone to the extent of removing his wedding ring before walking through the still-malfunctioning doors of the supermarket. He tried to reassure himself that the deception was necessary. As Dai had said: without anybody to talk to he might go mad. Maybe he had already. At least a little bit. And she was exactly the tonic that he needed. After just a short half-hour in her company, he felt better: happier, hopeful and even a little bit content. If anybody had asked him what they had eaten for lunch he wouldn't have been able to remember. He wasn't even sure what the restaurant they were sitting in was like. But he would remember every detail of Dai's face, her expressions and gestures, and how she smelt. It was an image that he planned to store in his head so that later, while at work, he could take it out and linger over it.

'Here I am, talking about myself all the time.' He put the cold cup of coffee back down in the saucer. 'I haven't let you speak at all. You must please tell me about yourself.'

Dai smiled, briefly. 'There's nothing to tell really. I live in a small apartment near the supermarket. I have a cat and I grow herbs in a window box. I've been working in the supermarket for just over a year. Before then I used to work at the hospital. In the canteen.'

'Are you married? Do you have children?' he asked, hoping that the answer to both questions would be no and surprised at his own impudence for asking.

'Yes, I am married.'

He couldn't help but feel disappointed.

'But sadly no children.' She paused and studied Kenji's face. 'I feel that I can trust you.'

He grimaced, hoping she didn't notice. He hated being dishonest with her.

'So I will tell you something that not many other people know. My husband is in prison.'

Kenji must have looked shocked because she went on hurriedly.

'He didn't kill anybody, before you think that you're having lunch with a murderer's wife.' She laughed self-consciously as he tried to look more sympathetic. 'He stole cars. He's always stolen cars. Ever since we first met when we were eighteen years old. Yes, that's how long we've been married. At first I thought it was fun and exciting. Then he got caught and sent to jail and it wasn't so much fun anymore. Each time we got settled down in a new area, I'd find a job and make friends, he'd steal a car and get caught. People found out. Sometimes he even stole from people we knew. There was gossip and suddenly people weren't so friendly anymore. I'd have no choice but to move on.'

'I'm sorry,' Kenji almost whispered. 'I had no idea.'

'Nobody does. In fact you are the first person I have told in a very long time. I cannot bear to see the look in people's eyes.'

This part of her story pleased him enormously. He had confided in her and she too had shared something of herself with him. This truly was two friends going through a difficult time, meeting to console one another.

'How long is he in prison for?'

'Three years. He is coming to the end of his sentence, though. This time he knocked over a young boy while driving a stolen car and the boy nearly died. He'll be out in a few months. When they took him away I told him I was leaving him and I haven't seen him since. I haven't been to visit him once. Not like the other times when I was a dutiful wife, waiting patiently for him. But he'll find me. He always does.' She smiled sadly. 'Now look at the time.' Checking her watch, she hurriedly stood up. 'I don't know about you, but I've got to get back to work.'

'Yes, of course.' Kenji stood up. He had already insisted on paying the bill, so they were able to walk straight out of the restaurant. 'If you ever need somebody to talk to,' he offered when they got out, 'I'm here.'

'That would be nice.' She nodded and kissed him delicately on his right cheek before turning and hurrying off down the street, back to the supermarket.

He stood there for several seconds. A foolish smile on his lips and his hand clamped to his cheek as if trying to prevent the kiss from escaping.

SIXTEEN

'A customer has complained about the condition of our fish tank.' Inagaki pointed at the glass walls of the fish tank, the insides of which were covered with a thick layer of green algae. 'It is an important matter that needs our immediate attention, so please begin at once.' He handed Kenji a key and pointed at the cleaning cupboard.

'It will be my pleasure,' Kenji smiled broadly, taking pleasure from the bemused expression on Inagaki's face. Nothing was going to get him down this afternoon.

Whistling the tune to a song that had been playing on the radio in the mail room, he collected the equipment he needed from the cupboard and began by transferring the fish from the tank into a bucket filled with clean tap water. Next he emptied the tank into a sluice sink in the cupboard where he began scrubbing at the slimy, green glass panes. Concentrating on finishing the job and doing so quickly, it took several seconds before he realised that there was a small, gaunt, bird-like man standing in the doorway, watching him. It was Akira Eto, Ishida's second-in-command at NBC.

'Yamada-san.' Eto inhaled deeply, his gaze lingering on the pink rubber gloves that Kenji was wearing. He still sounded like a man who was on the brink of suffocation.

Kenji froze, both arms submerged in the fish tank.

'I thought it was you as I came in the door. I said to myself, "That looks like Yamada-san." I didn't think it could be. I didn't realise that you worked here,' Eto continued cheerfully, but still Kenji could not speak.

'So you are well?'

Putting the fish tank carefully to one side, Kenji stood up.

'Of course you must be wondering about the old team. How rude of me. They are well. All working hard on the new series of game shows.'

'Game shows?' The pink rubber gloves made a loud snapping noise as he removed them from his hands. 'I thought that the network had decided not to make anymore game shows? That they would be specialising in news and documentaries.'

Eto laughed nervously. 'Really. That is odd.' Sucking deeply on the hot, heavy air in the cleaning cupboard, he continued more sombrely. 'The corporation went through a difficult patch for a while. I'm sure you remember. But everything is back on track now. In fact to celebrate, we are having our bi-annual social outing at the Maruhan Golf Club. Do you know it? It's not far from here. I just came by to pay the deposit.'

Kenji was stunned. It was a struggle to get his thoughts in order. 'I thought that the light entertainment division was being disbanded. The decision had been made by the board of directors.'

'No, it's doing very well.'

'And you'll be playing golf.' He grabbed Eto's arm, perhaps more forcibly than he should have done. But he needed to impress this important point. 'I always wanted to play golf.'

'Yes, well.'

Eto began to wriggle and squirm, attempting to extricate himself but Kenji would not let him go. Grabbing hold of Eto's other arm, he held his face up to the man who had tormented him with his proverbs every Monday morning for years. 'I always wanted to play golf.'

'My wife . . .' Eto was looking all around him, hoping that some-body might come to his rescue. 'My wife is waiting for me outside. I really must go or she will come looking for me.'

'Of course she will,' Kenji mumbled incoherently. 'My wife won't even speak to me.' Suddenly he dropped Eto's arms, who immediately fled out of the door. 'How could they do this to me?' He ran out after Eto, shouting, 'They took my job, they took my self-respect. Now they are all laughing at me and playing golf. I always wanted to play golf.'

Customers standing at the counter had turned to stare in his direction, while the bank clerks had climbed down from their seats and were standing on the tips of their toes to get a better view of what was going on. An elderly security guard approached Kenji and asked him what all the fuss was about. He felt trapped. Everyone was looking at him, talking about him. As the guard got closer, he looked for somewhere he could escape to. He was surrounded on all sides. If he ran they would surely catch him. So he grabbed the bucket and emptied it over the floor, spilling water and small, flapping gold bodies. The security guard and a number of customers rushed over, attempting to retrieve the goldfish. Meanwhile Kenji ran out, unnoticed.

Outside it was raining heavily. Within a few minutes his clothes were soaked. He did not notice as he followed the main road out of Utsunomiya heading towards the Maruhan Golf Club, running and walking. When he arrived, he spent some time circling the perimeter fence before finding a suitable point where he could slip under. Ducking down and crawling on his hands and knees through the muddied ground, he forced himself into a gap in the wire mesh fence and out through the thick vegetation on the other side. Standing up he looked around, not quite sure what to do or where to go.

Then he saw it glowing in the rain. On a hill in the distance stood a white hut. He half ran, half climbed towards it, his saturated trousers plastered to his legs and wet socks squelching in his shoes. The door to the hut was locked but the wood was weak and rotten, and by charging against it repeatedly he was able to smash his way in. Inside was exactly what he had been looking for: a large selection of golf clubs and balls. He grabbed a number of both and ran back outside the hut where the rain was coming down in sheets and the sky had become so grey that it could easily have been approaching night. He heard a loud rumbling and in the distance saw a small flash of lightning.

It did not stop him. As he had seen the professional players do on television any number of times, he stuck a pin into the ground and balanced a ball on top. Then he swung and missed the ball. He swung again and again, each time failing to hit the white sphere. 'Perfect,' he screamed, unaware that tears were rolling down his face. 'Why can't I get anything right?' Raising the club in the air, holding it high above his head just like the man in his golf ball ficus, he prepared to take another swing. High up above him the sky rumbled and a flash of white lightning broke through the clouds, hitting the tip of the golf club, travelling along the length of it and coursing through his body. He shuddered violently and passed out, vaguely aware of the smell of burning hair.

SEVENTEEN

'You're awake. I thought that maybe you were planning to sleep forever.'

As his eyes slowly opened, sleep receded and his conscious state struggled to take hold, Kenji noticed first that his mouth was parched and then that he could not lift his head. There were no physical restraints preventing him, it just felt heavy. Heavier than a lead weight and intense, sharp pains were shooting through it, exploding like fireworks behind his eyes. All he could see, on both sides and above him, was a bright white expanse of nothingness. Was it possible that someone was shining a light in his eyes? Or maybe this is what the afterlife looked like? He snapped his eyelids shut.

'I must be dead,' he thought, with a peculiar mixture of relief and dread. But if he was dead, then who was it that had just spoken to him and where was that slow, steady breathing coming from? The thought proved to be too much and as soon as it occurred to him, he fell back into a deep sleep.

When he next awoke, it was to the same expanse of white, although his mouth felt less dry and he found that he was able to lift his head fractionally, though it exhausted him to do so. He listened carefully, expectantly. There it was again. That same, heavy, laboured breathing: at once familiar and reassuring. It might not belong to someone else, he realised. Maybe it was his own breathing, and the fact that it sounded as though it was coming from somewhere else was because he was having an out of body experience. He had read about them in one of Eriko's magazines. It was entirely possible that he was, at this very minute, floating between the border of life and death and, if he looked down, would find that his spirit had been released from his body.

He lifted his head cautiously, but found to his disappointment that everything was as it should be. At least some of it was. Stretched out in front of him was his body shrouded in a light-green, woollen blanket. There were his feet, sticking up beneath it, and both arms resting on top. A plastic tag had been secured to his left wrist and his right hand was bandaged and appeared to be twice its normal size. Reaching up he groped his face with his unbandaged hand, and found one eyebrow missing. All that remained was a stubbly mass, while the other brow and the eye beneath it was covered with what felt like a patch. Cautiously, his hand inched further up his face, on to the top of his head where he found what could only be described as a turban.

'What are you doing?'

It was the same voice again: male and mildly amused.

'Death isn't what I imagined.' He tried to speak but found that his tongue would not move in synch with his lips. All that came out was a sort of mumble. Death was not something that he had thought a great deal about. But when he had, he imagined a sense of bliss. What he felt instead was numb and eerily calm, which in itself wasn't entirely displeasing.

'Don't worry,' the voice said reassuringly, 'it feels worse than it is.'

It was strange, but he didn't feel frightened. It was as though a switch had been flicked in his brain, turning a large percentage of his body function off. Maybe that's what death did to you. 'Am I dead?' Kenji asked the voice. He didn't know who he was speaking to, but the voice sounded friendly and he knew he could trust it.

The man chuckled. It was a familiar sound. He groped in the recesses of his brain for the memory associated with that chuckle but it flitted just out of reach.

'Here, drink some of this.'

A warm hand pressed against his forehead and his chin was tipped up, rather brusquely. Next, a plastic cup was positioned against his lips and water trickled into his mouth. He gulped it down greedily, surprised that he was even thirsty.

'Who are you?'

'Don't you know me?'

He blinked and then he blinked again. In the centre of the white nothingness a black dot appeared and from it grew swirls of bright vivid colour. They danced in front of his eyes and slowly began to settle until a shape formed and he was able to discern at least the outline of a man; a very large man. Slowly, more details began to appear. The face was large and round with full cheeks and a pair of black glasses sitting on the bridge of a small nose. Beneath the head a red sun was shining in a midnight blue sky, down on to a palm tree, water lapping at its base.

'Doppo,' he croaked. Now he knew that he was dead. 'It's you. I'm so glad to see you.'

'And me you, old friend. And me you.'

'I don't know what happened.' He tried to sit up but Doppo kept a firm hand on his chest until eventually he admitted defeat and sank back down. 'I don't know how I got here. Where am I? I'm dead, aren't I? I must be dead.' Although it was calm before, his mind was racing now, hungry for answers. 'I don't mind so much. You're here and things will be a whole lot easier now.'

'You were struck by lightning,' Doppo said.

'Lightning,' Kenji repeated. 'How did I get struck by lightning?' It seemed like such a bizarre suggestion. The last thing he remembered he had been at the bank, cleaning a fish tank. Not the best job in the world but he was unfazed by it. After all, he had Dai to think about. Of course, Dai. Realising that he would never see her again, he felt deflated. This admission seemed to trigger more memories. They came flooding back, playing in his mind like a slow-running, black and white film. He saw himself climbing up a muddy hill. It was pouring with rain and he was completely soaked. Looking down, he saw that he held a clump of grass in one hand and there was dirt

112

wedged beneath his fingernails. What had he been doing, he wondered?

As if he had a window into Kenji's mind, Doppo explained. 'They found you on the Maruhan Golf Course. You had a club welded to your right hand. They had to cut it away in the end.'

Looking down at the oversized bandage Kenji asked, 'What was I doing there?' His hand didn't hurt at all, which surely meant that he was dead. But then it started to itch and a dull throbbing pain formed behind his forehead. Here was Doppo talking to him and it wasn't like the other times he had imagined talking to his friend since his death. He didn't have to force himself to remember the details of his friend's face, it was here in front of him and he could hear him, see him, feel him.

'It looked like you had been trying to play golf.'

Another scene began to play itself out in his head; this one worse than the last. Eto standing over him, staring at him as he scrubbed at the glass walls of a dirty fish tank while wearing a pair of pink rubber gloves.

'Doppo,' he began, but started coughing.

'Have some more water.'

'No.' Kenji knocked the cup away. The intensity of his anger surprised him. 'They pushed me out.' The words tasted sour in his mouth, but he knew that they were true. Maybe he had always known in some corner of his mind. 'They told me that I wouldn't be the only one to go but I was. They wanted to get rid of me.' Now it seemed obvious. It was all because of the game show that had failed. He had tried to warn the production team. They might have listened if it hadn't been for the show's producer, Abe E. Kitahara. Then when the show did fail, Abe was not around. They needed someone to blame and they chose Kenji. He had seen it before; entire teams turning against one person. He just never thought that it would happen to him. 'They made a scapegoat out of me and didn't even have the courage to tell me to my face.' The reality hurt more than he imagined it would, especially now.

'That's a tough one.' Doppo sat down next to him.

As he studied his friend's face, Kenji suddenly became overcome

113

by emotion. 'I never thought that I'd see you again,' he sobbed.

'Hey.' Doppo stood up. 'Don't go getting emotional on me, salaryman.'

Kenji managed a small laugh. 'I'm glad though. I don't mind being dead. Especially with you here. Anything has to be better than that job in the bank.'

Doppo looked at him quizzically, opened his mouth as if to speak and then changed his mind. He sat down again. 'Tell me what happened. How did you manage to get yourself in this mess?'

'Ami found out,' Kenji began, describing the confrontation in the kitchen and the many mistakes that he had made leading up to it. 'I promised her that I would give up pachinko. Never play again. And I promised your daughter.'

Doppo bowed his head and stared at the floor. 'Maybe it was for the best. You weren't cut out for the pachinko life. You didn't like the deceit and in your heart you were always a salaryman. So why not get another job in TV? Why get an underpaid job as a mail room attendant in the bank? It is beneath you.' As he spoke, his voice grew louder, more animated.

Kenji shrugged. 'You think more highly of me than I deserve.'

'Pah,' Doppo pronounced. 'I don't believe that for one second. What happened to your dreams of promotion?' he persisted, leaning closer to Kenji's face. 'You told me once that you always wanted to be a producer. Make your own TV programmes. Why not take the opportunity? Be brave. Strike out. Take the risk.'

'How can I take a risk when I've never taken a risk in my life? I wouldn't know how.' Now Kenji was shouting.

'If you believe that then you'll never succeed. You deserve to work in a bank. Don't you understand how quickly time is slipping away from you? That one day it could be taken away altogether and then it would be too late to do all those things you dreamed of but never found the time or the courage to do.'

Finding that his head was no longer so heavy, Kenji turned away from Doppo and stared at the white expanse of space on the opposite side of him. The movement caused a tear that had settled in his right eye to roll down his cheek. 'Those dreams were foolish,' he all but whispered. He could not even remember having told Doppo about them. He had never told another living soul, not even his wife.

'Tell me about them again.'

Slowly, Kenji turned back and regarded Doppo for several seconds. His friend's face was crumpled with concern and his large, chubby fingers were clasped in front of him. 'I dreamed about making a TV show. A game show.'

'What kind of game show?'

Doppo pushed his glasses up the bridge of his nose. Beads of perspiration had broken out on his forehead. Kenji looked for the familiar outline of Doppo's inhaler in his shirt pocket, but it wasn't there. He guessed that his friend had no call for it anymore.

'I had many ideas. I used to keep them all written down in a notebook.'

'If you were to make a show now, then what would it be about?' Doppo's voice was quieter now.

Kenji struggled to organise his thoughts. It was not such a difficult question. When he worked for NBC, ideas often occurred to him.

'My mother-in-law enters competitions in magazines and news-papers,' he began, and saw that he had Doppo's full attention. 'Hundreds of them each week. And she wins. Not just small prizes, big ones worth lots of money. Some of them she keeps, others she sells. To torment me she often says that she could keep the family afloat just by the proceeds from her competitions alone. That her winnings would feed and clothe us in one way or another.'

'Go on.'

'I often thought about putting her to the test,' Kenji grinned. 'Locking the old battleaxe in a room with nothing to do and nothing to eat. All she'd have would be her newspapers and magazines. We'd see how she gets along then. See if she could survive just like she says.'

'And?'

'Well that's it. That's the game show. Lock a contestant in an empty room with no means of survival other than to enter competitions. Only when they win the equivalent of one million yen would they be let out.'

Doppo slapped his thigh. It resounded loudly beneath his enormous hand. 'That's a brilliant idea.'

Kenji agreed and smiled sadly. 'What use is it to me now though? Here. Now that I'm dead.'

Leaning over so that his lips were next to Kenji's ears, Doppo opened his mouth to speak. His breath felt icy cold and when he put his hand on Kenji's forearm a shiver ran through his entire body.

'You're not dead, Kenji. I am.'

'What?' Kenji struggled with this information. 'What do you mean? I must be. You are. You're here.'

'I've got to go now.' Standing up, Doppo looked down on Kenji, an expression of concern on his face.

'Please don't go,' Kenji pleaded even though he knew what Doppo had said was true. He was alive. As they had been speaking, the feeling had slowly started to return to his body. The throbbing behind his forehead was no longer dull, but an intense pain, and his bandaged right hand was itching beyond endurance. If he was dead then he wouldn't feel a thing.

'Goodbye. Look after yourself and don't forget just what a strong man you are. Look at everything you have been through and yet you're still here, hanging on. You can put your mind to anything you choose. Don't let your life slip by or you'll regret it.'

Doppo disappeared into the white expanse. Another form appeared in the place where he had been standing. She was wearing a white paper hat on her head.

'You're awake.' She picked up his wrist, rather brusquely. 'I thought that maybe you were planning to sleep forever.'

EIGHTEEN

Shuffling slowly along the black leather seat of the silver Honda, Kenji was able to reach the open door. His left leg – the lower half encased in plaster – was poking out, while the other was planted firmly on the black tarmac. Using the crutches the hospital had given him, and groaning with the sheer effort required, he was able to heave himself up and into a standing position. He hoped that getting about would become easier with time. Turning around, he positioned a reassuring smile on his face, just to let Ami know that he was okay. But she was at that moment putting her driving glasses in a blue leather pouch and then into her handbag. He turned back round and stared at the red brick wall facing him.

After Doppo's visit, Kenji had started to spend more and more time awake. With this came the gradual realisation that his injuries were much worse than the painkillers which he had been fed led him to believe. At some point during the climb to the top of the hill he had fallen on his left ankle, fracturing it. Thankfully the break was clean and he expected to be out of plaster in a few weeks. But it would take much longer for his hand to heal. Skin from his thigh had been grafted on to the palm, where the golf club handle had melted. Then there was his eye. The white surgical patch that he wore hid considerable swelling. A shard of metal had pierced his cornea and become embedded, and although it had been surgically removed, it would be several weeks

117

before they could tell if there was any lasting damage to his eyesight.

Throughout the journey from the hospital to their apartment, he had been telling Ami about Doppo's visit, but she didn't appear to be listening. She slammed the driver's door shut and came round to the passenger's side with a look of grim determination on her face, her lips pressed together in a hard, thin line. He noticed that she was completely without make-up and her hair, usually neat and tidy, was unwashed and had been tied up in a lazy ponytail. It did not even appear to have been brushed.

'I'm telling you, that's how it happened,' Kenji persisted, talking to the wall. 'He was there with me in the hospital and we spoke for some time. I told him about everything and it felt good.'

'So you said,' Ami replied coolly. 'Can you move over a bit, so I can close the door?'

He shuffled over and stood resting against the side of the car as she shut the door. The noise echoed throughout the basement car park. With Kenji's bag in one hand, Ami put her free hand around the small of Kenji's back as if to stop him from toppling over and together they walked slowly towards the door that led to the stairwell and a small lift.

'Is this too fast?'

He shook his head. It was harder than he had thought, walking with crutches, and beads of perspiration had broken out on his head. 'He told me that I should go back to television,' he said, becoming breathless. 'That I was too good for a job in the bank. I should make TV programmes just like I always wanted to. That's what I used to dream of doing. Then the twins came along and things changed. I forgot about myself. Well you do when you're a family man. It's only right and proper. But now they are older, at school, and you have a career of your own.'

'This way.' Ami manoeuvred them through the blue door into the stairwell and pressed the button for the lift. It soon arrived and they squeezed in. There was just enough room inside for the two of them and the bag.

'I've even had an idea for a TV programme. I really believe that it could work. Your mother was my inspiration. But don't tell her. I wouldn't want her to get any big ideas.'

'Please, Kenji, enough.'

If there was strain in Ami's voice, Kenji did not notice it. The last week had passed in a blur. At first he felt immensely depressed and disorientated. He was not dead after all. Even if the bank welcomed Kenji back after he'd made such a scene, the thought of returning to work was unbearable. But most of all he had worried about who had been there with him that day. Was it Doppo or entirely his imagination? Then the pain started to kick in and with it the doctors prescribed painkillers, and even a course of anti-depressants to help cure what was described as 'mild anxiety'. At first he had been reluctant to take them. It seemed like an admission of failure. The doctor had strongly advised that he should and now he was glad that he had. A few days later the fog that had settled on his brain had started to clear and he was thinking rationally. Of course it had been Doppo. He had come to give him a message and that message was that he had to be strong and take a leap of faith. And that was what he fully intended to do. As he stared at his reflection in the mirrored wall of the lift, he thought he looked like a very different man. And not just because of the bandages, although they did help. No, here was a man that had been through the wars, battled and come out on the other side. He was an inspiration and this wasn't the end. It was just the beginning.

'I'm going to call it *Millyennaire*.' He chuckled. 'It will have international appeal then, you see. I've been thinking about it all this time while I've been lying in that hospital bed.'

The lift stopped, the doors opened and Ami helped him out as he explained the show's format to her. The corridor leading to their door was too narrow to walk two abreast so he limped behind her, talking incessantly.

At the door Ami stopped and fished inside her handbag for the apartment keys.

'This will be the making of me,' Kenji continued happily. 'I'm glad I'm not dead now.'

His wife groaned audibly.

'Now I have something to look forward to. Something to aim for.'

'Please, Kenji,' she snapped. 'We are home now. I don't want to hear another word of this nonsense. Especially not in front of the children. They have been through enough already.' She opened the door and Kenji hobbled in behind her.

'It isn't nonsense. Doppo said that it was a brilliant idea. I can make it happen, I know I can. I need you to have faith in me. You're my wife. If you don't believe in me then what hope do I have?'

'Enough.' Spinning round to face him, Ami screamed loudly. Tears had gathered in her eyes and her hands were shaking. 'I can't take anymore. The lies. The deceit. The madness. Do you hate me so much that you would put me through this?'

'I don't hate you,' Kenji pleaded. He couldn't understand why she was being like this. Why wasn't she happy for him? He was doing this for the family after all. 'I love you. I love all of my family.'

'Well then.' Her voice was firmer now and less emotional. 'I will not have another word said on the subject in my home again. Now for once in your life act like a man and put your family first.'

Spinning back round, she marched down the corridor away from him. It was then that he saw it. A banner draped across the hallway that said 'Welcome Home, Dad'. Yoshi and Yumi were standing beneath it shaking like reeds by the side of a lake.

NINETEEN

The doctor shone a torch into Kenji's right eye. Her breathing was regular and shallow, and when she exhaled, he could smell coffee. She switched the light off and went back to her desk, where she began typing slowly, using one finger, on the keyboard.

'Your eye has healed very nicely. There is no reason why you shouldn't be able to see. Physically . . .' She stopped typing and turned her full attention on him. '. . . at least.'

'But . . .' he began feebly. 'It's been six weeks since the accident, and still I can't see a thing with it.'

She turned her attention back to the keyboard, leaving him staring at the poster behind her head. It warned, by way of schematic diagrams, about the danger of second-hand cigarette smoke to young children.

'Perhaps,' she continued, 'it is a psychological problem. I understand from your notes that at the hospital you were diagnosed as suffering from anxiety and prescribed a course of drugs. Are you still taking them?'

Kenji blushed furiously and shook his head. He hated any mention of anxiety or drugs. His was a physical problem. He couldn't see out of one eye.

'Are you under any undue amount of pressure at the moment?' She picked up a biro and began to twirl it round and round with her fingers.

'It has been a very difficult few months,' he agreed. 'I thought that things were starting to get better, but I was wrong. You see . . .'

'That must be it then.' She tapped the keyboard decisively. 'I'm going to prescribe you another course of anti-depressants and I think it's time you went back to work. It may well be the tonic you need. Continue wearing the eye patch if it makes you feel better. There is certainly some swelling left. We don't need to see each other again.'

It was obvious he was being dismissed. He stood up and put his jacket on. 'What about the pains in my eye and the headaches? They're not in my imagination.'

'As I said, I'm sure that they will disappear in time. Keep taking paracetamol in the meantime.'

Closing the surgery door behind him, Kenji had to accept that she was right. There was no medical reason why he could not return to work. The plaster had been removed from his leg three days ago and while he still walked with a slight limp, this was just because his ankle was weak and he had been advised not to put too much pressure on it. All of his hair and the eyebrow that had been burnt off during the thunderstorm had now grown back, albeit completely white. This caused much amusement among the twins, while Ami claimed it was a constant reminder of how foolish her husband had been and begged him to use dye. His hand was still bandaged, although healing, and he had become accustomed to relying on the undamaged one to go about his day to day duties. The only remaining problem was his right eye. The doctor seemed to be implying it was all in his mind.

'Why does nobody believe me?' he muttered, trudging through the crowded waiting room, down a flight of stairs and towards the exit. Outside he paused to look for a cigarette to find that he had none left. Spotting a convenience store over the road, he hurried across and joined a queue at the counter. As the row of people shuffled slowly forwards, he found himself staring at the long, straight black hair of the woman in front of him. When she moved her head, the light above reflected off it, creating the impression of a halo sitting on the crown of her head. As she paid for her magazine,

Kenji caught sight of her face: the familiar round cheeks and black, shining eyes. It was Umeko Suzuki, Doppo's daughter.

'Suzuki-san.'

After a long pause, she clamped one hand to her mouth. 'Yamada-san. How strange. I was thinking of you just this morning. I don't have your address or telephone number. I spoke to your friend and he said that he had not seen you for weeks. That your mobile number was out of service. I got terribly upset. You see, I have something I need to give you. I hoped to give it to you at the funeral, but you left suddenly.'

Kenji felt ashamed and changed the subject quickly. 'You didn't return to Hawaii?' It was all that he could manage to say. He had no idea why she wanted to see him. If he was in her position he would want nothing to do with her father's friends who had not helped him hold on to life. Who had, in fact, done the opposite.

'I did, for a while. Then my husband's company transferred him to their Tokyo branch. Just after Dad's funeral.' There was a hint of bitterness in her voice. 'May I ask what happened to your eye?' She looked inquisitively at the patch. 'And your hair? It's completely white. I'm sure it wasn't white the last time we met. I almost didn't recognise you.'

He touched his face self-consciously, feeling the patch with his fingers. 'It's a long story.'

'You must tell me all about it.' Umeko moved back, allowing Kenji to buy some cigarettes. 'Are you busy? Will you have a coffee with me?'

There was something almost pleading about her request and he had to agree, although he didn't know what they would have to say to each other. Even her appearance rendered him speechless. Judging by her clothes and jewellery, this was a woman of some wealth and taste. What would they have to talk about? Then he remembered Doppo.

'I would like that very much.'

'Two cups of coffee, please. Cream and sugar.'

As Umeko placed their order, Kenji looked around. They were on the top floor of a nearby department store, in what Umeko described as her favourite spot to while away a few hours flicking through the pages of a magazine. Kenji couldn't imagine wanting to spend any length of time here. The entire floor was bright and airy. He felt exposed and as he looked at the other women, wondered what they thought when they saw him. That he did not deserve to be here? That he was with a woman too young, too well dressed and too beautiful for him?

He opened his packet of cigarettes and took one out. 'Do you mind?'

'Please, go ahead.' She pushed the heavy glass ashtray towards him.

Lighting a cigarette, he inhaled deeply and blew a perfect smoke ring up over his head. It hovered and disappeared.

Umeko opened her mouth but hesitated before saying, 'Can I have one, please?'

'Sure.' Kenji smiled, sliding the packet across the table to her. 'Doppo always said you didn't like him smoking.'

'There were many things that I didn't like my father doing,' she agreed, coughing slightly. 'I realise now that I should have spent less time complaining and more time appreciating him.'

'That's what daughters do, don't they? Berate their fathers.' He smiled reassuringly. 'Doppo knew that you loved him very much.'

'Did he?' Her voice was hopeful. At that moment he realised she didn't blame him for her father's death. She was looking for reassurance from him. And it was the only thing he had to give. 'My biggest fear is that he didn't know how much I loved him.'

'Of course he did. He spoke about you all the time. He was very proud of you, Umeko. It was his intention to come and live with you in Hawaii. There wasn't a single person he met whom he didn't tell about it. And he was a man who knew many people. He just wasn't ready to leave them all behind.'

'And then he did.'

'Yes. And then he did.'

Leaning forward across the table, Umeko spoke in a hushed voice. Some of her hair was trailing in the ashtray. He wanted to brush it away, but resisted. 'You know, sometimes I still talk to him.'

'You talk to him?' To Kenji's own ears, his voice sounded high and squeaky.

'Two coffees.'

It took an eternity for the waiter to place one cup in front of Kenji and one in front of Umeko, a jug of cream and a bowl of sugarlumps between them. Kenji waited patiently, desperate to know more. 'You talk to him?' He didn't want to give too much away. Not after Ami's reaction when he had told her about his own conversation with Doppo.

'I don't know if he listens, but yes, I talk to him.' Umeko pulled on her cigarette once more.

'Is he there in the room with you? When you talk to him?' It was hard to keep the note of excitement out of his voice.

She hesitated. 'Sometimes I believe he is. Although my husband might disagree. He hates me talking like this. Most of the time I keep it to myself.'

'I cannot tell you how happy it makes me that you chose to tell me.' He grabbed her hands, no longer concerned about what the other women in the department store coffee shop would think. 'I am so happy to have bumped into you today. Over the last few weeks I have allowed myself to believe that I was going mad. Other people have led me to believe this. You see I also saw your father. I spoke to him. He gave me some good advice.'

She opened her mouth to speak, but he was in a hurry to get his words out and spoke over her.

'Exactly what advice doesn't matter. What does matter is that I ignored what he told me. I allowed others to influence what I thought. Now I know that I shouldn't have done that. So much time has been lost.' He adjusted his eye patch. 'But no matter. I'll make it up soon enough.'

She seemed to have caught his enthusiasm. When she spoke her voice was high and breathless. Reaching into her handbag, she removed a red plastic box and slid it across the table. 'I almost forgot. This is the reason I needed to see you.'

Wondering what could be inside, he opened the box. There,

sitting neatly on a sponge cushion covered with a layer of red velvet, was a gold medal on a chain. He picked it up and saw it was a St Christopher medal. 'Doppo's?'

'He would have wanted you to have it.' Umeko smiled for the first time since they met.

'I can't take this.' Kenji pushed the box back across the table to her.

'No, it belongs with you. I believe that absolutely. That's why I tried to find you. My father was very fond of you. He spoke about you all the time. And if he was here today I know what he would tell you. He would tell you to follow your heart. Don't let others dissuade you from your path. It may be difficult, but never give up hope.'

'Thank you,' he said and squeezed her hand. They drank the rest of their coffee in silence.

TWENTY

The attendants stopped what they were doing to stare at Kenji. Soga was the first to speak.

'Yamada-san, welcome back. We are very pleased to see you.'

Surprised by the warmth of his welcome, Kenji faltered. The swing door hit him in the back and he staggered forward as Soga hobbled over from the opposite side of the room. When he reached Kenji, the old man gripped his elbow with his bony, arthritic fingers and guided him inside, as if he was the invalid.

'Somebody, quickly, a chair,' he called as the two of them – one hobbling, the other limping – made their way inside.

It was still only 9.30 a.m. and the mail room was full of attendants who had yet to go on their rounds. A cluster of trolleys were waiting expectantly at the door. Nothing had changed in Kenji's absence. Everything was as it had been. The bright lights, the radio on quietly in the background, the peeling paint, the weathered table and the red telephone sitting in the corner of the room. The only thing that had changed was the faces of the men that now looked at him. Where before there had been open hostility, now there was sympathy and compassion.

A chair appeared in front of Kenji and all at once many hands forced him to sit down. Under their force he collapsed.

'How are you, Yamada-san?' Soga asked. The other mail room

attendants crowded expectantly around him, jostling for space with one another.

He found himself laughing. He was starting to feel like the star attraction. 'Really I'm fine. The doctor has given me a clean bill of health. There is no reason why I shouldn't return to work. So here I am.'

A cup of coffee was thrust into his hands. When he took a sip he found that it had been strengthened with a drop of brandy. A very fine brandy that he knew to be a favourite of Soga's, but when he looked into the liver-spotted face of the old man, Soga immediately looked away.

'Please, take one.' Yamanote had moved to the front of the attendants and was holding a tin open. Kenji peered into it. Unable to remember a single time Yamanote had spoken to him, he wondered what he could be offering him now. He smiled. The tin was full of butter cookies. He chose one and made an appreciative noise as he popped it into his mouth and it melted on his tongue. Yamanote snapped the tin shut; the other men raised their eyebrows and smirked. Everyone knew just how fiercely Yamanote guarded those biscuits. They were sent every month by his daughter from Europe and he had never, in all his years in the mail room, offered them to another attendant.

'What did it feel like?' one of the younger attendants called from the back of the crowd that had gathered around Kenji. 'To be struck by lightning.'

It seemed to be the one question that everyone wanted to ask, because immediately they moved forward and leant in more closely. Kenji began to fear that he might be crushed should they all topple down over him at once.

'Don't be so impertinent,' Soga admonished the young man. 'Can't you see that our colleague has been through a great deal?' He turned back and looked expectantly at Kenji.

'To be honest I didn't feel a thing,' Kenji shrugged. 'I just woke up in hospital and they told me what had happened. How I had got my injuries.'

A murmur of disappointment passed around the room. It was

evident that they had been hoping for much more and after such a warm welcome he did not want to let them down.

'Although,' he paused, his brow furrowed, 'just before it happened I did feel a strange tingling sensation. Maybe there was something in the air?'

'Like a charge,' a small voice offered helpfully.

'Exactly like that,' Kenji agreed. The other men laughed as though relieved. This was clearly more like what they had been expecting. Searching for inspiration, he continued. 'My head was buzzing. Every hair on my body was standing on end. My pupils were wide open. It was like the charge had heightened my senses, even before the lightning started. I wasn't afraid.' He paused as though thinking about it for several seconds. 'I was just very angry and wanted to get as far away from here, the bank, as possible.'

'Imagine,' he heard Soga mutter, 'a mail room attendant being asked to clean a fish tank.'

'And we thought . . .'

'All that time.'

'Inagaki has a lot to answer for.'

'Did it hurt?' Soga asked.

Kenji took a sip of coffee, savouring the brandy. 'The lightning hit the golf club, travelled along its length, down my arm and the full length of my body. At first it felt like a tingling sensation. Quite pleasant. Then it grew more and more intense. I could feel my body convulsing and I fell to the ground. The pain was immense by that stage. I clamped my teeth together. I was afraid of biting off my own tongue.'

Someone gasped.

'I felt a sharp pain in my eye.' He touched the eye patch. 'I would have cried out but my jaws were locked tight. I became aware of the smell of burning hair and flesh. I closed my eyes and saw a bright, white light. Then I passed out. When I woke up my hair had turned completely white and it has been the same ever since. I still cannot see out of this eye.'

At that moment the shrill ring of the red telephone in the corner of the room interrupted, causing everyone to jump. Soga hobbled over to answer it. When he returned he clapped his hands together loudly. 'Come on, men, back to work. There's mail to be collected.'

The crowd that had formed around Kenji reluctantly dispersed. He tried to join them, but a number of hands forced him back into his chair.

'No,' Soga spoke forcefully. 'You are on light duties. At least for now. Stay here, answer the telephone, help us sort the mail when we return.'

'I can't,' Kenji spluttered. 'I can't just sit here and do nothing while you all work.' He was both touched and appalled by the suggestion.

'You can and you will,' Soga replied firmly and would not listen to another word.

As the men left the mail room one by one, pushing their trolleys in front of them, Kenji wondered at the change in their attitude towards him. It was almost as if by sustaining these injuries, he had ceased to be a threat and instead become one of them. In his absence, stories about Inagaki's treatment of him had evidently spread and he was glad of it. It meant that the bank manager had lost respect among the mail room attendants and, keen to regain lost ground, he had offered Kenji his job back as soon as he received the doctor's permission to return to work. He even went so far as to come to the apartment to extend the invitation. Of course, for Kenji, returning to work, meant returning to the site of his humiliation, but it also got him out of the house. Under Ami's watchful eye he had been unable to further his plans, to make any progress. Whenever he picked up a pen, or if he even appeared to be concentrating on some private thought or other, she bombarded him with questions. 'What are you doing? What are you thinking?' If he ever looked remotely occupied and his mind in danger of drifting, she always found some job for him to do. 'Fold up these pieces of cloth for me. Wash the dishes.' He was not even permitted to leave the house unattended. If he went outside, even for fresh air, she would insist upon accompanying him and if she wasn't there, Eriko came with him. This had resulted in an embarrassing incident. While he was out with Ami one day, they had passed Dai. Thankfully a busy road separated them, so all that Dai could do was wave. A wave that Kenji had tried discreetly to return, but Ami saw it and her suspicions were immediately aroused.

'Who was that?' she had demanded angrily.

Kenji tried to sound nonchalant. 'Oh, her? She is just a customer at the bank.'

Coming back to the bank meant that he now had a legitimate reason to leave the house unescorted. Now he was being left in the mail room completely alone to do as he pleased. He couldn't ask for a better situation. The moment the other men left, he fetched his bag from the locker room. It contained his lunch box, notepad and a pen. Part of him had wanted to leave the house with his briefcase this morning. It would symbolise a return to form for him. Or at least a beginning. But Ami would certainly have noticed and insisted on looking inside, asking questions.

Sitting on a high stool at the sorting table, he opened the pad and stared at the blank page, the pen quivering in his hand above it. There was so much to plan, so much to get down on paper. Taking a deep breath he began.

Over the course of the week, whenever the other attendants left him in the morning and then again in the afternoon, he was able to plan the entire series of *Millyennaire* in great detail, just as he had seen the production teams at NBC do. Having worked with them for so long it was really no surprise that he had picked up some of their knowledge and expertise. It had just been lying dormant all this time, he realised, as his hand flew across the page.

Millyennaire would begin with the contestant being escorted blindfold into what he or she believed to be a real apartment in the centre of Tokyo. In reality it would be a temporary structure erected in a studio, but made to look and feel like an apartment. This approach was less expensive – specialist equipment for filming could be installed more easily – and there would be a big surprise for the contestant at the end of the series when the walls of the apartment fell down around them and they emerged to a live studio audience. Episodes would be screened once weekly, each lasting forty-five minutes excluding commercial breaks. Included would be live narration and pre-recorded footage of how the contestant had spent his or her time, what competitions they had entered, prizes they had won, how much they were worth. He thought about a presenter; someone glamorous and with charm. Hana Hoshino sprung to mind. He did not know why. Nor did he spend too much time worrying about that. He simply wondered, as he moved on to the budget calculations, what had happened to her and whether she would be willing to accept a reduced rate to revive her flagging career. The show would have to come in cheaply if it was going to pique the interest of the production teams. Everybody was under a lot of pressure at the moment.

It took two full weeks before his plans were laid out in detail and he was ready to make the call. Which he did during his lunch hour from a telephone box outside the bank.

'Miru TV.'

Kenji took a deep breath. 'Can I speak to Abe E. Kitahara.'

The last time Kenji had spoken to Kitahara, he had still been working at NBC. He did not have fond memories of the man. In fact, he held him responsible for his current position and on top of that found him to be vain, arrogant and not particularly talented. But in spite of all this, Kitahara had an enviable track record of getting TV shows made and if there was anybody who could find a way to make *Millyennaire* a reality then, although Kenji was loath to admit it, it was him.

Biting his tongue, he waited to be connected.

'Kitahara speaking,' a voice barked at the end of the line, catching Kenji off guard. He had expected to be put through to a secretary first.

'How can I help you?' the voice barked again and when Kenji failed to reply, 'Look, I'm a busy man.'

'Kitahara-san, this is Kenji Yamada,' he managed before being interrupted.

'Yes.' His response sounded vague.

'Previously of NBC. Programme research manager.' Using his former credentials made him feel uncomfortable, but getting his foot in the door was more important and he could be honest later if necessary.

'And?'

'I would be very grateful if you could spare me some of your time to discuss an idea for a TV show that I have. Perhaps over dinner.' As he spoke, Kenji purposefully passed the St Christopher medal that he wore on a chain around his neck back and forth over his fingers. It seemed to give him strength. He tried to imagine that Doppo was standing there with him, but was unable to conjure up an image of his friend.

'Are you buying?'

'Of course.'

There was a sound of papers being shuffled over the telephone.

'Tonight, 8 p.m. Don't be late. I hate being made to wait.' Kitahara mentioned the name of a restaurant in Roppongi and hung up.

TWENTY-ONE

'Kenji Yamada?'

'Kitahara-san.'

'Please, call me Abe.' The executive producer removed his brown leather driving gloves as he spoke. He was a short man who carried several kilogrammes in excess of what suited his frame. Kenji had heard from colleagues at NBC that Abe's father was American and as a young man he had spent several years living and working there. It was also rumoured that Abe had been trying for several years to achieve international success so that he might go and live in America permanently. Perhaps this was the project that could help him, and in doing so help Kenji.

'Abe-san.' Kenji bowed. 'It is very kind of you to see me at such short notice.'

'You mentioned that we worked together before, but I couldn't remember your name. Now that I see your face, it does look familiar. Have you done something to your hair?'

Kenji shook his head. It was easier than explaining.

Inclining his head towards the restaurant door, Abe asked, 'Shall we go in?'

Kenji dashed forward and opened the door. Immediately a warm blast of air carrying the odour of cooking food hit them full in the face.

Standing inside the doorway, Abe slipped out of the blue blazer he was wearing.

'Can I help you?' a young waitress asked from behind the reception desk.

Eyeing the waitress up and down, Abe stuck up two fingers. 'Two.'

When they had last met, Kenji had experienced two sides to Abe. One was exceptionally charming and persuasive, the other rude and bullish. He was obviously in the latter mood tonight.

'If you will follow me.' She hurried off, white clogs clattering loudly on the concrete flagstones.

Solid oak booths fitted with black vinyl cushions ran all the way around the outside walls of the restaurant, while the main space was completely taken up by three enormous rectangular tables around which diners were perched on low wooden stools. Each table was under the domain of a single chef, who stood at the top, commanding a vast array of raw ingredients and all manner of utensils that were set out on the cooking station in front of him.

'Please sit down.' the waitress indicated two empty stools at the very top of the table furthest from the door. They each selected a low stool: Abe next to the chef who was chopping raw vegetables with lightning speed, and Kenji next to a young man with a date who was giggling into the palm of her hand.

'Can I get you something to drink?' the waitress asked once they had settled themselves.

'I'll have a bottle of Kirin,' Abe ordered. 'And how about you, Kenji?'

'The same for me also, please.'

A few seconds later she returned carrying a tray and placed two bottles of Kirin, two glasses and a wooden bowl of lightly salted peas on the table in front of them. From the front pocket of her apron, she removed two pieces of card. 'The first game will begin in fifteen minutes' time. Please play one table of numbers at a time. If you cross off all your numbers, call out and you will receive 1000 yen off the price of your meal.' She clattered off again, to seat and serve another group of customers who were waiting by the door.

Taking a long draw from his bottle of beer, Abe appeared to be taking in Kenji. Looking at him from head to toe and then back again. 'What happened to your eye?'

Kenji touched the patch. 'Just a minor accident.' He did not like to think about it too much. Each morning he would get up, go to the bathroom and remove the eye patch. While staring at his reflection in the bathroom mirror, he covered one eye with the palm of his hand then the other. Every morning the same result. He still could not see out of the damaged one. Or rather he could see something, but it was just a continuous stream of bright, white light much as he had experienced at the hospital that day. It was painful and blinding, so he preferred to keep his eye closed and the patch over it.

Abe nodded dismissively and moved on to his next question. 'You work for NBC?' As he spoke he did not look at Kenji but all about the restaurant, finally pausing to stare at a young woman seated directly across from him. 'Hello,' he mouthed at her. She looked away.

It was hard for Kenji not to be shocked by Abe's behaviour. Judging by the fleshy pads that sat beneath the executive TV producer's eyes, the deep fissures that cut into his forehead, and the loose flesh hanging beneath his chin, he was somewhere in his early fifties. Old enough to be the young lady's father.

'I used to work for NBC. We have met once before.' Kenji leaned forward on his wooden stool, trying to catch Abe's attention. As he spoke a young man with bleached orange hair escaping from the confines of a stiff blue linen cap, spoke into a microphone at the front of the restaurant, next to the main entrance. 'Good evening,' he called.

'Good evening,' the other diners shouted playfully back. Had he not been here on business then Kenji might have joined in. But he was, and he was determined to walk away from here tonight with a deal.

Abe looked at Kenji. 'Hey now. Don't miss this.' He pointed at the young man with orange hair who was vigorously spinning a tombola filled with small balls with numbers painted on them. 'This is a hoot. You've never seen a room full of people get so excited by a stupid game. I like to come here just to laugh at them.'

'I now work for Fuji Bank in Utsunomiya.'

'Fuji Bank.' At last, Abe focused his full attention on Kenji. 'Those ATMs keep eating my card. Any idea why?'

Kenji admitted that he had not. Was this meeting going to be a waste of his time? he wondered as he struggled to get Abe's attention. He immediately pushed the thought to the back of his mind. It was too early for doubts.

'I mentioned on the phone that I had an idea for a TV show. Perhaps you'd be good enough to let me tell you a little bit more about it.'

'Of course you can. Let's order some food first though.'

Abe called out his order to the top of the table.

The chef, scanning the vast array of raw ingredients spread out in front of him, deftly selected pieces of chicken, beef, seafood and shitake. Piercing them with a bamboo skewer, he dipped the chunks of food into breadcrumbs, and then fiercely bubbling oil where they rapidly became a deep golden colour. The food was laid on a plate with a generous dollop of tomato ketchup and delivered to them on the end of a serving plank.

After they had finished eating this dish, Abe ordered again. This time the chef poured a circle of egg-based batter on to a grill, covered it liberally with octopus, cabbage and onion. When the light yellow mass had solidified, it was folded in half, cut into strips and served.

'So tell me your idea then.' Abe gobbled down the last bit of food on his plate, picked up the bingo card the waitress had given him, folded it in half and used the corner to clean out the dirt from his nails. The man with the orange hair had begun to call out the numbers and all around them people were intently studying their cards. 'Look at them.' Abe winked conspiratorially at Kenji.

Kenji took a deep breath. He had practised this speech a number of times and didn't want to get it wrong. 'The programme is called *Millyennaire*,' he began. He explained everything he had planned out: the set, the lighting, the presenter, the format of each episode. Breathlessly, he came to an end. 'Once the contestant has raised the equivalent of one million yen, they are allowed to go free.'

It was perhaps the first time all evening that he had succeeded in gaining Abe's full attention.

'You know something, Kenji, my friend. That isn't a bad idea. No, that isn't a bad idea at all. You've shocked me. Who would have thought it, eh? A bank clerk coming up with an idea like that.'

'Thank you,' Kenji beamed. 'But really I work in the mail room.'

'No kidding.' Abe no longer appeared to be listening. He stood up and took his mobile phone out of his back pocket. 'You're okay to get the bill, right? I've got to make a few phone calls.'

Kenji half stood. 'I have some detailed notes if you would like to see them. Some ideas for the presenter and the set. It's all in there.' He handed Abe his notepad.

'I'm excited about this.' Abe snatched the notepad and made to leave.

Kenji called after him. 'I can come and work for you at Miru TV. I can work on the show.'

'Sure. We'll sort something out. You've got my number right?' And with that he was gone, leaving Kenji sitting uncertainly on his stool. He wasn't sure what had just happened but thought it sounded good.

'*Banzai*,' the young man with the giddy date shouted, jumping up and waving his card in the air. The first game of bingo drew to a close.

TWENTY-TWO

Ami's cheeks were glowing and she had a dreamy smile on her lips. 'I will put on all the weight that I have lost,' she said, scooping the last of the raspberry sorbet out of the glass bowl and raising it to her mouth, 'after a meal like that.'

As she spoke, a large drop of crimson liquid formed on the underside of the spoon and detached itself, hitting the table with enough force to scatter small darts of red liquid over her white cashmere jumper. Kenji flinched, but Ami giggled. 'It serves me right,' she said, dabbing hopelessly at her jumper with a linen napkin, making the stain worse, 'for being so greedy.'

Kenji exhaled sharply, air hissing through his teeth. 'How could you possibly gain any weight when you are always so busy,' he spoke quickly, 'running around after everybody else?' Ami seemed pleased with this remark, so he went further: raising his cup in the air and proclaiming, 'A toast to us. Happy anniversary.'

'Happy anniversary,' she repeated, clipping her own cup off Kenji's and taking a small sip of sake before returning it to the table.

It was hard to believe, but this woman – the one sitting on the opposite side of the low, sunken table – was the same one that had accompanied him on the train to Takao Sanguchi station, where they had boarded one of the shuttle buses that ran to the restaurant. As the journey wore on, Ami had become increasingly tense and irritable, frequently turning on her husband and demanding to know exactly where they were going.

'How can I tell you that?' Kenji had said, his conviction slipping further away every time he was forced to repeat this statement. 'It will spoil the surprise.'

'I have work I should be doing,' she shot at him. 'Instead I am traipsing halfway across the country with you.'

He had laughed good-naturedly. 'It will not take so long and surely my company is not so objectionable?'

She did not reply.

'I have a story that is sure to make you laugh,' he offered tentatively, hoping to lift her mood.

Ami shrugged noncommittally, but he continued nonetheless. It was a tremendous relief to him, to be able to recount these stories: finding humour in the daily occurrences at the bank made working there more bearable. Although, these days, he did precious little work at the insistence of the other attendants.

'Nagasaki works at the bank and it is most unfortunate but he suffers from an involuntary tic that causes his right eye to squeeze shut and his tongue to protrude until it lolls from his mouth. Just yesterday . . .' Kenji shifted in his seat to face Ami who was twisting, viciously, the small pearl stud that pierced her right earlobe. '. . . he happened upon a new cashier who had mistakenly wandered down into the basement while looking for Inagaki's office. After encountering Nagasaki she ran up on to the bank floor screaming. "There is a mad man below," she wailed and all of the customers had to be evacuated while they searched for him.'

He chuckled and slapped his thigh.

Making sure that none of the other passengers could overhear, Ami leant closer to her husband and hissed in his ear, 'You are in no position to be so disrespectful about your colleagues.' Turning back to face the seat in front of her, she folded her arms across her chest and stared straight ahead.

The rest of the journey passed in silence. Not a word was said between them as the shuttle bus travelled deep into the lush green woods of Mount Tako, towards the restaurant. Descending deeper and deeper into the forest, Kenji studied his wife: her expression grew more thunderous all the time. Even the driver, whom they were seated directly behind, threw Kenji a number of sympathetic looks in his oversized rearview mirror.

'I don't know what you did to deserve the silent treatment, buddy,' he whispered to Kenji as they got off the bus, 'but I hope for your sake she thaws out pretty soon or you'll be in for a very frosty night.'

Kenji agreed and joined his wife. The restaurant had two large, wooden gates with rusty ring-shaped handles and pins nailed all the way through them creating a regular pattern of squares on both sides.

Together they followed the other passengers – about a dozen of them – along a path that led to a reception hut, passing on their way a quietly trickling stream, stone lanterns and polished rock walls with cushions of velvety soft moss nestled in the crevices. On one side of the path trees and conifers were planted: carefully pruned pine trees; chestnut trees; barberries and maples in burgundy, lime green and blue. On the other, pink evening primrose; gold plume; spruce trees; dappled willows and lotus flowers. Crossing over a small bridge, Kenji paused to admire the brightly coloured koi gasping at the surface of the water just below. Water lilies and irises grew in abundance.

'Look,' he said to Ami, indicating a heron that was perched on a rock, looking disdainfully at the new arrivals. But she had already passed over the bridge and was waiting impatiently on the other side, tapping her foot on the gravel. He hurried to join her, leading the way to the reception hut where they waited patiently in line.

'Can I take your name, please?' the receptionist asked.

'Yamada.'

'One moment, please.' A bell rang and another young woman appeared, dressed in a moss green kimono decorated with delicate pink flowers.

'Please come with me,' she beckoned and they followed her to one of the private tatami huts positioned at intervals around the garden.

It was nothing short of a miracle that Kenji had been able to secure a table at Ukai Toriyama. When he first phoned he was told that the restaurant was fully booked for the next six months but that they would put his name down on a reserve list in case any dining huts became available. He had almost given up hope until, yesterday, the restaurant called to say that there had been a last-minute cancellation. He snapped up the reservation immediately, though Ami seemed unimpressed.

'How can we afford to eat at a place like this?' she whispered as they followed the waitress.

Lowering his voice, Kenji explained, 'I have been putting aside a little money from my weekly allowance. So that we would be able to celebrate our anniversary.'

'How have you managed to do that?' Ami countered. His allowance was so small.

'Making cutbacks. Smoking less, walking to work instead of taking the bus.'

No sooner had he uttered these words than Ami stopped dead, placing her hands on her hips. 'Yoshi needs a new school uniform. You would have done better spending your money on that. Come on, let's go. If we hurry we may still be able to catch the bus.' She span round on her heel, sending a shower of pebbles flying up into the air behind her as she began marching towards the gate.

'No.' Kenji grabbed his wife's hand, bringing her back round to face him. 'We are eating here tonight.'

It was not a question, it was not a plea. It was an order and Ami's mouth fell wide open. Not once in twelve years of marriage had Kenji ever raised his voice to his wife. He had always allowed her to get her own way. But not tonight. Tonight he was determined to stand up to her. Shocked into submission, Ami allowed herself to be pulled along the path after her husband.

That was three hours ago and in that time they had consumed a delicious meal and some fine sake. Ami had – as the bus driver hoped she would – thawed considerably. How could she not? The hut in which they dined had a calming effect on both of them. It was constructed from a strong, lightweight wood and sat on a raised platform with a thatched roof supported by pillars. The floors were covered with soft tatami mats, and floor-to-ceiling windows covered with pale orange paper blinds flooded the room with warm sunlight. When the sun set, diffuse lighting in the hut was automatically switched on and lanterns were lit throughout the entire garden. Kenji felt peaceful and totally secluded even though he knew that they were not the only ones dining here tonight. Even the waitress was unobtrusive as she scurried in to bring them food, fill their glasses and take away dishes.

They had taken their time over the menu. In the end, Kenji allowed Ami to choose. 'I think we'll have walnut tofu to start followed by Kobe steak.' He cooked the steak himself, on an *irori* grill set over a sandpit in the centre of the table. It came served with an assortment of vegetable dishes, most of which Ami ate. When her dessert appeared, she was almost too full to eat it.

The truth was that he had lied to her. They could not afford to eat in a restaurant like this and he had not been putting aside a little money each week to pay for it. Instead, he had paid a visit to Tokyo where he played several games of pachinko, winning enough to bring them here. Dishonesty was not a trait that Kenji admired or even set out to practise. But – he had reasoned with himself – it was like plastering over the cracks in a crumbling wall until you had enough money to fix it properly. At the moment he could not afford to support his family but in the very near future he would. Until then he had to have Ami on side and in good spirits.

'Do you remember,' he began, 'I told you about my idea for a television programme?'

Ami dropped the napkin she had been using to dab at her jumper on to the table. 'Kenji, please do not spoil a lovely evening by talking about such things.' She sat up straight, her back rigid, but began to sway slightly owing to the large amount of sake she had drunk.

A flash of courage shot through Kenji. Tired of never being listened to, always being the one that everybody else walked over, he became emboldened. 'I am your husband and I will not be spoken to like that.'

Ami blinked furiously but did not say anything so he took a deep breath and began.

'Last week I met with a TV producer. A gentleman by the name of Abe E. Kitahara, who works for a production company in Tokyo. I know him from my time spent at NBC. We had dinner together. I told him about my idea for a game show. The one that I told you about. And he liked it very much.'

Ami sneered. 'I don't believe you.'

'Why would I lie?'

'You've done it before.'

Reaching across the table, Kenji cupped his wife's hands between his own but she pulled them away. 'I lied to protect my family from the truth. Now I have nothing more to lose. I have already lost everything. There is no longer any reason to lie.'

Ami stared at her husband intently across the table, her facial muscles relaxing fractionally. 'He offered you a job? This man. This Abe E. Kitahara.'

Kenji faltered. Exactly what had Abe offered him? Their meeting had ended so quickly that they had not had the opportunity to discuss such matters and Kenji did not feel that he could ask and thereby delay or inconvenience the TV producer anymore than he had already done so. He simply assumed that Abe would be in touch and while he hadn't – just one week had passed – there was still time.

'Yes,' he told his wife and swallowed deeply. 'Yes, he offered me a job. Of sorts. We will be making my TV show together. I will be the assistant producer.' It was not strictly the truth, but it was how Kenji hoped that things would work out and the effect of this news on Ami was startling. Gradually her entire body relaxed and she broke into a large smile.

'That is wonderful news.' She covered her mouth with one hand, anxiously patting her lips, bright red from the sorbet. 'What will my friends say? They will be very envious. Every time we meet I must endure their endless chatter about how well their husbands are doing at work, the promotions they are receiving and I must stay quiet. They pity me, I know that they do. But not anymore. Now I will be just as good as any of them. If not better. My husband the TV producer. Ha. What will they say to that?'

Kenji was perturbed by Ami's speech: she seemed to be happier for herself than for him. As he looked at her across the low sunken table, he found himself wondering what reaction Dai would have to his news and realised that it had been quite some time since he had last seen her. Maybe he should call by the supermarket. Just to say hello. They could have lunch and he could tell her. He thought about bringing her a present. Nothing big or showy. Just something small and pretty. She deserved to be treated well. Before he could dwell on this matter any longer, there was a light tapping at the screen door and the waitress slipped inside.

'If you would like to come outside,' she asked them, 'the festival will begin shortly.'

Ami looked quizzically at her husband as he helped her to her feet. 'Another surprise?' she asked.

He smiled mysteriously, leading his wife out of the tatami hut and on to the raised platform where they put on their shoes before making their way to the garden. All around them other diners were emerging from their huts and moving into the garden, gathering around the lake where a number of the waitresses were bent down, seemingly inspecting something on the ground.

Ami looked at Kenji expectantly. He squeezed her hand. Just at that moment the waitresses stood up slowly and disappeared into the shadows. A few seconds later a swarm of fireflies flew up from the ground and into the air where they formed undulating waves of greenish yellow light that rose higher and higher into the night-time sky.

A small yelp of excitement escaped from Ami's mouth.

'Make a wish,' he told her and kissed her softly on the lips.

TWENTY-THREE

'Goodnight, Soga-san,' Kenji shouted from the mail room door where he stood, one hand poised in mid-air, ready to push his way out. Shouting was necessary, especially when standing at a distance, as Soga's hearing – poor at the best of times – was worse at the end of the day when he switched off his hearing aid. 'See you tomorrow.'

'If I'm still alive,' the old man replied morosely as he locked a large, steel grey cabinet using one of the many keys on a long chain he wore around his waist and that clattered loudly wherever he went. Not – Kenji smiled – that he ever realised this.

Leaving the bank through the back exit where the deliveries were made and an orderly line of multi-coloured oversized bins were stored – one for each different type of material that bank employees discarded – Kenji passed a number of younger staff who had congregated, saying their goodbyes. He looked at their faces, smooth and unwrinkled, and found himself wishing that he was a young man: without responsibilities and worries. Where hope and aspiration had recently sat proudly on his chest, making him walk tall and hold his head high, there was now a heavy weight and a growing sense of desperation. He felt uneasy, and although he didn't like to admit it – at least not out loud – he knew why. It was four weeks to the day since his meeting with Abe and still no word. No letter or phone call. Nothing. The thought of being rejected kept him from calling. The silence could only mean one thing. Despite his initial enthusiasm, Kitahara had changed his mind about *Millyennaire* and with it went any hope that Kenji had of securing a respectable position in the industry he had been forced to leave.

He wished he had a friend to confide in, to help him allay his fears. If just for a short while. He did not feel quite ready to give up hope yet, but it was already slipping through his fingers. There was no point talking to Ami. Ever since their anniversary dinner, she had pounced upon him the moment that he arrived home from work and demanded, 'Is there any news?' Kenji would shake his head solemnly. At first she had been hopeful, supportive even. 'It's only a matter of time, be patient.' Then with time, her comments became increasingly derisive and caustic. Over dinner, and much to the confusion of the twins, she would ask the 'bigshot TV man' to pass her a dish or some sauce. Lately she had stopped talking to him altogether. If it so happened that they caught each other's eye, she would look away, a sneer of disgust all too evident on her face. At least – he reasoned as he left the rear enclosure of the bank and walked out on to the main road, scarcely missing a cyclist who trilled loudly on her bell – Ami was away this week, with the children and Eriko visiting her sister in Osaka.

As he walked further down the road away from the bank, he passed a phone box and stopped in front of it. The vague idea formed in his head that he might call someone. But who? The Professor or Michi? Both were out of the question, he realised sadly. If Ami ever found out that he had been associating with his former pachinko friends, she would make his life even more miserable then it already was. Even if he did call them, it was hard to imagine what he might say. Would they even understand? The Professor always adopted a supercilious air with others and while in the past Kenji had found it amusing and enjoyed bantering with him, would he know that he had something important and sensitive to discuss? As for Michi, he doubted she had ever had a serious conversation in her life and did not think that he was being overly unkind in this belief. Then it hit him. Umeko of course. Why had he not thought of her before? Just the thought of speaking to her made him feel calmer. Without even a hint of hesitation, he opened the concertina door of the phone box, squeezed inside and dialled. Her number was scribbled on a piece of card that had been sitting in his wallet ever since that day they had met and shared coffee in the department store, but he had never had a reason to use it. At least not until now.

The telephone on the other end of the line rang several times. Just as he was about to give up hope, a female voice answered. 'Suzuki-san?' he asked hopefully.

The maid informed him that the Suzukis were away on holiday. She asked if he would like to leave a message, but he declined.

As he pushed his way out of the phone booth, he contemplated the strength of his feelings. They surprised him. In the short space of time between deciding to call Umeko and being informed that she was away, he had built up an entire scenario in which they met for dinner and she told him to have hope, how things were going to get better any time soon. Now he was forced to give up this plan and face the thought of going home to an empty apartment where there would only be more time and space to brood. Determined to put this off for as long as possible, he decided to walk for a while. With nowhere particular in mind he set off, staring in the shop windows along the main street as he passed. It was not long before he found himself standing outside the supermarket where Dai worked. She was certain to make him feel better, look on the positive side of things. But what about the promise he had made to himself on the evening of his anniversary dinner with Ami? That next time he saw Dai he would do something nice for her. Looking around quickly, he spotted a florist across the road that was still open. He dashed across and bought a single flower – a white lily perched in a pyramidal glass vase filled with water and blue glass stones. It was unfussy and beautiful, just like Dai.

Running back across the road, it occurred to him that Dai might not be at work and his body grew heavy. He needn't have worried. He should have guessed that Dai wouldn't let him down. Even though it was twilight, he was able to discern a familiar form standing outside the supermarket. He called out. She looked up and raised her hand, where it hovered uncertainly in mid-air. Encouraged, Kenji started walking quickly towards her. The moment that he did, the expression on her face froze.

'Dai, it's so good to see you. Here.' He handed her the flower. 'This is for you.'

The force with which she thrust it back shocked him. 'Thank you. You're very kind, but I cannot accept such a gift.'

'It's for you.' Feebly he held the lily out to her, clasping the neck of the glass vase in one hand.

Again, she pushed it back. 'I cannot take it.'

They stood in silence for several seconds, the vase hanging between them, until Dai broke the silence and he saw a flash of the kind, gentle woman he had come here to see.

'Your eye. What happened to your eye? And your hair. It's completely white.'

Kenji had grown so used to both he often forgot his altered appearance might come as a surprise to anybody who hadn't seen him in a while. The hair he didn't mind so much. If he wanted to dye it – as Ami pressed him to – he could. His sight was not so easy to recover.

'I saw you once before. You were out walking with your sister and her children. You were wearing the same bandages then but I didn't like to come and ask since you were with company. Were you in an accident?'

'It's a long story. Perhaps we can get a coffee somewhere?' He looked hopefully across his shoulder at the coffee shop across the road next to the florist. 'I'd very much like to tell you about it.'

Dai shifted uncomfortably from foot to foot. Around them shoppers were entering and leaving the supermarket in a continual, steady stream. Occasionally they had to shift to one side to let a customer pick up or put down a basket or a trolley.

'I'm afraid that isn't possible.'

Kenji was crestfallen. 'I could really do with a friend to talk to. So much has happened since we last met.'

'To me too.' Dai stared at her feet. It had started to rain. It was a light drizzle and Kenji moved closer so that he was standing beneath the overhanging ledge. Detecting a hint of her perfume on the air, he inhaled deeply.

'I had an idea for a TV game show,' he offered brightly. 'A good one too. I was convinced that it was going to make my fortune. Now I'm not so sure. It came to me – the idea – after I got these injuries and was recovering in hospital. I was struck by lightning.'

He had been hoping to shock her into going for coffee with him. It didn't work. Dai wasn't even listening. She was looking at something over his shoulder.

He gave it another desperate attempt. 'There's so much to tell. Let's go and get a cup of coffee. Maybe even dinner. My treat.'

'Who's this then?' a deep male voice demanded, causing Dai to stiffen and Kenji to turn round. It occurred to him that the voice might belong to Rambashi, the young supermarket manager, and that he had got Dai into trouble by talking to her at work. Except that the voice was too deep, too authoritative and when he did turn round, he saw a man he did not recognise. Tall and balding, he wore what little hair he had long, set it in waves and combed back over his head. His shirt sleeves were rolled up to his elbows, revealing a faded tattoo of a naked woman sitting on a dolphin swimming down his right forearm.

'Tomo.' Dai spoke first. Kenji noticed that her voice was shaking. 'This is my friend Yamada-san. He was just showing me this lovely flower that he bought for his sister. She is staying with him at the moment. Kenji, this is my husband Tomo.'

'Nice to meet you,' Kenji offered stiffly, as he looked Tomo up and down. An unidentifiable feeling settled upon him, growing in intensity until he realised that he was annoyed. Maybe even jealous. It irritated him that this man had shown up and that his presence had such an effect on Dai's behaviour. Dai who was usually so kind and warm had been reduced to a frightened, quivering shadow. Next he felt angry. What was this man called Tomo doing here anyway? According to Dai their relationship was over. Unless maybe she had taken him back? The thought horrified him. Could she? Would she?

Tomo did not reply immediately. He simply stared at Kenji while chewing loudly on a piece of gum, snapping his mouth open and closed.

The supermarket door opened. This time it was Rambashi: wearing a rainmac and carrying a large golf umbrella in one hand. He stopped and stared at the three of them, opened his mouth as if to say something. But catching sight of Tomo, changed his mind and walked off quickly.

It seemed like a sensible idea, but before Kenji had the opportunity to do the same thing, Tomo positioned himself directly in front of Dai and said firmly, 'Come on, we're going.' Taking his wife by the elbow, he guided her down the street, whilst deliberately – or so Kenji thought as he watched him do it – dropping a cigarette lighter just outside the supermarket. When they had reached and rounded the corner, Tomo suddenly reappeared and strolled back towards Kenji, casually picking up the lighter on his way.

Leaning forward and down so that his face was within centimetres of Kenji's, he whispered, 'Stay away from my wife.' Then, flashing a smile and a mouthful of tobacco-stained teeth, he strolled off.

TWENTY-FOUR

He had been in such a hurry to get through the apartment door, Kenji forgot to close it. Almost as an afterthought, he reached out behind him and pushed the door with one hand so that it shut with a reassuring clunk. There was a grave need to be quick. It was rare for him to return home on his lunch break but having remembered only an hour ago that Ami, the twins and Eriko were due back from Osaka this evening, he had raced back. In their absence he had let things slip, been unmotivated to clean up. Large piles of dirty laundry and crockery had accumulated throughout the apartment, half-read newspapers lay strewn across the sofa, and empty cans of Kirin sat on the coffee table without coasters beneath. Worse still, he had been lax about where he smoked. Ami always insisted that he take his 'dirty habit' outside, but he had been less than faithful to this rule while she had been away.

Looking at his watch, he calculated that he had forty minutes in which to clean and maybe, if he was lucky, to grab some lunch. It would be impossible to do a thorough job. But if he tore through the apartment, throwing everything into large bin bags and hiding the evidence of his laziness, then it might be possible to clear at least the worst of it.

'I'll start with the kitchen,' he thought, walking down the corridor. No sooner had he done so than he froze in his tracks. Wasn't that Ami's voice coming from the sitting room and the sound of another's whom he did not recognise? What was she doing back so early? He turned slowly round. If Ami was home then she had seen the state in which he had left the apartment and was certain to explode. It was unavoidable. But he could put it off until this evening if he was quiet. Except as he put his foot down, the floorboard creaked beneath it and Ami called out, 'Mother, is that you?'

'It's me. Kenji.' His response was met by complete silence on behalf of his wife, but not her guest.

Rei Takai popped her head around the sitting room door and gushed at him with as much pleasure as if Kenji had been one of her husband's business associates. 'Yamada-san, it is nice to see you.' A large smile spread across her dumpling-like face before it disappeared back inside. 'Come in, come in.'

With considerable trepidation, he walked along the freshly swept hallway and into the sitting room where Takai, Ami's best and most demanding customer, was standing on a low stool immediately below the centre light. Her husband's company was hosting its annual ball and she was being fitted for the occasion in a midnight blue satin gown with a full skirt and halterneck top.

Looking up quickly, as if her head had been jerked back by an invisible length of string, Ami fixed her husband with a hard stare. Waving her hand in his direction, she oozed with false brightness, 'Kenji, it is not right that you should be in here during a fitting.'

Takai was in her early fifties, and Kenji had heard his wife say middle age had not been kind to her. It had completely ignored the lower half of her body – her two legs were as thin as a sparrow's – in favour of the upper half where a generous amount of flesh resided, now contorted into all manner of strange shapes by the tight material in which it was encased. The effect was not flattering but she would not be told.

Looking around cautiously, he could see that the entire room had been cleaned. The floors were vacuumed and the newspapers and cans were no longer in evidence. Every surface had been wiped down and was gleaming, while the windows had been thrown wide open and the air smelt perfumed. Apologising, he made to move off

153

down the hallway, when Takai stopped him, whining in a high-pitched voice.

'Please, Yamada-san, you must stay and talk to me. I am so bored. Your wife will not say a word to me; her mouth is so full of pins. Come in and sit down. You can keep me amused.'

Kenji hesitated. He knew that whatever he did – if he stayed or if he refused to – Ami would find fault. It seemed that less fault might be found if he stayed. At least this way he did not risk offending her best customer. So, ignoring the furious expression stamped on his wife's face, Kenji did as instructed: avoiding the pin boxes and scraps of material as he edged over to the sofa in the corner of the room and perched on the edge.

'Your job at Fuji Bank is going well?' Takai asked, smoothing the midnight blue satin over her rotund belly: the result of having borne her husband three healthy and – she repeatedly claimed – extremely successful children.

Kenji nodded. 'Yes, thank you.'

Sighing loudly, Ami stood up and turned on the sitting-room light in order to better survey her work.

'I see that your sight has still not returned?' Takai commented, her face creased in an expression of concern.

Instinctively, Kenji reached up and touched the eye patch. 'Not as yet, no.'

'I must give you the telephone number of my husband's doctor. He's a very good man. He'll be able to set you right. Please could you pass me my handbag.'

She pointed to an oversized brown leather handbag covered with all manner of pockets, buckles and straps that was sitting, as large as a cat, on the sofa beside him. He did as she asked, wondering if she would be able to find anything in it. He was wrong. Within seconds, she had located the card and handed it to him.

'Thank you,' Kenji said, sitting back down and pretending to study the card. He knew that he would never call this man, that he could not afford his services. But it would have been impolite to refuse.

'Ami tells me that you are heading for bigger and better things.'

Takai smiled benevolently at her seamstress, who pretended to be completely absorbed in her work: stabbing pins viciously through the hem of the dress. 'Another job in television?'

Kenji's top lip curled upwards as his thoughts fell to Abe E. Kitahara who had let him down so badly. 'It was a venture that I was considering,' he replied, staring straight ahead, trying hard not to look at Takai's bare, fleshy upper arms and ample cleavage. What had Ami done with the rubbish that he had created, he found himself wondering? How furious had she been to return home to the apartment as he had left it? Had she cursed him and sent the children out with their grandmother so that she could set about cleaning uninterrupted? Had she finished before Takai arrived? He couldn't find the answers to any of these questions by staring at the expression on his wife's face. Would she scream and shout at him tonight? The more he thought about it, the more he panicked. He began to have difficulty breathing. For reassurance, he grabbed his St Christopher medal and held it tightly between the fingers of his right hand. It felt warm. It began to grow hotter until it started to burn. He yelped, desperately searching for the clasp so that he could take it off. All the time it seared his skin. Eventually he had no choice and he tore the delicate gold chain from his neck and threw it to the floor.

The two women cast him anxious glances but otherwise pretended not to notice his erratic behaviour.

'Your husband is quite the entrepreneur, I think.' Takai looked down at Ami who, having stabbed her thumb with a pin, was sucking the flesh vigorously until the blood stopped.

There was an expression of the utmost sympathy on Takai's face and Kenji knew what she was thinking. She pitied Ami for being married to him. It was a relief when the intercom buzzed and he jumped up, calling, 'I'll get it.'

'Delivery for Eriko Otsuki,' a voice on the other end of the intercom announced.

'I'll be right out.' Opening the door Kenji made his way to the entrance where a young man in a royal blue jumpsuit, wearing a white baseball cap, was standing. It didn't look like anyone he knew.

'Sign here.' He thrust a clipboard at Kenji who signed his name at the bottom of the piece of paper.

'She's all yours.' The young man handed Kenji a set of what looked like car keys and then called out over his shoulder. 'Tani, let's get moving.'

Kenji looked over and saw a short, heavy-set man dressed in an identical jumpsuit climbing out of a gleaming, chilli red Toyota Celica with shallow-sloping, tinted windows and fifteen-spoke alloy wheels. 'She won this?'

'Don't ask me,' the young man replied as he climbed into the front of a small van. 'I just do the deliveries.'

'Those are for me, I think.' Appearing from behind him, Eriko snatched the car keys from Kenji's hand. 'I don't have much need for a car,' she continued smugly, 'but maybe I'll sell it. Do my bit for the family. You know I could . . .'

'Don't even say it,' Kenji interrupted her.

TWENTY-FIVE

Every seat was occupied when Kenji had boarded the train at Tokyo station. He was standing midway along the second carriage from the front: one hand clamped around a vertical chrome pole for balance, the other clasping a manila, A4-sized envelope elaborately inscribed with the name of the Harajuku Fuji Bank branch manager. Inagaki's secretary had instructed Kenji to deliver the envelope, stressing that this must be done in person. And while he struggled to imagine what message was so sensitive that it could not be trusted to a fax machine, a telephone, or even an email, he was glad to be out of the bank, if only for a few hours.

During the weeks that followed Kenji's return to work, Inagaki had not made an appearance. Nor had he on this occasion, pre-ferring to relay the errand for his former classmate through Naoko, his secretary with the plump calves. Thankfully this did not anger the other mail room attendants in the same way as it had done previously. If anything, it allied them more closely with Kenji. Was Inagaki such a coward, they wanted to know, that he could not come down to the mail room himself? Was he, they asked, afraid to look a man that he had broken in the eyes? While Kenji did not want to be written off just yet, he was glad of the support. There was so little of it to be had elsewhere. More importantly, it was looking increasingly likely that the mail room was all he had to look forward to for the rest of his working life. In which case it was better to be on good terms with his colleagues.

The train squealed as it stopped several minutes later at Harajuku station. He jumped out on to the platform and followed the other commuters towards the north exit and out on to the elm-lined Omotesando. It was several minutes before he reached Fuji Bank.

'I would like to see the branch manager please,' he told the young man behind the counter. 'I am here to deliver a letter.'

The bank teller jumped up and made a call from a red telephone on the desk behind him. After returning to the counter, he told Kenji the branch manager would be down in a few minutes. Kenji waited patiently until a man emerged from behind the counter.

'You wanted to see me?'

Kenji explained that he had been asked to deliver a letter and handed it to the branch manager. Thinking there would be a message to take back, he waited. At first it appeared the envelope was empty. Then the branch manager turned it upside down and a tie pin fell out on to the floor.

'Of course.' He grinned. 'I left this behind at the golf club. Although I don't see why Inagaki-san felt the need to have it delivered in person. We are playing again tomorrow.'

He walked off leaving Kenji fuming. It had been another of Inagaki's ruses. Did the man never tire of trying to catch him out? Was his own life so empty that the only pleasure he got was from trying to make Kenji miserable?

'I'm here now,' he reasoned, storming out, 'and I think I deserve the afternoon off.'

It was a warm, sunny day. Leaving the bank he headed towards a nearby convenience store where he bought a sandwich and a can of soda. Whistling a happy tune, he made his way back up Omotesando, towards Yoyogi Park. It was lunch time and the park was filled with office workers eating their lunch on the sun-bleached grass, joggers and bonneted children lurching haphazardly in front of their minders. He was glad not to be entirely alone. It helped to take his mind off Abe and *Millyennaire*. He had been foolish to think he could make a TV programme. Or that a man like

158

Abe would even take him seriously. Yet at the time, he had seemed interested.

Finding an empty bench he sat down and ate his sandwich. It was still too early to head back to Utsunomiya, so he decided to take a stroll round the park. The more he walked, the more relaxed he started to become. As he approached the park's main entrance, he noticed a group of men, squatting down around a loudspeaker. One was twisting a wire at the back of the amplifier, causing sound to cut in and out. The song was familiar. It was Elvis Presley. His favourite. It surprised him that all of them were dressed almost identically, in faded indigo jeans and a tight fitting T-shirt worn beneath a denim or black leather biker's jacket. Most wore their hair long on top and combed back into a large quiff with a generous amount of gel.

When one of the men managed to fix the speaker, a loud cheer went round the group and they started to dance, jitterbugging on long, pointed black leather boots. Black leather boots that were so worn the soles had to be held to the uppers with layers of black duct tape.

'Where have I seen that before?' Kenji wondered.

One of the men turned around and, after staring at him for several seconds, started to walk towards him. 'Hey, I know you.'

There was something familiar about him. Not just his boots, but also his suit – black with a faint silver dart detail running through it. As the man got closer he removed his sunglasses and Kenji could see his eyes: one was brown, the other green.

'Don't you remember me? My name is Izo Izumi.'

'Of course.' Kenji remembered now. Izo was the travelling sales-man he had met in the Shinjuku ramen bar all those months ago.

'How are you?' Izo slapped Kenji on the back and shouted to the other dancers, 'Look. It's my friend Kenji.'

They waved but did not stop jitterbugging.

Izo shrugged as if to say 'What can you do?', and then pulled on Kenji's arm, dragging him over to an empty bench. 'Come on, we'll sit down and you will tell me how you are. You must be working?'

Looking down at his ill-fitting uniform and then at Izo, Kenji nodded. He opened his mouth to explain that he was working in a bank. But much more came out. The whole sorry story, from beginning to end. Doppo's tuition and friendship, how his attempt at being a pachinko pro had to be aborted prematurely, his job as a mail room attendant. He even told Izo about the incident in the hospital: how it had led to his idea for *Millyennaire* and his unsuccessful meeting with Abe. Kenji didn't know why he found Izo so easy to talk to. Maybe Izo's mismatched eyes put him under some kind of spell. Maybe it was the fact that Izo seemed so genuinely pleased to see him. Maybe Kenji just desperately needed someone to talk to.

As Kenji told his story, Izo stopped grinning and he frowned. 'You haven't seen Abe since? He hasn't called you?'

Kenji found the question disconcerting. He had expected shock, disbelief, an uncomfortable silence. He hadn't expected to be believed.

'No,' he admitted and a wave of disappointment washed over him. It was the first time he had allowed himself to acknowledge just how upset he was. *Millyennaire* was a good idea. An excellent idea. At some point he had forgotten this.

'You haven't called him?' Izo's eyebrows furrowed.

The very idea was horrifying to Kenji. 'How could I?' he spluttered. 'Just to be dismissed again. I would rather not know. Maybe live in hope . . .' He shrugged. '. . . that one day I might get a phone call. Something out of the blue. And I could leave the bank.'

'I don't get it.' Izo shifted on the bench beside him. 'Something doesn't add up. Why would he bother to meet you in the first place? Why would he say that he was interested when he could easily have told you to go away and not bother him again?'

'That's the kind of man he is. He can be very charming. But what he says is not often what he does.' Kenji looked up just as a young child tottered past, its chubby legs working quickly against the ground. It was getting late and the office workers were starting to leave the park.

'That is,' Izo paused, 'exactly what I'm afraid of.'

'I could phone him,' Kenji offered tentatively, even though the thought of affirmative action terrified him.

Izo shook his head firmly. 'Too direct. This is not a man with whom you deal directly. You will have to be much smarter if you want to outwit him.'

Kenji did not understand what Izo was saying but nodded his agreement.

'Is he based in Tokyo?'

'Naka-Meguro.'

Izo laughed. 'That's a few stops from here. We'll go together. You have the time, don't you?'

'Now? Together? We can't,' Kenji protested. Izo didn't hear. He had already charged back to where his friends were dancing to another Elvis Presley song and his battered brown leather suitcase sat. Opening it he removed a white shirt, pulled it on over his T-shirt and secured a black tie around his neck. Dragging a comb through his hair and throwing on his suit jacket, he was ready to go.

'Come on, what are you waiting for?' Izo shouted, springing back and forth on the balls of his feet like a boxer.

Kenji didn't know, but followed Izo out of Yoyogi Park anyway.

TWENTY-SIX

'Abe-san is in a meeting and cannot be disturbed,' the receptionist confirmed, running a polished fingernail across the screen in front of her.

'It really is extremely important. If you could find a way?' Izo cooed, one hand resting on the milky-white glass desk at which she was sitting. It was circular and dominated most of the large reception room.

Kenji hung back, feeling more of a hindrance than a help. Although it did give him ample time to form an impression of the place. There were no piles of boxes stacked against the wall, or trailing wires as there had been at NBC. Everything looked new, tidy and uncluttered. The walls were painted stark white. Even the floor tiles were white. The only thing that was not in white was the receptionist's black dress and a single red lily in a vase on the desk in front of her. He wondered if Abe enjoyed coming to work here every day as much as he knew he would.

'Hmmm, what perfume are you wearing?' Izo sniffed the air.

Suki stared back at him. 'Abe-san cannot be disturbed. If you would like to leave a message, I will pass it on.'

'Maybe I can stay here for the rest of the afternoon and gaze at you instead?'

Izo would not be deterred. Kenji felt embarrassed just watching and dragged him away from the desk. 'Come on. Let's go.'

'It's been nice chatting with you,' Izo called as, together, they left the reception and entered a small lobby. Kenji pressed the down button to call an elevator, while Izo paced back and forth in front of a row of built-in cupboards.

'Of course, you're right. That wasn't getting us anywhere. But what do we do now?'

'We should just leave,' Kenji urged. He didn't care if he was whining. It was getting late and he would have to show his face at the bank before everyone clocked off for the day. The last thing that he wanted was for the other attendants to take umbrage that he had been gone all afternoon.

Izo wasn't listening, but was rattling the handles of the cupboards. Each was locked except for one at the very end. His head disappeared inside. When he finally did emerge, he threw something at Kenji. 'Here, try this on.'

The pale green jumpsuit landed at Kenji's feet. 'Why?'

'Just do it and don't ask questions.'

Kenji shook his head but pushed one foot into the leg of the jumpsuit and then the other. As he pulled the jumpsuit up over his body, pushed his arms through and fastened the buttons, he shot Izo an unhappy look.

'And this.'

A baseball cap landed on the ground. The name embroidered across the front was the same cleaning firm that they had used at NBC. No sooner had he put it on then Izo was thrusting a can of polish and a duster at him.

'What are we doing?' The jumpsuit was at least two sizes too small for Kenji and cut painfully into his upper legs.

'Look like you're supposed to be here,' Izo instructed, pushing an industrial-sized vacuum cleaner through the doors, back into the reception. The wheels rattled loudly across the tiled floor, and although Suki looked up, she allowed them to pass without comment, through the frosted doors behind her.

On the other side of the door, Izo whooped. 'We did it. We're in. Now look busy.'

'How do I do that?'

'Polish things.'

'What things?'

'I don't know. Anything.'

The nearest things to hand were the tubular chrome door handles. Kenji began polishing these as Izo bent down and pretended to be inspecting the vacuum cleaner. 'What next?' Kenji hissed.

'We find him.'

'How? This is a big office.' It was bigger even than NBC.

'Are you just here to moan?'

'Of course not,' Kenji replied angrily.

'In that case what we are going to do is walk very slowly throughout the entire office and look everywhere. And you're going to tell me if you see him.'

Determined Izo was not going to make him feel like a coward, an incompetent, Kenji set off walking along the aisle that ran around the perimeter of the office. Walking slowly, he stared intently into the face of everyone who passed or was sitting at their desk. Occasionally, when he wanted to get a better look, he would stop and polish whatever was closest to hand – skirting panels, door handles, light switches. He searched frantically for the face of the man he had met several weeks ago at the restaurant in Roppongi, and before then at NBC, but could not see him anywhere.

'It's useless,' he hissed at Izo. 'I can't see him anywhere.'

'Keep looking,' Izo said, banging the vacuum cleaner against a door that flew open.

'Can you do that some other time, please? We've got a meeting going on in here.' The man standing at the door was at least six foot and towered above Kenji.

'Another time.' Kenji nodded quickly.

'Yes. We can't hear ourselves think in there.'

The man disappeared back into the room. Once he was safely inside, the door closed behind him, Kenji tiptoed over to the shuttered window. He had seen something through the gap in the door and wanted to get a closer look. 'I think that was him. In there.'

'Really?' Izo pushed up behind him. 'You know you're doing the right thing. This would be a great place to work. I mean look at it. And did you see that guy's clothes. His suit was exquisite. Handmade almost definitely.'

'That's him. There he is,' Kenji whispered.

Izo pushed him out of the way. 'Where?'

'There. Sitting next to the elderly gentleman. To the right of the TV.'

'Are you sure?'

'One hundred per cent.'

Izo burst into an uncontrollable fit of giggles.

His enthusiasm was infectious. Kenji immediately felt his spirits lifting. 'What next? What will we do?'

'We need a plan.'

'What do you mean we need a plan?' Kenji was shocked. 'Are you telling me that you don't have one already? That you dragged me all the way here on a whim?'

'Give me a minute. I'll think of something.'

'I don't have a minute. Don't you understand? I don't have anything left at all? This was my last chance.' Kenji grabbed Izo by the shoulders. The strength of his emotions surprised him. Their faces were inches apart. Now that they were standing so close, Kenji could make out the outline of a contact lens on what he had thought was Izo's green eye. Of course. The man was a fraud, a fake, a conman. He had been foolish following him here today. He would be lucky if he had a job to go back to at the bank after this latest misadventure. When would he learn his lesson?

'I can't think with you crowding me like this.' Izo shoved Kenji in the chest so that he staggered backwards.

Kenji undid the buttons of the jumpsuit. 'I'm going.'

'You can't go. What about Abe?'

He shrugged. 'It's time to let it go. To get on with what I've got rather than dreaming about what I haven't.'

'Do you trust me?' Izo grabbed Kenji's shoulders firmly and stared at him.

'Yes.' Kenji wasn't entirely sure that he did but it seemed rude to say no.

'Okay, then will you give me a chance? Just one. I'm trying to help you. If it doesn't work out then we'll go home. Agreed?'

It seemed like a fair compromise. Kenji nodded.

'Wait for me here then.'

The last thing Kenji saw was the manic grin on Izo's face as he disappeared into the boardroom. As he waited for Izo to re-emerge, his face grew hot and flushed, and he started to feel very conspicuous so he knelt down and polished a plug socket. By the time Izo returned, it was gleaming.

'What happened? What did you do in there?'

Izo squatted down on the ground next to Kenji. 'I pretended I'd been sent to check the air-conditioning unit.'

'And?'

Placing one hand on Kenji's back, Izo spoke in a hushed voice. 'I don't know how to tell you this. But that guy Abe. At this minute he's pitching your idea to two representatives from NBC and they're getting pretty excited about it.'

'Really?' Kenji had obviously misjudged Abe. The TV producer just needed a bit more time to get things moving. He couldn't wait to tell Ami. She would have to eat her words. And Eriko? He would no longer have to put up with her jibes and barbed comments.

'I'm afraid he's taking all the credit for himself.'

This confused Kenji. 'Perhaps he has to. To sell the idea. They'll bring me in later. Maybe I know them, the people from NBC.' Standing up he attempted to look through the window but the blinds had been firmly shut.

'It didn't sound like that to me.' As Izo stood up his knees creaked loudly. 'He said that the idea came to him in a flash of inspiration. There was no mention of your name.'

Searching Izo's face for any indication this was a heartless joke, Kenji saw none there. 'In which case, we should leave.'

'Not so quickly.' Izo grabbed Kenji by the arm to stop him walking away. 'Can you prove that the idea is yours? Did you write it down anywhere?'

'No.'

'Did you tell anybody?'

'My family and they thought I was crazy.'

'That's a start. Okay, come with me and unless I tell you otherwise, don't say a word.'

'What?'

'Don't ask, just do.'

Abe did not notice the interruption immediately. 'As you can see from the pilot episode,' he addressed the elder of the two representatives from NBC, whom Kenji recognised as the senior commissioning editor and his assistant although neither would know who he was, '*Millyennaire* is going to put NBC back on the light entertainment map and win the ratings war for you. There is also the possibility of . . .'

Izo cleared his throat, loudly. Abe looked up and when he saw Kenji, a look of discomfort flitted across his face.

'Good afternoon, everybody. My name is Izo Izumi and this is my client Kenji Yamada.' The occupants of the room looked from Izo to Kenji, and then back again. 'I'm here today because I have every reason to believe that my client's copyright is being breached.'

'Hold on.' It was Abe who spoke. His voice had a strangled quality to it. 'Weren't you in here a minute ago looking at the air-conditioning unit?'

'His copyright?' The voice came from the tall, well-dressed man who had come out into the corridor to complain about the noise. 'My name is Aran Goto.' He shook hands with both of them, firmly and professionally. 'I'm the head of light entertainment here at Miru TV.'

Izo bowed politely. 'Goto-san, I am sorry to have to tell you this but *Millyennaire* was my client's idea.'

'Really?' Goto stared at Kenji who was standing in the corner of the room, hoping nobody would speak to him. This was madness, sheer madness. He couldn't believe he was here when he should have been back at the bank hours ago. At the same time, he couldn't help but admire Izo's audacity. If he had even a fraction of it he might not have got into this terrible sorry mess in the first place.

'My client came to your colleague, Abe-san, in the best of faith,' Izo continued. 'Hoping to have his idea made into a television programme. Abe-san informed my client that he was very taken with *Millyennaire* and would do his best to see it was made into a programme.'

'Can you prove that the idea belonged to your client?' Goto's voice was calm, coolly clinical.

'Of course I can. He copyrighted it before meeting Abe-san and there is a stamped and dated document describing the idea sitting in a bank safety deposit box at this very minute.'

'Liar,' Abe burst out. 'He wouldn't have the intelligence to do something like that.'

Goto stroked his carefully trimmed, greying beard. 'So you're not denying that you've met this man before?' His full attention was on Abe who was struggling to hide his fury.

'No. I mean, yes. I am denying that I've met him before. You can just tell by looking at him. He couldn't come up with an idea like *Millyennaire*.'

Everyone in the room turned to look at Kenji who did his best to look like exactly the kind of person who could come up with an idea like *Millyennaire*, and have the sense to deposit an important document in a safety deposit box.

The senior commissioning editor, who had been watching the proceedings unfold with obvious and mounting unease, stood up, gathered together his papers and put them away in a briefcase. 'NBC has been involved in a lengthy legal battle that has just come to an end. It is not an experience we wish to repeat. So if you will excuse us, we will leave you now.' His younger assistant jumped up from his chair and followed him.

Goto followed, imploring them to stay. 'Please, if you could just wait here for a few minutes I'm sure we'll have this situation sorted out. Perhaps we could talk some more over dinner?' He mentioned the name of an exclusive restaurant and both men hesitated, shared a few whispered words and agreed.

'If you will come with me.' Goto opened the door for them. Once they were outside, he hissed at Abe, 'Sort this out. I don't care how you do it. Just do it.'

Abe protested.

'*Now!*' the head of light entertainment barked before turning to leave.

Abe turned to face Kenji and Izo. His fists were tight balls at his side. 'What do you want? Money, is that it?'

'My client simply wants what is rightfully his.'

Abe guffawed. 'Rightfully his? What would he do with *Millyennaire*? What could he do with *Millyennaire*? No, it's better off with me. I'm the kind of person who can make things happen. Him? He's just a mail room attendant. Tell me how much you want and we can make this whole mess go away.'

'We don't want any money.' Izo remained calm, unruffled.

'Don't we?' It was the first time Kenji had spoken since they entered the boardroom and the words almost choked in his throat he felt so nervous. 'Why don't we want money? It sounds good to me.'

'If you will excuse me for one minute.' Grabbing Kenji forcefully by the upper arm so that he yelped in pain, Izo dragged him into the corner of the room. 'Have you seen the clothes these people are wearing? Tailormade, designer labels. That kind of thing doesn't come cheap. This business pays well and you deserve a shot at it. Not just a few small crumbs that fall off their plates. I'm trying to get you a way of life here. Are you with me? Do you trust me?'

Kenji nodded. If it wasn't for Izo, he wouldn't be here at all. He had to give his idea a chance, whatever it was.

'We are decided then.' Izo turned round and addressed Abe. '*Millyennaire* is my client's idea and he wants to be an integral part of the production team.'

'I – ' Abe put the palm of one hand on his chest. ' – am the executive producer on this show.'

'My client accepts that. Nor would he want to usurp your position. He will accept the title of . . .' He paused significantly. '. . . assistant executive producer.'

This was better than anything Kenji had hoped for.

'Excuse me?'

'Assistant executive producer.'

There was a long pause in which no one said anything. The only sound was of breathing.

'If I do that, if I give him a job then it will all go away? No one else has to know? As far as they'll be concerned *Millyennaire* was my idea.'

'Those are our terms.'

'In that case you've got a deal.' Abe swept out of the room, pausing at the door. 'Be here on Monday morning but lose the jumpsuit.'

TWENTY-SEVEN

'I am so proud of you.' Ami straightened the knot in Kenji's tie and made certain that it was lying flat against his chest. 'I can't wait to tell my friends how handsome you looked going off to work on your first day. They are already very jealous. "Ami," they say, "soon you will be mixing in fashionable circles and you will not want to know us." I laugh it off, of course.' She giggled.

It should have been an intimate moment: the two of them standing in the small kitchen, their bodies separated by a sliver of the yellow, early morning sunlight that was streaming in through the window above the sink. But as Kenji looked intently at Ami's face, he found himself struggling to recognise the woman that he had been married to for twelve years. Certainly this was her face. The curve of her cheeks, the line of her forehead and every crease and fold in her skin that had gradually emerged over the years were all too familiar to him. Yet sometimes she seemed like a different woman altogether. Everything it seemed, even when it was indisputably about him, his success or his failure, ended up being about her.

A comparison with Dai's reaction to his news when he had called in at the supermarket to see her was inevitable. Of course, he shouldn't have been there. Not after the last time, when her husband had warned him away. And she too had looked frightened and anxious when he first appeared from behind the display of

Tupperware boxes that she was in the process of stacking. But he had been feeling reckless that day, having just handed his notice in at the bank, and as excitable as a puppy. And his visit hadn't been wasted. When he told her, her face broke into a large smile and she gave him a big hug that embarrassed them both, saying that he had worked hard and deserved this opportunity more than anybody else. Neither of them mentioned Tomo.

Ami stopped giggling and became serious, running both hands across his shoulders, smoothing down the fabric. 'But you never know. Maybe we will'

The suit was old but the tie was new. A gift to mark his first day at work, it was dark blue and embroidered, in gold thread, with tiny television sets. He had laughed when she gave it to him. 'Where did you get it?' he asked, turning it over in his hands. Looking away shyly she admitted, 'The tie I bought. The television sets I embroidered myself.' It had struck him that it must have taken her a very long time and it was an extraordinary selfless thing of her to do. Hopefully, he grabbed her by the top of her arms and kissed her passionately on the lips. She had pushed him away saying, 'I can't have anybody thinking that my husband doesn't know how to dress.'

Today Kenji avoided her lips, and kissed her without passion on the cheek. He put it down to nervousness. His stomach had worked itself into knots at the thought of what was ahead. He was so anxious and excited that he'd been awake since four o'clock that morning.

'Have you got your lunch?' Ami enquired, following Kenji down the hallway towards the front door.

He rattled his briefcase.

Satisfied, she called the twins out of their bedrooms. They emerged, sleepy and rubbing their puffy eyes, still in their bed-clothes. It was only 7 a.m. but Kenji did not want to be late and Ami insisted that everybody see him off. Even Eriko had emerged from her room – her greying hair set in pink plastic rollers and covered with a net – to see him go.

'Dad.'

Yoshi tugged Kenji's arm as he surveyed his reflection in the hallway mirror. It felt good to be back in a suit. It was where he belonged. Looking down at his son, he could not resist ruffling the boy's hair even though he knew how much this annoyed him.

'What is it?'

'There's a Godzilla show on in Tokyo next month. Everybody in my class is going. Can I go? Will you take me? The tickets are selling out. We might have to buy some soon.'

'Yoshi,' Ami scolded, 'I told you not to bother your father with such things.'

Ignoring his mother, Yoshi climbed up on to the trays of dog food which Eriko had won several months previously and were still stacked on the floor beneath the mirror. This bought him up to the same height as his father's shoulders. 'Please can we go? Please. There's going to be a sixty-foot Godzilla there. No maybe eighty feet. Or even a hundred. They're shipping him in from America.'

'Sounds dumb to me.' Yumi pinched her brother's calf. For once he ignored her, so intent was he on getting Kenji's attention. This just served to make her crosser and she pinched him again.

'I tell you what.' Kenji leant down so their noses were touching. 'How about just you and me go? Leave the women at home? Does that sound good? I'll get the tickets this week. On my lunch break.' It was a long time since the family had gone cherry blossom-viewing, but he still remembered it with fondness. That feeling of together-ness, the way the children looked at him because he was responsible for bringing excitement into their life. Now that he was working again he wanted to build up as many of those images as possible so that when he was old and retired he had an entire bank to draw on.

Yoshi grinned, revealing a missing front tooth. 'Thanks, Dad.' Turning to go back to the kitchen, he stopped at the door. 'Have a good day, Dad. You deserve it.'

'Yes I do, don't I?' As he left the apartment, Kenji permitted himself a moment of self-congratulation. Yoshi was right. Dai was right. Doppo would say the same thing if he were still here. Izo had been saying it all along. He did deserve this piece of good fortune. He had struggled hard for it. Seeing his bus in the distance, he ran to catch it.

173

TWENTY-EIGHT

'Good morning. My name is Keiko Mifune. I am Abe-san's assistant.'

Kenji had been kept waiting in the stark white reception room for over an hour. There were no chairs, so he had been forced to pace anxiously back and forth. A number of times he had considered leaning against a wall but was frightened of leaving a mark. He was also frightened that he would be left here forever, that nobody would come to get him. All that was forgotten when, out of the frosted doors behind the reception desk emerged what he could only describe as a vision of loveliness. She had a pretty, heart-shaped face, framed by an elfin haircut.

'Do you speak English?' She looked at him intensely.

He shook his head.

'That's a shame.' Consulting the clipboard that she was holding, she ticked something on a piece of paper with a red biro. 'I like to practise whenever I get the chance. I want to go to America one day. Have you ever been to America?'

Beginning to feel inadequate, he shook his head for a second time.

'Never mind. Now if you will follow me I will show you to your desk.'

She turned to go, passing through the doors and into the office: the same one in which Kenji and Izo had been just last week.

'Everything is very orderly,' he commented as they passed through.

'We have recently undergone a refurbishment,' Mifune explained.

Despite the shaky start, this was a good sign. A refurbishment only ever meant one thing – a company was making lots of money and cared about the well-being of its staff over and above getting the maximum amount of work out of them as possible. Glancing admiringly at the new, varnished desks he wondered which one might be his. They continued walking, passing a number of people on the way. Kenji smiled at each and every one. Some smiled back, others looked at him curiously. Eventually they reached the back of the office where a row of filing cabinets had been stacked, forming an L-shape. Mifune stopped and he did too.

'These were left over after the refurbishment. We haven't had any opportunity to remove them yet.'

'I see,' Kenji replied, although he didn't at all. Why was Mifune showing him this?

'Your desk is right here.' Walking behind the filing cabinets, Mifune showed Kenji to a small desk on which there was neither a telephone nor a computer. That was neither new nor shiny. In fact one of the legs appeared to be shorter than the other so that it sloped slightly and a drawer would not close but kept rolling out when she leant down and tried to shut it.

'I don't understand.' He looked at her. 'It's so dark in here.'

'A bit gloomy, yes.' She looked overhead where there were two light fittings. One was dark, the other was flickering.

'Can't I sit outside with everybody else?'

'There is no room, I'm afraid.' Mifune ticked another item off her list.

'Abe-san. May I speak with him?' Kenji pleaded.

'He is busy right now but will be along to see you shortly. Please sit down.'

There seemed to be no other option but to do as he was told. It was his first day and he did not want to do anything to rock the boat. Sitting down he waited patiently for Abe to appear. Waited and waited. Occasionally he got up and looked over the wall of filing cabinets into the busy office. There were many, many people there but he could see neither Abe nor Mifune. Hours passed. Soon it was lunch time. Retrieving the box that Ami had prepared for him from his briefcase, he ate in silence. He had no appetite, but it passed the time. Where was Abe, he wondered, putting the box back in his briefcase? He was supposed to start work today and yet here he was, sitting alone, wasting time. It was too much for a man to bear. He jumped up and went in search of Mifune. He was surprised by how loud, bright and airy the office was. It had seemed so quiet, dark and stuffy behind his wall of filing cabinets. The opportunity to stretch his legs was welcome and it did not take very long until he found Mifune at a nearby coffee machine, deeply engrossed in conversation with a male companion. They both looked up as Kenji approached.

'I am very sorry to bother you, but I have been alone all this time. There has been no sign of Abe-san and I am anxious to start work.'

'He is a very busy man.' Mifune removed a steaming cup of black coffee from the machine. 'If you go back to your desk I will find him and send him over to you as soon as possible.'

Once again there seemed to be no option other than to do as he was told. At 5 p.m., when there was still no sign of Abe, he picked up his briefcase, put on his coat and left the office. At home that evening, Ami insisted the entire family sat down and ate dinner together, packed around the small kitchen table, so that Kenji could tell them about his day. He was too ashamed to admit the truth, so he embellished it. The office, he explained, was very modern and orderly, and he had been allocated a desk in the corner away from any disturbance so that he might get on with his work.

'They must think very highly of you,' Ami commented and he nodded, feeling a warm flush spread across his face. He took a gulp of beer to hide his discomfort. Luckily Yoshi was excited about a fight that had broken out between two boys in his class and it was easy for Kenji to divert attention away from himself. Secretly he wished that the next day would be better and he might have more to tell his family.

It wasn't. Nor the next nor the one after that. Abe could never be found. He was always out of the office, in a meeting or on a business trip. Soon the entire week had passed and Kenji had spent it alone, sitting in the darkened corner of the office behind the wall of filing cabinets, becoming increasingly desperate and frustrated. What would Doppo do in this situation? he wondered and tried to imagine his friend's face. Finding that he was no longer able to do so upset him immeasurably and to avoid bursting into tears – everything it seemed set him off these days – he stood up and went to the coffee machine. Only 11 a.m., it was already his third cup of the day.

There were two men standing at the machine, selecting their drinks, so he waited his turn. One was tall and wiry, the other short and fat. Neither noticed nor paid him any attention.

'Did you hear about Abe-san?' the short, fat guy asked as he selected a black coffee with sugar. The machine rumbled in response.

'No,' the tall, skinny one replied, leaning down because his colleague was so much shorter than him. On hearing Abe's name, Kenji also leant in closer.

'You know about the bonus scheme, right?'

'Sure. Whoever sells a show to a network and gets them to put up fifty per cent gets a bonus. Nobody has ever got it though.'

'Abe just did.' The short, fat guy took a sip out of the plastic cup of coffee he was holding and grimaced. 'That's hot.'

'How much?'

'Six months' salary.'

'No, it can't possibly be true,' Kenji exclaimed, alerting the other men to his presence. 'It isn't right. *Millyennaire* was my idea.'

'Hey, cool it. I'm only repeating what I was told.' The short guy tipped his colleague on the elbow and the two of them walked off down the corridor, casting Kenji a bemused glance over their shoulders. Then they turned away and he knew instinctively that they would be talking about him, laughing and smirking. How dare they? Pacing back and forth in front of the coffee machine, not caring if he got in anybody's way, a fury began to grow inside his head until it raged so much that he could not think clearly. Not since his encounter with Eto at the bank had he been so furious. When he

177

thought of how long he had sat at that desk waiting, he could have cried with humiliation. And all the while Abe was doing deals behind his back. Deals to the tune of six months' salary.

He thought about Ishida: his former boss and head of programme research at NBC. When Ishida had told Kenji there was no longer any job for him, he hadn't said a word. He had just sat back and accepted it. He sat back and took every bad thing that ever happened to him. He couldn't do that now. If only he could think more clearly. He couldn't breathe. Clutching at his stupid tie covered with gold televisions, he stormed away from the coffee machine, along the aisle that ran all the way around the perimeter of the office.

'I can't believe it,' he muttered under his breath and then more loudly. A number of people who were working nearby turned to look at him. At first curiously and then fearfully. He was long past caring. 'It's happened again. What am I? Do I have fool written on my forehead? Well, this is the last time. The very last time.'

Striding quickly down the corridor, he stopped the first person he saw. A young woman. 'I need to speak to Abe. Where is he?'

She looked terrified. He moderated his tone and asked more quietly.

'His office is at the end of this corridor. The last door on the right.'

Kenji ran off in the direction to which she had pointed. The door at the end of the corridor was solid and oak. It was also closed. He paused briefly before throwing it open. Abe was inside, sitting at his desk and cleaning the dirt out from his nails with a paper clip.

'Kenji.' He jumped up, surprised. 'How's it going? Are you settling in?' He walked around to the front of his desk, which Kenji noticed, was in a light, airy, spacious office. Not at all like the gloomy corner in which he had been hidden for the last week.

'You duped me.' He was shaking with anger. It was difficult to get the words out.

A sly smile spread across Abe's lips. 'What do you mean?' Sitting down on the corner of the desk, he inspected his fingernails. Behind him was an enormous window, sunlight streaming through it and lighting him up from behind.

178

'The bonus. The money for the show. *Millyennaire* was my idea. You passed it off as your own. You don't deserve that money. I do. I have a wife and children to think about.'

'Don't get so hot under the collar about it, Yamada. You know it really wasn't very much money. A drop in the ocean.'

'What do you mean?' he spluttered repeating the sum that he had heard from the fat man. 'How can you say that isn't a lot of money? What I would do with six months' salary. I would take my family on holiday. After the year we've had, we deserve it.'

'Like I said.' Abe crossed his arms over his chest. 'It wasn't a lot of money.'

'You . . .' Kenji was lost for words. How dare this man who had stolen his idea stand there and mock him. He wouldn't put up with it. Drawing his right arm back behind his head, his hand formed a fist and he prepared to swing it forward. He didn't know how he knew what to do. He had never thrown a punch in his life. But Abe, who was much stronger than he looked, stopped Kenji's punch in the palm of his hand before it had time to connect.

'What do you think you're doing?' he hissed, pushing against Kenji's fist until his arm was bent, twisted painfully around his back. 'Nobody ever questions me. Nobody ever challenges me. If you want to keep working here,' he laughed, 'then you'd better keep your head down. Stay out of my way and don't do or say anything to upset me. Do you understand?'

Kenji struggled, but it was pointless. The more he squirmed, the more Abe twisted his arm. He feared that the bone might snap at any minute.

With his free arm, Abe made a hook around Kenji's neck, restricting his breathing such that his face began to turn purple and he was struggling for breath.

'All right,' he yelped. 'Just let me go.'

'Do I have your faithful word that you won't try anything like this again?'

'My faithful word.'

Abe released his hold. Kenji hungrily gulped down air.

'Good.' Giving Kenji's arm one last, violent twist, Abe released it.

'Because you're not working at the bank now. You're swimming with the sharks and I could make your life around here very difficult if you don't start to show me a little bit more respect. Do you understand what I'm saying?'

He nodded dumbly.

'What's going on here?' A voice boomed cheerfully from somewhere behind Kenji. Goto was standing in the doorway.

'Just kidding around,' Abe shrugged. 'Boys will be boys.' He punched Kenji's upper arm.

'That right, Yamada-san?' Goto asked, twirling one of his diamond-encrusted cufflinks. 'I know what Abe-san can be like. He gets a little over-zealous at times.'

'Just kidding around,' Kenji nodded meekly, hating himself for it. The skin on his wrist where Abe had grabbed him was smarting, red and sore.

'That's right.' Abe threw an arm around Kenji's shoulders and squeezed them tightly. He was so close that Kenji could smell his aftershave. 'Where would I be without Yamada-san? He's my right-hand man. This new show, we'll be working on it together. Couldn't do it without him. Isn't that right, Yamada-san?'

Kenji agreed.

TWENTY-NINE

'Knock, knock.' A young man appeared at the end of the row of disused filing cabinets. 'Oh good, you're here,' he grinned, revealing two large protruding front teeth that, when his mouth was closed, pushed his top lip up and out. 'Do you think that there's anything you can do with this?'

He placed a toaster, almost tenderly, on the table where Kenji was sitting, hunched over a keyboard. The smell of burnt bread drifted upwards from the metal box and teased his nose.

'I was just toasting some bread in the kitchen when a blue spark flew out of it.' The young man laughed. It was a strange, breathless sound made by passing air in through his nose and out through his mouth, again and again. 'Now it doesn't work anymore.'

Kenji looked up from the keyboard that he had been fixing. Had been fixing all morning in fact – trying to unstick three keys that had become permanently stuck down, and also patch the exposed cable. Oversized with all manner of knobs and dials, the toaster was evidently an old model. Ten years old. Maybe even fifteen. It would make more sense to buy a new one than repair this one, but he was a man with time on his hands. 'Come back at the end of the week,' he grunted, returning his full attention to the keyboard. 'It will be ready for you then.'

The young man turned fractionally, but then hesitated: casting a long, thin shadow across the desk, obscuring what little light was to be had in this secluded corner of the office. Sighing loudly as though dealing with an insistent child, Kenji looked up.

'What is it?'

The young man who was by now shifting uncomfortably from foot to foot, quite clearly had something he needed to get off his mind.

'I've seen you around.' He chewed tentatively on his large bottom lip that, like the top one, stuck out. 'I often wondered who you were. Then somebody told me that you were the caretaker. I didn't realise.' He threw his hands open in a gesture of puzzlement. 'Caretakers don't usually dress so smart.'

Silence ensued as they both looked at Kenji's suit. It was Kenji that spoke first. Looking up at the young man he said firmly, 'It will be ready for you at the end of the week.'

Kenji was alone again.

How he had come to be known as the caretaker, he did not know. After Abe's threat he had kept something of a low profile, both here and at home. Losing another job was not something that he could afford to do. Nor could Ami come to know about his predicament at work. There was no other option but to come to work every day and sit at this desk, harbouring the vague hope that one day Abe might leave Miru and he would be able to emerge from behind the filing cabinets. Claiming a position more worthy of his skills and experience. In the meantime, he sat alone. Doing nothing and taking home a reasonable salary for it. This sat heavily on his mind. Just because Abe was morally reprehensible it didn't mean that he, Kenji, had to be. Looking at the various pieces of broken equipment and furniture that surrounded him – a wire rubbish basket with a hole in it, a keyboard on which a number of keys were permanently stuck down, an extension lead with a wire exposed through the cable – an idea started to form. He repaired each one and when they were back in working order, stacked them neatly outside the row of filing cabinets for anybody who might be passing. It wasn't long before they disappeared and word spread because people started to come and see him with their repairs.

Of course he was acutely disappointed. Not a day passed when he didn't stand at the wall of filing cabinets, looking out into the busy office, wishing he was one of them. Sharing in their excitement. Even stuck here in this secluded corner of the office, he could still feel some of it. There was an undeniable buzz in the air. People were laughing and joking with each other, and whenever anybody passed he heard snatches of conversation. Everybody was talking about *Millyennaire*. It was, they said, going to be the next big thing, and even more galling, Abe had achieved two feats which earned him incredible kudos amongst the other employees at Miru TV. He had found a sponsor to fund half the show and he had tempted the reclusive Hana Hoshino out of retirement to present it. There was talk of accolades and awards, international licensing, merchandising rights.

In time, the disappointment became easier to cope with. There was enough equipment to be repaired to keep his mind off it and at least he was able to support his family. Lying, however, never got any easier. Every evening upon arriving home, he was forced to make up a number of stories about how his day had passed, the people he had met, the work he was doing. Perhaps his stories were a little too good, a little too convincing, because Ami was steadfast in her conviction that he was an important part of the company. Her admiration was an admonishment to him. So now instead of going straight home at the end of the day, he found a hundred little jobs that might keep him occupied and away from home.

Tonight it would be the toaster. After dismantling the metal box and tinkering with the blackened innards, he decided that new parts were needed. At 5 p.m., he got up, checked his pocket for his wallet and made to leave the office, intending to head for a nearby hardware shop. He always followed the same route out: one that kept him away from Abe's office and took him by way of the boardroom. As he passed the glass windows, he could not help but notice that the blinds were fully closed. This meant one thing. That there was an important meeting taking place inside and under no account must the occupants of the room be disturbed. A secretary, dropping off an electric pencil sharpener to be fixed, had told him a story that did not make him doubt this. A number of years previously, the entire building was evacuated by the emergency services when news of an impending earthquake hit Tokyo. As the occupants of the twenty-second floor filed out past the boardroom they saw that the blinds were down and because of this nobody dared knock on the door to tell those inside about the evacuation. They remained, obliviously working away, as their colleagues gathered outside the building at the emergency meeting point. Thankfully, it turned out to be a false alarm.

Looking at the ivory Venetian blinds as he passed, Kenji wondered what was taking place in there when suddenly, without warning, they snapped open, revealing a pair of eyes. He hurried on. Did that set of eyes belong to Abe? It was difficult to tell. The best thing to do was to get away as quickly as possible.

'Yamada-san,' a voice called.

Could he pretend not to have heard, to keep walking? It was unlikely. The voice called out again from the now open door. This time it was louder and people were starting to turn and look in his direction. He turned round slowly. Standing in the doorway was Goto in yet another one of the suits Izo had so admired that first day they had come to the office, dressed as cleaners. This one was French navy and worn with a very pale lime green shirt and an emerald green tie.

'Who me? Now?' Kenji found that he was trembling as he walked past Goto into the boardroom where the other eleven members of Miru TV's senior management team were gathered. There was just one person missing, he confirmed upon quickly scanning the room. Abe.

'Please, take a seat.' Goto gestured at the table littered with take-away food boxes, paper cups, cans, bottles and sweet wrappers. This was a meeting which had obviously been going on for several hours. Even though the air-conditioning was on, the room felt hot and stuffy. Several people had removed their jackets, which were hanging off the backs of chairs. Ties had been loosened and shirt sleeves rolled up. Only Goto was perfectly composed and seemingly unflustered.

'Who is this?' a middle-aged man with a large mole on his right cheek, who was standing in the corner of the room, addressed Goto. Kenji recognised him. He was Takeshi Watanabe. Like Abe, an executive producer at Miru TV.

'This,' Goto announced, nudging Kenji into the room and closing the door behind him, 'is Abe's right-hand man. His assistant.'

'Why didn't you bring him in sooner?' a woman with large jowls asked from behind the electric fan she was holding to her face.

'I didn't know Abe had an assistant,' someone else commented.

'He always worked alone, I thought.'

All around Kenji, the room started to come alive and the sensation was not entirely pleasant. One by one, the occupants got up from their chairs if they had been sitting, or moved away from the wall that they had been leaning against, and began to advance on him.

'What does he have to say for himself?'

'Move over, I can't get a good look at him.'

'Did he say something?'

The further they advanced, the further backwards he went until soon he was standing in the corner of the room: completely surrounded and clutching the toaster tightly to his chest for reassurance. The smell of burnt bread teasing his nostrils for the second time that day.

'What's he got there?'

'A toaster.'

'Why's he got a toaster?'

Why, he wondered, were they so interested in the toaster? Had his secret been discovered? Had another employee told on him? Where was Abe, he wondered? He had been warned to keep his head down. This was exactly the opposite. But what was the worst that they could do to him? So he had fixed a few pieces of broken equipment and been paid for it. It was hardly a crime.

'Come now, Yamada-san,' Goto said kindly, laying a powerful hand on Kenji's right shoulder and guiding him through the wall created by the senior management team, to a now empty, black leather chair at the head of one table. 'Please sit down. We just need to ask you a few questions, that's all. Nothing to worry about.

A hush descended upon the room as a number of the management team sat down at the table. Others remained standing, leaning on the backs of chairs or the wall. All looked just about ready to tear Kenji apart. He loosened the knot in his tie.

'We have some news that may upset you.' Goto walked slowly over to where Kenji was sitting. Appearing to notice the toaster for the first time, he asked with a slight note of amusement in his voice, 'Can I take that for you?'

'No, thank you. That won't be necessary.'

'Fine,' Goto continued. 'There's been an accident. Abe, I'm afraid. He's dead. He died last night.'

Kenji studied Goto's expression. Was he lying to him? Maybe joking. But there was nothing about his demeanour to suggest that he might be. 'How?' he asked, trying to give away as little as possible about how he was feeling. Which was easy enough because he didn't know himself. A curious mixture of excitement and fear had settled in the pit of his stomach. With Abe gone he might . . . It didn't bear thinking about. He didn't want to get his hopes up in case they were dashed. A small job would do. Any job. Maybe back in programme research. A junior manager, he didn't care. He'd do just about anything except clean, deliver mail or do repairs.

'It's a delicate story and must remain within the confines of this room. At least for now.' Goto smoothed out the wrinkles that had formed in his trouser legs and straightened his shirt cuffs as he spoke. 'We're not yet sure what we will tell everybody or when we will tell them.' He paused and fixed Kenji with his eyes. 'There is a Godzilla exhibition in Tokyo at the moment. You may have heard about it.'

'Yes,' Kenji nodded, wondering what the exhibition had to do with Abe's death. 'My son wants to go.'

'The exhibition's showpiece is a sixty-foot Godzilla replica. It was shipped over from America where it was specially made for the occasion. When the replica arrived in Tokyo it was found to be too big to transport downtown by vehicle. So it was secured by ropes to the bottom of a helicopter so that it could be flown in and deposited in the plaza outside Shibuya station where it would act as an advertisement for the event. The plan had been to fly it in the night before the opening. At midnight when there would be very few people around. Only the exhibition staff were on hand to witness Godzilla's landing and they were standing back behind the safety line. Nobody saw Abe pass the line and by the time they did and had shouted their warnings it was too late. The ropes snapped and Godzilla fell to the ground. Abe was pronounced dead upon arriving at the hospital. The life had been literally crushed out of him.'

Overcome by a strong urge to laugh, Kenji slapped one hand across his mouth and pretended to cry out in distress instead. 'That really is most terrible.' It was evident that everybody in the room was studying him intently. He had to pitch his reaction just right. He had to appear to be upset. He was, after all, supposed to be Abe's right-hand man. 'Really very terrible. We were, as you know,' he addressed the head of light entertainment, 'very close.'

'Good, I'm glad to hear that.' Jumping up, Goto clapped Kenji loudly on the back. 'Because since this incident occurred we have started to uncover some very disconcerting facts about our friend and colleague, Abe. He was in a great deal of debt. He owed money all over Tokyo. The rent on his apartment has not been paid for six months and his car is about to be repossessed. Abe had, it seems, something of a predilection for hostess bars and backroom card games.'

'When I say that we were close,' Kenji interjected uncomfortably, 'I didn't mean personally. Rather at work.'

'Yamada-san, that's even better.' Goto was talking quickly, striding back and forth across the room as everybody followed him with their eyes. 'Because his work here at Miru TV has been left in just as much of a mess as his personal affairs. If not more so. Take *Millyennaire*. Abe assured me that everything was going according to plan. That he had secured a sponsor to fund half the production costs. That he had even tempted Hana Hoshino out of retirement to present the show. Yet I can find no record of this anywhere. NBC are getting nervous. Word of Abe's death has already spread in

187

certain circles and they want reassurance that they will not be affected. If they don't get it very soon, they may pull out. I have nothing to give them. This is a very tricky situation as I'm sure you can imagine.'

'Yes of course. I understand.' Kenji nodded solemnly although he was not entirely sure if he did.

'The show is in disarray,' Takeshi Watanabe pronounced passionately. 'There is less than one month to go before filming and we have no contestant, no presenter, no sponsor. What I want to know is can he fix this mess?'

This comment appeared to mirror the sentiment of the room because everybody agreed loudly and leant in a bit closer towards Kenji.

'Fix it?' he repeated, looking down at the toaster.

'Yes,' the woman with the hand-held fan joined in. 'You were his right-hand man. You must have known what was going on.'

'Please,' Goto addressed the room calmly. 'Allow Kenji to answer in his own time.' Then turning to Kenji he asked, 'Tell me, is it as bad as it seems?'

Looking first at Goto and then at the other eleven angry faces staring at him, Kenji knew exactly what he had to do.

'Abe's record-keeping was not the best that I have ever seen.' His voice was no more than a whisper. There was a bright white light flashing behind his bad eye. The one he still covered with an eye patch and out of which he still couldn't see.

'Can somebody tell him to speak up, I can't hear a word.'

Kenji cleared his throat and spoke loudly, more clearly. 'Abe's record-keeping was not the best I have ever seen. But I can assure you that everything is under control. You are right, Abe and I did manage to tempt Ms Hoshino out of retirement. I spoke with her last week and she is very excited by the project. I am also in the final stages of negotiating with a number of sponsors.'

'Excellent,' Goto enthused as the remaining occupants of the room relaxed visibly. 'In which case you will be happy to take this forward? To pick up where Abe left off? Of course you will not be alone. You will have Mifune to help.'

For the first time, Kenji noticed Abe's assistant sitting in the corner of the room with a notepad on her lap, her legs tucked beneath the chair. He addressed the room solemnly, 'It would be my greatest pleasure.'

Part Three

THIRTY

Dunkin' Donuts was empty except for a girl in school uniform sitting in the far left-hand corner and a young man slumped across a table next to the window, a polystyrene cup of steaming coffee on the table in front of him and a glowing cigarette resting in an aluminium ashtray.

'Refill?'

'Yes, please.' Kenji sat back and allowed the waitress to pour brown liquid into his cup. She did so with apparent carelessness, allowing the hot liquid to splatter on to the table. By the time she finished pouring, the cup was so full that he had to take the first few sips without picking it up.

'Thank you,' he said politely, wiping up the drops of coffee with a paper napkin.

'I like your hair,' she said, opening and closing her mouth as she chewed on bright blue bubblegum. 'And your eye patch. I wear one too, sometimes.'

'I was in an accident.' He took a sip of coffee.

'Too bad.' Chewing furiously, she turned towards where Izo sat and tipped the coffee jug.

'No more, thank you,' Izo said, putting one hand over the top of the cup.

It was already too late. The scalding liquid flowed out of the jug and all over the back of his hand, causing him to yowl in pain.

'Hey, watch it.'

'You shouldn't have put your hand out,' she retorted, blowing an enormous blue bubble.

'You should have asked before you poured.'

She considered this suggestion before responding. 'My manager isn't here today. You won't be able to make a complaint.'

'I wouldn't dream of complaining.' Izo stood up suddenly. Startled, she staggered backwards. 'I couldn't bear for you to lose your job when you obviously bring joy into the lives of so many others.'

Izo marched off to the washroom while she went back to lounge on the counter.

Kenji lit a cigarette and took out of his pocket a magazine article he had torn from one of Eriko's magazines, unfolding the piece of paper on to the table. He had read it many times, the creases were starting to fray and he could recite the opening paragraphs word for word. The journalist promised an exposé of a woman who, twenty years previously, had been a household name – a TV presenter – but for many years shunned publicity of any kind. Once the owner of homes in Tokyo, Paris and New York; the driver of fast European sports cars and the fiancée of an up-and-coming film director, she now lived alone in an undisclosed location in Tokyo.

'I became appalled at the way in which Japan was heading,' she was quoted as having said. 'At the height of my career I was being offered obscene amounts of money to have a personal audience with men who wanted to make me their wife, or to sing at parties where men – who should have known better – were running around with girls young enough to be their daughters when they had families waiting for them at home. I tried to speak out against it, but my voice was small. So I gave up all the trappings of my success and am trying to lead a frugal life.'

The journalist's interpretation of events was much less kind. Ms Hoshino and the handsome film director, he claimed, had embraced their fame and wealth with gusto, throwing lavish parties where drugs, alcohol and sex were freely available. They enjoyed an open relationship that suited both parties until she became embroiled with a well-known political figure who had visited their home on a number of occasions. Her feelings for the politician were unrequited and it was not long before she started to make a nuisance of herself. Endless telephone calls, letters and gifts preceded a suicide attempt. And when this failed she retreated from the spotlight to lick her wounds and had never re-emerged.

This account did not give Kenji much hope. He still did not know where she lived or how he would find her, and if he did, what would she say to his proposal? No, surely. In the cold light of day his plan seemed crazier than ever. The best thing that he could do was to go and see Goto now; confess everything. But how could he? To do so would mean losing his job – again -and the respect of his family. They were all so proud of him. Everyone except Eriko, but he did not expect miracles. To admit the truth – that there was no job, never had been – was unbearable. He had to make this work. This was the opportunity that he had always been waiting for. He would rise to the challenge and show everybody who had ever doubted him what he was made of. He had to.

He kneaded his temples. His head was throbbing and a bright light was flashing in the back of his right eye, as it had been doing ever since the evening of the showdown in the boardroom. Hopeful that it was an indication that his sight might be returning, he had made an appointment with his doctor.

From behind came the sound of a closing door. Looking up, Kenji saw Izo crossing the floor towards him. The waitress, who was slouched over the counter, stared defiantly at him. He smiled sweetly and told her to cheer up.

'Any ideas?' Izo asked, throwing himself down on the blue plastic seat opposite Kenji who was studying the main photograph in the article more closely with a magnifying glass. Izo was not in the best of moods as his suitcase and its contents had just been stolen by a rival salesman who was attempting to take control of the areas he covered. It was – Kenji learned – a cut-throat business.

'You know, I've seen this picture somewhere before. I just can't remember where.' Kenji pulled the magnifying glass away from the picture as though looking at it from a distance might jog his memory. It was on the very edge of his recollection. The bright light flashed in the back of his eye and as it faded an image appeared. A black and white photograph. The very same as in the article. He squinted. There was a large, elaborate signature scrawled across the bottom of the photograph. A frame. Crystal perhaps.

'I remember now.' He beat the table with the palms of both hands – a habit he had picked up from Izo. 'It was in Inagaki's office the day that I went to see him about the job at the bank. In a frame on his desk. I knocked it over and he became very agitated.'

'Must be a fan.' Izo looked up but continued shredding the rim of his polystyrene cup. 'What am I going to do without my suitcase. I have to get it back.' He brushed the bits of polystyrene back and forth across the table.

'No, it wasn't just that. He told me at the time. I'm sure of it. Yes, that's right. He told me that he was the secretary of her fan club.'

'In that case, what are we waiting for? Let's go.' Izo stood up with the single-minded determination Kenji had come to admire.

THIRTY-ONE

'Are you ready?'

Kenji was crouched down behind a long row of multi-coloured dustbins at the back of the bank, talking to Izo, who was inside, on his mobile phone. From this position, he could just about see the post van and the driver who, as always, was lying across the front seat, listening to music on an oversized pair of headphones.

'Just give me a few minutes,' Izo instructed Kenji. 'Enough time for Inagaki to get down to the ground floor and then you can go up.'

'How long is a few minutes?'

'I don't know. Three, maybe four.'

'Okay. I'll give you four minutes precisely and then I go up. Are you ready now because I'm about to hang up? And the four minutes starts from the very second I do. Do you understand?'

The line went dead.

Their plan was that Izo would create a diversion inside the bank, demand to see the manager, while Kenji sneaked in through the back door and up to Inagaki's office. They had timed the incident to coincide with the arrival of the post van as the back door was always left open at this time and the driver was not at all vigilant. Still Kenji felt nervous. Anything could go wrong. He might be recognised. To reduce the possibility of the latter he had dressed for the occasion in a dark blue jacket and trousers of the type worn by maintenance. He was also carrying a tool box.

After exactly four minutes he stood up and, keeping close to the walls, crept into the bank through the back door. The lift was too public so he took the stairs up to the fourth floor where he looked out of the small glass window in the fire door, making sure that nobody was outside. Walking quickly along the corridor to Inagaki's office, he was relieved to find that Naoko – his secretary with the plump calves – was nowhere to be seen. She always took lunch at midday. Looking at his watch he saw that it was now 12.10. More importantly, the door to Inagaki's office was wide open and papers were spread across the desk as if he had left in a hurry.

Closing the door behind him, Kenji walked stealthily towards the desk where, as he had remembered, Hana Hoshino's photograph sat in a crystal-glass frame. He put on a pair of gloves – Izo had laughed, but Kenji insisted – and picked up the frame. Inscribed across the photo were the words: 'Thank you for all your kindness.' He put the frame back in exactly the same position and then sat down on Inagaki's chair. Tucked beneath the desk there was a small filing cabinet. He pulled at the first drawer but it would not open. None of them would. He stood up. Three grey steel filing cabinets were arranged in a row behind the desk and he tried each one in quick succession. They all opened but contained reports and documents relating to the bank.

Kenji returned to the small cabinet beneath the desk. Whatever he needed – and he wasn't sure yet – was in there. He was certain of it. He began searching for the key. Was it taped to the underside of the table, in the pencil tidy or plant pot? It was nowhere to be found. Then he had an idea. Picking up the frame he tried to remove the back, but his hands were shaking too much. He checked his watch – it was now 12.14. Time was running out. He had promised Izo that he would be in and out of the office as quickly as possible. He had also promised him that he wouldn't leave empty-handed.

He fumbled with the frame until the back came away and a small key fell out, exactly the right size to fit a filing cabinet. He tried the key in the lock. It turned. He pulled the top drawer out and almost shouted with glee when he found each file referred to Ms Hoshino: her discography, press cuttings, fan club membership. Losing no time, he went directly to a file marked 'letters' and pulled one out. It was handwritten, signed by her and had an address scribbled across the top right-hand corner of the page. The address was in a run-down part of Tokyo, which struck Kenji as odd. Why would she be living in a place like that, he wondered? But every letter bore the same address so after taking a photocopy of one, he returned it to its folder and locked the cabinet. He replaced the key and, making sure that everything was left in exactly the same position as he had found it, he opened the door, hurried out into the hallway and down the stairs.

As he approached the back door on the ground floor he froze. Soga was standing there, just about to close it, his back more painfully hunched than Kenji remembered it to be. What was he going to do now? If he got locked in then he was done for. He no longer had his key and people would want to know what he had been doing here in the first place. There would be questions, accusations and suspicions.

Turning around, Soga saw Kenji. If he was surprised, he did not show it. 'Some people should really lock these things,' he said, leaving the door on the latch and walking off, 'anybody could get in.'

Kenji marvelled at just how lucky he had been and passed through the open door into the sunshine.

THIRTY-TWO

Both sides of the street were lined with games parlours, adult video shops, magazine shops and hostess bars. He tried hard not to look in through the doors, but their sights and sounds spilled out on to the narrow street and when Izo stopped to ask a fat man with damp patches underneath both arms for directions, Kenji was forced to stand in front of a rack of videos. The covers depicted young women in various states of undress, but always with the same surprised expression on their face. He turned away, thankful that the more explicit images had been blurred out.

They moved on down the street. Bags of rubbish had been dumped outside the shops and large brown rats were rummaging through them. Horrified, Kenji watched as one beast with an enormous pregnant belly, dragged a half-empty take-away box across to the other side of the road, while another disappeared down an alleyway with a worn tennis shoe. The rubbish had been festering in the hot sunlight for days and, together with the drains, gave off a rancid, sulphuric smell. Reaching into his pocket he withdrew a clean handkerchief and, holding it over his mouth and nose, inhaled the smell of fabric conditioner.

Neither he nor Izo had said a word to each other since leaving the station, although Kenji suspected that they were both thinking the very same thing. This cannot be where she lives. At the height of her fame Hana Hoshino had featured in the lists of Japan's wealthiest.

So how, he wondered, had she sunk so low? He had imagined her tucked away in a modest, but tidy apartment; venturing out in headscarf and sunglasses for her grocery shopping; involved in charity work; older but still elegant and conducting herself with dignity. Of course, the address he had lifted from Inagaki's office might be wrong. Perhaps it was simply a correspondence address and she did not actually live there.

'Here we are.'

Izo had stopped and was looking up at a small apartment block. Its walls were covered with turquoise tiles and a dark green moss grew over the grouting. The ground floor of the building had been extended into a patio across which were arranged boxes of fruit and vegetables, pot plants, trinkets and lucky charms. An old man was sitting in the corner of the porch on a rocking chair that creaked loudly as it rolled back and forth across the wooden boards. He stared at them through the porch windows.

'Are you sure?' Kenji grabbed the piece of paper from Izo's hand.

'Apartment four, it says here. I guess she must live above the shop.'

'How do we get in?' Kenji looked from one side of the building to the other. There were no stairs or alleyway to be seen.

'It must be through the shop.' Izo pushed him gently towards the building. 'You go first. I don't like the look of that guy.'

The steps leading up to the patio creaked loudly beneath Kenji's weight. Inside it was dark, humid and musty.

'We're looking for apartment four.' A fly buzzed around his head as he spoke. He flicked it away but it came back immediately.

The old man pointed at a half-open door opposite the one through which they had just entered.

'Thank you,' Kenji said and bent down to pick up as many apples as he could carry from a box on the floor. 'How much?'

'One thousand yen,' the old man answered, half-rising out of his chair.

Kenji gave him a five-thousand yen note and walked away.

Beyond the patio was a hallway. A single door led off the right-hand side and stairs ran up the wall on the left. They took the stairs, climbing to the fourth floor, and stopped outside the only door. A name was written on a piece of paper that had been taped just beneath the bell but, faded with age, was now unreadable. Knuckle-shaped chips were missing from the door in several places and the area surrounding the lock was heavily scratched. They said nothing to each other, uncertain what to do, as a young man came sliding down the banister from the fifth floor, ran past them and slid down the banister to the third. A baby was crying somewhere behind a closed door and the smell of boiled rice hung in the air.

'Go on,' Izo whispered encouragingly. Kenji reached out, withdrew his hand, reached out again and then rang the bell. Several seconds passed in silence so he rang it again. This time the sound of movement came from inside the apartment followed by a voice screaming: 'I thought I told you to go away.' Startled, he contemplated running as quickly as possible in the direction from which they had come but just then the door flew open and a woman appeared. Although much altered, there was no denying that the person standing in front of them was Hana Hoshino.

'Hoshino-san.' Kenji spoke first. He tried to keep his eyes on her face, but he could not help but take in the former TV presenter's stained, blue satin dressing gown. It hung open at the waist to reveal a matching nightdress and an emaciated frame. Her collarbones jutted out at a sharp angle, paper-thin skin stretched across them forming a concave at the bottom of her throat.

'Who are you?' she slurred. In one hand she clasped a tall, thin glass containing a clear liquid. The ice cubes in it clinked lightly as she spoke.

Kenji looked at Izo. They had agreed Izo would do most, if not all, of the talking. There was, after all, no woman in Japan who could resist his charms. Or so he claimed. But when Kenji turned to his friend he observed an expression entirely new to him. Izo was terrified.

'What do I say to her?' he hissed. 'I don't know what to say to her.'

As he watched Izo struggling, Kenji knew he had to act. He had to muster up enough courage to speak to her and he had to get it right. 'This may seem crazy but . . .'

Before he could finish, Hoshino screeched loudly, 'I have no money. If it's money you're after I've got nothing. It's all gone. Gone for good.'

Her hair had been wrapped round large rollers and pinned in place. While most sat securely, some had partially unravelled, forming heavy ringlets that bounced off the side of her face as she swayed, struggling to maintain her balance, in the doorway.

'No,' Kenji soothed, 'it's not money that we want. I want to talk to you about a TV programme that I am making. I would like you to present it. The network would like you to present it.'

She did not appear to have heard him. Bottom lip trembling, her eyes filled with tears that threatened to wash away her false eyelashes, one of which was already sitting on her cheekbone like a spider. 'Every last yen. Gone. Gone for good.'

Izo leaned across and whispered in Kenji's ear, 'Look, I think we'd better go. We can come back another time. When she's not so . . . so drunk.'

'Leave? But we've just got here.'

'I know, but look at her. She's not making any sense.'

Reluctantly, Kenji agreed and after bidding Hoshino goodbye they turned to leave.

'Where are you going? I didn't say that you could go anywhere.' Reaching out to grab Kenji's shoulder, Hoshino forgot she was holding a glass and it fell to the floor. The glass shattered and the clear liquid spread out into a viscous puddle. Dropping on to her knees, she made a half-hearted attempt to pick up the shards scattered about the worn linoleum.

'Please, you'll cut yourself.' Grabbing her bony shoulders, Kenji attempted to haul Hoshino up.

'Get away from me.' She struck out at him. 'Who do you think you are, touching me like this? Do you have any idea who I am?'

'Please, you must get up.' Ignoring her protests Kenji pulled her into a standing position and turned to Izo. 'Help me get her inside.'

Izo looked horrified. 'I can't. I mean look at her. She's . . . she's drunk. In a few minutes she'll start crying and screaming. If there's one thing I can't stand it's to see a woman cry.' He shuddered, visibly upset.

'Oh go then, go. I can manage on my own for all the help you've been,' he snapped, exasperated.

He didn't need to be told twice and as Izo ran down the stairs, Kenji struggled to help Hoshino into her apartment. They went down a narrow corridor, the left-hand side of which acted as a galley kitchen. As they squeezed by, Kenji put the bag of apples down on the counter. Beyond the kitchen was a small studio containing a single futon on a low beech frame, a small round table with a single chair, and a large dresser on top of which sat a portable television and miniature CD player. Every square inch of the walls in the apartment were adorned with framed pictures of a younger, smiling Hoshino surrounded by admiring fans, many of whom were famous in their own right: actors and actresses, soap stars, classical musicians and politicians. There was even a photograph of Hoshino shaking hands with a former prime minister. Handling her all the more carefully because of this, Kenji eased her tiny frame down into the small chair at the round table. When he turned her hands over, so that her palms were facing upwards, he moaned – 'Oh no.' They were bloodied where the glass had pierced the flesh.

'I'll get a cloth.' He started to panic. What if she had really hurt herself? Needed stitches? She would surely blame him. 'Where's the bathroom?'

Looking up at him like a small child, she pointed towards the end of the corridor.

The bathroom was tiny. He had to close the door, standing pinned to the wall, just to use the sink and when he turned on the hot tap, overhead pipes screeched, propelling a murky brown liquid into the basin. It took several seconds to clear and while he waited, Kenji searched for a small bowl to which he added a few drops of disinfectant. He rinsed and wrung dry a grubby, white hand towel that hung from a rack above the toilet. Filling the bowl with water, he turned the tap off and tried to determine the best way to squeeze out of the bathroom while carrying the bowl, cloth and packet of plasters he had found. Overhead the pipes grumbled and then

204

quietened down. In their place was the sound of raised voices. At first he thought that they were coming from another apartment. Then he realised that one of the voices belonged to Hoshino.

'I told you I have no money,' she sobbed.

'We told you that you have a week to pay or we'll have to think of another way to extract the money.' This time the voice was male: deep and menacing.

Kenji panicked. What should he do? The voices were quite evidently not friendly and if he stayed in the bathroom, didn't move a muscle or make a sound, then whoever was outside would have no reason to know that he was here. But what if the owner of the voice intended Hoshino harm? Could he really stay here and listen to it happen? Would he ever forgive himself if he did? I have to go to her, he resolved, putting down the bowl and bandages. He flung open the door and propelled himself out and down the corridor, picking up the first thing he saw and could use to defend Hoshino.

'What do you think you're doing?' he shouted. 'Take your hands off her.'

There were two men in the apartment: both extremely well dressed and standing over the chair in which Hoshino was cowering. One of the men was stroking the side of her face with his right hand while the other watched.

'Who's this then?' one of the men asked, turning to Kenji. 'You didn't tell us that you had company.'

Hoshino did not reply, just sobbed as the man stroked her face with his fat hand. He wore a thick gold band on his little finger.

'Leave her alone.' Kenji spoke clearly, sounding braver than he felt. But the man did not stop stroking Hoshino's face, even though his hand was now wet with her tears.

'What are you going to do about it?'

'Leave her alone this very minute.'

Both men laughed and it was as though the sound tripped a switch inside Kenji's brain. He no longer felt frightened or intimidated. He just felt very angry and determined to do something about it.

'I'm sick of people like you. Charging into people's lives. Thinking that they can do as they please. Treating people how they like. Well you can't, you just can't.' Raising his right arm, he aimed and threw the missile that he was carrying at the man stroking Hoshino's face. His aim was good, better than he could have hoped for. The apple hit the man straight in the chest and because it was completely rotten, exploded on impact, smattering the fawn Italian fabric of his suit with its brown flesh.

'Look at what you've done.'

The man with the fat fingers stared down at his chest as his friend advanced. Kenji threw another apple. This time aiming for the man's smile but catching his bulbous nose instead.

'Get out. Now,' he shouted, throwing the rest of the rotten apples at their feet where they exploded, splattering their expensive Italian leather shoes.

'Okay, okay. We're going.'

The two men edged out past Kenji, both wiping down their clothes with handkerchiefs. At the end of the corridor they turned to look back.

'This won't be the last you hear from us.'

The door slammed shut behind them.

The apartment was silent. Several seconds passed before Hoshino looked up at him. Tears streaked the white powder that covered her face. She looked incredulous. He shrugged helplessly. What could he say when he was shocked by his own behaviour. Where had all that anger come from? Then she smiled. At first it was only the briefest hint of a smile and then it widened into a broad grin. Soon she was laughing and he found himself joining in with her; laughing so loud and for so long that eventually his belly began to ache.

'I can't believe you just did that,' she spluttered. She seemed very, very sober now.

'I don't know what came over me.'

'Do you have any idea how well connected those people are? And you threw rotten apples at them?'

'It was the first thing that came to hand.' He liked to see her smile. When she smiled it reminded him of the Hana Hoshino he had admired as a young man.

Then, as suddenly as she had started laughing, she stood up and pulled the blue dressing gown around her. 'If you'll excuse me for a moment.' She walked carefully down the corridor and disappeared into the bathroom, emerging a few minutes later, face washed clean and wearing a fresh gown. She swayed slightly as she walked, and had to lean against the walls for balance, but was evidently more coherent than when he had first arrived. 'I must give you something for your trouble.' She blustered around the apartment, opening and closing drawers, picking up piles of paper. 'But I have no money. A signed photo perhaps?' She opened the door of the cabinet running along one side of the room and removed a thick brown envelope. It was filled with black and white signed photographs. She removed one and handed it to him. It was the same black and white print that Inagaki had on his desk. Scrawled across the bottom was the message: thank you for all your kindness.

'That is very kind, but really what I wanted . . . Why I came here today . . . Was to ask you to present a TV programme that I am making.' He liked the way that he sounded. He felt confident, in control.

'Ah yes, your TV programme.' She looked vague. 'Tell me about it.'

Which he did as they sipped the hot, sweet tea that she made for them.

'I agree that it sounds like an unusual show. Very exciting. But I . . . I couldn't possibly present a TV programme. I mean, look at me. I'm not the beauty I once was.'

'You're as lovely as you ever were.'

She laughed self-consciously. 'I'm in a lot of trouble. I have taken out many loans to finance projects. A chat show to re-launch my television career. Acting lessons. Plastic surgery even. None of which worked. Now they . . . the people who loaned me the money want it back. I am nothing but trouble.'

'We would pay you to appear. We could pay off your debts.'

'You could do that for me?'

'Yes, I'm sure we could.' Kenji was not at all sure. NBC were very much sold on the idea of getting Hoshino out of retirement to present the show. It was on this basis that they had agreed to part-fund the project. But would they want to pay off her debts too? Was there any other way? 'How much do you owe?' When she told him, he tried hard not to look shocked. 'Well, in that case we have a deal.'

They had another cup of green tea to mark the occasion.

THIRTY-THREE

A warm orange glow filled the kitchen as the afternoon sunlight streamed in through a small square window above the sink. A cup of black coffee – now cold – sat in the middle of the table where Kenji was slumped, his forehead resting on the brown-chequered tablecloth as his feet beat out a slow, monotonous rhythm on the floor.

It was Saturday: one of the few days of the week when the apartment was empty. The children were at their lessons – he did not know which ones. Ami was buying cloth in Tokyo and Eriko was shopping with her friend Wami Inagaki. As he sat there, staring at the brown squares, Kenji marvelled at the sense of euphoria that had gripped him yesterday evening as he left Hoshino's apartment. It took until this morning before reality hit and in place of the euphoria came a creeping, cold, dark fear. What had made him promise her Miru TV would pay off her debts? *Millyennaire* was entirely dependent on finding a suitable sponsor to match NBC's contribution, and no matter how many times he went through Abe's records, he could not find a mention of one anywhere. If there was no sponsor there was no show. Unless of course he could find one himself.

Worse still, in a fit of excitement, he had telephoned Goto last night. Hoshino had been signed, he'd claimed. His work on the sponsor was progressing nicely and he fully expected an agreement to be in place by the end of the week. Goto's enthusiasm had taken him by surprise and it was all that Kenji could do to rein in Goto's plans for launching the show.

The apartment door opened and closed. Kenji looked up. Eriko was making her way into the kitchen, pulling a shopping trolley behind her which creaked and rocked. Since winning the chilli red Toyota Celica she had, if it was possible, become more unbearable than ever. She had sold the car using some of the cash to pay off outstanding debts and put some towards a modest family holiday later that year. The rest she had put to one side 'in case anything happens to me or . . .' She had looked in Kenji's direction. '. . . to him.'

'What are you doing just sitting there, wasting space?' she muttered, removing a brown paper bag of carrots – the green leafy tips were poking out of the top – from her shopping trolley.

Ami had told her many times not to buy fruit and vegetables from the neighbourhood shops, that they were of an inferior quality and did not last more than a few days. But Eriko insisted she was getting a bargain and her daughter should not pay the extortionate supermarket prices.

'Thinking about your TV shows?' she mocked.

'You won't be laughing when I tell you who I met yesterday,' he retorted angrily and regretted it immediately because now the old woman's attention was focused solely on him. Usually he did not discuss work at home. His family had no idea what it was that he did every day and it was better that way. Should anything go wrong, which seemed likely, then there would be fewer expectations to shatter. But Eriko's comments had infuriated him. Just once he wanted to prove her wrong. To show her that, contrary to what she might think, he was capable of being a successful producer.

'What do you mean?' she demanded. Ami had applied a perm to Eriko's grey hair last night and the curls on her head were tight and unyielding.

'A former television presenter. She used to have her own chat show, but that was a number of years ago. Fifteen, I'd say. If not more.' He knew that this description was more than adequate. Eriko had been an admirer of Hoshino's shows when they were first screened in the 1980s and still watched the re-runs on TV.

Her forehead creased into a frown as she clasped a bag of runner beans to her chest. 'I don't believe you.'

'It's true,' he shrugged nonchalantly. It was enjoyable, teasing the old woman, and he was disappointed when the intercom buzzed and he had to get up to answer it. 'Hello,' he said into the mouthpiece.

'It's me, Izo. Can I come in?'

'What do you want?' Any sense of fun that he had felt immediately drained away. He had not forgiven Izo for deserting him yesterday. The walk back to the station from Hoshino's apartment had been even worse than the walk there. Not just because he was alone, but because twilight was quite obviously the time when the surrounding streets really came to life.

'Come on, my friend. I'm sorry about last night. Let me in. I want to know how things went.'

Reluctantly, Kenji hit the red button to open the apartment door. Izo appeared, seconds later, carrying a familiar battered brown leather suitcase.

'You got it back?' Despite himself, Kenji could not help but feel happy for him.

'I did. It was empty though. But that didn't really get me down.' He smiled encouragingly. 'Because from now on I'm going to start making my own merchandise. Wait till you see this.' Laying his suitcase ceremoniously on the floor, he opened it and removed a knife with a sharp blade and a small battery pack attached to the wooden handle. Thin metal arms extended from the handle to the blade and when he turned the battery on, the blade moved in and out of the handle with a cutting action. 'It's a steak knife. For the diner who doesn't want to have to cut the meat himself.' The battery died and the blade stopped moving.

Kenji frowned.

'Of course it's not quite perfected yet. But give me time. I'll do it. I almost forgot. This is for you.' Izo grabbed something from inside

211

the suitcase and handed Kenji a gift-wrapped parcel that looked and felt like a book.

Slightly embarrassed, Kenji hesitated. He had nothing to give Izo in return.

'Please open it. It's a book. An apology for running out on you last night.'

Ripping off the delicate tissue paper, Kenji revealed the front cover of *Japan's Best Ever TV Shows*. He smiled. 'Thank you. It's very kind of you.'

'Hey.' Izo looked over Kenji's shoulder and spotting Eriko hovering in the kitchen, lowered his voice. 'How did it go last night?'

'She agreed.'

'That's fantastic.'

'Is it? I promised her money, money to pay off her debts and I don't know if I'll be able to raise it.'

Izo put a reassuring arm around Kenji's shoulder. 'Come on. Make me a coffee and we'll come up with something.'

As they made their way towards the kitchen, the apartment door through which Izo had just come, opened once more. Kenji turned to see Ami enter, followed by the children. Both of them carrying a shopping bag in each hand.

'Yoshi, leave your bags on the floor and get the last one from the car.' As she instructed her son, Ami walked the full length of the hallway, eyeing her husband's companion with distrust. 'Hello,' she said coolly, but spotting the brown paper bags Eriko was unpacking from her trolley, quickly forgot about Izo. 'Mother,' she muttered, putting her bags down on the kitchen table, 'have you been buying rotten vegetables again?'

It was evident that Ami suspected Izo of being a former pachinko associate, so Kenji lost no time in introducing him. 'This is my friend Izo Izumi. He has called by to help me with the show.'

Assuming that this meant he was a colleague of Kenji's from Miru TV, Ami immediately thawed. 'I get to meet so few of my husband's colleagues and he is always so secretive about work. We never know what he gets up to. Perhaps you will tell us.'

'Top secret, I'm afraid.' Izo shook his head and Ami laughed, almost flirtatiously.

'Why don't you men sit down. Let me move those bags. There, that's better. Now can I get you anything? Coffee perhaps?'

'Kenji was just about to make some.'

'Please, let me. You must get on with your work and I promise not to listen.'

The moment Ami turned her back on the kitchen table and began unpacking the shopping bags, Eriko sidled up beside her, whispering in her ear.

'Mother, please, I'm busy,' Ami snapped loudly. 'I can't hear you anyway. You'll have to speak up. Don't be so silly. Kenji – ' She turned to face her husband. 'Mother says that you are trying to make her look foolish by claiming to have met Hana Hoshino yesterday.'

Kenji and Izo exchanged a long look. 'It's true,' they both said in unison, squeezing their chairs further under the kitchen table as the twins struggled to get past with yet more shopping bags. Soon there would be no room left in the tiny kitchen. Even if Kenji had wanted to get up and leave he couldn't have done so. He was completely hemmed in.

'Oh my.' A hot flush appeared on Ami's neck and spread quickly up to her face. 'Imagine that.'

'What is it?' Yumi asked.

'Your father met a very important person yesterday, which means that he must be very important.' Taking the shopping bag from her daughter, Ami put it down on the counter.

'You don't believe him, do you?' Eriko demanded as Yumi began jumping up and down on the spot singing, 'Daddy's famous. Daddy's famous.'

Watching his sister with distaste, Yoshi muttered, 'Don't be so stupid. Stop that now.'

As the sound of the voices around him grew and grew – people shouting to make themselves heard, interrupting each other – Kenji's head started to pound. The kitchen was starting to feel hot and stuffy. He needed to get out, get some fresh air. But the twins

213

were standing immediately behind him, bickering and he was stuck.

'Who did he meet?'

'Somebody very important.'

'Who's very important?'

'I sincerely hope that you're talking about me.'

It took a split second before the Yamadas realised that the voice – female and softly spoken with perfect diction, almost as if she had been trained to speak like that – did not belong to one of them. Everybody went quiet, stopped whatever they were doing and turned to look at where Hoshino was standing in the kitchen doorway.

'I hope you don't mind,' she said with a coquettish smile, 'the door was open.'

Everybody stared at her. Nobody moved or said a word. It was several seconds before Kenji realised his mouth was slightly agape and he snapped it shut. Never before in his life had he seen such real-life glamour and here it was in his kitchen.

Eriko was the first to speak. 'I must make a phone call,' she apologised, fighting her way out of the kitchen.

Ami regained her composure. 'It is a pleasure to meet you, Hoshino-san. I am humbled that you would come to our home, if not slightly embarrassed. You find us in something of a mess, I'm afraid. I am Ami Yamada. I believe that you met my husband yesterday. Please can I take your coat?'

'Thank you.' Hoshino removed her coat, revealing a brightly patterned dress and silk head scarf, placing them across Ami's out-stretched arms. She also took off her large sunglasses. 'The pleasure is mine. Your husband has done me a great service.'

Everybody looked at Kenji. He knew they were expecting him to say something, but he found himself unable to speak. The woman who stood in front of him had not simply had a make-over, she had had a make-back, almost becoming the celebrity she once was.

In the ensuing silence, Ami left the room. When she returned a few seconds later, she pressed Hoshino to take a seat at the table with Kenji and Izo.

'How about a drink? Some coffee, tea, cakes? Mother.' She clapped her hands together until the old lady appeared. 'Help me see to our guests.' Turning to address Hoshino, she enquired, 'Perhaps your colleagues in the hallway would like to sit in the living room?'

'Colleagues?' Kenji asked suspiciously, standing up and looking out into the corridor where the same two men that had been in Hoshino's apartment last night were squeezed. 'What are they doing here?' he demanded angrily.

'Kenji, don't be so rude,' Ami chastised.

Reaching across the table, Hoshino patted Kenji's hand lightly with her own. 'Please don't worry yourself. It's okay. They're my bodyguards.' Giggling, she whispered conspiratorially, 'I called their boss last night after you left and explained my situation. That I was hoping to pay off my debts very soon. He was keen to protect his investment, you might say, and sent the boys over this morning to look after me. We've had an enormous amount of fun ever since. Haven't we, boys?'

She looked at the two oversized men in the Yamadas' hallway. They did not react. Their expressions remained virtually unreadable. Not just because of the lack of any light in the hallway but also because of the sunglasses that they were wearing.

'We've even been shopping.' She stood up and performed a small twirl. The hem of her dress flew out in a high circle before she collapsed into the chair. 'I can add it to my existing debt, you see and I do need a new wardrobe if I'm going to be a star again.'

'Hoshino, we need to talk.' Kenji leant across the table, laying both palms flat on the surface. 'There's something I need to tell you.'

'Kenji, please,' Ami tutted loudly as she laid out her best china in front of him.

Again, Hoshino laid one hand over Kenji's. Her skin felt cold and smooth and he noticed that she was wearing an enormous diamond ring. 'I can't thank you enough for what you have done for me. You have given me hope. Yesterday all was bleak. Today it is bright.'

'Excuse me,' Izo coughed politely. 'Hoshino-san, we met briefly yesterday.'

'Did we?'

'Yes. I'm Izo Izumi. Kenji's personal advisor, you might say.'

'Lovely,' she smiled, tucked a stray curl under her head scarf and adjusted her sunglasses.

'There may be a problem.' Kenji did not want to lie to her. He did not want to promise her anything that he could not deliver. But before he could say another word, Izo kicked him fiercely in the shin. 'Owww,' he yowled. 'What was that for?'

'Is there something the matter?' Hoshino looked anxiously at Kenji.

'Kenji just wanted to tell you,' Izo interjected, 'how excited he is to be working with a professional such as yourself.'

'I . . .'

'It concerns him that he will not be able to maintain such high standards as you are used to.'

'Never.' Hoshino appeared aghast at the very idea, but before she could say another word the intercom buzzed.

'My, it is a busy house today.' Putting the coffee pot down on the table, Ami went to answer the door, fighting her way out of the kitchen and past the two enormous men that blocked the corridor. 'I'll just be one minute.'

A few seconds later a small, croaky voice could be heard calling, 'Let me through. Room for a little one.'

As far as was possible, Hoshino's bodyguards flattened themselves up against the wall, allowing Wami to squeeze past them. Limping slowly behind her was her son.

'Mother, what do you think you're doing? We can't just charge in here like this,' he was saying.

'You said that you wanted to meet her, didn't you?' the old woman shot back. 'Now here's your chance. So do as I say and I don't want to hear another word out of you.'

'You're mistaken if you think she's here,' Inagaki spat angrily. 'I've already told you that this is bound to be another one of his ruses to . . .' He broke off upon entering the kitchen and looked for the first time, at least in the flesh, into the smiling face of Hoshino.

'And who is this handsome man?' she asked demurely.

THIRTY-FOUR

'Dad, I don't want to go to sleep,' Yoshi whined, rubbing his eyes with a balled-up fist while suppressing a yawn. 'I'm not tired.'

'It's late.' Kenji spoke firmly, bending down and brushing back his son's hair to reveal a jagged scar on his forehead that he kissed lightly. 'I have important things that I need to sort out. And you need to go to sleep.'

The scar dated back to an incident that had happened when Yoshi was four years old. Ami had gone out shopping, taking Yumi with her and asking Kenji to look after Yoshi so that she wouldn't have both children pulling at her while she bought groceries. Kenji and Yoshi had been sitting at the kitchen table, Yoshi drawing in his book, Kenji looking on, occupied and thinking about work. Some thought had occurred to him. What that thought had been, he couldn't now remember, although it was almost certainly an idea for a TV programme because he had jumped up to look for his notebook, convinced that if he didn't write his idea down at that very second he would forget it. He hunted all through the apartment for the notebook but couldn't find it anywhere. Then he heard a chilling scream that made him stop what he was doing and rush back into the kitchen. Yoshi had been standing on a chair, trying to reach a carton of juice on the kitchen counter, and had fallen and hit his head on the corner of the table. When Kenji reached him, his body felt limp and Kenji was terrified he was dead. Kenji had taken

Yoshi to hospital where he was subjected to several tests but was soon given the all-clear and sent home the next day. When Kenji and his wife were alone together in bed later that night, Ami had been barely able to contain her anger. Where had he been? What had he been doing when he was supposed to be looking after his son? Kenji had never been any good at lying and it didn't occur to him to tell anything other than the truth. When he told her, she shook her head. When was he ever going to get it into his head that he was an ordinary salaryman with a family to look after, she asked, not some hotshot TV producer. After that she rarely left him alone with the children and Kenji felt it was safer to leave anything that related to them to her. And he did not mention his dream of becoming a TV producer ever again.

The scar had faded with time, though was still visible now. After he kissed his son goodnight, Kenji turned on the small mushroom-shaped lamp next to Yoshi's bed, which cast a warm, pink glow over his son who reluctantly settled down. Yumi was already fast asleep in the room next door – arms thrown up above her head like a ballet dancer. So as not to wake her, Kenji tip-toed along the length of the hallway, breaking into a light-footed run when the telephone started to ring.

'Hello.' He turned away from the laughter and chatter that was coming from both the living room and the kitchen. 'Mifune-san? Yes, this is Kenji.'

He listened carefully as Abe's former assistant explained that Goto had scheduled a press conference to launch *Millyennaire* at the Cerulean Tower Hotel. It would take place tomorrow. A room had been booked at the hotel for Hoshino, and Kenji was to make certain that she arrived safely and help prepare her. It had been some time since Hoshino had appeared on TV and Goto wanted to feel confident that she was up to the job and would make a good impression.

'This is all very fast,' Kenji muttered, kneading his forehead. He had expected more time. Much more time.

'Goto is adamant,' Mifune explained, 'that this project should get underway as quickly as possible.'

'Yes,' Kenji replied, agreeing that he would get Hoshino to the hotel and ensure that she was prepared. To be fully prepared, however, she would have to know the truth. His conscience would not allow him to stand by and watch as she got herself further into debt: spending money that was not hers on fur coats and diamonds. Feeling clearer in his own mind that this was the right thing to do, Kenji headed to the kitchen, pausing momentarily at the sitting-room door.

Ami pushed past him, carrying a tray of drinks. Grabbing her lightly by the elbow, he stopped her. 'Your mother,' he whispered, nodding at the scene unfolding inside the room. 'Look at her.'

'Busy, busy, busy,' Ami sang out shrilly.

Instinctively he knew that it was not irritation that heightened her voice, but happiness. Playing the accommodating hostess clearly suited her. Especially when there was a celebrity amongst the guests. Perhaps most surprising of all was that it did not seem to alarm Ami that inside the sitting room, her mother and Wami were playing cards with Hoshino's two enormous minders. Kenji watched as his wife happily topped up the two women's empty glasses with freshly made lemonade and removed the men's empty beer bottles, replacing them with fresh ones. That they had not been using the coasters she provided did not seem to bother her even though he would have been severely chastised for such behaviour.

'I win again,' Eriko announced, laying her cards face up with a flourish and sweeping the pile of matches that had built up in the centre of the table towards her already sizeable pile. 'Go on.' She looked at the two minders, their large frames perched uncomfortably on the edge of the canary yellow sofa. 'Deal another hand.'

Wami sucked air sharply through her teeth, while the two bodyguards shook their heads from side to side.

How exactly this had happened, Kenji was not sure. It wasn't just the card game that perplexed him, but the fact that his home was filled with all these different people. He could not remember a time when there had been so many gathered here together. If indeed there ever had been. Then it hit him. They were here because of him. 'I am the reason,' he said out loud and it sounded both wonderful and terrifying. Adjusting his eyepatch, he left Eriko to her game and continued to the kitchen where he found Izo lingering, just outside the doorway.

'Can you believe this?' he whispered. 'A star in your kitchen. In your own home.'

Kenji nodded. 'I'm very lucky.'

'Lucky? Luck has nothing to do with it. You deserve it.' Izo turned around to face him. 'You're not going to do anything foolish, are you?'

'What do you mean?'

Izo whispered, 'Tell her about the sponsor. That you haven't got one.'

'I have to. It's the only honest thing to do. But,' he shrugged, 'if things go well tomorrow then it may no longer be an issue.'

'What's happening tomorrow?' Izo frowned.

'A press conference.' Kenji touched Doppo's St Christopher medal. 'I've got a good feeling about it as well. I don't know why, but I'm certain we're going to find a sponsor.'

'Glad to hear it. Now listen to this.' Izo nodded in the direction of the kitchen. 'I think we've got a love match.'

Looking inside, Kenji witnessed the sight to which Izo was referring. Sitting on one side of the table was Hoshino who had removed her head scarf, revealing long, loose curls. Opposite her, both elbows resting on the table and chin balanced on the palms of his hands, was Inagaki. His hair had been swept back with a considerable amount of styling gel but under the heat of the kitchen lamp, it had started to wilt and kept falling into his face. Sweeping it back, he never for a second allowed his brown, adoring eyes to leave Hoshino's face.

'Tell me again about the time that you met Prime Minister Nakasone,' he begged. 'What questions did you ask? What did you wear? What did he say to you?'

Kenji found it disconcerting to see the usually rigid bank manager behave like this. That he was even capable of appearing so relaxed and content was a surprise.

Hoshino sipped on a glass of lemonade. Although it was not very obvious, Kenji noticed that her hand was shaking.

'Again?' she feigned mock surprise. 'You must be bored of the story by now.'

'Never,' he exclaimed loudly. 'Every time you tell it I learn something new. A detail that was forgotten in the last telling. A jewel that you wore. A compliment that was passed. So please tell me again.'

'Well.' Picking up a piece of watermelon with a toothpick, Hoshino nibbled on it. As she ate, she retold her story, addressing not only Inagaki, but also Kenji and Izo. Looking at each of them in turn, her curls bounced lightly off her shoulders. It was almost as if Inagaki found this breaking of her gaze painful and whenever she looked away he would call her back to him with some question or other.

When she had finally finished her story, silence descended upon the kitchen. Suppressing a yawn, Hoshino made to stand up.

'I have outstayed my welcome. It is time for me to go.'

Inagaki looked stricken. 'Don't go, not yet.' He cast a cautious glance in Kenji's direction. 'How can you leave when you haven't told me about this new TV programme that you're going to appear in?'

'Perhaps my associate is in a better position to explain,' she said, inclining her head in Kenji's direction.

'I'm glad that you mentioned the TV programme.' Kenji deliberately avoided Izo's stare. 'I need to tell you something, Hoshino-san. You should be aware that we do not yet have a backer for the show. NBC have offered to meet half of the production budget. I must find a sponsor for the other half. If not the entire project will fail.'

Her face crumpled revealing for the first time today the worn face that Kenji had met yesterday.

Her disappointment pained him and he tried hard to lighten the mood. 'There is a risk we will not find one. I cannot lie to you. But there is a press conference organised for midday tomorrow and I am very hopeful.'

She looked troubled. 'Tomorrow. So soon.'

'At the Cerulean Tower Hotel. I am certain that this will be the ideal opportunity for me to find a sponsor. Many influential people have been invited to attend.' He thought of the long list that Mifune had reeled off over the phone. 'With your charm and good looks we will not fail.'

'But I am not ready. What will I wear? My hair, my make-up.'

'Don't worry.' Ami appeared at Kenji's shoulder. 'I can help. And I do believe I have the perfect outfit for you. It will suit your colouring exactly.'

'You will be in the hands of a very talented seamstress.' Inagaki patted Hoshino's hand reassuringly. 'And there are many people who would be very interested in a project of this kind. People who have means. I'm sure that Yamada-san will be able to find them. Won't you, Yamada-san?' He glared pointedly at Kenji who, in that second, saw the return of the same rigid man that he was used to.

THIRTY-FIVE

Reaching down, Kenji grabbed his wife's hand. Holding on to it firmly, he negotiated their way towards the exit. Outside the station he paused, allowing them both to catch their breath. Ami smiled up at him. Shyly, or so he thought. The heat caused by so many bodies pressed up together in one train carriage had flushed her cheeks. Letting go of her husband's hand she removed a small, battery-operated fan from her handbag – a gift from Izo – and held it in front of her face for several seconds as the blades struggled to turn in one direction and then the next, before flopping limply down to the side of the base unit. They both laughed. She returned the fan to her handbag and patted her hair self-consciously.

'You look lovely.' Kenji spoke softly and grabbed his wife's now empty hand again. The arrival of Hana Hoshino last night seemed to have given his marriage a new and much needed lease of life. All morning he had felt like a new husband: always touching and glancing admiringly at Ami, cooing compliments. 'Just like a lovesick dove,' he thought, smiling to himself, before turning and walking swiftly across the bus lanes that ran alongside the station. In turn Ami had been receptive and playful; confiding in her husband that she felt less tense in his presence. There was no longer anything to be angry about and she had even started to look towards the future. Perhaps they might move into a new apartment? Something bigger and more modern. They might even think of going abroad this summer rather than staying at home as they always did. 'Why the sudden change?' Kenji had asked his wife who, after some prodding, eventually admitted that Hoshino's appearance had put to rest a fear that had been gnawing at her for several months. A fear that her husband was deluded, going mad. That he would never be the executive TV producer that he aspired to. Just a salaried man. Or worse still a mail room attendant. Now she could hold her head up high and never be ashamed to talk about him in the presence of her friends or customers.

He had never quite realised that she was ashamed to talk about him. But he pushed this thought to the back of his mind as they reached the bridge that spanned the busy freeway, along which early morning traffic was crawling bumper to bumper.

'It's not much further now,' he murmured as they climbed the bridge and crossed to the opposite side of the road. The Cerulean Tower, in sight since they had left the station, grew larger and more imposing until they were standing in the driveway that approached the multi-storey building, surrounded by lush, green, exotic vegetation densely planted in marble walled beds.

Inside the lobby, Kenji felt some resistance pulling against his hand. Turning around he saw that Ami had faltered to a stop behind him and was staring at her surroundings, blinking rapidly.

'Oh my,' she announced, 'I always knew I deserved to come to places like this. That we deserved to. Perhaps now?' She looked at her husband questioningly who admitted that, yes, the Cerulean Tower was an impressive establishment.

The floor was a continuous, uninterrupted flow of white marble. All around them dark grey, flat matt walls towered, reaching up to a milky white ceiling. To their left stood a highly polished walnut wood reception desk – a large, sweeping counter with bevelled edges. Vast windows stretched from floor to ceiling along the length of the wall opposite the reception desk and, clustered in front of them, were compact wicker chairs with moss green cushions. Each was positioned next to a small, cubic, walnut table bearing a heavy glass ashtray in which were placed complimentary strips of matches.

'Good morning.' A young man standing just inside the entrance bowed politely. 'Welcome to the Cerulean Tower. How may I be of assistance to you today?'

'I'm here to see a guest. A business associate is staying at the hotel.' Kenji felt the need to justify his presence. Unlike Ami, the hotels of Tokyo were not unfamiliar to him. Business associates visiting NBC frequently stayed in establishments such as the Excel, or the Park Hyatt, and the duty had often fallen upon him to ferry them back and forth; act as a guide; a dinner companion; a drinking buddy. This was his first visit to the Cerulean Tower, however. For the simple reason that any guest lodged here would have expected to deal with and be entertained by the most senior executive. And, of course, he had never been one. Until now.

'Please.' The young man nodded at the sweeping walnut counter. 'One of my colleagues will be able to assist you.'

There were three young women standing behind the reception desk. Each appeared to be occupied, but as he approached the desk one looked up at him.

'Good morning, sir. How may I be of assistance to you today?'

'I have an appointment to see one of your guests. Hana Hoshino. She is a business associate.' Kenji anxiously studied the young woman's expression. She thinks I don't deserve to be here, I'm an intruder, he feared.

'Can I please take your name?' the young woman asked politely.

'Kenji Yamada.'

'If you could wait a minute, please.' Inserting an earpiece, the receptionist dialled a number on the switchboard hidden beneath the overhanging ledge that separated them. He turned away politely.

Although it was Monday morning, 8 o'clock, the lobby was buzzing with activity. The hub of wicker chairs opposite were largely occupied by men in suits, reading newspapers, drinking cups of coffee and smoking cigarettes in quick succession. Other guests cut across the lobby, porters dragging their luggage. One in particular caught his eye. A man whose hair was suspiciously black, with the exception of a streak of white running like a mane from the front to the back of his head. Kenji watched as, dressed all in black and wearing on his feet what appeared to be a pair of ballerina pumps, this man waltzed across the marble floor cooing at a small white dog that lay cradled in his arms, its small tongue flicking in and out of its mouth like a lizard's.

'I'm afraid,' the receptionist coughed politely, 'that there is no answer.' Looking at the time on the delicate gold watch hanging off her slim wrist she offered, 'Breakfast is still being served. Perhaps your friend is dining and will return to her room shortly.'

'Perhaps.' Kenji knew that Hoshino rarely ate breakfast. She had told him that last night when they parted and made their arrangements for meeting up the next day. Anxiously he cast a sideways glance at his wife. Unconcerned by this news, she was staring at the guest with the white streak running through his hair and the miniature dog.

'Will you wait? If you would like to order some coffee, I will send a waiter over,' the receptionist suggested and Kenji nodded.

Nudging Ami, he led the way to the cluster of wicker chairs and selected two on the outermost edge. Almost immediately a young man in a white tunic and black trousers with a sharp pleat running down the front of both legs appeared.

'Good morning.' He bowed, handing a small leatherbound menu embossed with a gold outline of the Cerulean Tower to both Kenji and Ami.

Turning first one page and then the next, Kenji did not take in the contents. He could stand it no longer. He jumped up and returned to the reception desk.

Room 1401 was still not answering.

Trying to look unconcerned, he returned to his wife who had ordered coffee and pastries. Where could Hoshino be, he wondered? Panic rose inside him. She was supposed to be here. They had agreed to meet at 8 a.m. The press conference did not start until noon, but they would need plenty of time to prepare what they were going to do. It was supposed to be Kenji's big day. The day when everything finally came together.

'Still eating breakfast?' Ami enquired, brushing at the shower of icing sugar that had landed on her skirt.

Kenji nodded forlornly and continued to stare at his wife as she deliberated over the rapidly diminishing plate of pastries. 'It's 8.45.' It was getting harder to keep the note of panic out of his voice. 'How long does it take one person to eat breakfast?'

'It is,' Ami acknowledged, dabbing the corners of her mouth with a napkin, 'very good food. Please,' she begged, asking her husband to sit down as his pacing was starting to get on her nerves.

He couldn't. He was worried now, very worried. What had happened to Hoshino after she left their apartment last night? Her bodyguards had driven her back to Tokyo, to her hotel room. They would have made sure that she had got here safely. What if she had slipped out afterwards? Gone to a bar? More likely she had continued drinking in her room. It was exactly this possibility that he feared when he had witnessed her hands shaking. It was all too much too soon for her. Had she had a little something to calm her nerves? Had that little something turned into a lot of something?

An hour crawled past, during which time he asked the receptionist to phone her room several times. Eventually it was Ami who called for decisive action.

'Come on,' she said, putting her magazine in her handbag, 'we'll go up.'

'We can't. I mean we haven't been announced.'

'What else will you do? Stand there and wear your shoes out pacing back and forth?'

'Yes, you're right. Of course you're right. Let's go now before I change my mind.'

They took a lift to the fourteenth floor. Following wooden signs mounted on the walls, they walked to the very end of a magnolia corridor lit overhead by spotlights flush with the ceiling. Their footsteps were soundless on the lush, red, deep-pile carpet, flecked with spots of gold and blue. Upon arriving at room 1401 Kenji tapped lightly on the door. There was no answer.

'She'll never hear that,' Ami scolded and, reaching across, rapped her knuckles repeatedly against the door. Still there was no answer. At exactly the same moment they both leaned forward, giggling like teenagers, and pressed their ears against the door.

'I can't hear anything.'

'Knock again.'

'No, you knock.'

A chambermaid emerged from the adjacent room – an elderly Korean lady – causing them both to jump back. Ami was the first to regain her composure.

'Oh no,' she cried, rooting in her handbag. 'I left the key card inside. I can't believe I did that. Right on the counter next to the sink. Now we'll have to go all the way to the ground floor.' Pretending to notice the chambermaid for the first time, she turned to face her. 'Unless . . . I don't suppose you could let us in? Save my legs?'

The chambermaid shrugged and muttered something in Korean. Turning to go, she revealed knotted veins running up the backs of her legs.

Ami persisted, tapping the maid's shoulder and miming the action of opening the door. The old lady looked at them suspiciously – Kenji was certain that she suspected him of some wrongdoing – while his wife acted out leaving the room and closing the door to realise that she had left the key inside.

'Ahhh,' the chambermaid grinned.

'That was lucky,' Kenji whispered to his wife as the door closed heavily behind them, submerging the room in darkness. The air smelt sweet and stale.

'Stay where you are,' he whispered and holding his hands straight out in front of him, began to walk forward. He didn't want to risk opening the door again should the maid still be outside, and a cursory grope of the surrounding walls failed to reveal a light switch. He would walk in a straight line. Walking in a straight line from the door in any hotel room anywhere always led to a window. That much he knew. Walking cautiously, his feet became tangled in something – possibly an item of clothing – and he stubbed his toe on something hard – an armchair. The sound of deep, heavy, irregular breathing filled the room. His own, but also someone else's. Then the palms of his hands hit something solid – the window – and he pulled first at what felt like a curtain and then the blackout blind, flooding the room with sunlight.

228

Ami cried out. Lying sprawled across the bed, fully clothed but with the hem of her brightly coloured dress caught unceremoniously round her waist, revealing laddered tights, was Hoshino. The bedcovers were rumpled. An empty champagne bottle lay beside her. A number of others on the floor.

'Hoshino-san,' Kenji called but she did not stir. Wide-eyed with panic, he turned to his wife. 'What do we do? She's out cold.'

'Get her up,' Ami ordered, moving towards the bed. 'She'll have slept off most of what she's drunk by now. Get her up and help her into the bathroom.'

Although it made him extremely uncomfortable to do so, Kenji eased one hand behind Hoshino's back and helped her up into a sitting position. She groaned. Closing his eyes to protect her modesty, he turned her slightly and then, wrapping his arms around her, pulled her into a standing position. She flopped in his arms like a broken doll as they shuffled in an awkward waltz towards the bathroom where he propped her up on the toilet seat.

'Leave us now. I will see to her.' Ami closed the door, opened it again and called out after her husband. 'Order plenty of coffee, scrambled eggs and dry toast.' This time when she closed the door it was immediately followed by the sound of running water.

Precisely twenty-nine minutes later – he knew because he had counted each one – Ami emerged from the bathroom, followed by a very repentant and shell-shocked Hoshino. Her black hair was damp, her face washed clean of make-up and she was enveloped in a white towelling dressing gown.

'I am extremely embarrassed,' she repeated again and again, failing to meet his eyes. 'That you should see me like this. I can't believe that I let you down after all the kindness you have shown me.' She spoke slowly as if the effort was too much. He suspected she had been crying.

'Don't worry,' Kenji reassured her. 'We still have time before the press conference. Sit down and have something to eat.' He pulled out a chair at a round table next to the window and she sat down.

'I'm really not very hungry.'

Ami would not take no for an answer and soon Hoshino was

spooning small amounts of tepid egg into her mouth as Ami pulled and tugged at her hair, securing it into an elaborate bun.

The phone shrilled, breaking the silence that had descended upon the room, causing them all to jump.

'My head.' Hoshino was close to tears. 'Please can someone get the phone for me.'

Rushing forward, Kenji picked up the phone and said good morning. 'It's the events manager,' he whispered covering the mouthpiece. 'The room is ready for the press conference and we can go down any time we like to do a dry run.'

Hoshino looked aghast. She put down her cup of coffee as she could no longer hold it, her hand was trembling so much. 'I can't do it,' she muttered, at first softly and then more loudly, 'I can't go through with it.'

At first Kenji thought she might be joking, but seeing the look of sheer panic on her face, he realised that she was very, very serious. 'You have to. You can't let us down. Everything has been arranged. This is our big chance to get the show known. To get a sponsor. Without a sponsor there's no show. Without a show I have no job.'

'I know. I'm sorry. But I haven't got it in me. Please, you must understand.'

'It's just nerves.' Ami patted Hoshino reassuringly on the shoulder. 'Once you get out there it will be like you've never been away.'

'It's been such a long time I'm worried I will have forgotten how to do it.' Her voice trembled as she spoke. 'I was never very good in the first place.' A fat teardrop rolled down her cheek, followed by another and another. 'I can't do it,' she wailed, jumping up out of her chair and running into the bathroom, locking the door behind her.

Kenji looked at Ami. 'What now?'

They both stared at each other in silence and then at the locked bathroom door. The telephone began to ring. Again. Kenji tried to ignore it but the shrill persisted. It would not stop so he snapped up the receiver.

'Inagaki-san . . . No, now isn't a good time . . . It's a delicate situation . . . No, I haven't done anything to her . . . She's locked herself in the bathroom and she won't come out . . . If you must.'

He replaced the handset. 'He's coming up. I couldn't stop him.'

'Perhaps he will be able to convince her to come out,' Ami said, shrugging helplessly.

Minutes later Inagaki was standing at the door, quivering with rage. 'What have you done to her, Yamada?' He limped past Kenji into the room. 'How did she get in this state? Do you have any idea what a precious, fragile, delicate woman you are dealing with here? If you have hurt her feelings in any way, I swear I will . . .'

Before he had any opportunity to finish his threat, Ami inserted herself between the two men. 'My husband did nothing, Inagaki. He has been nothing but patient and kind.'

Not used to his wife defending him – she was usually on the other side – Kenji looked on in bemusement.

'Hoshino-san is nervous. She has stagefright and must be encouraged gently to come out. She needs her confidence boosted. But now that you are here, I can think of nobody better placed to do this than you.'

Inagaki straightened his tie. 'I am sure that I can try.' He limped towards the bathroom door. 'Please give us some privacy.'

Kenji and Ami retreated to the corner of the room where they sat in a pair of small armchairs next to the window, casting anxious glances at Inagaki who was tapping lightly at the bathroom door. They could not hear what he was saying. His voice was a whisper. But in time the bathroom door opened a crack and then more widely. He slipped through the door and closed it sharply behind him. Several minutes passed.

'What do you think they're doing in there?' Kenji wrung his hands anxiously in his lap.

'Give them time.'

'We don't have time.' Looking at his watch he saw that it was now 11.30. 'I'm going to get them out of there.' Standing up he strode towards the bathroom and was ready to knock on the door when it opened. Hoshino emerged, smiling shyly, Inagaki in her wake.

'I'm ready.' She clapped her hands together and looked up at Inagaki who was smiling benevolently. 'Tell me what you want me to say.'

He could see that her hands were still shaking.

THIRTY-SIX

'You want to buy all those?' The young sales assistant leafed through the pile of newspapers Kenji had placed on the counter between them, pausing to study the covers on a number of them in more detail. 'There's a lot here. Oh, I didn't know that had come in yet. I've been waiting for this.'

From the bottom of the pile she slid out an A4-sized newspaper that specialised in gossip stories about celebrities, soap stars, politicians, and had large-scale colour photographs. Kenji watched as she flicked through the pages, making various noises to display either her shock or amusement. 'I didn't know that they were a couple . . . What does she think she's wearing?'

'Who's that?' A slim man with a high-pitched voice, wearing a tight white T-shirt attempted to see over Kenji's shoulder. 'Fuchsia-pink. How awful. And with her colouring.'

Kenji coughed – loudly – and grabbed the newspaper back, placing it down firmly on the pile. 'Excuse me, but if I could just pay for these. I have to be at work.'

The man in the tight white T-shirt recoiled.

'I was just looking.'

'Some people can be very rude.'

'Especially first thing in the morning, I find.'

'If I could just pay.'

More slowly than was bearable, the sales assistant picked up each newspaper in turn and keyed the price into the cash register. Some prices it took longer to locate on the front covers than others and the keys on the till appeared to be just as elusive to her. Adding everything up she pressed a button that pinged loudly and quoted a price to Kenji. He baulked, looking down at the pile of papers. Certainly a mistake had been made somewhere. But he had neither the time nor the inclination to correct it and he thrust a banknote at her.

She stared at it and at the pile on the counter. 'Wait a minute. There must have been some mistake. That is too much. Let me try again.'

'Just take it.' He pushed the note into her hand. He knew he was being abrupt, rude even, but did not care. It wouldn't be the first time today. This morning he had chastised Yoshi for brushing his teeth 'the wrong way'. Then, running for a bus, had charged past an elderly lady, knocking the shopping bag from her hand, sending apples and oranges rolling across the ground. Not stopping to help her pick them up, he jumped through the open doors of the bus and narrowly beat a heavily pregnant woman to the one remaining seat.

There seemed to be no way that he could control his behaviour. He was being propelled forward through the morning by a curious mixture of anger, anxiety and apprehension. Yesterday – he flung open the shop door and walked out on to the street – had been an unmitigated disaster. Unable to stop turning the sequence of events over in his mind last night, he had a fitful sleep, dropping off at 4 a.m. and then failing to hear the alarm. Now, on top of everything else, he was going to be late for work when he had so desperately wanted to be among the first to get in. An hour without disruption was all that he needed to go through each of these newspapers. To see if the story had appeared anywhere and if it had, then he could think about formulating a response to the questions Goto was certain to ask. Now, though, it was already 9.30 a.m. His colleagues would have started to arrive at their desks over an hour ago. News would have trickled through the office. People would be talking to each other.

The shop was part of a small, grey concrete complex at the base of the twenty-five-storey tower block in which Kenji worked. Usually he bought a newspaper followed by a coffee and muffin from the place next door before taking the short walk across the concrete slabs to the building's entrance. Today there was not enough time. Skipping breakfast, he rode the escalator to the twenty-second floor, sneaking in past Suki by keeping his head down and walking quickly and as close to the wall as he could get.

It was no longer in the darkened corner of the twenty-second floor that he worked, but in the office that Abe had once occupied. At first Kenji had refused the space, afraid that it would in some way jeopardise the project. But Goto had insisted, and when he started to ask questions about why Kenji – Abe's right-hand man – had been assigned such a paltry space in the first place, it seemed prudent to accept. Now he was starting to wonder if his gut instinct hadn't been right.

The office was more than he could ever have hoped for. It was large, bright and airy with an enormous window spanning the entire length of the wall running immediately behind his desk. If he ever needed a distraction, Kenji would simply spin around in his black leather chair, flick the blinds open and stare at Mount Fuji in the distance (if it was a clear day and the humidity was low). If a fog hung in the air, he studied the traffic on the ground instead and occupied himself by wondering where everybody was going.

Mifune had methodically removed every trace of Abe from the room. His belongings – reports, journals, books and magazines, videos of old shows, a bag of golf clubs, snapshots of him playing with colleagues or posing with minor celebrities – had been boxed up and delivered to his one surviving relative, an uncle living on the remote island of Shikinejima, who had promptly sent the parcels back. A note found inside stated that he had no need for any of these items and asked what had happened to the enormous wealth he had been led to believe his nephew had acquired? Was it not true that Abe was a successful TV man? Goto wrote back – the elderly man did not have a telephone – explaining that all of Abe's estate had to be sold off to pay for his debts. That was the last they heard from the uncle.

With all of Abe's possessions gone, the room felt empty. At Mifune's prompting, Kenji had started to fill it with his own belongings. Even then the two enormous, solid oak bookcases positioned against both the left and the right wall, looked bare. Anybody entering the room might not have even realised that it was occupied, had it not been for the few personal mementoes that sat on the matching oak desk: a photograph of the twins in the sunglasses he had bought them on the day the family went cherry blossom-viewing, and one of Yoshi dancing in a shower of petals; a good luck charm; a drawing that Yoshi had done for him.

Now, standing at the open office door, holding the pile of newspapers under his right arm, Kenji wondered if he should pack up his few possessions here and go home now. Certainly it would save Goto the pain and embarrassment of having to tell him to do so.

Throwing himself down on his leather chair, he tossed the newspapers on to the table. How he would miss this chair, this office, this view. It was such a short time that he had been in here, but already he was attached.

He looked at the newspapers. He could take a quick look. There was still time. Goto was attending a breakfast meeting with the board and would be unavailable at least until mid-morning. His hand hovered over the pile as he wondered which one to start with. Picking up the *Mainichi News* he thumbed quickly through the pages. Too quickly because a number were stuck together. Dampening his thumb, he started again. It was on page seven that he found what he was looking for.

'Fallen Star' the title proclaimed, and beneath it a black and white photograph of Hoshino taken the very moment that she had tripped over the microphone cables snaking across the conference room floor at the Cerulean Tower Hotel and landed on her hands and knees. The accompanying piece was written by Leiko Kobayashi, a popular journalist with columns in several dailies who specialised in entertainment news including TV and film reviews. Occasionally she wrote more 'serious' pieces. Seeing her name on the page Kenji knew that trouble lay in store. Leiko Kobayashi was renowned for her acid tongue and uncompromising stance. 'Why treat people with sensitivity,' she was once quoted as saying after the young star of a film she had savaged checked herself into a well-known retreat specialising in disorders of the nervous system, 'when you can treat them with contempt.' Her indomitable style enthralled and appalled people in equal measure. And while the public couldn't get enough of her, she was a thorn in the side of the industry. During his time at NBC, she had broken at least five fledgling shows with a single review – and, it appeared, she had not changed.

Taking a deep breath, he began to read.

'Despite having fallen to the floor and being in a considerable amount of pain, former TV presenter Hoshino, 44, insisted on continuing with the press conference to promote her new game show, *Millyennaire*. One could not help but think that she shouldn't have bothered. Sometimes mumbling, sometimes rambling, always incoherent, she seemed to be suffering from some kind of concussion. Sadly the reality was much worse. It appeared that Hoshino, one-time fashion icon and much loved star, was drunk.'

It was far worse than Kenji had feared. Wincing, he read on.

'*Millyennaire* sounds like a solid concept for a game show but the executive producer – an unknown Kenji Yamada – may have bitten off more than he can chew if this fiasco they called a press conference is anything to go by. It was not long before Hoshino burst into tears explaining that the show was under-funded and calling upon "anybody, somebody" to come to her aid. If, after this, she remains to present it, one can only hope that nobody hears this call to arms.'

'That's it.' He stood up and threw the newspaper down on the desk. There was no point staying now. Once Goto and the executives at NBC whom he knew to be extremely conservative and didn't like scandal of any kind saw the article, he would be asked to leave. Why wait? Why not just go now without suffering another indignity? Opening the drawers to his desk he quickly scooped out a number of personal belongings and threw them into his briefcase. Taking one last look around, he closed the blinds covering the window and prepared to leave.

'What's going on in here?'

One arm already in his raincoat, the other struggling to find the other hole, Kenji froze. Goto was standing in the doorway with what could only be described as a wry smile playing on his lips. Kenji was reminded of a cat toying with a mouse.

'Are you going somewhere?' As he spoke, Goto pulled the arms of his black suit jacket down over the cuffs of his grey shirt. A fat black tie hung round his neck.

Still struggling with his coat, Kenji managed to thrust his other arm into the other hole and pull it up around him. It was on inside out, but he didn't have time to remedy it. He had to get out of there as soon as possible. 'I thought it would be for the best. Yes.'

'You did?' One hand resting against the door frame, Goto's eyes lingered on Kenji's desk and the open newspaper. 'Is that the *Mainichi News*?'

He nodded, shamefully.

'I believe that we received quite a bit of coverage from the lovely Kobayashi.'

'We did.' Kenji picked up his briefcase and strode purposefully towards the door; determined to retain as much of his dignity as he possibly could with his raincoat on inside out.

'Excellent news.'

Kenji froze. Not just because he had reached the office door and had no way of getting out past Goto, but because he wasn't entirely sure if he had heard correctly. 'Perhaps you haven't had time to read the article yet.'

'No, I've read it.' Goto did not move even though he could see Kenji wanted to get past.

'But . . .' He couldn't understand. 'You're happy?'

'Of course I'm happy. This is a new show. We need to stir up some publicity. Good or bad, it's all the same to me. Or at least that's what I told Hoshino-san last night.'

'You saw her?' Kenji felt dizzy and had to put his briefcase down on the floor so that he could reach out and rest one hand on the wall.

'Yes. When I dropped off a case of champagne. Just a small token of my appreciation.' He stroked his chin thoughtfully. 'As a young man I was a great admirer of Hana Hoshino.'

Thinking about the empty champagne bottles he had found littered across the floor of Hoshino's hotel room, Kenji exploded. 'You did what? But she shouldn't drink. She can't handle it.' It was evident to him that not only should Hoshino abstain from alcohol, but also that whenever she did drink, the effects of this combined with whatever prescribed medication she was taking were explosive.

'So I heard,' Goto chuckled and moved away from the door, coming into the office and sitting on the chair opposite the window.

Kenji had no choice but to join him, sitting down at the opposite side of the desk, although he did so reluctantly, absentmindedly running his fingers around a coffee stain the cleaners had missed. He knew that they had been in because the entire room smelt of lemons.

'By the way, it looks like you've sewn up the sponsorship deal.'

'Er, yes?' Kenji leant forward in his chair. The smell was starting to make him feel dizzy. Or perhaps it was the lack of sleep and skipping breakfast.

'I got a call this morning. Fuji Bank want to sponsor the show. It seems they believe that it could help encourage saving amongst the younger age groups whom they are having difficulty reaching through traditional advertising. A gentleman named Inagaki called. Although he did ask me not to mention his involvement to you. It's not a problem, is it?'

'It's not a problem.' Kenji shook his head slowly from side to side.

'Glad to hear it.'

'Well that's everything I had to say.' Slapping the palms of his hands against his thighs, Goto stood up and moved soundlessly across the carpet to the door. Even though he was no longer sitting opposite him, Kenji could still smell his aftershave. It lingered in the air.

'You've done a very good job, Yamada-san.'

Kenji looked up, his forehead creased in a frown. It appeared that he had, although he was not entirely sure how.

'You've saved my neck and I'm not about to forget that in a

239

hurry.' Goto patted his tie. 'How about a game of golf next weekend?'

'Golf?' Kenji spluttered.

'Yes, I'm a member of the Maruhan club.'

'I would love to. My game though . . .' He self-consciously patted the eye patch that he still wore. '. . . is not very good.' Would he even be able to play with only one good eye?

Goto paused and for a few dreadful seconds Kenji feared he might be about to retract the offer that meant more than anything. More than even the job, the office, the chair and the view.

'In that case.' Goto pulled on the cuffs of both his shirtsleeves so that the diamond-encrusted links were visible to Kenji. 'We need to think about getting you a membership card of your own. So that you can get up to scratch.'

THIRTY-SEVEN

'There it is,' the driver shouted, swinging the taxi into the parking lot and screeching to a stop outside the one-storey building sandwiched between two tall tower blocks.

This was the third time they had driven down the road. They had both been looking upwards and missed this modest building with no windows and only a single, recessed red door.

Kenji got out and paid the driver. In the darkened recess he groped along the brick wall until his hand found something cold and metallic. An intercom. He pressed a small square button and the intercom buzzed loudly, although several seconds passed before it was answered.

'Who is it?' a voice barked.

'Kenji Yamada.' His voice sounded croaky, barely audible. Turning away he cleared his throat and turned back again. 'Executive producer on *Millyennaire*.' It was the first time he had uttered those words out loud and found that in spite of his nerves he was smiling.

The sound of paper rustling was followed by another loud buzz and a curt instruction to enter the building. Pushing against the red door, he found himself in a small atrium, off which ran three corridors. Each one was identical – coarse grey carpet covered the floor; the walls were painted white and the ceiling covered with yellow polystyrene tiles, punctuated at regular intervals with the plastic guard of a fluorescent light.

Cautiously looking down each corridor in turn, he wondered which way was the right way and whether there was anybody around that he might ask.

'Yamada-san.'

He could have burst into song when he saw Mifune striding down the corridor towards him, carrying a red clipboard. The heels of her shoes clipped together as she came to a halt in front of him.

'We are running behind schedule and there is much to do. Please come with me.'

She was capable of being extremely bossy but, he had found, it was exactly what he needed.

'The taxi driver could not find the address,' he began to explain but Mifune had already turned around and was walking away from him, along the length of the corridor down which she had come. Scurrying after her he wondered if maybe it was better not to divulge the reason why he had been delayed. The last thing he wanted to do was appear incompetent. It was 3 a.m. before he had gone to bed. He had been preparing for today: what he would say, how he would act. The minor details such as how he would get to the studio, what he would wear, were forgotten. Consequently, upon waking this morning, he had lost valuable time that he intended to use performing some deep breathing exercises, on running around the bedroom, deciding what tie would create the best impression and making frantic phone calls, trying to obtain the correct address for the studio.

The corridor, it seemed, stretched on forever. They turned left and then right so many times that he began to wonder if they might not end up exactly where they had started. Looking at the building from outside, he had never imagined that it could be so big.

Mifune stopped at a double set of white doors. How many such doors had they already passed? He hoped very much Mifune did not intend to leave him alone. It was doubtful he would be able to find his way out of here.

'This is studio four.'

As she spoke, Mifune opened one of the white doors and together they walked into the darkness.

'It is the largest of Miru's studios with an audience capacity of six hundred and where *Millyennaire* will be filmed.'

The white door closed soundlessly behind them and for several seconds all was in complete darkness. Kenji could sense Mifune standing to his left and heard the sound of several switches in quick succession as a number of bright spotlights suspended from a high ceiling were illuminated. The studio itself was not too dissimilar from others Kenji had visited while he worked for NBC, although it was almost certainly bigger, putting him in mind of a large, dark, cavernous warehouse. The floor was black, as were the walls, the ceiling and the rows of seats that were arranged in three sections at 45-degree angles and rose sharply up in tiers that could be reached by steps running up either side. The only difference between this and those other studios was that positioned to the back right of the large space in front of the seating area was a cabin. At least 24 feet long, 12 feet high and 12 feet wide, it was completely windowless and looked utterly out of place.

'Is this it?' Kenji felt a surge of excitement rising up through his stomach. It was amazing. Everything was exactly as he had planned and recorded in the notebook that he had foolishly relinquished to Abe that night in the Roppongi restaurant. Thankfully, he had managed to retrieve the notebook from a safe in Abe's office when he moved into it.

'This is the contestant's apartment where they will be living for the duration of the show.' Mifune walked towards the cabin door.

'Seeing it here makes everything seem so real,' he smiled.

Mifune frowned fractionally. 'It is to your liking? It is as you planned? I followed the notebook exactly.'

'It's perfect.'

She smiled and went into the cabin, ducking down slightly to avoid hitting her head on the low door frame. 'Watch your head as you step inside.'

He followed her. Once inside he inhaled sharply. It was truly amazing. Had he not known this was a cabin, he would not have believed it. It felt every bit as real as any other high-rise apartment in downtown Tokyo. Although perhaps darker and dingier, not to mention sparsely furnished. Worn tatami mats had been lain across the floor and the walls throughout the entire cabin were covered with a garish paper – velvet hexagons set against a shiny gold backing. At regular intervals throughout the room, paintings of rural scenes in mahogany wood frames had been hung.

The apartment was open-plan: sleeping, eating and living areas clearly denoted by the presence of a few, humble pieces of furniture such as a rolled-up futon; a low rectangular table and cushion; a battered armchair. In many ways it reminded him of the apartment in which he had lived before his marriage. The absence of any real furniture, a television set, a radio, had not bothered him as he was so rarely at home. But how would the contestant feel trapped in here twenty-four hours a day, seven days a week with nothing else to do? It would drive them mad, surely?

'The audience will be sitting just outside?' he asked incredibly, rapping his knuckles against the walls. 'How can that be?'

'It's fully soundproofed. In here you can't hear anything of what's going on outside. Wait just a minute.' Mifune ran outside, closing the door behind her. She returned several seconds later, looking flushed. 'Did you hear anything?'

'No.' He shook his head.

'I was screaming at the top of my voice.'

'That's amazing. I didn't hear a thing.' Taking one final look around him, he rubbed his hands together. 'What's next?'

'If you would like to come with me.' Mifune turned and left the cabin, 'Hoshino is in the dressing room getting ready for some publicity shots. Your wife is with her. They have both asked to see you when you arrive. Afterwards I have arranged for you to brief the production team.'

He stumbled out after her, just missing hitting his head on the cabin door.

'I spoke this morning with NBC regarding the scheduling of the show,' she continued, striding towards the studio door, 'and they have decided to give us a Sunday slot at 7 p.m. As I'm sure you are aware, it's not the best.'

He nodded. They had called it the 'graveyard slot' in the days when he had worked at the network. Largely because it was sandwiched between the news and a weekly soap opera: both of which attracted high viewing figures. It was an unwritten rule that whatever came between these two programmes was not of much merit. It did not have to be. Those people who tuned in for the news often stayed for the soap opera, watching whatever came in between with little regard for its merit and for no reason other than that they were too lazy to pick up the remote control and switch over. The slot was typically reserved for low-budget filler productions. It had, on occasion, been used for a fledgling show that the network wanted to launch before boosting it to a more demanding slot where it would have to command an audience in its own right. Kenji hoped that his former colleagues regarded *Millyennaire* as the latter.

'Ishida-san in programme research has also been in touch to discuss the pilot episode.' Mifune handed Kenji a piece of paper with a telephone number written on it. He didn't need reminding, the digits were firmly engraved on his memory. They belonged to his former boss at NBC.

They left the studio, walked further down the corridor and turned right. No sooner had they done so than Kenji became aware of loud, cackling, female laughter. He cast a surreptitious glance at Mifune but either she did not notice, or if she did, was too polite to pass comment.

'Here we are.' She opened another white door. Light, smoke and laughter spilled out.

The make-up room was as small as the studio had been large, although mirrors running along the length of the longest wall opposite the door created some sense of space. Sitting in front of the mirror on a high, black leather chair that both reclined and rotated, was Hoshino, tissue paper tucked in around the neck of her blouse. She was holding a half empty champagne flute in one hand and a long, thin cigar in the other. Ami, her face flushed, was also drinking from a glass and sitting on a chair in the corner of the room. The two women were gossiping like old friends as another applied Hoshino's make-up and yet another combed and teased her hair. They were discussing a soap star both favoured who frequently appeared in the celebrity columns of newspapers, always with a different woman.

'I don't believe for one second that he is as much a ladies' man as he likes to pretend.' Hoshino took a sip of champagne. 'He must be hiding something.'

'Really?' Ami looked shocked.

'Oh yes.' Hoshino sucked on her cigar. 'I've seen it many times before. I can tell you now, nobody pulls the wool over my eyes.'

Spotting her husband's reflection in the mirror, Ami squealed. 'Kenji, you must have a glass of champagne with us.'

'I can't,' he protested. His stomach already felt sick without making matters worse. 'I'm working.'

'Look, here are my dresses.'

As Hoshino jumped up, Kenji noticed that she was swaying slightly. Clutching his arm – he thought perhaps for balance – she led him to the far corner of the room where a temporary clothes rail had been erected with a number of dresses, each covered with a transparent plastic bag hanging on it.

'So they are,' he nodded.

'We have agreed that I will supply Hoshino's wardrobe for the entire show.'

'That's wonderful news,' he confirmed, pretending – because he knew that his wife would want him to – to study the silk material beneath the plastic covers; the reds and blues and greens; the patterned and plain fabric; the sequins and diamante stones.

'They look even better on,' Hoshino interrupted, her voice slightly mumbled because the make-up artist was in the process of applying her lipstick. 'Better made than any other dress I have ever worn. The fabric is exquisite, the cut perfect.'

'I'm glad you like them.' Ami clapped her hands together in front of her.

'Like them,' one of the make-up artists roared. 'She loves them. She has been trying them on all morning.'

'Really?'

'You'd better believe it.' The woman continued. She had a

gravelly voice and it sounded as though it might be painful for her to even speak. Kenji suspected she had supplied the cigar. 'She couldn't make up her mind which one to wear in the photo shoot so she has decided to wear them all. One after the other.'

Unable to hide her delight, Ami clapped her hands together in front of her chest like an excited child.

'Hoshino-san, time to go.' Mifune popped her head in through the open door. 'The photographer is ready for you now. Kenji, if you will come with me. The team are assembled.'

THIRTY-EIGHT

The small room was square and windowless. There were about half as many chairs as there were people and those who had not been able to find seats were left leaning against the walls or perched on the edge of tables that had been pushed up against the back of the room.

Kenji paused in the doorway. Seemingly to permit Mifune to enter ahead of him, but in truth to take the opportunity to study the members of Abe's production team before they had the opportunity to study him. There were many more than he had expected. At least thirty. It was difficult to count, everybody was packed in so tightly and all talking among themselves until Mifune – taking the only unoccupied space at the front of the room – cleared her throat. Gratitude flooded through him. It made everything so much easier to have her there beside him, leading the way and showing him what to do. It was a great effort not to thank her profusely at every opportunity. But to do so would have made him appear inexperienced.

'Thank you for coming,' Mifune said.

Everyone looked at her, silently. Then someone spotted Kenji and the low murmur of conversation spread throughout the team.

'As mentioned in my previous memo I asked you all to gather here today for two reasons.'

Even though she was addressing the production team, they were all still looking at Kenji.

'First, so that our new executive producer can meet the entire team. Second, so that you can receive your instructions.'

Mifune turned to look at Kenji who nodded in what he imagined was an authoritative manner and said, 'Please go on.'

It was the only signal the occupants of the room needed. Now everyone looked at Mifune. Away from their intense scrutiny he relaxed a little.

'Please, will each person stand up in turn, say their name and what they do. Ito-san, if you could begin.'

A man in his forties, with round cheeks and a paunch to match, dressed from head to toe in denim, stood up. 'Gaku Ito, cameraman.' He sat down heavily and nodded at the woman next to him.

Standing up, she created a gust of air that inflated and lifted the skirt of her floral print dress. 'Iva Yoshida, scriptwriter.'

One by one everyone stood up, giving their name and job title before sitting back down. There were cameramen, lighting technicians, scriptwriters, set designers. Even the make-up artists, now that they had delivered Hoshino to the photographer, slipped into the meeting room, introducing themselves after everybody else and apologising for being late.

Would he be expected to remember everybody's name, Kenji wondered fearfully, as he walked from the doorway towards the centre of the room, talking as he went.

'Thank you all. Thank you for coming here today.' Breathing deeply and slowly he brought to mind the speech he had prepared last night, writing it out word for word on pieces of card. It had been a last-minute decision not to bring the cards as, he imagined, he would command more respect without them. Each word was delivered with what he liked to think of as measured passion. He stood tall, head up straight and used the minimum of gesticulations. Those he did use were carefully chosen, smooth and fluid. In short he was modelling himself on a man he had once admired: the head of the programme research unit at NBC – Ishida.

'My name is Kenji Yamada and while I regard it as my greatest fortune it could also be called a grave misfortune that I have come to be assigned the role of executive producer on *Millyennaire*.' He paused, allowing the team to digest not only what he had said, but what he hadn't said by avoiding any mention of Abe's name. 'You are probably wondering who I am. What my credentials are.'

Two men in the front row exchanged a look that told him everything that he needed to know. That he had struck exactly the right note. To do so had been easy enough. He had simply imagined how he might feel in their position. What questions he would want answered if the team in which he worked was suddenly taken over by a complete stranger: someone who did not work for the company, whom they knew nothing about. He would want to know: who had he worked for? Why didn't he work for them anymore? What was his experience?

'I have worked in the television industry for twenty-two years,' he continued as the men smiled hopefully at each other. 'My career has been what you might call unremarkable.'

The smiles turned to frowns. A low murmur spread around the room as people shifted in their seats. It was exactly the response he had aimed for. Whether it would achieve the desired effect was another matter.

'Work hard, get good results for the company and you will be rewarded. That's what I was told in my former position at NBC.' It was not necessary to go into the detail of what his position had been, just to establish himself as at least having worked for a leading network. 'I followed these instructions to the letter. I waited patiently for my promotion.'

Someone coughed.

'Then, in spite of everything, in spite of my loyalty and devotion, I was pushed out. At just forty years of age I found myself without a job.'

The scriptwriter became visibly upset and, taking a lace-trimmed handkerchief out of her bag, held it to her mouth.

'But my story does not end there.' Tipping backwards and forwards on his toes, Kenji clasped both hands firmly behind his back. 'My career may have been unremarkable, but then I had a remarkable idea and that was *Millyennaire*.'

'I thought it was Abe-san's idea,' he heard someone whisper.

'But they gave him the bonus.'

'You don't think he . . .'

'He wouldn't have. Would he?'

He paced over to the right-hand corner of the room and stopped. 'It would be easy for me to tell you about what I have done in the past. About the shows that I've worked on. What viewing figures they achieved. Budget costs. Income generated. But is any of this important? All that matters now is *Millyennaire*. It has taken me months of hard work to get this far. Real physical and emotional struggle.' He touched his eye patch.

'To understand *Millyennaire* you must understand what it was born of, not what I have done. That is why I am telling you my story. I don't want you to feel sorry for me. I want you to feel inspired and hopeful. *Millyennaire* is about the ordinary man and woman. People like you and me who have to battle and work hard to succeed every day. It's about success in the face of adversity. It's about saying that no matter what is thrown at you, you will get up and start again. It's about the light at the end of a long tunnel.'

The two men in the front row turned in their seats and began whispering excitedly to each other.

'Everyone in this room has a vital role to play and I don't want you, even for a minute, to underestimate your importance. Fujiwara-san,' he addressed the make-up artist who looked shyly at the floor, 'you will deliver Hana Hoshino to us looking flawless. She will gaze at her reflection in the mirror and feel beautiful thanks to you. This will give her the confidence to do a good job. Ito-san, your steady hand will capture Hoshino's luminance on film while her words, the scripts, will amuse and capture the audience's imagination. Ashida-san,' he addressed a more junior member of the production team, 'every day you will deliver magazines and newspapers to the apartment. A small job you might think, but without this there would be no show.'

'Together we will make a programme that will change the face of game shows as we know it, not just here in Japan but across the rest of the world. I have only one question for you.' Standing in the centre of the room he fell silent and looked down at the floor. When he spoke it was quietly. 'Are you with me?'

'What did he say?'

'I didn't hear him.'

Looking up, Kenji stared at a number of people in turn, holding their gaze before moving on to the next person. When he spoke again it was louder and clearer. 'I said, are you with me?'

A few voices, quiet but strong, replied, 'We're with you.'

He clapped the palm of his right hand to his chest as his face crumpled into a frown. 'I'm disappointed. Are so few people up for the challenge? I will ask you one more time. Are you with me?'

By the time he asked a third and then a fourth time, the entire room was standing on their feet shouting, clapping and stamping, 'We're with you.'

THIRTY-NINE

It was not Kenji's habit to work on Saturdays. Over the short space of the last few weeks, it had become his habit to devote as much of the weekend as was possible to his family. On Fridays, he got home no later than 8.30 p.m. and brought with him an extra-large pizza. Walking through the apartment door he would shout, 'Come and get it.' At which point the children, who had been listening out for him, came dashing out of their rooms. The entire family ate together sitting around the kitchen table. Eriko would take only a single slice, claiming that her dentures could not cope with more, and Ami insisted the kitchen window was held wide open and the door firmly shut. 'Otherwise I will be getting rid of the smell for weeks.' But on Saturday morning the apartment was empty. So Kenji took the opportunity to catch up with work, but the moment that the twins returned with their mother, he put his papers to one side and they did something together as a family. Last week they had enjoyed a picnic and a game of baseball in the park. The week before that they had gone swimming. Although this change to the Yamadas' weekend routine was a recent one, already it had become established. The twins began pestering him from Wednesday onwards, besieging him the moment that he got home from work, even if it was late and they were supposed to be in bed, sleeping.

'What pizza will we get for dinner on Friday, Dad?'

'I liked the one we got last week.'

'You always say that.'

'Can we go swimming on Saturday?'

'I want to go to the cinema.'

This weekend, though, was different. It was this weekend that Miru TV was holding auditions at the Cerulean Tower for a contestant to appear on *Millyennaire* and Kenji was already running late.

Exactly three weeks ago, he had personally placed an advertisement in the classifieds section of the *Mainichi News* for one day only. Much to the surprise of the entire production team, it had attracted thousands of applicants. Evidently he was not the only person who trawled through the back pages of newspapers: looking for what he was never quite sure, but certain that he would know when he found it. If he had seen the advertisement would he have responded? Maybe, he shrugged, as he walked down the road away from the apartment. The wording would almost certainly have attracted his attention – he had spent a great deal of time getting it just right. 'Ever dreamed of making a million?' the advertisement asked. 'Ever watched game shows on TV and thought, "I could do better than that"? Then here's your chance. Apply today.'

Would-be contestants were invited to send in a videotape putting forward – in any way that they saw fit – why they deserved to win a million, while demonstrating any special talents that they might have. Mifune and Ashida had sifted through the original batch of tapes, getting them down to a manageable one hundred. The pair had seen most of these applicants last week. Both reporting back how surprising it was that an individual – so funny and confident on tape – became so nervous and inarticulate in front of an audience. The list rapidly dwindled to ten. All of whom had been asked to attend a final audition at which, unbeknownst to them, they would be observed by the wider production team including Kenji.

Looking through the list that Mifune had provided him with, Kenji saw that the final ten included an equal mixture of men and women. One in particular, he had been told, stood out. In his early thirties, he was known only as 'Endo' and had given his occupation on the application form as 'actor and voice-over artist'. The production team was confident that Endo was by far the best contestant – he was witty, funny, articulate and handsome. But they had to be certain that he would be all these things under the extreme conditions of the show. Which was the purpose of today's audition.

Each contestant had been invited to the Cerulean Tower where they would be kept waiting in a room for an hour. Maybe even more if the team felt it was necessary. The room had been stripped bare of all but a chair and a number of props including a brightly coloured set of children's building blocks; a pair of women's high-heel shoes; a raincoat; a tricycle; a large tyre. All of these items Eriko had won by entering competitions and they might be all that the contestant, if they were similarly successful, would have available to keep themselves occupied during their stay in the *Millyennaire* apartment. The team would be judging not just their ability to keep themselves amused, but also others who might be watching. The test was simple enough. Any contestant who made use of the props in the allotted timeframe would be considered suitable for stage two of the audition. The team – watching by way of a hidden camera – dearly hoped that it would be Endo. Stage two, which would take place on Sunday, saw the contestant left alone in a room with a large pile of competitions that had been cut out of magazines and newspapers. They would have an hour in which to enter as many as possible: answering questions, devising slogans and spotting the odd one out. At the end of which they would be scored on their performance.

It was going to be a long weekend, but he was looking forward to it, Kenji thought, as he quickened his pace. He would have to hurry if he was going to make the 8.01 a.m. train to Tokyo. As he passed the supermarket, his thoughts turned to Dai. He had seen her last week, waved and crossed the road to talk to her, when he had spotted Tomo. Since her husband's return it had seemed sensible to stay away and while he missed their chats, her pleasant manner, he knew it was the best thing to do. At least that's what he told himself when he saw her again – standing outside the entrance to the supermarket, pressed up against the wall as far as she could go – and crossed over to the other side of the road. Standing behind a parked delivery truck where he knew he could not be seen, he stopped and watched her. She was wearing her uniform and the thick quilted jacket usually worn by staff packing freezers. He wondered she did not feel overdressed given it was such a warm summer's morning. Her head was bowed, her face hidden, and in her right hand she carried a plastic shopping bag that appeared to be empty. In the short space of time since he had last seen her, Kenji observed that a dramatic change had come over Dai. Previously a plump, pretty woman she had lost several kilogrammes and despite her jacket, looked underweight, gaunt even. She was wearing a large pair of black sunglasses.

He thought about the train he had to catch and began to walk off. There was not enough time to go and talk to her, he reasoned. Nor was it a good thing to do. Life was going well at the moment and he didn't want to put anything in jeopardy. But could he really walk away? There was a time when she had been a good friend to him. Surely he should return the favour?

Running quickly across the road, he came to stand before her. 'Dai,' he said softly.

She did not respond so he repeated her name, more loudly.

'Dai. It's me, Kenji.'

She looked up at him, but he could not see her eyes through the dark lenses of her sunglasses.

'Kenji.' Her voice sounded artificially bright, forced even, and he wondered if she had been drinking. There was something about her manner that put him in mind of Hoshino. 'You look well. Your new job must suit you.'

'It does. Very much so.' When Kenji felt nervous, he was inclined to talk too much. Which is exactly what he did now. He told her about anything that came to mind: the show, the production team, the auditions that were planned for the weekend. Several seconds passed before he realised that she was not listening and behind those darkened sunglasses she was staring at the floor. 'Dai, is everything all right? You look different, distracted.'

She lifted her head again slowly. It was almost as if she were drugged. When her face was in line with his, he saw that her bottom lip he had always found so full and shapely, was quivering. A large tear rolled out from beneath her sunglasses and down her cheek. Rummaging in his pocket for a handkerchief, he implored her, 'Please don't cry. It is my very last wish to see you cry.'

'I'm just being silly.' Refusing the handkerchief, she wiped the tear away with the back of her hand and then again as another one fell down after it. 'Now you must go. My husband will be here any minute and he must not see us talking. He was very angry last time.'

A horrible thought struck Kenji. 'Take off your glasses so that I can see your eyes.' He was aware that his voice was shaking.

She withdrew from him as much as was possible given that her back was already pressed up against the wall, and shook her head. 'They are tired and puffy. I did not sleep well last night.'

'Why are you standing here? Why are you not inside at work?' he persisted.

'I have been inside,' she admitted. 'They sent me away. They said that I was no good to anybody this tired.'

When her voice faltered, he knew immediately that she was lying. Why though? What had happened to turn this once vibrant, outgoing woman into a quivering, frightened creature? From someone whose openness was her most attractive feature to someone who was quite clearly hiding something? A desire to know the truth took hold of him. He reached out, even though a voice was shouting inside his head, 'Don't do it.' It was rude, inconsiderate, hurtful to a woman whom he cared about and yet he could not seem to stop himself. Reaching out, he grabbed the glasses from her face revealing that her right eye was bruised and swollen, the lid forced closed. 'Who did this to you?' His voice was calm and measured, although with each word he spoke the anger grew inside him.

She snatched the glasses back. 'How dare you. It is none of your business. Absolutely none of your business.'

'Please don't be cross with me. It is only because I care about you. Who did this to you? Did he?'

Standing rooted to the spot, she began to rock slowly back and forth, her head bowed.

He wanted to grab her, make her stop. She was frightening him now. Then suddenly a thought occurred to him. He was a man of means. Miru TV paid him handsomely. If he couldn't use it to help his friends then what was the point?

'I cannot let this go on.' He held her firmly by the shoulders. 'You must come away with me. I will find you somewhere safe to stay. Somewhere he can't find you.'

Looking up at him, she laughed. Dismissively, or so he thought. 'What about your job? Your life? Your wife? Your children? Would you forget about them so quickly and come away with me?'

He spluttered. 'I didn't mean . . .' How could he explain without hurting her that he didn't mean that he would go away with her? That his only intention was to place her somewhere safe away from her husband. And how did she know about Ami and the children? Certainly it was a mistake to have lied to her that first day, to pretend that he was divorced. But the longer the lie persisted, the harder it had been to tell the truth.

It appeared that she knew the questions he was asking himself. When she answered, her voice was cold and distant. 'I saw you with them. In the park having a picnic. And don't tell me that it was your sister again because I saw you kissing her.'

He remembered the kiss. He had instigated it. Thirsty from their game of baseball, Ami had quickly consumed the contents of a can of fizzy drink and promptly burped. Embarrassed, she had clamped a hand to her mouth as the children rolled around on the blanket laughing. He had found the entire incident charming and leant across to kiss her on the lips, until she finally batted him away saying, 'Enough of your nonsense.'

'You men are all the same.' Dai laughed mirthlessly. 'Now stop bothering me and go away.'

'I'm sorry I lied. It was a stupid mistake.' He tightened his grip on her shoulders. 'But that doesn't change anything. I still want to help you.'

Shaking herself free she hissed, 'It's for your own good. Go away. You will only make things worse. Please, for my sake.' Her loud sobs were starting to attract the attention of passers-by.

'What's going on here?'

Spinning round, Kenji found himself staring up [ ]
Dai's husband, Tomo. Anger and loathing boiled up ins[ ]
looked from Dai – who was whimpering – back to her hu[ ]

'Yamada-san was just leaving.' She pushed Kenji away. '[ ]
you? He was just passing. On his way to work.' She pushed him
again, more forcibly this time, so that he stumbled into a nearby
trolley.

'You can't treat her like this. I won't let you.' Kenji was enraged
by Tomo's smug expression. He looked like an old lizard, dried and
wrinkled by the sun.

'Come on, let's go.' Tomo grabbed Dai's arm and pulled her
towards him.

'Don't do this,' Kenji pleaded with Dai, grabbing her other arm.
'You don't have to go.'

There were tears falling freely down her cheeks now. 'Don't you
understand? You are making things so much worse.' The expression
on her face was so terrified, he dropped her arm and watched as she
was dragged away, stumbling after her husband.

He stared after them as they rounded the corner and disappeared
from view. Minutes must have passed in which he did nothing but
stand there. In time he realised that there was nothing left for him to
do. He turned and crossed the road. The first thing he heard was
squealing wheels as the car came racing around the corner. Then he
saw their faces – Dai's terrified, Tomo's smug, determined.

FORTY

'Dai.' Kenji tried to speak but his mouth felt dry and the words that emerged were barely decipherable. She must have heard him though, because through the fog that surrounded his head, a soft, friendly voice came.

'It's Ami. Your wife Ami.'

A hand – smooth and warm – touched his. At first lightly and then with a firm grip, kneading the fleshy pads on the palm of his hand. The sensation lulled him back to sleep.

'Kenji, I'm sorry, so very sorry.'

'Ami?' He was awake again. This time the words he spoke were clearer although still mumbled.

'Kenji, it's Dai. I had to see you. To say how very sorry I am for what happened. For what he did to you.'

Very slowly, he opened his eyes. Dai was standing in front of him against a background of blinding white light. Or was it a dream? The plumpness had returned to her face, and she was smiling down at him. He had never seen her wear her hair loose like that before and wanted to tell her how pretty she looked, but the words would not come.

'It made me see things more clearly,' she continued.

Reaching out, he tried to grab her hand, but her fingertips slipped through his and she began to drift away, her voice growing softer.

'I'm leaving him. This time for good. I'm going to go somewhere he'll never find me. I can't tell you where. It's better that way. I wanted to say goodbye first. And sorry. I am more sorry than you will ever know. You are a good man, Kenji. I will miss you.'

Even after she had gone the smell of her perfume lingered. It was fresh like cucumbers.

To protest was too much effort. Floating was much easier. And pleasurable too, he realised, as he allowed himself to drift slowly down what appeared to be a tunnel filled with bright white light, rolling first one way and then the next, bobbing up and down.

'Kenji.'

Somewhere below, his name was being called. Rolling over, he looked down. On the ground beneath, there were a number of people running along after him. He recognised Ami first. Then Eriko, Mifune, and Hoshino. None of them could reach him, he realised with a chuckle, watching as they ran after him, futilely jumping up and down, attempting to catch the hem or the cord of his chequered dressing gown. It occurred to him that Dai would not have tried to drag him down, would have happily allowed him to float, and with this thought he sank down suddenly and Ami was able to catch his ankle. But she was not strong enough to hold on to it and so he drifted away, laughing.

'I need to talk to you about my dresses,' Hoshino called. 'Red or blue for the opening show. What do you think works best?' She held two dresses up in front of her as he turned his back and heard her stamp her heeled foot in fury.

'Do what you want,' he shouted down at them. 'I don't care anymore.' It felt too good to be this weightless and unencumbered to give it up. There was nothing that would make him want to come back down. Except perhaps Dai, and she was gone now.

Ami grabbed the belt of his dressing gown and ran along with him. 'It's time to come down,' she demanded, impatiently. 'You have been asleep for long enough and there are important things that need to be done.' As Ami pleaded with her husband, Eriko pulled at her arm, forcing her to stand still. As Kenji drifted away from them, Mifune ran forward to take their place, running along below him. Neither smiling nor frowning, her pretty face was perfectly placid as she clamped a red clipboard firmly to her chest. 'I have a number of pieces of theme music I need you to listen to. You must make a choice. The music department must know by tomorrow at the very latest.'

Each demand was like a small weight hanging off him and he felt himself sinking lower and lower, until he landed softly on the ground. Fighting against an enormous sensation of having lost something wonderful, his eyes opened. The white walls; the narrow bed that creaked underneath his weight; the vague smell of disinfectant. It was all horribly familiar. He was back in hospital. How had he got here? Hearing a noise to his left, he called out hopefully, 'Doppo, is that you?'

'Yamada-san. You're awake.'

It wasn't Doppo. It was a nurse, dressed in white.

'Please don't try to speak.' She popped a thermometer in his mouth while consulting a small watch pinned to the front of her uniform.

'Dai.'

'Pardon?' she removed the thermometer and allowed him to repeat what he had said before popping it back in. 'Dai?' She frowned. 'Ah yes, she did come. After you first arrived. She wanted us to let you know that she'd been here. She hasn't been since. Of course your wife is a regular visitor with your colleagues from work, Mifune and Hoshino. I must say that we are very excited to have a person of such importance in our hospital. But . . .' She looked vaguely disapproving as deep frown lines cut across her forehead. '. . . you need to rest and Mifune is waiting to see you outside. I will allow her a few minutes but nothing more.'

Kenji nodded and the nurse disappeared through the white curtain. Moments later Mifune appeared.

'Yamada-san. You are awake. I am so happy to see you looking better. We have all been very worried.'

Kenji struggled to sit up in bed. Noticing his discomfort, Mifune helped him to adjust the pillows.

'Where am I?'

'You're in hospital.'

'But how? I was . . . The auditions. I was on my way to the auditions. I can't be late. Will you take me? If we leave now we'll get there.' Kenji pulled the bedcovers back and was surprised to see his left leg stretched out in front of him, completely covered in plaster. 'Oh no,' he moaned, looking down at it. 'Not again. Why must this always happen to me?'

'The doctors said that the bones were still weak from your previous fracture. They also said that you were lucky just to break a leg,' Mifune soothed as she patted the pillows behind his back.

'The accident,' he repeated blankly, looking up at her.

A small frown wrinkled her otherwise perfectly smooth brow. It was such a minute movement that he would almost certainly have missed it if he hadn't been studying her face.

'What is it?' he demanded, starting to feel frightened. 'What's the matter?'

'They haven't told you?'

He shook his head.

'You were run down by a car.'

'Run down. No, I can't have been.' He searched his brain for a memory, anything that would confirm what she was saying, but there was nothing there. The last thing he remembered was that he had been on his way to the audition when he had seen Dai. They had spoken. Then her husband had arrived. Of course, Tomo. His face through the car windscreen was the last thing Kenji had seen. Just thinking about it terrified him. Where was Tomo now? Was he still free, roaming the streets? Would he want to come back and finish Kenji off? Or would he be satisfied with the job he'd done? Kenji struggled to push these thoughts to the back of his mind. He couldn't think about them at the moment. All that mattered was that he had to get to the auditions.

'The auditions. We will still make them if we hurry?'

Mifune hesitated.

'What is it? What's the matter?' he demanded. He had never seen her lost for words before.

'The auditions have been over for some time.'

'How long?'

263

'Four weeks.'

He could hear the blood pumping in his ears. 'The show. I must . . .' A cold sweat broke out all over his body. 'I was floating. I should have come back down. I knew I could have come back down but I didn't want to.' Grunting, he attempted to swing one leg off the bed on to the floor, and then the other one, but the effort was too much. He felt dizzy and sank back down on to the pillows.

'Please, Yamada-san, do not over-exert yourself. You are not well enough. Rest assured that everything is in order. The police have even arrested the man who did this to you. There was a witness. A woman who worked in the nearby supermarket. He was a petty thief and had stolen the car he was driving in when he knocked you down.' He is in prison now.

Kenji's pyjamas felt damp and clammy against his skin. He scratched his neck absentmindedly. 'What about the auditions? How did they go?'

Pulling up a nearby chair, Mifune sat down. 'The auditions went well. Endo was, as we expected, the better contestant. We filmed a pilot episode and tested it with some focus groups. Their reaction was extremely positive. We were ready to start filming the series when Endo pulled out.'

'No.' How could things possibly get much worse? he wondered.

She nodded. 'He was offered a role in a soap opera.'

'What happened? What did you do?'

'Ashida-san and I went back to the shortlisted candidates, but none of them were appropriate or available. So we returned to the initial applicants and auditioned ten more. Of those one stood out. A woman. More mature than we had imagined the contestant might be. But she has a certain eccentricity.'

'Do you have any stills?'

'I thought I did.' She searched in her file. 'But I must have left them at the office.'

Beyond the curtain that surrounded his bed, someone coughed: a painful, racking sound that left them both silent until it had finished.

'We didn't have time to record another pilot episode with the new contestant, but NBC did not mind so much. Given the reaction to Endo they were keen to get the first episode out. In fact they are so confident it will be successful they want it to go out live rather than pre-recorded as previously agreed.'

'When does the first episode go out?'

'Tonight.'

'Tonight?' Kenji repeated disbelievingly. 'How could so much have happened in so little time?'

'You briefed the team well.' She gave a rare smile. 'They wanted to do this for you while you recovered.'

The curtain opened and the nurse came back in. 'Your ten minutes are up,' she told Mifune sternly. 'Yamada-san must rest now.'

'Of course.' Mifune promptly stood up. 'I will call your wife immediately and tell her that you are awake. She was very concerned that you would miss the first episode.' The chair scraped loudly across the floor as she pushed it back against the wall. 'I will see you again tomorrow. Goodbye for now.'

'Goodbye,' Kenji said, allowing the nurse to place two white tablets on the tip of his tongue. He had also wanted to say thank you and that he did not know what he would do without her if, as she was always saying she wanted to, she went to America .

FORTY-ONE

There was the sound of humming: a cheerful, melodic sound that eased him slowly from sleep into wakefulness. He lay there for several seconds, listening to the tune with his eyes closed. When he did open his eyes, he noticed a familiar spotted blouse out of the corner of his eye and turned his head to where Ami was arranging several large, round, pink apples in a plastic bowl on his bedside cabinet.

Putting the last apple in the bowl, she surveyed her work. A small smile of satisfaction stayed on her lips as she wiped her hands on a square, chequered cloth, a fresh supply of which she kept in her bag. She turned and saw that Kenji was awake and looking at her.

'I thought they were better than flowers.' She hesitated and then sat down on the bed next to him, brushing the hair back and planting a large kiss on his forehead. When she drew back to look at him, the smile disappeared from her lips, which formed a thin line, and her brow puckered. 'You had us all very worried. When I think of what that man did to you I shiver. He could have killed you.'

'Well, he didn't,' Kenji offered reassuringly. He didn't want to waste anymore time than he had already done on Tomo. He was in prison where he belonged and Dai was gone, somewhere safe. It was over now. 'I'm very much alive. Maybe even a little bit smarter. Think I must have banged my head. It is a shame it didn't do the same thing for my eye.' He touched the black leather patch.

'The man is a monster.'

'He is better forgotten about. Now . . .' Kenji leant forward, straining to see past the curtain that had been left fractionally open. '. . . where are the children?'

The metal bedframe creaked loudly as Ami shifted to find a more comfortable position. 'Wami-san is looking after them. They will be along later this evening.'

Kenji frowned as he lay back on the pillows and took the plastic cup of orange juice Ami held out to him. He had managed a little food earlier, but had nothing to drink. Now he felt dehydrated to the point of dizziness and gulped down the juice, allowing Ami to refill the cup. 'Where's your mother?'

'Staying with my sister in Osaka. She has been gone for a few weeks and will be away a few more. How do you feel?' Stroking Kenji's stubbled cheek with the palm of her hand, she smiled. 'Someone needs a shave.'

He was aware of how bad he must look and if he hadn't felt so drowsy would have been embarrassed. His hair felt oily and unwashed and his scalp itched. The corners of his mouth were dry and cracked, and his mouth tasted like his teeth could do with a good brush. 'I need more than a shave. Oh no, not again.'

'What is it?' Ami sprang up from the bed as if she'd been electrocuted.

'It's nothing,' he grimaced. 'It's just that occasionally my leg itches and I really want to scratch it. But I just can't get at it.'

'I thought . . .' Without warning, her face crumpled.

'What is it?' It suddenly occurred to him that maybe the doctors had shared with her some news to which he had not been party. Maybe his leg was more seriously injured than he had been told. 'My leg.' He looked down at it, laid out on the bed in front of him. 'I will walk on it again, won't I?'

'Yes, of course you will. It was a clean break. Just like the other one.' Ami sobbed, tears flowing freely down both cheeks. From beyond the curtain came the hum of the nurses' voices as they started their evening rounds.

'Then what is it? Why are you crying?'

'It is just me. I am being silly. You see when Mifune-san rang I tried to get here as quickly as possible, but I was delayed. By the time I arrived you were asleep. I thought that maybe you would sleep for a long time again and I wouldn't see you.'

'You're here now.'

'I'm a terrible wife.' She sniffed loudly. 'When I think of the way that I have treated you, I am ashamed. When all that you were trying to do was to make a life for us, your family.'

Stunned, Kenji watched as Ami dabbed at her face with a handkerchief. It did little to stem the flow of tears that just kept falling. He noticed that there were dark shadows beneath her eyes and her wrists looked slimmer than usual. Had she lost more weight? Had she not been sleeping?

'You have been a loyal and patient wife,' he whispered softly, this time stroking her face. 'Even when I pushed you to the limit, you stayed by my side.'

'You have made me very proud,' Ami gulped.

'And you me. The way that you have coped with everything that has happened. Look at you. A successful businesswoman.'

She sniffed dismissively.

'You are. Now dry your tears. I can't have my beautiful wife getting upset. But isn't it just our luck?' he chuckled, thinking about Eriko. 'We finally get the old battleaxe out of the apartment, have the chance of some time to ourselves and I'm stuck in here.'

Allowing herself a small smile, Ami slipped out through the white curtain surrounding Kenji's bed explaining that she was going to throw some water on her face. As Kenji watched her go, he understood that he was truly a lucky man. He had taken it for granted before. Being a husband and a father. But now he saw. There was nothing more that one man could ever hope for than to be surrounded by a supportive and loving family. Dai had shown him that and wherever she was now he made her the faithful promise that he would cherish them forever.

A few minutes later, when Ami returned, he held out his hand to her. 'Ami, I just wanted to say . . .'

'Look at all the cards your colleagues have sent,' she interrupted, patting his hand and putting it back down on the bed as she walked past and began picking up a number of cards arranged neatly on the side cabinet and the bed rail that ran behind Kenji's head. 'Wishing you a speedy recovery, Mifune.' She replaced the card and picked up another, showing him the cover – a man in plaid trousers, a matching cap and a red jumper, poised to swing a golf club. 'Looking forward to that game of golf you promised me when you get out, Aran Goto.' This card seemed to please her more than the rest and she squeezed Kenji's hand. 'Your former colleagues from NBC even sent a gift. It came with a card signed by Shin Ishida. Look.' She pointed at a house plant sitting on the trolley that stretched across his bed.

'It's a ficus.' He stared accusingly at the plant.

'Isn't it lovely? I seem to remember . . .' Ami's sentence trailed off into mid-air.

Kenji took the opportunity to push the trolley away, and in doing so remembered something else; something very important. 'What about the show? It's on tonight. I can't miss it.' For the second time that day he pulled back the bedcovers and attempted to stand, only to collapse back down on to the pillows again when the effort proved to be too much.

'Don't worry,' Ami soothed. 'I've asked the doctors and they said that it is okay for us all to watch it here with you in the hospital's television room. The twins will be coming. Your friend Izo. I have also asked mother's friend Wami-san and . . .' Ami paused. 'Her son, Inagaki.'

Kenji groaned. He wouldn't have chosen to spend time with the man who had taken such pleasure in tormenting him while he worked at the bank.

'Please don't be angry,' Ami pleaded. 'It will be a small party to celebrate your recovery. I have prepared some food.'

'When do we go?'

'We can go now.' Ami stood up and grabbed a wheelchair that had been sitting at the bottom of the bed.

He protested but, looking at his legs, he knew that it was useless.

FORTY-TWO

Kenji stared at the television in silence as his brain stumbled over words that might describe how he felt. Not only had he been drifting in and out of consciousness for the last four weeks and missed all of the preparations for *Millyennaire*, but one of his legs was broken and he was about to watch the first episode of the game show that he had created being screened on a 13-inch, black and white portable set with a wire coat hanger acting in the place of an aerial. There was not even a proper stand for the TV. It had been set down on a metal trolley of the same type that was used to deliver meals on the wards.

'I'm sorry,' Ami apologised, testing that the brake had been applied to his wheelchair. The note of irritability in her apology was evident. 'It's all that was available. The patients' TV stopped working last week. This one had to be borrowed from one of the junior doctors. If I'd have known I would have arranged to bring our own. But I didn't. Not until an hour ago. By then it was too late.'

Kenji felt frustrated but knew there was no point getting upset about something he couldn't change. Anyway, he didn't want to put Ami under anymore stress.

The television room was long and narrow, with metallic grey windows running along the length of the two longest walls. One set overlooked the car park below. The other provided a view of the corridor and any patients or staff that passed through it. Vertical slatted blinds were supposed to prevent people from seeing in or out, but they had started to fall apart and were hanging haphazardly at intervals along the top of the window frames. Low, cushioned chairs were arranged around the perimeter of the room, at the far end of which sat the television on top of the trolley.

'It could be a lot worse.' Kenji patted his wife's hand that was resting on his right shoulder. Outside, an elderly man passed by, shuffling down the corridor. He was wearing a hospital gown, gaping at the back, and was completely bald except for a few strands of stray, wispy hair that were standing up about his scalp, waving like antennae. There was a large, weeping wound on his head and although a nurse was standing beside him, guiding him along, he appeared to be confused and disorientated. As he passed, the old man's eyes locked with Kenji's who quickly looked away. 'Where are the children?' he asked with a sudden, involuntary shudder. 'I thought that they would be here.'

Ami, who had walked over to the furthest corner of the room where she began removing plates of food from two blue coolboxes, unwrapping and lying them across a long table, looked up over her shoulder. 'They should be here any minute. Look here they are now.'

The door to the television room flew open. Yumi and Yoshi came bowling through it, chattering excitedly.

'I told everybody at school. Taka wanted to have a sleepover so that we could all watch it together, but I said I couldn't go. She was very upset, so I said we could have one next week.'

'You're so stupid.'

'I am not.'

'She's just saying that because she thinks that you will take her to the TV studio and she'll meet lots of famous people. I know because her brother's in my class and he told me.'

They did not see Kenji at first. Ami had left his wheelchair at the front of the room, near the television, and he was struggling to turn it round. By the time he realised that the brake was still on and finally managed to face the chair in the opposite direction, the twins were both staring at him in silence.

271

'It looks worse than it is,' he soothed, although doubted very much that it did. His left leg was covered in plaster from the base of his toes to the top of his thigh and stretched out horizontally in front of him, supported by metal rests. The effort of turning the wheelchair had left him breathless, panting and sweating.

Yumi was the first to approach her father, moving cautiously. 'Does it hurt?' she asked, staring at his leg.

'Just when I try to kick a ball,' he said.

She giggled and moved closer, prodding the plaster with one finger.

'Yumi,' Ami scolded, 'your father is not a specimen to be studied. He has been through a tremendous ordeal.'

'Never mind her,' Kenji whispered, grabbing his daughter's hand and pulling her towards him, where he clasped her firmly with one arm around the waist and to the side of his chair. 'Yoshi, you too,' he beckoned and then lowering his voice to a conspiratorial whisper said, 'If you get some pens I'll let you write on it.'

Large smiles broke out on the twins' faces and they both dropped down on to the ground, where Yoshi tore open his rucksack and removed a pencil case, distributing the contents between him and his sister. As they bickered over who would have what pen, Kenji greeted his remaining two visitors. Ami had told him that they were coming, but he had not believed that they would.

'Inagaki, Wami. It is very good of you to come.'

'Yamada-san.' Leaning heavily on his walking stick, Inagaki limped over to the wheelchair. 'How are you feeling?'

'That I am a very lucky man to be here, surrounded by my lovely family.' He grimaced as Yumi leant heavily on his leg and began to draw a picture of a cat.

'It's a terrible business,' the bank manager continued with genuine feeling. 'To be run down in your own neighbourhood. One that is normally so safe.'

Kenji nodded again and, bending down, asked the twins to go and help their mother. He wanted to talk to Inagaki in private. He did not want there to be any awkwardness between them. At least

272

not tonight when so much else had already gone wrong. 'About the sponsorship. I've been meaning to say . . .'

'Please. Not another word.' Inagaki raised one hand in front of his chest. 'Call it a favour for a friend. Two friends. Now . . .' He turned away and in one expansive gesture took in the table of food that Ami had laid out. '. . . look at all this lovely food. Ami, you have surpassed yourself and I for one am hungry.'

To pursue the subject was futile, Kenji realised, as he watched Inagaki piling a paper plate with food as Ami pushed dish after dish at him. It seemed entirely plausible that Inagaki had intended his role in orchestrating the sponsorship deal to act as way of an apology for how he had treated Kenji. In fact, Kenji strongly suspected that it was. But the bank manager was too proud to admit it.

'Kenji, some of your favourite food.' Ami handed Kenji a paper plate and although he took it and said thank you, he knew that he would not eat it. Whether it was nerves or the absence of any discernible appetite after having been kept on a liquid diet for the last four weeks, he did not know. Certainly the doctors had said that it might take some time to get back to how he was before and not to expect too much too soon.

'What time is it?' he asked anxiously. His own watch was lying on top of his bedside cabinet and there did not appear to be a clock in the room.

'Six fifty-five,' Ami replied, clapping her hands together. 'Time for everybody to sit down. Quick, Yoshi,' she bid their son as she wheeled Kenji back to the front of the room, 'turn the television on.'

The set was so small that in order to get a good view, any view, everybody had to pull one of the chairs away from the wall and squeeze in on either side of Kenji, as tightly as possible. Just as they had got comfortable, they were disturbed by a loud banging on the window. Izo was running down the corridor.

'Sorry I'm late,' he called, throwing his suitcase in the corner of the room and clambering over Kenji's wheelchair to sit cross-legged on the floor in front of him. 'Have I missed anything? Has it started?' he demanded.

'We've just turned the television on.' Kenji bristled. Did it really take this long for people just to sit down? They were going to miss the start of the show.

'Shhhh,' Ami whispered, leaning across the small circle of chairs to turn up the volume knob.

They had sat down just in time. From the two small speakers on either side of the screen, *Millyennaire*'s synthetic theme tune began to play: at first softly and then building to a loud crescendo of drums and keyboards. What would have appeared as multi-coloured lights began to flash in a random sequence as a deep male voice announced, 'Ladies and gentlemen, welcome to *Millyennaire*. Your host for this evening is – ' He paused as the applause from the frantically clapping studio audience grew so loud that the small television began to vibrate on the trolley. ' – Hana Hoshino.'

At that very second, Kenji forgot he was in hospital. So great was his excitement he imagined himself there, sitting among the studio audience, and began to clap and cheer along. All around him, his friends and family joined in.

'Look, she's wearing my dress. The red one, I think. It's difficult to tell.' Ami squealed, clapping her hands in front of her as she bounced around on her seat. 'It looks perfect. Just as I imagined it would.'

The theme music gradually quietened until it was barely audible. At which point Hoshino uttered her first words on live television for twenty years. Everybody in the room held their breath.

'Good morning, ladies and gentlemen.'

Kenji looked at the clock on the wall. It was 7 p.m. 'Did she just say what I think she said? Tell me she didn't,' he demanded, looking all about him at the horrified faces of the others.

Inagaki, the palm of his right hand clamped across his forehead, groaned and nodded. Ami simply stared at him, her mouth hanging open, as the children tittered loudly on their chairs.

'But . . . How . . .' Kenji spluttered. 'It's scripted. With an autocue. They would have done a dry-run.'

'Stage fright,' Inagaki suggested and it seemed that he was right because Hoshino quickly and professionally corrected her mistake.

Putting it to the back of his mind, Kenji listened as she explained the show's format. He was leaning so far forward in his wheelchair that his back muscles were starting to painfully cramp and it was becoming increasingly difficult to stay in any one position.

'I can't hear her. Can someone turn the TV up,' he snapped as Ami turned the dial another notch and the trolley now continuously vibrated underneath the reverberations from the set.

He was not alone in appearing uncomfortable. The others did too and the atmosphere in the room was starting to become increasingly oppressive. Everyone had expected great things from Hoshino. She had once been a great TV presenter – smooth, polished, confident and above all glamorous. Whatever she had then she appeared to have lost now. Her presentation style was awkward, she paused at the wrong cues, repeatedly gave a high-pitched nervous giggle, and stumbled over her words. The audience, though, was kind. They clapped appreciatively at appropriate intervals and when she showed them the cabin in the corner of the studio where the contestant was now living – had been living for the last two days – they gasped.

'Our contestant has no idea that we are all sitting outside. As far as she is concerned this is a real apartment in downtown Tokyo.'

As she spoke, two men appeared. Dressed in black jumpsuits, they were pushing a large TV screen, at least four feet by three feet, mounted on two long legs, out from the shadows towards the studio audience. It stood blank until a spot of light appeared in the centre and an image flooded the space. It showed the small, sparsely furnished apartment inside the cabin, lingering on the luridly patterned wallpaper and the worn tatami mats. Next the camera passed over the kitchen, the sitting area and the bathroom before zooming in on a figure sleeping soundly, snoring loudly, on a futon.

'This footage was taken three, no, that was two days ago.'

There was another gasp as the screen cut to the contestant being blindfolded, guided into a black car with darkened windows and driven to the red studio door, at which Kenji had first stood a few weeks previously. The door was opened and she was guided by a hand he recognised as Mifune's through many long corridors and finally to the studio and cabin door. It was the first time that Kenji had seen the contestant and although her face was being deliberately hidden from view, he could tell she was an elderly lady; much older than he had expected.

'Upon arriving, our contestant spent some time exploring the apartment.'

Footage filmed from overhead showed the elderly woman exploring the apartment, opening various cupboards and tut-tutting loudly as she found them empty. Her hair was grey and curly and she was wearing a floral housecoat over the clothes in which she had arrived. When she had finished exploring she sat down heavily in the apartment's only armchair and another camera cut to her face.

'Mother!' Ami screamed.

'It's grandmother,' Yumi and Yoshi giggled.

Kenji rocked back and forth in his wheelchair. His head was reeling. 'This is impossible.'

Wami was the one person who did not say anything. Who had not said anything since she first arrived.

Hoshino, too, struggled to maintain her composure. It was evidently the first time she had seen the contestant or else she would have been more prepared. 'What a surprise.' Several seconds passed in which she said nothing at all. By the time she focused on the autocue, it had already moved on and she struggled to keep up. 'Our contestant Eriko has been making good use of her time in the apartment. Catching up on some much needed sleep.' Various clips appeared on screen: some depicting Eriko sleeping on her left or right; sometimes on her back snoring; sleeping on the futon; sleeping in a single armchair. The studio audience laughed loudly.

Kenji saw Ami flinch and look away from the television.

'What does she think she's doing? She will disgrace us. The entire family,' she wept into a handkerchief.

'She must have seen the advertisement in the paper,' he said through clenched teeth. 'You know what your mother's like. Always looking for ways to make money. She thinks she's doing you a favour. She couldn't have done anything worse. This will ruin my reputation when everyone finds out who she is. They'll think I put her in there.'

'I can't bear to watch.' Ami stood up and left the room. The door banged loudly behind her.

'She awakes only to eat,' Hoshino's narration continued, as more clips of Eriko were shown: slurping noodles; hungrily gobbling rice; lingering over small cakes.

'That's not like Grandma,' Yoshi whispered loudly, looking at Kenji.

He had to admit that this was true. While living with the Yamadas, Eriko had subsisted entirely on a few hours' sleep and a diet that would not have satisfied a small bird. It was, she repeatedly told anyone who would listen, one of the symptoms of old age that she had to endure. To look at her now was like looking at a different woman. But more importantly it made for very dull viewing. The contestant was supposed to keep him or herself entertained and in doing so, the audience. Now, not only would people think he had rigged the show, they would think he had made a bad choice as well.

The camera cut to Hoshino. 'Yes, well,' she laughed nervously, 'our contestant certainly does seem to be tired. And hungry. And she doesn't appear to be interested in entering a single competition.' The camera lingered on a large pile of newspapers and magazines.

Kenji couldn't bear to watch anymore and to know that anybody else might be watching it. 'Switch it off,' he demanded, wheeling himself out of the room.

FORTY-THREE

'Snooze TV.'

Mifune dropped another newspaper on to the pile on Kenji's lap. It was folded open at *Last Week's TV*: an article that ran every Monday in some of the more established publications. In the bottom right-hand corner of the page, a grainy, black and white photo taken from last night's episode of *Millyennaire* depicted Eriko fast asleep on a futon: her head lolling backwards and mouth slightly agape. In a small glass on the floor next to her head, it was just about possible to make out a set of false teeth soaking in water.

When Eriko had first moved in with the Yamadas, it had been a source of great irritation to Kenji that she left her dentures out to soak anywhere around the apartment. He was always happening on them, in a glass on the kitchen counter, next to the telephone on the low-rise table. Once even in the fridge. Each time he had groaned and complained to Ami. Now he was beginning to wish that he had been nicer to the old woman, kinder and more patient. If he had, then maybe she would not have felt the need to respond to his advertisement in the classifieds section of the *Mainichi News* and his wife would still be talking to him.

'I spent the time cleaning out my children's fish tank instead.' Mifune handed him another newspaper, another and then another. 'Dull . . . Don't waste your time . . . I thought that this was supposed to be a game show? Where's the competition?'

278

He shuddered. It was evident that Mifune was just doing what she believed to be her job. And she was, with the greatest attention to detail and efficiency. But did she have to be so brutal? At least the newspaper critics hadn't picked up on the fact that the contestant was the producer's mother-in-law. Or that his wife made the costumes.

'That is enough.'

Putting the rest of the newspapers and magazines down on a nearby chair, Mifune looked down at where Kenji was sitting in his wheelchair, with one leg stretched out in front of him. It was obvious that she was waiting for her next instruction. He was beginning to wish he hadn't called her after last night's show, asking her to visit him in hospital, and bring a few key members of the team along. They were waiting outside the television room now; trying hard not to look in through the windows that were barely covered by the broken blinds. Of course the ward sister had strongly objected: both about the patients' restroom being taken over for a meeting and about Kenji working when he was supposed to be recuperating. It had been necessary to promise her many things, including Hana Hoshino's autograph for her and each of the other nurses, before she agreed to turn a blind eye.

'Ah.' A thought suddenly popped into Kenji's head.

'What is it?' Mifune asked.

There was one person who could turn the tide of public opinion in their favour. No matter what everybody else was saying, one good word from her could transform the entire situation. No matter how diabolical it seemed. 'What about Leiko Kobayashi?'

Mifune picked up the *Mainichi News* from the pile of newspapers that she had put down. 'It's not good news, I'm afraid.'

'Read it to me.'

'Are you sure you want me to?'

'Yes, read it to me.'

With an exaggerated movement, Mifune opened the newspaper and began flicking quickly through the pages. When she found what she was looking for, she folded the entire paper in half, and then in half again before she began to read. ' "*Millyennaire* – it was claimed, by whom I don't know – would change the face of modern Japanese game shows, sending ripples of excitement through the international world of television. If this is the future then stop the bus, I want to get off. Where to begin? With the contestant is best, I think. My own grandmother could have done better and been more entertaining. Surprising since she has been bedridden for the last seven years following a severe stroke that left her speechless and paralysed down the left side." ' Mifune looked up.

'Go on.' He nodded.

' "Hoshino's performance was shambolic. After twenty years' absence from our television screens, one cannot help but wonder why she didn't stay away? She stumbled through her lines with as much elegance as an elephant on ice skates. And who could blame her? Perhaps she was dazzled by the sequins that covered literally every inch of her dress. Much like the contestant may end up being if last night's performance was anything to go by, I suspect the clothes designer listed in the show's credits as 'Ami' has been trapped in an apartment herself for the last twenty years. How else would she have failed to realise what is currently fashionable? Or that Hoshino is no longer the beauty she once was no matter how many fake gems you pin to the front of her dress?" '

'Enough, enough.' Kenji waved a hand about his head. 'Maybe, if the second episode is better Kobayashi will come round?'

Mifune laughed. 'Leiko Kobayahsi never reviews a show twice. Once is usually enough.'

Outside the room, a few members of the production team had formed an orderly queue. 'The team are very down since last night's show. Reading these reviews did not help matters. I know that they are looking forward to seeing you. Your words stirred them greatly last time and they are hoping for the same again to get them through this difficult patch.'

If a long, thin blade had been plunged deep into his chest it couldn't have hurt more. He exhaled sharply. Did he have it in him to be what they wanted him to be? Certainly the last speech had gone well, but that was with adequate time to prepare. Kenji had always been a man that could shine if he was given enough notice.

To perform well on the spot, without notice, was something that his extrovert colleagues had been better at. Surely, though, he could do it, turn things round? If there was no show then what else did he have? It would be back to the mail room and he couldn't bear that. Which is why he had to do it. For his sake as much as theirs.

'Bring them in.'

Mifune crossed the room to open the door.

'Come in. Yamada-san is ready to see you now.'

The first to appear in front of him and, at his bidding, sit down was Yoshida, the scriptwriter. She was followed by Ashida who, from what Kenji could ascertain, had risen to the ranks of Mifune's second-in-command over the last few weeks. The boy looked tired and his hair was unbrushed. According to Mifune he had been at work since five this morning dealing with press enquiries. Both gave Kenji lingering looks, oozing with so much sympathy he was obliged to look away. Also accompanying them was one of the show's cameramen, a make-up technician and one of Hoshino's bodyguards.

Kenji pulled Mifune's arm to attract her attention. 'What's he doing here?' he whispered when she had crouched down to his height. 'Why the bodyguard? Where's Hoshino-san?'

'She is unwell. I tried to speak with her first thing this morning, but she is suffering from a migraine and refuses to see anybody other than your friend, the bank manager. She asked that one of her bodyguards attend this meeting instead as she does not want to miss what you have to say and assures me that she will be fit for the next show.'

He nodded. Everyone had now sat down and was looking at him expectantly. It was not possible to delay the moment any longer. He wheeled himself round to face them better. It was a slow process that left him sweating and evidently made everyone else uncomfortable because when he finally did manage to turn round, they were all half standing, half sitting. As if they had been uncertain as to whether they should assist or watch him struggle. Using the wheelchair was bad enough, but having one leg stretched out horizontally in front of him meant he had to give himself at least an additional few feet of clearance before undertaking any manoeuvres. The nurses, however, had insisted upon it until he was certain that the spells of dizziness that afflicted him had passed.

'Thank you for coming.' He wiped his forehead with a handkerchief as a plastic cup filled with cold water appeared at his side. Mifune had fetched it from a cooler in the corner. He drained the cup in one go, allowing Mifune to take it away from him before she joined the others on the chairs.

It was difficult to meet their gaze so he toyed with the belt of his dark blue towelling dressing gown. This had to be good. This had to be better than the last time. Putting the belt to one side, he looked up, going so far as to linger on each person in turn. Then, very slowly, very deliberately, he clapped his hands together: at first softly, then more loudly. The hollow slap of flesh against flesh echoed throughout the room. He liked the way it sounded – strong and brave. Stronger and braver than he felt. He didn't want to stop.

At first the expression on their faces did not change. Everybody continued to look at him as if clapping was the most natural thing in the world to do, given the present circumstance. Ashida even smiled in encouragement, while Yoshida nodded her head along as though she had detected some hidden rhythm. But the more he clapped, the more visibly uncomfortable they became. Fujiwara, the make-up technician was the first to crack. She turned and glanced cautiously at Mifune. At her side, Yoshida tittered nervously into the palm of one hand, while Ito the cameraman's forehead creased into deep, angry frown lines. Even Hoshino's bodyguard, who had been idly picking at something on the leg of his trousers, stared hard at Kenji. Only one person appeared to be unperturbed by his behaviour and that was Mifune. She regarded him coolly. But he could tell enough from her poise – the way that she was leaning forward, listening to him, the way that her hand was holding a pen poised over a notebook, ready to write – to know that she had complete and utter confidence in him and his ability to turn this situation around. Imagining himself to be the man she saw, he felt powerful and brave.

He started to chuckle. It was not that he felt much like laughing, but the more he did, the easier it became. His muscles – at first stiff and tense – began to loosen and he started to enjoy himself although very much aware that if the clapping had cast doubt on his sanity, laughing would make matters worse. Which it had done, judging by Ashida's jaw, which was hanging open, and Ito, who was angrily rubbing his thigh as though it might prevent him from storming out of the room.

'Come on,' Kenji shouted at them. 'Join me.'

Not one of them responded or showed any indication of wanting to. Even Mifune was silent.

'Come on, just try.'

Ashida was the first to join in. His was a quiet, polite clap and the palms of his hands barely made contact.

'You're not at a classical music concert now,' Kenji cajoled until the young man grew braver, and clapped more loudly. He looked surprised and a large grin broke out on his face. It was not long before he was whooping loudly and because he looked like he was having so much fun, the others could not help but smile. A smile turned into a laugh, turned into a clap, turned into a whoop and soon everybody was making as much noise as they possibly could. Several seconds passed before they realised that Kenji had stopped clapping and laughing. When they did, they stopped too, abruptly.

'That was good.' Kenji felt and sounded breathless. 'Better than I could have hoped for.'

'Yamada-san.' Ashida's face was concerned. 'Please excuse my impertinence, but what was good?'

A murmur of agreement rippled among the others.

'Life is good.' Catching the wheels of his chair, Kenji attempted to tip himself backwards and forwards. It didn't work so instead he pretended to roll the chair forward slightly. 'The show was better than I could have hoped for.'

'The reviews . . .' Ito stared pointedly at the newspapers and magazines sitting on the empty chair. '. . . were awful.'

'Awful. You think?' It wasn't easy, but Kenji managed to act as if it was the first time the thought had occurred to him.

'Yes, awful.'

The cameraman, who was the oldest of the team and had seen it all before, was evidently growing impatient. It was time to start drawing them in.

'Different is the word I would use. We said that *Millyennaire* would be different and it has been just that. Let me share something with you that I have learnt over the years. The best way to upset people is to change something and that's what we're doing here. Of course they'll complain. Of course they'll say they don't like it. This isn't the kind of game show that they're used to. It will take some time before they understand and come to appreciate it. But give them a few weeks and they won't be able to get enough of it. *Millyennaire* will be all that everybody talks about.'

'You really think so?' Yoshida asked, blowing a stray strand of hair that had escaped from the bun on her head away from her face.

'You might even say that it's all they're talking about at the moment. Have you ever known a show to attract so much attention by the opening episode alone? They normally build up slowly. Not *Millyennaire*. We don't ask for attention. We take it.'

'I suppose that's right.' Yoshida nodded, curling the same stray strand around one finger. 'I never thought about it like that.'

Even Ito and Hoshino's bodyguard, appeared to be mulling this suggestion over. This was not enough, though. There was more to be done. He may have reeled them in. Now it was time to ensure that they were firmly hooked.

'There is one thing that upsets me.'

'What?' Ashida leaned forward in his chair.

'Tell us,' Yoshida pleaded.

'I can't.' He turned away, pretending to be hesitant.

'You must.'

'You can't not.'

'Well, I suppose. It's just . . . You see, I thought that you were all made of stronger stuff. I thought that you were in it for the long-haul. And yet at the first sign of trouble you're ready to give it up, admit defeat.'

Ashida frowned and shook his head. 'Never. Not me.'

'Of course not.'

'I'm in for the long-haul.'

'Me too.'

'Then . . .' His voice became deeper and more authoritative. '. . . don't come to me with petty concerns and worries. There may be worse yet to come and I need you to remain strong. Beyond this is more glory and recognition than you could ever have thought possible and a little bit of it belongs to everybody here in this room.'

For the first time since she had arrived, Mifune smiled and he knew he had said exactly the right thing. As her shoulders relaxed visibly, his did too, and he became aware of the painful knots that had worked their way into his shoulders and back.

'Excuse me.'

Kenji nodded at Ashida who had put his hand up.

'There is one thing that we – ' He looked at the others who nodded. ' – have been worried about. We have heard that the contestant is your mother-in-law. It must be wrong, surely.'

It was a question Kenji had expected much earlier and already had an answer prepared. 'She is, I'm afraid. Although please let me reassure you, neither my wife nor I had any idea what she was up to. If we had we would certainly not have allowed it.'

Everyone looked at the floor. He knew, instinctively, by their reaction, the appearance of his mother-in-law as a contestant in the show had been a topic of great debate among the wider team. To his face they were too polite to voice the true extent of their disquiet. All he could do was reiterate what he had said and hope they believed him.

'In fact, how could I have known? For the last four weeks I have been barely conscious, lying in hospital. Before my accident, Endo was due to be the contestant. I woke up believing that he still was. I sincerely hope that you believe me. This show means so very much to me and I would never do anything to jeopardise it. My mother-in-law acted on her own initiative. Perhaps even without being aware of my involvement in the show. I can appreciate that is not how it looks. But that is how it is.'

'If once again you will excuse my impertinence,' Ashida continued, the quaver in his voice revealing his nervousness, 'much of

285

the show's problems have been attributed to the contestant. Your mother-in-law. She does nothing except eat and sleep.'

'You are exactly right and I had some ideas about how we might solve this.' He pulled a notepad from the pocket of his dressing gown and began to read. 'The old lady eats too much. Cut her food rations. Make her realise that the only way she will eat is if she wins food. I can guarantee she will start entering those competitions a whole lot faster. She sleeps too much? Wake her up. The means are at your fingertips.'

As he spoke, Mifune scribbled furiously in her own notepad.

'Yoshida-san, I want you to make sure that Hoshino has her scripts at least twenty-four hours in advance and . . .'

Kenji looked at the bodyguard realising that he did not even know his name.

'Ronin Muto.' His voice was barely audible and he appeared remarkably shy for such a large man.

'Ronin-san, you must make sure that she practises.'

'I will.'

'Ito-san.'

The cameraman looked up expectantly.

'Get the multi-coloured flashing lights turned down. It dates the show. And – ' He turned to the make-up artist. ' – you might want to suggest to wardrobe that Hoshino opts for some of my wife's less flamboyant creations. Now – ' He struggled to turn the wheelchair around so that his back was facing them and began to wheel himself out of the room. ' – you said that you are with me. What are you waiting for? Get on with it.'

FORTY-FOUR

It was dark by the time Kenji's train pulled into Utsunomiya. He left the station with all the other commuters, but unlike them he was not going home. First, he had to find a copy of the *Mainichi News* and went into the nearest convenience store. 'Have you got it?' Kenji demanded. One of his elbows was resting heavily on the counter as he attempted to look over it. He would have climbed over it too, if it was not for his broken leg which was planted firmly on the ground. There were no copies on the shelves, but it was getting late. Perhaps they might be stacked up by the feet of the sales assistant, bundled up with twine, waiting to be taken away with the other returns. Finding none there he struggled back into an upright position. Even with both crutches planted firmly beneath his armpits, he still swayed gently from side to side.

'Got what?' Nonplussed by Kenji's appropriation of the counter, the young sales assistant adjusted the baseball cap on his head.

'The *Mainichi News*.'

'Didn't arrive today.'

'Hmmpff.' Swinging violently round so that he was facing in the opposite direction, Kenji hobbled to what was thankfully an automatic door – he had never been more grateful of such things than during the last week – and out into the street. No sooner had the cool night air hit him full in the face than a cyclist came hurtling towards him. Trilling angrily on her bell, she swerved, just missed hitting him, and continued down the street.

He threw one hand up in the air at her back as she disappeared down the road. 'How is it possible?' he muttered under his breath, moving slowly down the road in the same direction as the cyclist. How was it possible that every single shop, stall and vending machine he had visited today did not have a copy of the *Mainichi News*? Nor had anyone that he had stopped to ask, and there had been many. By all accounts there was a Tokyo-wide shortage of the newspaper: either because it had not been delivered or, within an hour of arriving, had sold out. He simply had to get a copy. The frustration of not being able to find one was making him grind his teeth loudly together and he had already bitten his nails down to their quick. Time was fast running out. It was already 8 p.m. and any shops that did have copies would at this very minute be packing them up for the supplier's truck to collect.

He stumbled forwards. 'What now?' he muttered, realising too late that the rubber tip of his right crutch had become trapped in the grille covering a drain. Pulling and grunting fiercely at the other end, he was unable to dislodge it. It was only when a young school-boy, urged on by his mother, rushed to help Kenji, that he managed to free his walking aid.

'Thank you.' Bowing curtly – he hated people to see him so indisposed – Kenji carried on down the street, keeping as far away from the drain covers as possible. Several people stared at him as they passed. A young man in dark blue denims and a tweed peaked cap, a young woman whose shoes were at least one size too big for her and slapped against the tarmac as she walked, even a child being pushed by her mother in a pram. They looked at him with sympathy, maybe even fear. It was then he realised he had been growling. Was this what he had been reduced to? A shambolic figure, stumbling around the neighbourhood, forced to accept help from children.

The second episode of *Millyennaire* had been aired. There was no hiding from it. It had been just as dismal as the first, if not worse. The production team couldn't be faulted. Everybody had followed his instructions to the exact letter. Hoshino had her scripts well in advance of screening, which gave her plenty of time to practise, although perhaps too much. Whereas previously her performance had been spontaneous and full of errors and omissions, now there was a wooden quality to her delivery. Although technically correct, there was no sense of passion or personality coming through from her. Eriko, meanwhile, had generated even less footage this week than last and had yet to enter a single competition. The newspapers and magazines delivered daily to the 'apartment' were forming an ever increasingly large pile by the door immediately beneath the letter box. Cutting her food rations evidently had no effect upon her motivation. The only effect was to make her sleep more and no matter what they did to rouse her – bright lights, loud noises, continuously dripping taps – she appeared to be completely impervious.

Earlier that day he had gone to work, worried to the point of sickness in case he was called to bear witness to Goto and the other members of the senior management team, let alone the production crew. Mifune had informed Kenji that Goto knew Eriko was his mother-in-law and had taken the decision not to make an issue out of it. If they didn't, then hopefully nobody else would notice and so far this had been successful.

Arriving at the twenty-five-storey office block early, he had managed to make his way to his office, tucked away in a corner of the twenty-second floor, without being waylaid. It appeared that a black cloud followed him as he attempted to negotiate the deep-pile carpet – the rubber tip of his crutches dragged over the surface so that he had to pick them up with each step. How grateful he was to arrive and close the door behind him. How reassuring it was to see his beloved oak desk; to look out at the sprawl from his window; touch the few small possessions that were dotted about the office. How it would sadden him to give them all up, he thought, sitting down on his black leather chair.

The first thing he intended to do on arriving was to read every major newspaper from cover to cover. Last week *Millyennaire* had been a hot topic. This week, he realised, throwing the last newspaper to one side, it was nowhere to be found. This realisation stirred up in him a mixture of relief and wounded pride. Was his show not good enough for them, he raged, at the same time hopeful that the absence of any negative reviews might permit *Millyennaire* to limp along for some time yet. In that time who could tell what might happen? The natural presenter in Hoshino might wake up. Eriko could reconnect with her insatiable appetite for winning. The show could be the success that he dreamed of.

A loud rapping interrupted his thoughts. The sound of knuckles being bashed repeatedly against wood. As they played out their demanding, repetitive rhythm, Kenji wondered if he might somehow escape or hide. Perhaps under the desk? Then the office door burst open and Ashida ran in.

'Yamada-san, please excuse me for this interruption. I am very sorry, but Mifune told me that she had seen you. I had to talk to you. You see . . .' He was almost breathless with excitement or exertion, Kenji could not tell which. Small beads of perspiration had broken out on his forehead and he was wringing his hands repeatedly.

'Leiko Kobayashi has reviewed *Millyennaire* in her column.'

'The *Mainichi News*? She can't have. I would have seen it.' Suddenly feeling very hot, Kenji began to rifle through the newspapers sitting on the desk in front of him. 'There was nothing. I found no reviews.' It was when he reached the end of the pile that it hit him. Of course, he remembered now. He had not bought a copy of the *Mainichi News* this morning. Standing in front of the newspaper racks in the store this morning, his hand had hovered over it. Certainly. But he had changed his mind. He already had enough newspapers to carry on the train and given that Leiko Kobayashi never reviewed a show more than once there seemed little point. That she had broken with tradition must mean something surely. Did he dare to hope that it might be good news? 'Have you got it?' he demanded, holding his hand out to Ashida.

Ashida shook his head. 'A friend told me they had seen it.'

'What did it say?'

Another shake. 'I'm sorry, she did not read it. I thought that maybe you might have a copy.'

'Come on.' Grunting loudly, Kenji heaved himself out of the chair and, using the crutches that were propped up at the side of the desk, hobbled round to where Ashida was standing. 'We've got to find a copy.'

And that was how the search for the *Mainichi News* began. Together they swept throughout the entire office that at mid-morning was buzzing with activity. Kenji moved more slowly than Ashida and covered less space, but still managed to stop at each desk, leaning over the partition or, if it was high, banging his crutch at the base until a head appeared over the top and demanded, 'Who is that making so much noise?' Everybody that passed he accosted with a similar lack of grace and good humour, demanding: 'Have you got a copy of the *Mainichi News*?' The answer was inevitably no and so expectant of this did he become, that sometimes he hobbled off before the person whom he had so rudely stopped even had the opportunity to answer. 'Why are you looking for it?' they might ask, but he did not answer, moved straight on to the next person. An hour later, they had asked everybody in the entire office and Ashida had visited all of the local stores without luck.

'I'll try tonight, when I get home,' Kenji had told him, confident that the drought would be limited to downtown Tokyo, only to find, when he left work that evening, that all the local shops in Utsunomiya were also without copies. The shop that he had just visited had been his last hope. Now there was no other option but to head home, and while he was angry that his search had proven to be fruitless, he was secretly pleased. The less he knew about the content of Leiko Kobayashi's review, the more that he could hope.

Rounding the corner at the end of the street, he happened upon the cyclist who minutes earlier had swerved to avoid him. She had come to a stop underneath a street lamp and was talking animatedly to a young man. On her back she wore a rucksack, sticking out of which was . . . He couldn't be sure, but it looked very much like the thing that he had been looking for.

'Hey you,' he called out, waving one hand high above his head. 'You on the bicycle. Don't go anywhere. I need to talk to you.' He hurried towards her. Again the rubber tip of his crutch got trapped in the grille covering a drain and he had to prise it free. This time cursing in case the cyclist would ride off by the time he reached her. 'Wait. Just a minute. Stay where you are.' When he did finally reach her, a thin film of perspiration covered his face and there was a damp patch running down the back of his shirt, along the length of his spine.

The cyclist – who had one foot planted firmly on the ground, the other resting on the pedal of her bicycle – looked at him quizzically. 'Have you run all this way just to apologise?'

'The newspaper,' he panted. The exertion had left him dizzy and nauseous. 'I'll buy it from you. How much do you want for it?'

She frowned and looked at her friend who sniggered but, seeing the expression on Kenji's face, immediately stopped.

'You're serious, aren't you?'

'Of course I am.' With some difficulty, he pulled his wallet from the back pocket of his trousers and extracted the first note that came to hand. He didn't care how much it was. He just wanted that newspaper. 'Take it. Ten thousand yen.' He stuffed the note into the cyclist's hand. Shrugging, she took the newspaper from her rucksack and gave it to him. Losing no time, he shuffled quickly over to the nearest shop doorway where he was able to see beneath an overhead neon light and started searching for the article. On page sixteen he found exactly what he was looking for.

'Will this torture ever stop? Quite literally.' From these few words he knew all was lost. 'Last week innocent viewers were forced to endure thirty minutes of what was at best painfully embarrassing television, at worst mind-numbingly boring. This week the production team responsible for this debacle has, obviously heeding my comments, raised the game.'

He moaned, attracting further curious glances from the cyclist and her friend. Who did Leiko Kobayashi think she was? The arrogance of the woman. How dare she think that she in any way yielded power over him. That he had listened to her suggestions. Knowing now that worse was yet to come he contemplated tossing the newspaper to the ground. Unable to do so, he read on.

'What a sad, sorry game it has now become. In a bid to rouse the contestant, to force her to enter competitions as is the show's basic premise, daily food rations have been cut. The old lady appears unbothered and passes much of the day asleep. Failing to wake even in response to all manner of torture techniques including flashing lights, loud noises and a constantly dripping tap.'

Sufficiently dismayed, he found that he was now able to ball the newspaper up and threw it to the ground. An old lady wearing a pink mohair hat looked at him disapprovingly as she walked by. Ignoring her he hailed the first taxi that passed.

FORTY-FIVE

The moment he walked into the apartment he realised everything was not as it should be. Getting through the door was a lengthy and protracted procedure in itself that consisted of swinging his plastered leg over the threshold, extricating his key from the lock and then finally moving out of the way so that he could close the door behind him. All of which was performed while balancing on a pair of crutches. It was not until he had finished that he became aware of the ominous silence that filled the apartment. Ominous because, returning home at this time, he should have been met by the excited sound of chatter as the children, dinner eaten, argued over what thirty minutes of television they should watch before returning to their homework. Argued so much that by the time they decided, the thirty minutes were up and they had not watched a single thing. Standing perfectly still, he listened hard. But there was nothing. More worrying still, every single light in the apartment was on. Almost as if someone had run from room to room, flicking each switch in turn. Ami would quite simply not have allowed it. If she was here.

So where was she, he wondered, limping along the corridor. It had never seemed so long, his movements so slow. Looking down he saw that the hairs on his arms were standing on end and that his flesh was covered with small goosebumps. It was when he heard the sound of his wife's voice coming from the sitting room that he realised just how anxious he was. *She hasn't left me.* He almost whooped with joy.

'You're here.' He wanted to say more, to express his tremendous relief, but the words lodged in his throat as he took in the view that met him. Sitting in the middle of the canary yellow, faux-suede sofa, her feet clearing the ground, head bowed and shoulders convulsing, was Yumi. Crying fit to break her heart and sending judders along the length of her body. Crouched down in front of her, the tips of their heads touching, was Ami: whispering soothing words that he could not quite make out and stroking their daughter's soft, wispy hair.

'What is it? What's the matter?' he blurted out and although he hated himself for it, wanted to bolt back out of the front door. At least as fast as his plastered leg would allow him. Ami was, after all, best placed to deal with matters of this nature. She shot him a look filled with recrimination and loathing. He wanted to quit the apartment even more so but stayed.

'Darling, you must tell me what happened,' Ami pleaded, wiping the tears away from Yumi's face. No matter how many she wiped away, more came to replace them. 'How can I help you if you don't tell me what happened?'

'He . . . he . . . he . . .' Unable to get the words out, Yumi sounded painfully out of breath.

'What's happened?' Kenji eased himself down on to the sofa beside Yumi.

'Dad.' Yumi clutched her father's hand with a strength that surprised him. Her hands felt small and smooth in his.

'What is it?' Kenji cajoled. 'Tell us what happened. You can tell us anything.' He looked at Ami, hoping that she might return a gesture of solidarity, but his wife looked away.

'He said that he'd hurt me if I told anybody.'

'Who did, darling?' Using the palm of her right hand, Ami gently turned Yumi's face away from her father's. This did not stop Yumi looking at him, however. Fat tears cascading over the bottom of each eye, pink now, and down her cheeks.

'I don't know his name. He's in the class above me.'

'Well, it's just not true,' Ami stated firmly.

Kenji noticed that the television set was on in the background with the sound turned down. The news was on.

'If you tell me what happened I will make very sure that he never hurts you again.'

Kenji's legs were starting to feel numb. He put one arm around his daughter's shoulders, where it hung limply. She felt as fragile as a small doll and infinitely breakable. 'Please tell us what happened?' he begged, more for his sake than hers. It somehow occurred to him that if he could just solve this one problem, make everything all right for his daughter, then everything would be okay.

The young girl sniffed and looked down at her feet that were encased in white plimsolls. The toes were scuffed. 'He said that Grandma was a stupid old lady and that my parents must have no morals if they send an old lady out to work for them.'

'I knew it,' Ami snapped, jumping up. Her lips were pursed and he could hear her breathing heavily through her nostrils. 'I knew that this would happen. How did they find out?'

'It slipped out.' Yumi's sobs grew louder.

'Please.' Kenji's arm no longer hung limply, but became a protective embrace. 'Not in front of the child.'

'For once you're right.' Recovering herself, Ami crouched back down on the floor. 'Grandma may be a little bit silly at times.'

Yumi smiled weakly.

'But we all know that she isn't stupid. Look at the car she won for us. Someone that stupid couldn't have done something like that, now could they? What about the computer and all that food? As for forcing Grandma to appear on the show that simply isn't true,' Ami continued, stroking Yumi's hair. All the while the young girl's sobs grew quieter. 'We had no idea. The first time we realised was when we saw her on TV at the hospital. Do you remember?'

Yumi nodded sombrely. Now that her tears had subsided, she was hungrily gulping down air.

'It sounds to me like this boy is just jealous that you've got a famous grandmother and he hasn't. That's what you must remember. People say hurtful things because they feel bad about themselves. Now how about we wash your face and I read you a story? I'll stay with you until you go to sleep.'

Taking her daughter by the hand, Ami led her to the bathroom and later to her bedroom. Neither said another word to Kenji and he remained sitting on the sofa until, over an hour later, Ami returned. She closed the sitting-room door firmly but quietly behind her.

'I knew it would turn out like this.'

Opening his mouth to protest, he realised it was pointless.

'Don't say another word.' Ami stood in front of the television set, hand on hip. She was wearing a beige tracksuit with two pink stripes running down the side of both legs. It was usually what she wore when home alone: cleaning or sewing. She changed into something smarter when one of her customers was due, or she had to leave the apartment to run errands or collect the children. On her feet she wore a pair of white plastic, open-toed sandals and in her left hand she was jangling a set of car keys.

'Are you going somewhere?' he asked.

'Never mind me,' she bit back. 'Just get my mother off that show and get her off now.'

'I can't,' he tried to explain, feeling more ineffectual than ever. Was it really his fault that his daughter had been crying like that? he wondered as he ran his right thumbnail back and forth over the garish yellow nap of the sofa. Had he done this to his family?

'What do you mean you can't? You're the producer, aren't you? You can do anything.'

'She signed a contract. She knew what she was getting into. It's legally binding.'

'Now,' Ami repeated, 'I don't want to hear another excuse. I just promised our daughter that I wouldn't let another bad thing happen to her. Don't make me have to break my word.'

Throwing open the sitting-room door, she marched out, returning a few seconds later with a large pile of bedclothes crammed beneath her right arm. She threw them down on top of him with so much force that they sent a full glass tumbler of milk that had been sitting on the coffee table, flying to the floor. Luckily the glass did not break, although the contents spilt out on to the carpet.

'You're sleeping in there until this gets sorted,' Ami spat angrily. 'And clean that mess up.'

FORTY-SIX

'In light of these viewing figures – ' Goto's head tipped fractionally in the direction of a line chart projected on to a white screen at the front of the boardroom, ' – we have a tough decision to make.' Straightening his tie, he cleared his throat. 'We may even have the decision made for us. If our sponsors pull out.'

Someone groaned as all around him was the sound of quiet muttering. Were they talking about him, Kenji fretted? Were they writing about him? Passing notes to each other. Blaming him. Saying that it was all his fault. It was starting to feel very familiar.

Effortlessly and with one fluid motion, Goto pulled a black leather chair from beneath the table and sat down. In front of him he positioned his elbows and formed a tall, thin triangle with his hands. Over the tip he studied the occupants of the room, lingering on each one in turn. His gaze was neither offensive nor defensive. It was simply searching. Kenji made every effort to avoid it, helped by his broken leg, which meant that he had to sit some distance away from the table, outside the ring formed by the other members of the production team.

From this secluded position, he stared hard at the chart. The last twenty-two years of his career had been spent dealing with numbers. As he studied the unforgiving black line and square data points a few flashed before his eyes. Seventy-five per cent of viewers agreed that the length of the show was suitable, 85% said that they would watch it again, three in five forty- to fifty-five-year-olds watch game shows regularly. Numbers told stories. That's what he liked about them. And if it wasn't the story that you wanted them to tell, they could be massaged, stretched a little. But not such that it might compromise a research manager's position. There were simply standard tools that a person in his position would have at his disposal. Remove an outlier, use the median rather than the mean, opt for a 90% confidence limit instead of a 95% one. All would prove useless here. No matter how long he stared at the chart, there was no escaping the story it told. The black line was clearly demonstrating a downward trajectory. *Millyennaire* was losing viewers at an ever increasing rate. It wasn't a temporary blip. There were no signs of recovery. The game show . . . his game show was an abject failure.

Even though the air-conditioning unit was on, blowing cold air down on to his head with such velocity that it ruffled his hair, the room felt stuffy and Kenji was obliged to loosen his tie and undo the top button of his shirt.

The chart depicted viewing figures over the last six weeks since the show had started. Everybody agreed that the results for week one – when over ten million viewers had watched – showed promise. Certainly it was unlikely that they had been attracted to *Millyennaire* in its own right. It was more likely that they were left over from the news that had just finished. Reluctant to either turn over or turn off, they were content to watch and wait for the network's most popular soap opera to start after *Millyennaire* had come to an end. It was less important how they got there. It was more important that they liked what they saw, stayed and returned next week. That they maybe even told their friends. Or at least that was the theory that he had been labouring under.

In their analysis of the viewing figures, the programme research team at NBC – the very same one that Kenji had once worked in – broke viewing figures down into five-minute time slots. In doing so they revealed a sharp peak towards the end of episode one when even more viewers tuned in. They too intended to watch the soap opera, but a motto at NBC had been that getting them there was half the battle. A battle that had evidently been lost. Viewing figures for

Millyennaire dropped by half during week two and again during weeks three and four. Word was spreading and it was spreading fast, thanks to Leiko Kobayashi and her now weekly reviews of *Millyennaire* in the *Mainichi News*. It was not the kind of word they had been hoping for.

Flicking through the pages of the report that was sitting on his lap, prepared also by Ishida's programme research team, Kenji searched desperately for some sign of hope. Some small indication that *Millyennaire* was worth saving. He found no comfort there amongst the neat black print and colourful graphs. Only more distress. There were, it appeared, many dimensions along which the show failed to please its viewers. Where was the contest? they wanted to know. In the last four weeks Eriko had failed to enter even a single competition despite the piles of magazines and newspapers that were accumulating by the 'apartment' door. She had not won a single thing. Instead she continued to spend vast amounts of time sleeping, waking just to use the bathroom and eat those small rations of food available to her. Hoshino's performance was described as erratic: veering within the short space of an episode from stiff and wooden to ridiculously spontaneous. Viewers felt that she dated the show – a younger presenter would have been better – while the lighting, theme music, and wardrobe all added to the feeling that this was a format that belonged to another era. Kenji was, it appeared, ten years too late. The report concluded that *Millyennaire* should be withdrawn as quickly as possible before further damage to the network could be done.

As he tapped his biro on the front page of the report, he studied the list of names and their contact details. There was one he didn't recognise. Was it his replacement, he wondered, tapping the pen more furiously? People were starting to look at him.

It was no longer the big production team it had once been. Gradually, the more senior, experienced team members had been taken out to work on other more successful shows and had not been replaced. Those who remained were staring at him now. He avoided their gaze. He felt unable to cope with the expression that lingered on their faces, the thoughts dancing just behind their eyes. An expression so subtle that he might have missed it, had he not known, guessed even, that it was there. After all, he had seen it before and it frightened him.

After it first emerged that Eriko was his mother-in-law, there had inevitably been a considerable amount of gossiping, staring and hushed conversations that stopped the moment he would enter a room. As soon as he was out of hospital, and had called the entire team together he had a hard time convincing them that he had not rigged the selection process and did not want the prize money for himself. He pointed out that he had been lying unconscious in hospital when Eriko was auditioned for the show and that when he woke up he was under the impression that Endo, their first choice, was still due to appear. They saw the logic and came round one by one. Thankfully they had also been able to keep his relationship to Eriko under wraps and out of the media.

He was grateful for the cold air blowing over his head as he spoke now. 'I don't understand. At home she entered competitions all the time and never lost. Something must be wrong with her. She must be sickening. Perhaps we should send in a doctor?'

'It's not just that she doesn't win anything,' Mifune offered from the opposite corner of the room, 'but that she's so . . .' Hesitating, she shifted uncomfortably in her seat. '. . . boring.' As those people seated on either side of her nodded their heads in agreement, she appeared to gain confidence. It was unlike Mifune to say a word against him, although recently she had been less staunch in her unconditional support for him. With her right hand, the gently rounded nails on which were painted a delicate shade of peach, she brushed the hair from her eyes. 'All she does is sleep and eat. The most interesting footage that we had to show last week was of her searching on the floor for stray grains of rice that she might cook.'

Kenji's face burned with shame and he sank even lower in his chair, beginning to feel like a specimen that was being dissected by a classroom full of junior school biology students. His chest had been left wide open and his entrails, coloured with deep shades of red and purple, were quivering.

'It is all my fault,' interjected Hoshino who had been whimpering softly ever since Goto first showed the chart. She was sitting on a chair beside him and had a white handkerchief clamped to her face, the rest of which was obscured by long black curls that had fallen from the bun on top of her head. She had not removed the mink coat in which she had first arrived and had repeatedly, throughout the meeting, cast anxious glances at Muto who was pacing back and forth outside the room. This did not surprise Kenji as Inagaki had already confided in him, in a rare moment of comradeship, that Hoshino was borrowing money again and her lender, at first glad to give it and charge a healthy interest rate in lieu of *Millyennaire*'s success, was now getting jumpy and calling in what he owed.

'If only that odious woman Kobayashi would stop writing those awful reviews,' Yoshida spoke up, her voice shaking with emotion. Today she was wearing a purple jumper with short sleeves, made of mohair that kept drifting in the air around her and making her sneeze.

Hoshino's sobs turned into a wail as everybody looked uncomfortably at the floor. 'If only I could explain, you might understand,' she managed in between gulps of air. 'It's all my fault. But I can't. It's all too much. Really it is.'

Removing the handkerchief, she revealed a face blackened with streaks of mascara. She stared hard at each person in turn. Was she looking for someone to jump to her defence, Kenji wondered? Nobody did. Himself included. How could they? It was true. Kenji knew ten minutes into the first episode of *Millyennaire* that whatever talent Hana Hoshino, Eighties icon, had once possessed, it was all gone now. She was washed up and washed out. There was not one episode in which she had got all her lines right. In the beginning she had handled her mistakes professionally, correcting them discreetly and without making a great deal of fuss. Recently each mistake was accompanied by a nervous fit of giggles that lasted several seconds and occasionally ended with a bout of hiccups. It had become necessary to pre-record her clips. They had even enlisted a voiceover artist who sounded like her when Hoshino had started to turn up at the studio evidently under the influence of alcohol, increasingly late, sometimes on the wrong day.

'NBC are anxious. Very anxious,' Goto intoned, still looking out over the tip of the triangle he had formed with his hands and that showed off the square gold cufflinks he was wearing in his light blue shirt. 'They want to pull the programme immediately. It shows them in a bad light. But they have already invested heavily and I was able to convince them to hold back on making any decision at least until after this weekend. Our sponsors are also upset. They too want to withdraw. I managed to convince them that I had something that would change their mind.'

'You do?' It was the most animated that Kenji had sounded in weeks and he sat forward expectantly in his chair.

'I don't. Perhaps you might have, though?' Goto threw his arms wide open in an expansive gesture as though trying to embrace everybody in the room. He didn't stop looking at Kenji for a single second. Suddenly and without warning, he stood up. 'You have until the end of this weekend. Be back here first thing Monday morning. If nobody has come up with a plan we will lay *Millyennaire* to rest. There is no point in prolonging the misery. Agreed?'

It was an ultimatum and as Kenji stared up into Goto's face, he nodded his head slowly.

'You are free to go.'

Before he left, Goto offered Hoshino a fresh handkerchief that she grabbed and replaced with the one that was at that moment clamped to her face, releasing a high-pitched whimper into the room. At the door he paused. 'Please be with your families over the weekend and share good times with them. But remember what decision awaits us on Monday morning and be prepared. I'm sure I don't need to tell you how disastrous it would be for us to have to pull the show. Not once before in the entire history of Miru TV has this happened.'

Kenji waited until the room had emptied, which it did quickly. Nobody wanted to be alone with him, and who could blame them. He was beginning to feel like he might be cursed. He pulled himself out of the chair and, using his crutches that dragged on the deep pile carpet, made his way slowly to his office, racking his brains for some idea, some plan for how he might save *Millyennaire*. He had to think of something. His job depended upon it. There was one thing. His last chance. He had been thinking about it for days, mulling it over. Did he dare? Did he have any choice?

Back at his office he looked at the pile of newspapers and magazines which sat in the far right-hand corner waiting for Ashida to call by later and take them to the apartment. Quickly, in case there was a knock on the door that put an end to his plan, he sat down at his desk, scribbled a note on a piece of paper and slipped it between the pages of a magazine that he knew to be Eriko's favourite and that she still read. If the team found out that he was communicating with the old woman, it would be the end for him. But if he sat back and did nothing it would also be the end. He chose his words carefully.

There was just one more thing left to do. Before he could think too much about what he was doing, Kenji picked up his telephone and dialled the number written on a bright pink Post-it note stuck to the table, its edges curling with age.

FORTY-SEVEN

Kenji had reserved a table at Aoyama for his meeting with Leiko Kobayashi. One of Shibuya's more ostentatious restaurants, bright lights flooded an immense interior formed by soaring white walls on which hung several pieces of modern art. As the waiter showed him to his table, he paused to study one of the paintings, but was unable to understand what the orange blobs on the white background were intended to represent. Looking at the price beneath, he baulked and moved on. He could not understand it, let alone afford it.

'Here?' Kenji asked the waiter who was waiting for him at a small circular table covered with a crisp white cloth. Kenji negotiated his way through the restaurant, apologising to diners whose meals he interrupted with an ill-placed crutch or by knocking into them. There were two chairs positioned on either side of the table even though it would struggle to accommodate one diner. It was hardly the discreet corner that he had requested, positioned in front of the restaurant's immense windows through which passers-by could not help but look: staring at the diners and whatever they were eating.

'There were no tables left when Goto-san rang. This one was squeezed in as a special favour to him,' the waiter explained in a measured tone of voice.

Biting the tip of his tongue, Kenji decided that it was best to say nothing else. He politely thanked the waiter for being so accommodating and sat down.

An hour of research on the Internet had told him everything that he needed to know about Leiko Kobayashi: what path her career had followed, what newspapers she wrote for, where she lived, where she ate, even her favourite colour. Aoyama was, according to a recent interview, her favourite place to dine in all of Tokyo – an easy enough fact to find, whereas getting a reservation had proven to be much more difficult. At least until he hit upon the idea of claiming to be Goto. Lying created a distinctly uneasy feeling in the pit of his stomach. It had worked though and he couldn't help but feel elated by this stroke of good fortune. The maître d' faithfully promised him a spot and although they recognised immediately that Kenji was not Goto when he arrived at Aoyama, it had been easy enough to explain.

'An emergency at the studio . . . called away suddenly...asked me to come in his place.'

As he stretched his broken leg out in front of him, finding a position where it would get in the way as little as possible, Kenji went over in his head – one last time – how he would handle this meeting. To begin, he would scrupulously avoid any talk of why he had asked Kobayashi to join him at Aoyama. Instead he would flatter the journalist, for she was – he had discovered – more than a TV critic, she was also a serious journalist who wrote under various pseudonyms about all manner of social injustices and natural disorders. He would encourage her to talk at length about herself; taking every available opportunity to applaud her writing skills and obvious determination not to shirk from the truth. The food would be excellent and the wine would flow, loosening her lips if they were at all tightly sealed. Meanwhile, Kenji would sip only water; preferring instead to remain in full control of his senses. Then before the end of the meal, when they were both in good spirits, he would broach the subject. The small matter of her weekly reviews of *Millyennaire* and what effect it was having upon the show. How much better if she could just ignore that it even existed, or – dare he say it – were a few good words too much to hope for?

'Kenji Yamada?'

By the time Kenji managed to struggle to his feet, Kobayashi had seated herself at the opposite side of the table and was unfurling a crisp white napkin on to her lap. It was the first time that he had ever seen her. Even the articles that he had read failed to carry a picture of the journalist. Of course his imagination had filled in the gaps. In his mind, he had seen a mature woman, thin and severe in a tailored suit with long hair centrally parted and pulled back into a tight knot. He could not have been more wrong. It was difficult to judge how old Kobayashi was because she was so very fat. Her head was round, her upper body was round and her arms too would have been round if they had not been long. Her girth was undeniable, although the true extent of it was difficult to gauge because she wore a black, tent-like dress thrown over her body. An entire family could easily have camped under the garment, he thought, unkindly. Her hair was not long and black as he had imagined, but cropped close to her head and dyed red to match her lipstick and the polish she wore on her bitten-down nails.

'Thank you for agreeing to meet with me.' Kenji quickly sat down, carefully rearranging his leg as Kobayashi looked on in amusement but did not say anything.

'I was hungry.' She removed a silver case from a red leather handbag, selected a cigarette, tapped it on the table and lit the end with a thin silver lighter. The smell of mint drifted up from the end of the cigarette and hung in the air between them.

'Hi.' The waiter appeared at Kenji's side. 'This is your food and drinks menu.' He placed two black leatherbound menus, one fatter and wider than the other, on the table in front of them. 'I'll give you a little time to look over these and will come back to take your order.'

He turned to leave, but Kobayashi stopped him in his tracks with a loud, sharp voice that arrested not only his progress but any conversation taking place in the immediate vicinity. 'I'll have a vodka and slimline tonic. One ice cube only.'

The waiter went to the bar. Meanwhile, Kobayashi consulted the menu, smoke curling up into her eyes. 'So,' she said, batting it away and smiling thinly. Either her teeth were genuinely yellow or made to appear so by the harsh contrast with her red lipstick.

'So,' Kenji repeated. 'Kobayashi-san, I must admit . . .' He attempted to look bashful. '. . . I've always been a fan. Your articles are very interesting . . . perceptive . . . incisive.' From what he had read, Leiko Kobayashi had started out on a women's magazine, but rose up quickly through the ranks to become editor. From here she began to write for the daily newspapers and now in addition to her TV columns, wrote more serious feature articles. Assuming different identities for different subjects helped protect what she called her 'brand' identity.

'You think? Leiko is complimented.'

Kenji was about to discover that she had a disconcerting habit of talking about herself in the third person.

'The stories are not always so good. Take, for example, the one I am working on most recently . . .'

'I'm sorry to hear that.' Kenji considered lighting a cigarette but realising that his hands were shaking, resisted. He had not appreciated just quite how nervous he was until now that she was sitting here in front of him. So much depended upon this meeting. If he could just get it right, then he felt certain that many good things would come from it. 'What . . .'

'Crows, yes. You've seen the crows?' Kobayashi flapped her arms about her head in a bizarre imitation of a crow, almost knocking over the frosted glass of vodka that their waiter had just brought over. She grabbed the glass and took a sip. ' "Leiko," they said. "We want an article about Tokyo's crow problem." So I say, okay, how do you want me to pitch it? My brain – ' She tapped the knuckles of her right hand against her head and banged so hard that Kenji winced on her behalf. ' – is working ahead of them. The government as corrupt, failing to tackle the problem head on because they are too busy taking backhanders from businessmen that want to get planning permission? No, they say. We want a human interest article. Speak to the people that have been attacked by crows and find out what effect this has had on their lives. Tsk, I tell them. Leiko is a serious journalist. She does not write about little black birds. They say she has no choice. If Leiko wants to get paid, then she must. And besides. The birds. They are not so little.'

The waiter had returned and was hovering next to their table with a pen poised above a notebook. 'Are you ready to order?'

'Do you need a few minutes?' Kenji enquired politely as Kobayashi had not yet consulted the menu.

'No need. I always have the same dish.' She stabbed her cigarette out in the heavy glass ashtray, the end of which was covered with a thick layer of red lipstick. 'Please, you go first.'

While Kenji ordered Caesar Salad to start and turkey chilli for his main course, Kobayashi lit another cigarette, exhaling the smoke out through her nostrils as Scott prepared to take her order.

'I'll have a Bloody Mary to start. Followed by spare ribs with fries. Lots of barbecue sauce.'

'Would you like any wine with your dinner?'

Without attempting to consult Kenji, or even looking in his direction, Kobayashi ordered the most expensive bottle on the menu.

Taking their menus, the waiter walked away, the soles of his black leather shoes clipping loudly on the gleaming black floor tiles.

'What was I saying?' Kobayashi paused. 'The crows. So have you seen them?'

Kenji thought about this for a few seconds. 'Now that you mention it, I have. They sit on the electricity wires on the street outside my apartment. They start cawing at dawn. I did not really think about them as being a problem.' He shrugged.

'Then I have a little fact that may surprise you,' she continued animatedly, inhaling deeply on her cigarette. 'An employee of the Japanese Wild Bird Federation told me that the number of crows Tokyo residents can abide with comfortably is three thousand. How many do you think there are at present?'

'Four thousand.' Kenji frowned as from somewhere behind a white swing door with a porthole window that he assumed led into the kitchen, there was a loud crash and the sound of a man's voice raised in anger. The buzz of conversation in the restaurant dropped momentarily before regaining its former level. His mouth felt dry. He took a sip of iced water wishing he could have a proper drink. It might calm his nerves.

310

'There are thirty thousand crows in Tokyo alone.'

'So many?'

'It's the rubbish,' she shrieked and then continued more quietly, leaning across the table and whispering conspiratorially like they were old friends. He noticed with ill-concealed disgust that her expansive bosom was pressed up against the table and covering most of it. 'The rubbish left out in bags on the streets every night that they feed on. Tearing through them with their powerful beaks. The terrible rules and regulations that are forced upon us in this country. You must sort your rubbish into an endless number of categories: recyclable, combustible, aluminium, glass. And if we weren't already making things easy enough for them, they insist that we must then put each category into a different transparent bag so that the refuse men can tell the difference. The crows cheered that day.' Leiko made an odd sound, halfway between a whoop and a caw. 'Now they don't have to tear the bags open to find out if there's any meat in them. All they have to do is sit on the sidewalk and look. They see something they like, they attack, strewing rubbish all over the sidewalk. Leave it to the refuse men to sort out, I say. But my neighbours, they complained about me. Now I have no choice but to clean up after those blasted birds have dined.'

'Your salad.' The waiter placed Kenji's starter down in front of him and a tall glass with a long celery stick in it in front of Kobayashi. He opened the bottle of red wine and stood it in the centre of the table. 'I'll just leave this to breathe for you.'

Kenji couldn't resist it any longer. Pushing the bowl of crisp salad leaves to one side, he ordered a double whisky. 'Ice. No water.'

'We have an extensive collection. Can I show you the menu?'

'Just house, please.' He didn't care. He just needed a drink. This woman was more odious and self-obsessed than he had ever imagined that she might be. It made him feel tired just listening to her. As the waiter went away to the long, well-lit bar, running behind which were thin glass shelves that climbed all the way to the ceiling, Kenji looked back at Kobayashi who was crunching loudly on her stick of celery. 'What is being done about it? The government perhaps . . .'

Twirling the half-eaten celery stick in the glass of red liquid, she interrupted him. 'They have a trapping and gassing campaign. A recent report claimed that it had got rid of seven thousand birds. Each ward has even got its own team of volunteers that go round smashing crows' eggs in their nests. You should see those things. Crazy bastards. They build their nests out of coat hangers. Coat hangers, can you believe it?'

'Has it helped?' Kenji took a large sip out of the glass Scott had placed in front of him, as he waited for Kobayashi, who was searching in her bag for a photograph she wanted to show him. The amber liquid left a hot trail in its wake as it trickled down his throat and immediately he felt a lot better. Not quite so nervous. Certainly no longer in awe, but still fearful of this woman. He took another sip, and another. Maybe he felt a little bit angry. Yes, certainly angry. How she had maligned him and his show. Ruining things for his family and his colleagues, he thought sourly, knocking back the whisky. In no time it was gone and he ordered another one. At least his plan appeared to be working. Kobayashi was talking unremittingly about herself. Did she have gills? he wondered, checking the side of her neck and giggling to himself. He did not see any there, but was certain that she had not even paused for breath. Oh, how his mind was wandering. He had to get it back on track. All he needed to do was continue to steer the meeting in the correct direction and tonight could be his night. He imagined telling the team and the look of admiration return to Mifune's eyes.

'I can't find it.' She put the bag back down on the floor. 'But never mind. You asked if it had helped? Not at all. The food is always there for them to take, so their numbers keep growing and growing. They put nets over the rubbish now. If the crows can't get through, they go to Ginza or Roppongi and feed on food thrown out by restaurants. They've even started stealing from the animals at Ueno Zoo and they've been picking off prairie dogs, boring holes in the backs of deer.'

'Despite your initial reluctance,' Kenji noted – he was beginning to feel in control and with it maybe even a little bit smug and powerful, 'you seem very passionate about the subject.'

As she shifted her enormous bulk on the small wooden chair, it creaked loudly beneath her and scraped across the floor tiles. 'Leiko must get passionate. If she is to write an article, she must get passionate about the story even if at first she does not believe in it.'

'What exactly is your story about? What's your hook?' He looked around the restaurant, hoping to attract the waiter's attention. Eventually he reappeared and Kenji was able to order another double whisky and Kobayashi's wine glass was filled.

'I have been interviewing members of a support group: Victims of Tokyo Crows. Each has been attacked. Some while they sat on park benches eating a snack from the bakery. Others while they rode their bikes to work or were going about their daily business. Most have been dive-bombed and pecked. Some seriously, others less so. Now they are very nervous people, afraid to walk the streets. They always carry umbrellas even if it is not raining and their pockets are weighed down with projectiles in case they need anything to throw at the crows.'

'Why do the crows attack?' Feeling wind rising rapidly up his oesophagus, Kenji kept his mouth shut and pushed the whisky away. Drinking on an empty stomach was not such a good idea. 'They've got all the food they need.'

'This is the time of year that they mate. They are protecting their nests from those that unwittingly stray into the vicinity. Most victims talk about having seen the crow several seconds before the attack. To have been looking at it. And that, my friend, is the worse thing that you can do. If you see a crow, keep your eyes trained to the floor. Do not under any circumstances make eye contact.'

'Can I clear those away for you?' The waiter indicated Kenji's barely touched Caesar Salad and Kobayashi's empty Bloody Mary glass. They both nodded.

'So Leiko has spent an entire day writing about this. Writing about crows when she is supposed to be a serious journalist. I do hope that you have a much more interesting proposition for me.'

As she fixed him with her beady black eyes, the thought occurred to Kenji that she resembled a crow in a not insignificant way. He wanted to laugh out loud but took a deep breath instead.

'I want to talk to you about *Millyennaire*.'

'I suspected that might be the case.'

The smile on her face was cruelly playful. If he hated her before, he loathed her now.

'One turkey chilli with rice.' An enormous dish was placed in front of Kenji. It was covered with a generous helping of chilli, rice, tortilla chips smothered with guacamole, salsa, melted cheese, sour cream and a mound of refried beans. 'And your ribs. Can I get you anything else?'

'More barbecue sauce. This is nowhere near enough,' Kobayashi ordered as she tucked a linen napkin into the neckline of her tent-like dress.

The waiter returned a few seconds later carrying a large bowl full of a thick brown liquid.

Picking up his knife and fork, Kenji began to eat. The whisky had taken the edge off his appetite but he had to show willing. Looking up he smiled at Kobayashi who had already started, tearing the meat off a spare rib that she was holding with both hands. Putting the shredded rib back on the plate in front of her, she wiped her fingers on the napkin, staining it with reddish brown barbeque sauce. It was evident that she did not wish to talk and she rebuffed any attempt that he made to start a conversation until every last rib on her plate had been stripped clean of its meat.

The waiter reappeared.

'Can I get you any dessert or coffee perhaps?' After handing them each a dessert menu, he set about clearing the table, revealing a white cloth heavily stained with debris. 'The key lime pie and blue berry swirl cheesecake come highly recommended,' he said, carefully and expertly balancing the plates in the crook of his right arm.

Kenji declined as Kobayashi ordered cheesecake with a large helping of vanilla ice cream. Once this arrived and was rapidly demolished, she went on to order a cognac and cigar. Kenji was starting to flag. The whisky had at first given him confidence but was now making him feel heavy and lethargic. He had to pick up the subject of *Millyennaire* now or it would be never. Taking a deep breath and a slug of water, he opened his mouth to speak.

Kobayashi got there first. '*Millyennaire*. You wanted to talk about it?'

Kenji retrieved his well-rehearsed speech. 'As you are aware I am the executive producer on *Millyennaire*. It means more to me than I could ever put into words for you. But it is not just me that it means something to. Others have invested so much of themselves in the show despite having a great deal to contend with already. Our script-writer has a five-month-old baby. Our cameraman recently returned to work following his wife's death from a long and painful illness.'

He had hoped that by personalising the show, making the people that worked on it real for her, he could win Kobayashi over, but she made no attempt to hide an exaggerated yawn.

Not allowing himself to be put off so quickly, he continued. Every word he said was truthful and honest. She would have to be made of stone if she didn't see this, if she wasn't affected by his plight. 'We are a family that has worked very hard together to create *Millyennaire* and your every word, your every review is injurious to us.'

'Ah yes.' Leiko smiled. 'Leiko's reviews. I wondered when you would get to them. Really it's out of my hands. Leiko's public expects it of her. What else can she do? Her hands are tied.'

The waiter reappeared. 'Can I get you anything else?'

'No, just the bill, please.' Kobayashi smiled at Kenji, revealing pieces of meat stuck between her teeth. 'This one's on you?' Picking up her handbag from the ground, she packed her cigarette and lighter away. 'There really is no more that Leiko can say on the matter.'

Leaning across the table, Kenji lightly covered her podgy fingers with his hand even though it repulsed him to do so. 'Please,' he begged and despised himself for it. 'You have never reviewed a show more than once. Why *Millyennaire*?'

She snatched her hand back, bent down and lowered her voice to a sharp hiss. 'Once is usually enough to make or break them. Yours continues to drone on like a fly at a window. No matter if you open the window, it refuses to find its way out and just stays there, banging up against the glass. It annoys me and I must do something about it.'

'If you could just stop reviewing the show, then maybe we would stand a chance.'

'Why would Leiko do that?'

'As one human being for another?'

She stood up. 'Perhaps your friend Hoshino could have shown me the same compassion when she ran off with my husband all those years ago. Really you have her to thank for this mess.'

Spinning round, she attempted to march out of the restaurant, but her progress was slowed by having to squeeze between tables and chairs. As he watched her go, Kenji's mobile phone began to ring. Automatically, he picked it out of his pocket and hit the answer button.

'Yes. What is it?'

Seconds later, he too was hurrying as best as he could out of the restaurant and down the street.

FORTY-EIGHT

'Is it true?'

Reaching out blindly, Kenji swatted the microphone, pushing it away from his face. It continued to hover in front of him like a persistent fly and it was not alone. There were many others buzzing around him. Some so large he wondered if they might pick up the sound of his laboured breathing as he staggered out of the hospital, across the sidewalk and into the waiting taxi with as little drama and as quickly as was possible for a man with a broken leg and a pair of crutches. The journalists moved with him to the stationary vehicle.

'Did Hana Hoshino attempt to take her own life last night?'

'Will she recover?'

'What is the relationship between Hana Hoshino and the TV critic Leiko Kobayashi?'

'No comment.' Sliding backwards across the seat of the taxicab that smelt overwhelmingly of pine, Kenji reached forward and pulled the door shut behind him. Outside the window, the bright white bulbs popped repeatedly, adding a sense of excitement to the grey flagstones and the brownstone front of the hospital building.

Kenji gave the driver the address of Miru TV's headquarters in Naka-Meguro and they pulled away, edging the car slowly into the continuous stream of traffic.

It was 8 a.m. He knew that much because the time was flickering in blue digits from the clock in the centre of the dashboard that shone as if it had just been polished. It was probably Monday, although he couldn't be certain. Maybe it was Tuesday. The last few days had passed in such a blur he had lost all track of time. After receiving Inagaki's telephone call at Aoyama on Friday evening, he had rushed straight to the hospital and been there ever since, sleeping fitfully on a hard plastic chair in the waiting room.

'Go home. Get some sleep and a change of clothes,' the nurses had repeatedly advised but he politely and resolutely shook his head. He owed it to Hoshino to stay. With every hour that had passed on that plastic chair, the more tormented with guilt he had become. All the way to the hospital he had been silently berating her as he turned Leiko Kobayashi's words over and over in his head. So Hoshino's infidelity was the reason why *Millyennaire* had been put under such intense scrutiny by the TV critic, why it was publicly panned week upon week. How he had cursed her. Her vanity, her stupidity. What names he had called her. And how he intended to tell her exactly what he thought of her the moment that he saw her. The foolish woman.

Inagaki had been virtually incoherent on the phone, but he felt certain that vodka and champagne had something to do with the TV presenter landing herself in hospital. Kenji himself had run out of compassion for her. At least until he saw her, asleep in the tiny hospital bed that she made appear large. Her too-black hair was spread out in wild tendrils across the stark white pillow, her face was smeared with make-up and there were black stains caused by charcoal solution at the corners of her mouth. As he looked at her lying there, it occurred to him how very fragile she was. Vulnerable too. And he had put her there, by exposing her to ridicule and misery. Now he owed it to her to call an end to this entire sad, sorry mess. It was, as Goto had said only days previously, time to pull the plug on *Millyennaire*.

The driver stared at Kenji in his rearview mirror. 'Don't I know you from somewhere?'

'I don't think so.' Kenji yawned into his hands and shook his head vigorously from side to side.

'Tired?'

'I can hardly stay awake,' he conceded, meeting the taxi driver's eyes in the rearview mirror before looking away. Outside it was raining heavily: the rain beating out a steady rhythm on the back window. Up front, a small cat with one paw raised in the air was glued to the dashboard and a jade stone swung from red string tied around the rearview mirror.

'Been at the hospital all night?'

Kenji watched the jade stone swing back and forth. The effect was almost hypnotic. 'All weekend.'

The taxi driver opened his mouth to speak but was prevented from saying anything by a silver Mercedes that cut sharply in front of him. A string of expletives escaped from his mouth. Despite himself, Kenji smiled as he stared out of the window at the buildings as the taxi inched slowly past, caught up in the rush-hour traffic. He was aware that the windscreen wipers were on. The monotonous sound of the blades sweeping back and forth across the window and the heat in the car were making him feel sleepy. He felt that he might easily drift off, but when his eyes closed and his head fell backwards, he saw Hoshino lying in the hospital bed.

As they had waited for news, on the dark orange plastic chairs in the waiting room, with a television on above their heads, Kenji and Inagaki carefully pieced together the events of that evening: from what they each knew and what others had told them. After the meeting at Miru TV had ended on Friday evening, Kenji had gone to Aoyama. Hoshino, on the other hand, had returned to her hotel room and taken an overdose of paracetamol, washed down with an entire bottle of vodka. It was a stroke of good luck that before losing consciousness she had made an incoherent phone call to Inagaki who had rushed straight over, and found her slumped across the marble tiles on the bathroom floor, her head resting against the base of the toilet, a trickle of blood congealed on her forehead. At the hospital her stomach was pumped while they all waited for news. At last some came. Thankfully the drugs had not had the opportunity to work their way into her bloodstream and no permanent damage had been caused. Kenji, on the other hand, would never forgive himself. The guilt was an enormous burden, pressing down heavily on his chest. But now he was going to do something about it. It was the only way that he might be able to breathe again. He refused to leave until Hoshino was sufficiently awake to receive visitors. When she was, he apologised profusely, begged for her forgiveness and immediately left for the office.

'Did you hear about that television presenter?' the taxi driver asked, seeking out Kenji in the rearview mirror. Not waiting for an answer he continued. 'Took an overdose of pills or so I heard. I wonder if she was staying at that hospital? I bet that's what all those reporters were there for. What do you think?'

Kenji shrugged.

'I'm certain they were. Maybe that's where I've seen your face before. On TV. They've been there all weekend and you look very familiar. Maybe they caught you going in and coming out.'

'Possibly.'

It didn't seem to bother the driver that Kenji did not respond properly and although he did not say a great deal by way of conversation, Kenji found that he was glad of the company. The sound of someone else's voice drowned out his own, intrusive thoughts.

'You did it to her.' The same words kept rolling around in his head again and again. 'You as good as gave her the pills.'

'They're blaming Leiko Kobayashi. You know her? The TV critic with the reputation for the acid tongue. She gave this presenter's new game show a bad review. Not just one, but lots of them. She wouldn't let it drop it seems. Something of a personal vendetta. I meant to watch the show myself last night to see what all the fuss was about.'

'Last night?'

'That's right. Every Sunday at 7 p.m.'

Of course, Kenji had forgotten. *Millyennaire* was on last night. He had assumed that it would not have been possible with Hoshino in hospital to do a live performance. But the team were used to her not showing up, had a catalogue of clips and a voiceover double that sounded just like the real thing.

The driver indicated to turn left. 'I was working. My wife watched it. She said it was pretty bad, but in a fun kind of way. They've got this old lady on it doing all sorts of weird stuff.'

'Weird stuff?' The driver had Kenji's attention now. He leant forward, resting one hand on the lace cover draped over the head rest. 'What do you mean by weird stuff?'

The taxi stopped at a set of traffic lights. Two schoolgirls walked slowly in front of the car. They were wearing French navy, pleated, A-line skirts and blazers to match. Underneath their blazers, both wore a white T-shirt with a face printed across it. The face looked familiar, although he could not be sure. It was raining and the windscreen wipers were going. As the schoolgirls got closer, he was able to make out some of the details on the face. It was heavily wrinkled and belonged to a woman. A woman he knew. It was Eriko, he was almost certain of it. Opening the window, he tried to get a better view but the girls had passed and the taxi pulled off.

'Wait, stop,' he called. 'I have to get out.'

'Not here you can't,' the taxi driver shouted back and by the time he did stop – further down the road – the girls were long gone.

'Just drive on,' Kenji muttered, massaging his temples. His head was in turmoil, tired from lack of sleep. He must have been hallucinating. That was the only explanation for it. But then there was the taxi driver. What he had said. 'Weird stuff. You said that the old lady was doing weird stuff.'

'That's what the wife said. Cleaning in a leotard. Doing aerobics. And she's eighty-two years old. Crazy, like I said. Here we go.'

He pulled up outside the office block where Kenji worked. Paying the driver, Kenji got out and hurried towards the office, taking the lift to the twenty-second floor. Passing through the reception, Suki looked up from her milky white, glass desk. On the counter in front of her was a long, thin glass vase containing a white lily with a thick, green stem.

'Goto wants to see you as soon as you get in.'

'Where is he?'

'In the TV room.'

That was good. Get it over and done with as soon as possible. But he had to freshen up first, splash some cold water on his face. He headed straight for the men's washroom, past the neat rows of desks and a number of colleagues. Each of whom stopped him and relayed the same message. Goto was waiting to see him in the TV room. As he stood at the sink in the washroom, splashing cold water over his face, Ashida emerged from one of the cubicles and opened his mouth.

'I know.' Kenji dried his hands on a towel. 'I'm going now.'

He made his way to the TV room noticing that a number of the desks that he passed were unoccupied. This was unusual. It was 8.30 a.m. now. A time when most of his colleagues would already be at work. Perhaps they had been called to deal with some crisis? He sincerely hoped it was nothing to do with Eriko. After what the taxi driver had said he was feeling increasingly uneasy.

It was only when he was within a few feet of the television room, when he saw that the door was open and people were spilling out into the corridor, that he realised where everybody was. As he approached, he heard his name being whispered. By the time he reached the door Goto, who was standing in the far right-hand corner of the room, was shouting loudly, 'Make way, everybody make way.'

The TV room was more full than he had ever seen it before. There must have been at least thirty people in there, but they all made way for him. Squeezing back against the wall, forming a pathway through which he could pass. As he did so, someone started clapping. Someone else joined in. Soon the entire room had exploded into riotous applause and cheers.

'What are you doing?' he spluttered. 'Why are you clapping? Do you have any idea?' His voice was growing louder and more angry, but it didn't matter, they could not hear him. They simply cheered him on, clapping him on the back, until he reached Goto in the corner of the room and everybody stopped. 'Goto, I must speak to you immediately. We must . . .'

'In a minute, Yamada-san.' Goto clapped his enormous hands together. 'Quiet everybody. It's on.' He nodded at the large TV screen at the front of the room.

'About what you said on Friday,' he whispered.

Goto smiled down pleasantly at him. 'Not just yet. I think you need to watch this first.'

Reluctantly, Kenji joined the others, staring at the TV set.

'Turn it up,' someone shouted and the volume gradually rose.

On screen a female newscaster appeared. 'Reports that Hana Hoshino took an overdose last night are as yet unconfirmed by her colleagues and friends.'

The newscaster was replaced by footage that showed first Kenji leaving the hospital and then Inagaki. Both of whom offered a 'No comment' to the waiting journalists.

'The presenter of a Sunday evening game show called *Millyennaire* has been blighted by personal difficulties recently.' The newscaster continued. 'Battling with alcohol addiction, her recovery has been made worse by *Millyennaire*'s failure to win over viewers. In the show, a single contestant competes to win one million yen by entering competitions in magazines and newspapers. Prizes are converted into their cash equivalent but so far . . .' Eriko's face appeared on a screen immediately behind the newscaster. '. . . the contestant has done little but sleep and eat.

'Hoshino herself has attracted an unprecedented amount of attention from TV critic Leiko Kobayashi who is renowned for breaking many fledging shows. Hana Hoshino's dress sense and presentation skills have come under attack and it is believed that on Friday night the former star, who has recently returned to the lime-light, took an overdose. Leiko Kobayashi was unavailable for comment.'

The screen cut to more footage. This time showing Kobayashi entering an apartment block, wearing a large pair of sunglasses and shielding her face with a copy of the *Mainichi News*.

The newscaster paused, indicating the end of the story.

'Last night a flock of crows in Yoyogi Park attacked a . . .'

Pointing the remote control at the TV set, Goto switched it off. 'Yamada-san, how is our patient?'

Silence descended on the room as everybody turned to look at him.

'She is fragile but better. There is no permanent damage. Perhaps it is her pride that will be hurt the most. She would rather the press not have found out about this.' He shook his head. 'I can't understand how they did. I told nobody other than the studio.'

'Yes, well,' Goto coughed and straightened his yellow tie. His black and white beard looked neat, as though it had been recently trimmed. 'Nothing we can do about that now.' He clapped his hands together loudly. 'Come on everybody, break over. Let's get back to work. Yamada-san, please walk with me.'

Once the room had cleared, the two men were able to leave. Goto had to bend down so that he was in line with Kenji's height. He whispered conspiratorially, a smile playing on his lips. 'When I asked if you had something up your sleeve, I had no idea. Why, this is genius in its design. Did the two of you come up with it together? You and Hoshino-san? And the bank manager? Was he in on it as well?'

Kenji paused, 'I don't understand.'

Goto looked quizzically at him for several seconds, smiled and then walked on, casting glances at the nearby bays to make sure that nobody was listening. Everybody was looking up at them as they passed. Smiling at Kenji and clapping their hands together. Goto lowered his voice even more. 'Of course you don't understand. I can see that you'd want to play that card. The less I know the better. I couldn't agree with you more.'

'Goto, you must listen to me. This has to be the end of *Millyennaire*. Things have got out of hand. People's lives have been put at risk. This isn't what I wanted.'

'The end? Are you joking?' Goto laughed loudly. 'Did you know that viewing figures doubled last night?'

'Doubled? Why?'

'Why do you think? There's an enormous amount of public sympathy for Hoshino and the viewers wanted to support her. The reviews coming in today are more favourable than they have been in the past. This is exactly what we needed. More importantly, it looks like your mother-in-law may be picking up as well. I don't know how you managed that, but she was like a new woman last night.'

Kenji thought about the note that he had popped inside the pages of Eriko's favourite magazine. It had occurred to him that the one important thing missing from the apartment was the old woman's rivalry with her son-in-law. So he wrote her a few words to remind her that he was watching. It had seemed like a good idea at the time. Now everything seemed pointless.

'I appreciate that you probably haven't seen last night's show, but ask Mifune-san. She's prepared you a recording.'

They stopped in front of Goto's office and he laid a hand on Kenji's right shoulder. 'I must admit that for a while there Kenji you had me worried. I didn't think you had it in you. I even got to thinking that maybe you were a fraud just as old Abe claimed you were. It would have spelt the end for me. But I was wrong. You were probably biding your time all this while. Well done.'

Goto walked into his office, closing the door behind him.

FORTY-NINE

Kenji pressed play and sat back in his chair. *Millyennaire*'s familiar opening credits began to roll down the TV screen as the theme tune throbbed from the speakers. From amidst the multi-coloured flashing lights, Hoshino emerged. Of course he expected it, but seeing her there when really she was lying in a hospital bed unnerved him. Nor did she look anything like the woman he had just left who had been dressed in a white regulation hospital gown thin as paper. The woman on the screen in front of him was wearing a midnight blue silk dress. The audience clapped wildly. It wasn't a real audience, just a soundtrack. Not only were they unable to fill the studio, Hoshino had started refusing to perform live.

'Welcome to *Millyennaire*,' Hoshino gushed. A stranger may have put her effusiveness, the high-pitched tone to her voice, the way it cracked as she spoke, down to nervous energy. He saw now that this, and the drinking, were all signs of a woman under an enormous amount of pressure. He had been too selfish to see it for himself, too concerned with *Millyennaire* and making it into a success. How laughable that seemed now.

On screen the picture changed, showing the apartment. In the background Hoshino's voiceover double began to narrate. The transition was seamless. He could not even tell the difference even though he knew it to be so.

'It has been a busy week in the apartment,' the voice explained as an image of Eriko's heavily lined face flooded the entire screen. Kenji, who had been leaning forward in his chair, elbows resting on the table and chin on the palm of one hand, recoiled sharply, sending the chair flying back into the wall on its four legs. Not quite sure what had caused him to react like that, he pulled himself back to the table and studied the screen closely for some clue. What had startled him so much? Staring at the old woman's face, it gradually dawned upon him. Over the past weeks, her performance in the apartment had been nothing short of pathetic. Despite their previous acrimonious relationship and the fact that she was ruining the show, his show, he had found himself starting to feel pangs of sympathy for her. After all, she was to all intents and purposes a harmless, fragile old woman only capable of sleeping and eating: suspended in a state of inertia by the conditions that prevailed in the apartment. Had he even started to feel guilty? Possibly. If he had been able to provide for his family as he should have done in the first place, then his mother-in-law would not have responded to the advertisement and she would not be on the show now. But that was then. The face on the screen before him now no longer seemed fragile and vulnerable. Certainly it was old and lined. But the steely glint of determination in her eyes had returned. There was the same mouth that had criticised him so many times, and he recognised the proud way in which she held her head upright, crowned with the grey curls over which she took so much trouble each night, pinning them in rollers and covering them with a hairnet. This was the same familiar battleaxe.

The camera tracked her through the apartment. Dropping down to the floor, she placed two folded hand towels beneath her knees and began scrubbing the bathroom tiles with a hard wire brush. Washing it out in a bucket of soapy water.

Mouth agape, he watched as she went on to clean the taps with a toothbrush and painstakingly polished them with a cloth until they were gleaming. The transformation in her – and the bathroom by the time she had finished – was remarkable.

Chuckling loudly, Kenji clapped his hands together in delight. 'Mother-in-law, are you finally going to show us what you are made of?'

'It has been a busy weekend for Eriko,' the narrator continued. 'The cleaning equipment she won arrived on Saturday morning and is worth a total of 5,000 yen. It was followed later that day by an exercise ball and clothing worth 10,000 yen.'

'What,' he spluttered, looking about him as though he might find an answer to his question. 'Why did nobody tell me about this? She was entering competitions. I should have known.'

Another image of Eriko filled the screen: wearing an aquamarine lycra catsuit, much like the one that Ami owned. It was several sizes too big for the old woman, the legs and arms were too long and it hung loosely from her tiny frame. Not that she appeared to care or even notice as she stretched her limbs in all manner of strange contortions causing the joints to crack so loudly that he often grimaced. Some of the movements that Eriko completed, Kenji did not think a woman of her age should even be capable of. Sitting down on the floor she lifted her right leg up and lowered her head towards it. Several attempts later and with much groaning and panting, the old woman succeeded in placing her leg behind her head. Granted it was neither elegant nor without a certain amount of cheating and coaxing, but Kenji could not help but applaud the determination that she showed to succeed. Next she got up and slowly easing herself down managed to perform the splits, getting to within about a foot of the ground.

As the disc ran, Kenji picked up and began to leaf through the newspaper cuttings that Mifune had given him with last night's episode. He scanned over them quickly.

'There is no good reason why *Millyennaire* should be a quiz show. The prizes are hardly worth winning. The contestant to date has shown little aptitude for winning. But in spite of all this it works. It is infinitely watchable and immensely enjoyable. Due in no small part to Hana Hoshino's comedic skills and her self-deprecating style.'

'This is genius. How can something so bad be so good?'

'We've watched her lose, now watch her win.'

Struggling up out of his chair, Kenji stuffed the newspaper articles in his jacket pocket and left the office, heading straight for the hospital.

FIFTY

'Guess what?' Ami sounded breathless, almost as though she had run up several flights of stairs without stopping.

'Hello Ami, how are you?' Kenji teased good-naturedly. 'I am very well. Thank you for asking.'

On the other end of the telephone line, Ami sighed loudly. It was a sound that he knew well and decided immediately that it was prudent to resist from further joking.

'Can you give me a clue?' Balancing the telephone receiver in the crook of his neck, he scanned the surface of his desk, picking off any papers that he would need for his meeting with Mifune later that day. They were supposed to be discussing the party to celebrate the final episode of *Millyennaire*. Eriko was just 250 yen off the prize mark of one million and would be emerging to a live studio audience in a matter of days. But he seemed to have lost the list Mifune had given him among the files strewn across the surface of his desk. The list detailed what tasks had been done and what remained. He had to find it, if only to avoid the look of mild annoyance on her face when he told her he had lost it. It never said anything to indicate she was annoyed. She just clamped the red clipboard she went everywhere with firmly to her chest, twirled the biro she was holding between thumb and index finger fractionally faster, and shifted her weight from one foot to the other. All of these things told him that she was annoyed. And he hated more than anything to annoy her because without Mifune none of this would have been possible. And soon she would be leaving him – going to America. So where was that list?

'What did you say?' Ami demanded.

'Me?'

'Yes, you.'

'I didn't say anything.' He shook his head.

'What are you doing?'

'Nothing.'

'You're breathing heavily.'

'I'm just sitting at my desk. Please go on.'

Ami paused. He knew that it could go either way at this point. She could find his response, his manner lacking in some way, become cold and distant before eventually hanging up. Or she could continue, propelled by her own momentum. Thankfully it was the latter.

'Angelique Besson called.'

'Angelique Besson,' Kenji repeated blankly. Evidently Ami expected him to know who this person was, but he had no idea.

'I told you. Several times. She owns a boutique in Harajuku. It's called Sophistique.'

'Of course, yes.' At last, he had found the list sitting underneath an empty coffee cup and covered with several brown rings. As Ami recounted her story, he scanned it quickly: crossing out a few tasks and adding others. This party was going to be one of the most important social events in Tokyo this year and it was essential that everything was not only right but perfect. In conjunction with Goto, they had identified several important people to invite to the party. People that worked for the big networks and had the power to commission new projects from Miru based on the strength of *Millyennaire*. Kenji already had a few turning over in the back of his mind.

'I took a number of my dresses to show her several weeks ago but when I didn't hear back from her, I assumed that she wasn't interested. It turns out that she was called away to Paris at short notice and she does want to stock my dresses after all.'

Ami was squealing with excitement. Kenji knew that he should summon up enough enthusiasm to match hers, but found it a struggle. Dresses didn't excite him in the same way as they did his wife. Or Hoshino for that matter.

'That's fantastic news. We'll go out this weekend to celebrate. As a family. Anywhere. You choose.'

'Angelique said that retrospective designs are becoming chic. The Eighties are back in fashion. Everyone is clamouring for shoulder pads, costume jewellery and full skirts. Angelique said that she wants me to design exclusively for her. A one-year contract to start. Then, if it works out . . .' There was a loud buzzing noise in the background. 'That's the intercom,' Ami explained. 'I'd better go. It will be Takai-san. I can't wait to tell her. She'll be so jealous. See you tonight.'

Before Kenji could utter a word, Ami had put down the telephone. Looking incomprehensibly at the receiver, he replaced it in the handset. He marvelled at his wife. She was like a whirlwind these days: never stopping, always full of energy, darting from one project to the next. He was only glad that she was happy. He, too, was happy now that he had found the list. If only he could find the time to work on it, he muttered to himself, as a single tap sounded on the door.

'Come in.'

Mifune moved soundlessly across the office. 'Some mail for you.'

Smiling, he accepted the large pile of envelopes. As he flicked quickly through them, Mifune picked up the remote control sitting on his desk and pointed it at the TV set in the corner of the room, suspended by a bracket from the ceiling.

'It will be starting in a few minutes,' she commented, referring to the news item that he had asked her to remind him to watch. 'Can I get you some coffee?'

'No coffee, thank you.' He shook his head wistfully. 'What will I do without you when you're gone to America? How will I cope?'

Mifune frowned. 'I'm sure that Suki-san will do just as good a job if not better.'

'I'm sure she will.' Sighing loudly, he stopped flicking through the envelopes. Caught between them was a postcard. On one side, a pencil drawing of a cat lying on its side, looking well fed and contented. On the other, handwriting that he did not recognise. 'Thanks, Mifune-san. That will be everything.'

'Okay.' She looked at him quizzically, but when he did not respond, walked away, pausing at the door. 'I'll be back at 2 o'clock to go over the details of the party with you. You haven't lost the list, have you?'

He waved the coffee-stained piece of paper at her, barely able to hide his impatience. The urge to know what was written on the card was almost unbearable. 'Go, Mifune-san. Go quickly,' he whispered and when she had finally gone, he flicked the card over and began to read.

'Dear Kenji, I have found peace and solitude in a beautiful corner of our island. I can't tell you where.' Immediately he looked to the postmark, but it was smudged. 'It's better that way. Enjoying the show. You must be very proud. Fond regards.'

It was unsigned.

Looking at the picture again, he held the card up to his nose and inhaled deeply, convinced that he would be able to capture a hint of her scent. If it had ever lingered there, it was gone now. Lost in thought, he jumped when there was another tap on the door – this one louder and more forceful than the last. Hurriedly, he put the card in the top drawer of his desk, closed and locked it, putting the small silver key in the pot where he kept all of his pens and pencils.

'Come in.'

'Good, you're here.' Goto strode into the office and pulled up a chair next to Kenji's desk. 'How's the leg?' he asked, glancing behind the table.

'The plaster was taken off yesterday. It feels a bit weak and they've given me exercises to do, but I'm glad to be free of the thing. It was very restrictive. You don't realise until you have one.'

'Yes, I can imagine.' Smoothing the creases out of his trouser legs, Goto looked up at the TV set. 'When does it start?'

'Any minute now. Here we go.'

Kenji turned up the volume, and both men leant forward in their chairs. The newscaster's voice grew louder as behind her a still of

Eriko's face appeared. It was an all too familiar image now. Taken from the show in which Eriko had first showed signs of life – cleaning in her floral housecoat and exercising in an aquamarine catsuit – this image was used on an almost daily basis by news broadcasts, magazines and newspapers.

'As *Millyennaire* fever sweeps the country, viewing figures have peaked at an all-time high of 17 million,' the newscaster explained, her voice placid and unemotional. 'Meanwhile the show is coming to an end. The contestant, Eriko Otsuki, is only 250 yen short of reaching the jackpot of one million yen. Critics are hailing the show an unprecedented success and Eriko has become a national icon. Earlier today, we went out on to the streets of Tokyo to find out what exactly her appeal is.'

At Kenji's side, Goto spoke quietly and evenly. His eyes never left the television screen. 'This is getting big. I'm fielding calls from the States and Europe. There's a lot of interest in licensing the format. With the profit from merchandising this is going to make Miru a lot of money. I don't mind telling you that the board are very happy.'

Kenji nodded. It was all that he could do. With each day that passed, *Millyennaire* bought with it some development or success that far exceeded all of their expectations. Every morning, when he took the train to work, he overheard snatches of conversations between friends and colleagues. *Millyennaire* never failed to feature in some way. Merchandise was flying off the shelves faster than they could put it on. The most popular piece being a twelve-inch replica of Eriko wearing a floral housecoat and a hairnet over her greying head. No gossip magazine was without the old woman on its front cover. Ami had even been approached by several authors who wanted to write Eriko's biography. There was even talk of a film. Meanwhile, Hoshino was featured regularly in women's style magazines and on TV chat shows.

It was real. It was happening to him. And yet at the same time, everything seemed surreal.

Taking a deep breath, he turned his attention back to the television screen where a group of three teenagers in school uniform were being interviewed. Shy at appearing in front of the camera, they were giggling self-consciously and bumping up against each other just like the penguins that he had seen at the zoo.

'Do you watch *Millyennaire*?' a voice asked off-camera.

They all nodded their agreement.

'Tell me,' the voice continued, thrusting a microphone into the face of the tallest girl, 'what makes it such a good programme?'

'I don't know.' she stared hard at the ground as if there was something interesting down there. 'It's pretty bad really. Like watching my grandmother dancing at my sister's wedding. Sometimes I get so embarrassed for her, for Eriko, I can't even bear to watch it. I cover my eyes. But you never stop watching. Each week you turn on to see if it has got worse. And it always has.'

Encouraged by her friend and evidently not wanting to be left out, the next girl – shorter and heavier with a long, thick fringe that fell into her eyes – leant forward and spoke into the microphone. 'Like the episode she won a football and taught herself to keep it up in the air for three minutes. Imagine an old woman like that. My brother can't last nearly as long and he's eleven.'

'Or what about the time,' the third friend who was wearing braces on her teeth interjected, 'she won a mouth organ and taught herself to play. The same song over and over again till it drove me mad.'

As she erupted into a fit of giggles, the camera zoomed out; showing all three girls in frame at once.

'I notice that you're all wearing rather distinctive T-shirts,' the voice commented as the schoolgirls opened their blazers to reveal T-shirts with Eriko's face printed across them.

'I've also got a doll,' the girl with braces boasted proudly, showing off a plastic doll fashioned to look like Eriko. That never failed to send a shiver down Kenji's spine no matter how many times he saw it. It was so very much like the old woman.

Not wanting to be outdone, the girl with the thick, heavy fringe pushed herself towards the microphone. 'On Sunday, I'm having a sleepover at my house. It will be the last episode and we want to celebrate.'

This statement appeared to dampen the mood amongst the

hitherto jovial girls. They were no longer so eager to talk and appeared visibly downcast. The interviewer took the opportunity to hand back to the studio, whereupon there was a brief pause before the newscaster moved on to the next item.

'A refuse man in Chiba ward was left hospitalised after being attacked by a crow.'

Kenji pointed the remote control at the TV and switched it off. Meanwhile Goto jumped up out of his chair with enthusiasm and energy, striding around to the other side of the table where he faced Kenji. 'This is far better than we could ever have hoped for. Which is why the board of directors have asked me to give you this.' He slid a white envelope across the table. Kenji simply stared at it.

'What is it?' he asked fearfully.

'Call it a token of their appreciation,' Goto offered, smiling broadly, and then left the room.

Several minutes passed before Kenji finally built up the courage to open the envelope. He was not quite sure what it was that he was so frightened of. Could it be that he thought the envelope contained papers that spelt the end of his new career? It was possible. Ever since his dismissal from NBC, he had become extremely wary of those around him. He always knew that the company came first. Now he knew that this could be at the expense of the employees and had learned to watch his back. So anxious was he about the contents of the envelope, he put off opening it until the end of the day, when he was just about to leave the office. Using the silver plated envelope opener – a gift from Ami – he slit it open with one sharp movement, turned the envelope upside down and shook the contents out on to the table.

He caught his breath and sat back down when he saw what was inside. One permanent contract of employment with Miru TV, a corporate membership card for the Maruhan Golf Club and a company cheque for one million yen.

FIFTY-ONE

Kenji studied his reflection in the mirror that ran the full length of the tiled wall immediately behind the row of sinks. Like every other room in the studio building, there were no windows in the men's bathroom. The only light came from a quartet of spot bulbs, arranged in a two-by-two formation in the centre of the low ceiling. Of the four bulbs, two were gone, one flickered, while the other cast a grey light over the room including the mirror and his reflection staring back at him.

At first Kenji feared he might be sickening for something: he had never seen himself look so lifeless, deprived almost of oxygen. Like a cold, dead fish laid out on a slab. Yes, that was it. The last few days must have taken more out of him then he realised. They had passed in such a blur of incessant activity, affording little opportunity for either sleep or food as the preparations for the final episode of *Millyennaire* and the celebratory party got underway. Now, or at least it appeared so under the strange grey light, he was paying for it. Still, he reasoned, pinching his cheeks until some colour returned to his complexion, tonight would breathe some life back into him.

He adjusted his eye patch and wondered what he would look like without it. He never took it off these days and, much to the bafflement of the doctors, the sight in his eye had not returned. But even with the eye patch, and a full head of white hair, he still looked better than he had done eighteen months ago. He felt more relaxed, healthier, younger even. Thinking about the night that he had spent at the Gas Panic bar in Roppongi, he shuddered. It was almost as if one of the drops of condensation that hung off the air conditioning vents that snaked across the ceiling in the bar had fallen off, past the neck of his shirt and dripped down his back. His raincoat had been ruined after a night spent trailing in spilt drinks, and drinking cheap whisky on an empty stomach certainly hadn't done him any favours.

Those days were behind him now, though, and if he could he would lock even the memories of them away in a room with a heavy iron door and a rusty lock that once shut would not open. How different things could have been. It was frightening to think what might have happened if he hadn't met Doppo that day in the pachinko parlour. He had been a big man with a heart to match; his personality as loud as the shirts he wore. It was Doppo who had given him the courage to act. Instinctively, he grabbed the St Christopher medal hanging round his neck. As he held it, he thought he heard a voice echo around the men's bathroom, bouncing off the tiled walls.

'Salaryman, I am honoured that you would think of me like that, but you know it's not true. It was you all along. You're the reason why this happened, not me.'

Spinning around so quickly that he almost lost his balance, Kenji was certain that he caught a flash of black hair and a lurid shirt reflected in the mirror. Or was it a trick of the light and his over-active imagination, sharpened by lack of food and sleep? No, it couldn't have been. Bang. The door to the toilet cubicle at the end of the row swung shut. The leather soles of his shiny, new, brown Italian leather shoes clattered loudly against the white floor tiles as he raced towards the cubicle door and pushed against it. It opened easily. There was nobody inside. Nor was there anyone inside any of the other cubicles. He was completely alone in the men's wash-room. Well maybe not completely alone, he thought, touching the St Christopher medal.

Taking a deep breath he walked out of the men's washroom into the maze of corridors.

He always managed to get lost among the long, featureless corridors of Miru TV's studio. The coarse grey carpet and the polystyrene ceiling tiles gave nothing away. There were no landmarks or clues as he blundered first in one direction and then another. He usually wandered around helplessly until finally he happened upon someone who knew where they were going and could show him the way. Not tonight, though. Tonight he simply followed the noise spilling out of the open doors to studio three. It was small in comparison to studio four where *Millyennaire* was filmed, but this suited the atmosphere they wished to create among the one hundred specially selected guests who had been invited to join the pre-show party. Another five hundred guests would join them for the after-show party in studio four after Eriko's emergence to the audience that she didn't know was waiting for her.

Just thinking about the look on the old lady's face when she emerged from the apartment sent a shiver down Kenji's back and made the hairs on his arms stand on end.

Just outside the door to studio three he paused and adjusted his tie. Looking down at his suit, which was tailored from a coffee-coloured, superfine, woven wool, he felt every inch an executive TV producer. He wasn't a fraud, he was the real thing. His shirt alone was testament to that – beige linen, imported from Italy – as were the gold cufflinks set with small rubies that matched his tie pin. 'You're award-winning,' he told himself, before sweeping into the studio that was buzzing with excitement, conversation and music. Waiters in white jackets and black trousers were moving among the clusters of guests, dotted across the cavernous space, filling glasses with champagne and handing out party snacks.

He looked hard, studying every face that he could see in the room. Everyone who didn't have their back turned to him. There was someone he very much needed to talk to and he had to talk to her now. Later, things would only get busier and the demands on him would be greater. There would be no time for a small aside. Then he saw her, standing over at the opposite side of the studio, her black hair shining under the bright lights. Making his way to her proved difficult. People – many of whom he recognised but did not know – stopped and congratulated him. There were several well-known baseball players amongst the guests, soap actors, pop stars and society people. Everybody, it seemed, wanted to talk to him, place a familiar hand on his shoulder as if they had been friends all his life.

'Great show.'

'Best I've ever seen.'

'What's next?'

'Don't tell me you don't have another great idea up your sleeve because I just won't believe you.'

He just wanted to get over to the other side of the studio to see her, to tell her, to thank her. If he could thank her, then it would feel as though he had thanked Doppo, her father. Maybe tonight, he could lay Doppo's memory to rest and move on. As he fought his way across the studio floor, a glass of champagne found its way into his hand. Draining the contents quickly, he handed the empty glass straight back to the next waiter who passed. Finally he reached her. All around, loud conversation was buzzing in his ears like angry flies. The moment he said her name it died away. It felt almost as if there were just the two of them in that room.

'Umeko-san.'

As all other noises and sounds receded into the background, she turned to face him. A large smile broke out on her face, pushing up her apple-shaped cheeks that were so very much like her father's.

'Kenji, it is so good to see you.' In a sudden and impulsive movement, she grabbed him in a warm embrace. Where there may have been awkwardness and unease, there was only a sense of two people with a unique bond. It was almost as if they had known each other all their lives. 'You are well?' Pulling back she held him by the shoulders and admired his suit. 'You look very well.'

He nodded. 'Better than ever. That's why I needed to talk to you. You see none of this – ' He waved his hands about in an expansive gesture. ' – would have been possible without your father. I never got to thank him for anything that he did for me.'

'I'm sure he knew.' She brushed out the creases that her grip had left in the upper arm of his suit.

'No, you don't understand.' Taking her gently by the elbow, Kenji led Umeko to a secluded corner of the studio. Gradually, the sights and sounds that surrounded him were coming back and he was aware of the fact that too many people were listening to what he had to say, hanging on his every word like barnacles to the side of a ship. 'I never told you this before, but your father gave me the idea for *Millyennaire*. All this. I feel like something of a fraud. It was his idea really. You see he came to visit me in hospital and it was he who gave me the idea. Without him I would have nothing. I would be nothing.'

For a moment her face looked stern and he was gripped by a fear that he had offended her.

'I do not believe that you had no part to play in this.' Her voice was calm and measured, though there was force to her words. 'My father was always telling me what a creative and talented man you were. That you had big ideas but didn't allow yourself to recognise them or have the courage to believe in yourself. He said one day you would be a success and he was right. Look.' Taking Kenji by the elbow she turned him around to face the packed room. 'These people are all here today for you. Not my father. Enjoy your success. You deserve it.' She squeezed his hand affectionately. 'Now if you will excuse me I must find my son. He has run off somewhere. He is very excited to see so many stars gathered together in one room and I am afraid he may be making a nuisance of himself.'

As Umeko moved off into the crowd, her long, black, silky skirt floated behind her. Kenji watched her go. Suddenly his stomach growled hungrily. He felt more ravenous than he had done in days, months even. Accepting another glass of champagne from a waiter, he made his way to a large table where a buffet had been laid out and started to help himself, piling his plate high with food and popping bits into his mouth as he did so.

All around him, the sound of laughter and chatter pealed like small bells. For the first time he realised how very much he wanted to be a part of it. He wanted to celebrate. He deserved to celebrate. But first things first. He had to get something to eat.

'Yamada-san.'

A polite smile fixed firmly on his face, Kenji looked up from the table. It was several seconds before he realised why the man standing next to him looked so familiar. The peppered hair, the thick glasses, the polka-dot handkerchief poking out of the top of the breast pocket of his suit jacket. It was Ishida, his former boss at NBC. The smile immediately slid from Kenji's face and he was obliged to put the plate of food back down on the table because his hands were shaking so much.

'Ishida-san. It's been a long time.' He was amazed how calm his voice sounded. There was not a hint of the immense resentment that was bubbling up inside him.

'Eighteen months.' Ishida's response was as prompt as if he had painstakingly counted every day. 'I have been following your career with interest. Congratulations on the show.'

'Thank you.' Kenji nodded, curtly. 'It would not have been possible without the hard work of all the men and women here. My family and friends.'

'I like to think . . .' Ishida removed his glasses and began to rub them with his white cloth covered with polka dots. '. . . that I too have played some small part in your success. After all if it had not been for me – ' He looked up and smiled self-consciously. ' – none of this would have happened.'

At first Kenji thought that it was hunger or tiredness, maybe even both, that made him feel suddenly so violently agitated. Then he realised it was the sight of the polka dots. How dare Ishida claim one small part of his success? He had nearly broken Kenji and done so without a second thought.

When Kenji spoke his voice was quiet, but every word was clear and firm. 'Everything I have achieved, I achieved alone. Please rest assured that you had absolutely nothing to do with it.'

'I . . .' Opening his mouth to respond, Ishida was interrupted by the public address system.

'Can everybody please be seated. Five minutes to show.'

FIFTY-TWO

'The front row has been reserved for you,' Mifune explained as she ushered Kenji along the corridor. 'There are enough seats for you and your family, and your friends.'

The only lights on in the studio were those suspended from the high ceiling and pointed at the cabin, creating a luminescent orb all the way round it that was visible from the moment he passed through the door. In the background, jazz music was playing softly. He had never been a fan of jazz but the music, carefully selected by Ashida to reflect the mood as *Millyennaire* came to an end, was perfect. The sound of the saxophones made him long for something he didn't know he had lost, while the persistent drums heightened his anxiety. He was still furious at Ishida. But he pushed it to the back of his mind, soaking up the atmosphere instead. Those few people already seated in the studio spoke in hushed voices, reverent whispers. The effect of everything coming together – the lights, the music, the people – was otherworldly and made him stop in his tracks, oblivious to the fact he was holding up those waiting to get in behind him. This was a moment he wanted to savour and remember forever.

'This way please, Yamada-san.'

Kenji dropped into pace beside his assistant and, after looking round to check nobody was in earshot, whispered, 'How is she?'

'Nervous, but generally okay. Inagaki-san is with her now. They are practising some breathing exercises, I believe.'

'She hasn't been drinking?'

'Not a drop.'

At least that was something. They were already taking a big risk as it was, broadcasting tonight's show live, but it was one Goto had insisted on. It would, he claimed, add a raw energy to the show that was absent from pre-recorded versions. If the team pulled it off, the effect could be spectacular. 'It would feel,' Goto had declared at a meeting last week, 'like watching history in the making.' If, on the other hand, it failed, Kenji would be reeling from the after-effects for a long time to come. The reputation he had spent months building and nurturing would be in tatters. Like Goto, though, it was a risk he wanted to run. So what if Hoshino made a few mistakes, botched her lines, laughed in the wrong places? It had come to be expected of her and the public loved her all the more for it. Her ineptness had become her trademark and one of the keys to the show's spectacular success.

When Kenji reached the front row he thanked Mifune and sat down. His family was already there – Ami and the twins, also her sister from Osaka who had arrived several days ago with her three children and husband. Sitting at the very end of the row was Wami, Eriko's best friend. When Inagaki joined them a few minutes later he took the empty seat next to his mother. The only person who wasn't there, Kenji noticed, was Izo, who had been busy talking to a young attractive researcher at Miru TV at the party next door and arrived a few minutes later, looking flushed.

'Sorry I'm late.' Izo sat down.

Kenji nodded.

Waiting became unbearable. How would the show end? Would it go with a bang, just like the small display of fireworks they had planned? (It was nothing too big because Health and Safety wouldn't allow it.) Would the reviews be positive? Would Kenji be remembered favourably in the annals of TV production? He hoped so. This was the job he had always dreamed of and he wanted to hold on to it for a long time to come. Not that he was the only one who had done well out of *Millyennaire*. Ami's dresses were now in boutiques throughout Tokyo. Even Inagaki had tasted success. He had met his heroine, the woman he most admired (and maybe even adored), and been promoted to regional manager by Fuji Bank for orchestrating the successful sponsorship deal.

The lights trained on the cabin in the corner dimmed and then expired completely as the jazz music faded out. In its place came the familiar background theme tune to *Millyennaire*, building to a crescendo of keyboard and synthetic drumbeats. An intense spotlight illuminated a white cross on the studio floor as Hoshino emerged, to rapturous applause, from behind the cabin wearing one of Ami's most flamboyant creations yet: a cream satin dress, trimmed with white lace and spotted, faux fur cuffs.

'Ladies and gentlemen, welcome to *Millyennaire* and the episode you have all been waiting for.'

The response she received was rapturous. The sound of clapping and cheering resounded in Kenji's ears. Hoshino continued.

'Three months ago our contestant entered what she believed was a real apartment in downtown Tokyo. During this time she bored us to tears and moved us to cry with laughter. She captured the nation's heart and in the process won a year's supply of rice, a garage filled with power tools, an all-expenses paid trip to Taiwan, a motor boat, a make-over. Tonight all of Eriko's prizes will be converted into their cash equivalent and a total of one million yen will be deposited in her bank account. Remember, Eriko knows that she was being filmed, but has no idea how successful the show has become. She does not know that she has been watched for the last two months by in excess of seventeen million viewers, and that she will be emerging to a live studio audience.'

Eriko's face appeared on the screen behind Hoshino. The studio audience clapped with appreciation, Kenji more so than most. His relationship with Eriko had never been the easiest in the world, but part of him would be glad to see the old battleaxe again. Especially now that the family could afford to move into another apartment; somewhere bigger where he could turn a corner without bumping into his mother-in-law. He noticed that the old woman had even dressed up for the occasion and was wearing her best outfit. A lilac dress and jacket she usually wore for weddings, and a small hat with a purple feather attached to the side. Her wrinkled hands were clamped to her face.

'Eriko, tonight you have won one million yen and you are now free to leave the apartment.'

The old woman removed her hands from her face. 'Thank you,' she repeated over and over, bowing.

'Please stand in the centre of the room and someone will be in to collect you in a few minutes.'

As Eriko went to stand in the centre of the 'apartment', Hoshino began a countdown. 'Ten, nine,' the studio audience counted with her, 'eight, seven, six, five, four, three, two, one.'

Suddenly, and without warning, the walls of the cabin in which Eriko had been living fell away and the ceiling was hoisted clear off, leaving the old woman standing amongst its remains as fireworks went off all round her, whizzing and cracking. She opened her mouth and screamed loudly, a strange strangulated cry, and flapped her arms about her side like a small bird who had yet to learn to fly. The audience stood up, their cheers growing louder and louder. A number of people began whooping and chanting her name, or stamped their feet on the ground.

'Eriko, Eriko, Eriko.'

This only made the old woman worse. She screamed louder, flapped her arms even more. Then very suddenly she stopped screaming. Nobody noticed at first, not even Kenji. It was not until she clutched her right arm across her chest and her face contorted with pain that he began to think something might be wrong. He looked on incredulously as she fell down on to her knees, wondering if this was part of the plan but understanding, almost implicitly, it was something far more serious.

In front of a studio of 600 people and a viewing audience of more than seventeen million, Eriko swooned, falling flat on her face.

'Mother,' Ami screamed, running towards the remains of the cabin.

It was already too late.

FIFTY-THREE

It was hot and stuffy in the fibreglass capsule. Kenji woke gasping for breath and sat up violently, pulling the sponge plugs from his ears and the eye mask from his face. There was a clearing of several inches between his head and the ceiling of the tube-like capsule, but it was only a few feet wide, which made turning and crawling to the end difficult. He did manage it though, and flung the door open, not thinking that there might be somebody on the other side. Quickly, he stuck his head out. The corridor – lined on both sides by an upper and lower row of capsules – was empty. Even the slippers that last night had formed a neat row on the ground were gone. That usually meant so too had the other patrons – men, mostly like him, who worked in Tokyo, although not like him, had families to be with and who they would have woken up with this morning if they had not missed the last train home.

What time was it anyway? He inched round as quickly as he could on his hands and knees and began scrambling among the covers, looking for his watch. At last he found it and, checking the time, threw it back down on to the mattress in disgust. It was 10 a.m. He was going to be late. Wasting no more time, he climbed down the ladder outside the capsule door and ran to the washroom, where he quickly freshened up and dressed.

It was only by accident that he even knew Eriko's funeral would be taking place in Utsunomiya today. Since the last episode of

346

Millyennaire, Kenji had been living in a capsule hotel in Shibuya. It was close to the station so that if Ami called him home he would be able to get there reasonably quickly. Although it was looking increasingly unlikely with each day that passed. He telephoned, repeatedly. She would not talk to him, had not spoken to him, in fact, since the night they left the hospital where Eriko's body had been kept until Ami was able to make the necessary arrangements with the funeral parlour. That night she had gone home, telling him definitively, he would not be welcome to come with her. He had been in the capsule hotel ever since.

Last night, he had been lying on the thin mattress in his capsule, watching the small TV set attached to the fibreglass wall directly above his knees, glumly drinking a can of beer, having already finished three others. The programme he was only half watching finished and the news started. Seeing Eriko's face on the screen made him sit up and increase the volume so much that the man in the cubicle next to his had banged on the partition wall shouting, 'Turn it down.' Kenji ignored him. The news item was about Eriko's wake. He learned it had taken place earlier that day in Utsunomiya. It was attended by her immediate family and close friends, although hundreds of fans had descended on the funeral parlour, holding up the traffic for miles around. The newscaster announced that even more mourners and fans were expected for the funeral that would take place the following day at 11 a.m., after which the body would be transported to a nearby crematorium.

The prospect of going to the funeral terrified Kenji. How could he face Ami at her mother's funeral knowing he had been responsible for her death? Or for that matter, how could he look his children in the eyes, or his sister-in-law? They too had lost someone they loved dearly. His cowardliness didn't matter though. All that mattered was that he did the honourable thing by going to pay his respects and begging for his wife's forgiveness. Except now he was going to be late and there would not be time to buy the black suit as he had planned. The only clothes he had were the ones he had worn on the last night of *Millyennaire* – a coffee-coloured suit and beige linen shirt. Such an outfit would look disrespectful, and on top of that they were stained and crumpled. But it was all he had. If only he hadn't woken up late. He cursed the other men who had slept on the same corridor as him last night; the ones who had rolled in drunk at 2 a.m., and then the one who had kept him awake with his snoring until 4 a.m.

It was their fault he would be late, he thought, as he hurried from the hotel. Luckily, when he arrived at Tokyo station he had to wait only a few minutes for the next train to Utsunomiya. Once he was on the train he thought he would start to feel better, less anxious, but found he could not settle. He stared out the window the entire way, occasionally taking sips from a bottle of whisky in his pocket to calm his nerves. It didn't seem to be doing him any good. When he arrived in Utsunomiya, he hailed a taxi, asking to be taken to the funeral parlour. When the driver muttered under his breath, 'Not another one', he should have been worried, but he had other things on his mind. It was only when the car was a mile from the parlour and could not get any closer that he started to panic. He paid the driver, jumped out of the taxi and ran the rest of the way.

The funeral parlour was a white, nondescript three-storey building with large glass windows and a big piece of card mounted on an easel outside, on which Eriko's family name had been painted with fat brush strokes. As the newscaster had predicted last night, the building was completely surrounded, mostly by young girls. Many of them wore T-shirts over their school uniforms with Eriko's face on the front, and carried pictures of the old lady or prayer beads in their hands. There was a strong smell of incense and even though there were so many people, the atmosphere was subdued, reverent even. Kenji passed several young girls who were sobbing uncontrollably and had to be consoled by their friends who too had tears in their eyes. He pushed his way through them, to the building's entrance where two men were standing. They looked familiar.

'Muto-san,' he said, recognising one of Hoshino's bodyguards but not knowing the other's name.

They greeted him politely, but when he tried to squeeze through, they blocked his way by moving closer together.

'I'm sorry, but only family and guests of the family are permitted,' Muto said, not meeting Kenji's eyes.

'But I am family,' he protested. 'You know me.'

They maintained a stony silence. He tried to push through once more but was bounced back. It was obviously pointless. He would have to try and find another way in. He set off, circling the building, but could find no open door or window. Eventually he gave up and began walking away from the parlour, hoping to pick up a taxi, which he soon did. He asked to be taken home, to the family apartment. He knew he had no key to get in – that was in the apartment – but was happy to wait outside, sitting on a low wall opposite until Ami and the twins returned, which they did, several hours later. He had to wait all day, by which time it had grown dark and his muscles were stiff and painful. But that was okay. He regarded it as small punishment.

Ami climbed out of the taxi, the children came after her. They made a solemn party – Ami was dressed in a black kimono, Yumi was wearing a black pinafore dress over a white blouse while Yoshi wore a smart black suit. Kenji only wished he had been there to comfort them today. He stood up and made to cross the street, hesitating when he saw what Ami was carrying – a large urn clamped to her chest. His legs wobbled beneath him, but somehow he found the courage to walk across the road.

'Ami,' he called gently.

Ami's reaction was the same as if he had shouted her name at the top of his voice. The expression on her face was one of pure loathing and he trembled before it.

'What are you doing here? I told you not to come. I never want to see you again.'

'Please, Ami. Let me talk to you. Let me see the children.'

'No, never.' Ami grabbed Yumi by the hand and pulled her along the sidewalk to the apartment door. Yumi, who was looking over one shoulder at her father, began to cry. Even Yoshi's bottom lip was trembling. 'Come on, hurry up,' Ami chastised them, walking so quickly they struggled to keep up with her.

'Ami, you have to forgive me. I am truly sorry for what happened to your mother. If I'd had known she had a weak heart I would never have allowed the show to end in such a way. You have to believe me.'

'I don't have to do any such thing.' Ami reached the building and presented the key card to a panel mounted on the side wall which beeped. She opened the door, ushered the children inside and closed it firmly behind them. Helplessly, he watched through the glass as his family moved further and further away from him, before disappearing around a corner. When he could no longer see them, he pressed the doorbell for the family's apartment and wouldn't stop pressing it until he heard a door inside open – they lived on the ground floor – and footsteps marching down the corridor. When Ami appeared she was carrying a half-shut suitcase, clothes spilling out of it. She opened the door and threw the suitcase at him.

'Here you are. Now you have no reason to come here ever again.'

Kenji failed to catch the suitcase. It landed on the ground, opened, and his clothes went flying everywhere, including his underpants. Embarrassed, he bent down to pick them up. By the time he had, Ami was gone. It was obvious there was no point trying to talk to her. She had made her feelings perfectly clear. She hated him. No, he would go even further than that. She loathed him. His only hope was that the strength of her feelings might diminish with time and she would at least allow him to see the children.

He retraced his steps, heading back to the station where he caught the next train to Tokyo. Once in Tokyo, he made straight for Naka-Meguro and Miru TV's head office. It would be the first time he had been there in the week since Eriko's death. Once the newspapers had got hold of the story it was impossible to show his face. Not only had they reported Eriko's death in minute detail, they had discovered she was the producer's mother-in-law. Shortly after, the story also broke that the producer's wife had made Hoshino's dresses for the show and that his former classmate had orchestrated the deal that provided the show's financial backing. One newspaper accused Kenji of being a megalomaniac; another reported Inagaki had been suspended from his job pending an investigation. Meanwhile sales of Ami's dresses soared.

Although it had never been his intention, Kenji had brought shame on Miru TV and he had to put things right. That's what he was intending to do now. He would go to the office where he would write a letter of apology, thanks and resignation to Goto, collect his belongings and leave. Now would be a good time because it was getting late and the building would be deserted. There was little chance he would be seen, except by the security guards.

When he finally got to his office, he collapsed down into the chair at his much loved desk and with great sadness looked out the window on to the blinking lights of the traffic below for what would be the last time. Turning back round, he switched on his computer and began to type his letter when the door flew open and Goto strode in.

'Yamada-san, where have you been? I've been trying to phone you for days. I've left countless messages.'

Kenji was too embarrassed to even look at Goto and stared at his desk as he spoke. 'Please accept my apologies for what happened. I am very sorry that my actions have brought shame on the company.'

Goto pulled up a chair and sat down at Kenji's desk. 'No harm done. In fact, this is the best thing we could have hoped for.' He paused, momentarily. 'Of course, I am sorry for your loss. Eriko was your mother-in-law. Please accept my condolences. I sent a wreath to the parlour and a number of our employees attended the funeral. But her death was a stroke of good fortune. Since last week we have sold the rights for the show to fourteen different countries. Everyone, it seems, wants to be a *Millyennaire*.' He chuckled. 'And you, Yamada-san, have made Miru TV very rich indeed. The board are exceptionally pleased with your performance.'

'But the newspapers.'

'Don't worry about them. It will all calm down soon. Especially now that Leiko Kobayashi is no longer reporting. Anyway, we'll look after you. Just keep your head down for a while. Where are you staying? I know you're not at home because we tried to find you there.'

Kenji blushed, mentioning the name of the capsule hotel.

'Well look, here's the address to the company apartment. Take this letter with you – ' He scribbled a short note on a piece of headed paper. ' – and you can stay there until you're ready to come back to work.'

'Thank you,' Kenji said, clutching gratefully on to the piece of paper. He was ready to die for a good night's sleep.

'Don't mention it.' Goto stood up and smiled. 'You're one of us now.'

FIFTY-FOUR

'Are you excited?' Kenji asked Yumi, who was on the other end of the telephone line.

It was two years since they had last lived together as a family – the twins, Kenji and Ami. Time had passed quickly. It seemed hard to believe that in a few weeks' time the twins would be starting junior high school. From what Yumi had said, they were well prepared for this event. New uniforms had already been bought, bags, pencil cases and stationery. Even tennis rackets as they would be taking lessons from the start of the new term. Yumi had been practising.

'And how is your mother?' Kenji asked as he did every time he phoned, on Wednesday and Saturday evenings at 6 p.m., except for alternate weekends when they came to stay with him in his apartment in Tokyo. To phone on any other day or at any other time was strictly forbidden by Ami, who had made it clear from the outset that she wanted to know when to expect his calls, so she wouldn't accidentally pick them up. Yumi's answer was vague, as always, and since Kenji did not want to make her feel any more uncomfortable than she already did talking about her mother with him, he decided to drop the subject.

'Okay then, I'll see you at the weekend. The cherry blossoms are on their way. Did you see the news? Maybe we could go to the park?'

Yumi said she would like that and, once they had said goodbye, hung up the phone.

As Kenji replaced the receiver in its cradle, he exhaled loudly hoping to dispel some of the loneliness that always settled on him after talking to the twins. At least he would not be alone this evening. It was now 6.30. In half an hour he would be meeting Izo in the same Shinjuku ramen bar where they had first made each other's acquaintance. Though, given that he couldn't remember where he had left his wallet, or his keys, getting there on time could be difficult. Being a freelancer had its advantages. He could work from home, for one thing. But it also meant his apartment was permanently cluttered with books, files, tapes, discs and various pieces of electronic equipment. He started rooting around on his desks, lifting tall piles of papers and magazines and putting them back down until he found what he was looking for.

After Eriko died, Kenji had stuck it out at Miru for six months. They were six long months. After a respectable interval of three weeks, Goto, enthused by the success of *Millyennaire* (the concept had sold worldwide), had started to press Kenji for his next big idea. Kenji had searched inside himself, but everything he came up with seemed pointless and frivolous. (The team liked many of the ideas, though, and he understood that they were being made now.) Back then he used to sit in his office, staring at Mount Fuji through the window, feeling like a big fat hen. 'They come, they steal my eggs and they go away,' he'd said. 'I want more than this.' He thought about all the people who passed him on the street every day. A light burned in their tired eyes, but no one saw it, no one except him. He had been like that once. When he'd come up with the idea, he'd gone straight to see Goto, who'd looked at Kenji as if he had gone mad. Kenji had no choice but to leave. If he was going to do something extraordinary, he was going to have to do it alone.

He left Miru and put an advertisement in the classifieds section of the *Mainichi News*. The result was a series of documentaries currently being shown on TV, late on Sunday evenings. The first had followed a salaryman during his normal daily activities. He rose at 5.30 a.m., commuted two hours to work, sat at his desk, attended meetings, ate lunch. Day in, day out he followed the same monotonous routine. There appeared to be no interest in his life, only drudgery, and the viewers pitied him for it. Perhaps they even congratulated themselves for being so much better off. Then, in the final half of the documentary, things started to pick up and the viewers' assumptions were challenged. It emerged that in the evenings, at the end of a long day, the salaryman was a volunteer fireman and while some evenings he did little more than sit around the station with other fire fighters, on others he was battling fierce blazes and rescuing young children. No matter how he spent his evenings though, he still got up at 5.30 a.m. the next day and went to work, his colleagues none the wiser and he an uncomplaining hero.

Then there was the forty-five-year-old office lady who was happily married with two children of whom she was very proud and a job that, for the most part, she enjoyed. Yet in spite of this, she felt there was something missing from her life – a thrill, a passion. So once a month she went shoplifting. She never kept the things she stole; the thrill of taking them was enough to keep her satisfied.

Initially, he had experienced great difficulty getting the networks even to look at the documentaries. Being the man who had made Japan's most successful game show, and whose mother-in-law died on it, opened many doors but it didn't stop them from being slammed again in his face. The executives who agreed to meet him expected more of the same, they didn't want anything solemn, so it wasn't until *The Salaryman's Story* was shown at the Yamagata International Documentary Film Festival, that people started to take him seriously. The documentaries were bought by one of the smaller TV networks. Viewing figures for the first two documentaries had been low and critics were bemused. Kenji was not overly worried. He knew things had a tendency to turn themselves around and he was a man used to waiting.

Now that he had found his wallet and keys, he put on his jacket and left the apartment, pausing briefly to straighten the two photographs by the door, both of which he had taken. One showed Yoshi dancing in a shower of cherry blossom petals at Ueno Park. The other was of the twins, wearing the brightly coloured sunglasses he had bought them that same day.

As Kenji walked towards the station, he wondered how long it had been since he last saw Izo. It was at least a year, almost certainly. And even after this long, it was unlikely he would spend more than a few hours in his friend's company. Izo was in Tokyo for one day only. It was a happy coincidence because today was the second anniversary of Eriko's death and Kenji had wanted to mark it in some way and did not want to spend it alone. Before Izo called, he had even invited Hoshino and Inagaki to join him for dinner. Unfortunately, they were unable to accept as Hoshino was busy filming for her new chat show on location in Hokkaido and her new husband, Inagaki, who was also her manager having left the bank following his suspension, went everywhere with her. Kenji had apologised about the suspension, repeatedly and profusely, only to be told it didn't matter. Inagaki, it seemed, was glad to be free from Fuji Bank and even happier to be married to a busy, successful woman.

When he arrived, Kenji found the ramen bar exactly as he remembered it. The only difference was the chef. He was younger and fresher than the one Izo had known, although the apron he wore was equally stained. Nodding politely at him, Kenji took a place on a tall stool at the end of the bar and studied the menu. In the back of his mind, he knew he was expecting the door to fly open at any minute and Izo to come blustering through it carrying his battered brown suitcase. The reality was that his arrival was a much more sedate event and he was carrying a black leather briefcase.

'Yamada-san.' Izo greeted Kenji warmly and sat down next to him. 'How have you been?'

'Good,' Kenji responded with equal affection. 'You look well. Very smart.'

Izo looked down at his clothes self-consciously. 'You think I've sold out?'

Kenji was surprised by how respectable his friend looked in a smart dark blue suit with his hair neatly cut, though there was still a hint of the old Izo about him. Even though the sun had set, Izo was wearing a big pair of black sunglasses, but when he took them off, Kenji noticed his eyes were still two different colours: one brown, one green.

'Not at all,' Kenji said quickly. 'Never.'

'Sometimes I worry. But a man gets old. He can't spend the rest of his life travelling around the country, living out of a suitcase.'

'Of course.' Kenji nodded. 'How is your job going?'

Izo explained as they both ordered the same dish they had eaten the day they first met – Chinese noodles in broth with sliced pork and a leek garnish. Kenji already knew some of the story. A year ago, Izo had created yet another one of his crazy household appliances. This was perhaps the weirdest yet – a small, battery-operated jacket that if placed round the shell of an egg, heated up, slowly cooking the inside. When the egg was done the jacket switched off and the result was a perfectly soft or hard-boiled egg depending on the diner's preference. While drinking in a bar in Kyoto one evening, Izo had got talking to a man and tried to sell him the egg jacket. It transpired the man was the chief executive of a manufacturing company in Kyoto specialising in household appliances. He was so taken with Izo's invention that he bought it and asked Izo if he wanted to come and work for him.

'Sometimes it feels strange to be in an office, wearing a suit, working with the same people every day,' Izo elaborated. 'But they let me do pretty much what I want. If I want to go and think in a coffee shop, that's fine. Or maybe look for ideas in department stores. Sometimes I just sit in the park or lie on the grass, staring up at the sun. The only things I am judged on are the ideas I come up with and I've always had plenty of those.'

'You have,' Kenji laughed, tucking into the bowl of steaming noodles that had been set down on the counter in front of him by the chef.

'But enough about me. How are you, my friend?' Izo asked, shifting on his stool. Kenji thought he looked embarrassed and seemed to be struggling for words. 'I saw your documentaries on television. They were . . . interesting.'

Kenji smiled. He was used to this reaction. But it was important for him that Izo understood why he had wanted to make the documentaries. 'When I was a boy my mother and I made up stories about the people we passed in the street. Mine were always exaggerated flights of fancy about pirates and smugglers or bank robbers. My mother's were about men and women who looked ordinary on the outside, but actually had some extraordinary ability or did extraordinary things. "If you are very lucky," she used to tell me, "you will meet these people when you grow up. You may even be one yourself."'

Izo laughed and ate some more noodles. 'It's a nice sentiment.'

'It's more than a sentiment,' Kenji continued passionately. 'When I was a salaryman it kept me going. The idea that I could be extraordinary helped me get up every day. And in the end I was . . . I did something extraordinary. Although . . .' He paused. 'Whatever way you look at it, *Millyennaire* has been sold worldwide. It was my idea. I was responsible for it. Only some people aren't as lucky as me. They don't get the chance to shine. I wanted to give it to them.'

'Is that why you left Miru?' Izo asked.

Kenji nodded.

'And you are happy in your work?'

'More than I have ever been.'

Izo thought about this for a few seconds. 'Then I am happy for you. But what about Ami?' he asked.

Kenji shook his head sadly and changed the subject to talk about happier things, promising Izo that he would visit him in Kyoto one day soon.

'Who knows,' Izo smiled, 'maybe you will meet some of your extraordinary people there? With hair like that and your eye patch –' He pointed at the patch Kenji still wore as the sight in that eye had never returned no matter how many times the doctors said it would. ' – they'll know where to find you.'

When they parted, later that evening, outside the ramen bar

Kenji waved his friend off and told him to keep watching the documentaries, there was better still to come. When Kenji turned round to walk away in the opposite direction, he spotted a cherry blossom petal float by on the breeze.

It landed on the ground by his feet.

ACKNOWLEDGEMENTS

I would like to thank Unilever for sending me on secondment to Tokyo and colleagues at Nippon Lever who made me feel welcome.

Thanks also to Dr Alf Louvre for his comments on an early draft of this novel, and to Alison Samuel and Poppy Hampson who helped me refine the finished version.

Finally, I would like to thank Bill Hamilton and Corinne Chabert, and all my family and friends for their encouragement and support.